PRODUCTION VALUES

A Hollywood Satire

E.V. Hayes

Creative Nudge Press

CONTENTS

Pre-Production

The trouble started, as trouble often does in Hollywood, with someone trying to make history more commercially viable.

CHAPTER 1

Victoria Martinez was engaged in what her therapist called "shelf therapy." She'd denied it three sessions running before finally admitting that yes, fine, sometimes she did rearrange her awards collection when stressed. The therapist had nodded, validated her coping mechanism, and charged her $375 for the breakthrough.

Today, Victoria was deep in shelf therapy mode, adjusting a mid-tier festival prize that kept sliding to the left.

"You stay where I put you," she muttered, wedging the crystal obelisk between a Producers Guild nomination plaque and the Oscar she'd won for *Backhand*, a lesbian tennis biopic that had lost $14 million but secured her reputation as "one of the good ones" among industry progressives.

Through her floor-to-ceiling windows, the Pinnacle Pictures lot spread out like an aging resort desperately clinging to its four-star rating. Once the crown jewel of independent studios, Pinnacle now occupied that awkward middle ground: too small to compete with conglomerates, too big to claim scrappy underdog status. Rather like Victoria's career itself.

Her office door opened without a knock, and Lucy Chen, her assistant of three years, entered with the facial expression of someone who'd just witnessed a seagull steal a baby.

"Dr. Friedman quit. Again," Lucy announced, clutching her tablet like a shield.

Victoria placed the award down with careful precision. "Which one is Friedman again?"

"The historian. The *actual* historian. The one whose book we optioned."

"Right," Victoria said, weighing this development. "That's the third time this month."

"He says 'If Eva Braun is going to be rewritten as a proto-feminist who tried to moderate Hitler's policies through pillow talk, then I cannot in good conscience remain attached to this project.'" She paused. "Those are his exact words. He made me write them down."

Victoria smoothed her custom-tailored blazer, a power move she'd perfected over fifteen years of climbing from assistant to executive. At forty-five, she wore her success like armor: designer clothes that said "I earned this" rather than "I inherited this," and the kind of understated makeup that took forty-five minutes to look effortless. "It's a historical drama. We're not making a documentary."

Lucy cleared her throat. "He also said, 'Historical accuracy in media has civic importance because most Americans' understanding of World War II comes from entertainment, not education.'"

"Sounds like a personal problem. Has he looked at TikTok? Half the platform thinks Hitler was secretly Black."

"Actually, TJ Jackson just hit a million followers with that theory."

Victoria paused. "The one who does those history rants to dramatic music?"

"That's the one."

Victoria filed this information away for later. "Fine. Tell Legal to look at Dr. Friedman's contract. How much will it cost us to have him quietly hate us from his university office?"

Lucy consulted her tablet. "He's technically fulfilled his consultant requirements. His credit is locked."

"Perfect. This won't be the first time someone's name appeared on something they found morally repugnant." Victoria lifted an Emmy and turned it so the figure faced the window. "Welcome to Hollywood, Dr. Friedman."

The Emmy, Best Limited Series for *The Cartographer's Daughter*, had been her first major win, the validation that transformed her from "diversity hire" to "rising executive." Three years of sleep deprivation and antacid addiction had gone into that sixteen inches of gold-plated legitimacy. A legitimacy that still felt conditional, as her lunch with Sean would undoubtedly remind her.

Lucy hesitated. "There's more. Kennedy Oswald's team sent over her latest script notes."

Victoria's shoulders tightened. "Kennedy Oswald is playing Eva Braun, not writing the movie."

"She prefers 'story architect' to 'actress' now."

"Of course she does," Victoria muttered. "What are her demands this time?"

"She wants Eva and Hitler to have met earlier in his life, possibly during his struggling artist phase. She says, and I'm quoting, 'Eva coming into his life after he's already established looks bad for the character arc.'"

Victoria blinked. Twice. "Has anyone on her team mentioned that Eva Braun would have been about two years old during Hitler's Vienna period? Or that she wasn't even born during his 'struggling artist' phase?"

"Her note says, 'Historical ages are flexible when the emotional truth is more important.'"

Victoria closed her eyes briefly. "Has no one told her Hitler is the bad guy? Who wants to boss-babe this evil?"

"She's also refusing to sign her final contract until these changes are approved. And she's threatening not to promote the film if, in her words, 'they silence Eva's voice.' And HerStory Films wants approval rights on all marketing materials."

"HerStory Films is Kennedy's Instagram account with an LLC. Is that all?"

"She's leveraging her social following. Fifteen million followers."

Victoria moved to her desk, shuffling papers that didn't need shuffling. The original vision for this project, a serious historical drama examining the human capacity for evil, felt like a distant memory now, lost beneath Kennedy's relentless pursuit of "character arc" and "empowering representation."

It didn't help that this WWII project had been handed to her after she'd successfully shepherded *Daughters of War*, a female-focused Vietnam story, to critical acclaim. The studio's thinking was transparent: give the "diversity hire" the prestige historical pieces because they checked award season boxes.

"When I greenlit this project, it was a serious historical drama about the rise of fascism with prestige awards potential. Now it's turning into 'The Devil Wears Panzers.'" Victoria sighed. "And let's be honest: a story set in Nazi Germany? It's too white for today's award committees anyway. We'd need to completely reinvent history to make it remotely competitive."

"I could mock up some diversity numbers for potential casting," Lucy offered.

"Don't bother. This project is a headache Sean's team handed me because no one else wanted to touch Hitler with a ten-foot pole. And now it's falling apart." Victoria grabbed her antacid bottle from the desk drawer. "I'm thinking we let the option lapse."

Lucy looked surprised. "Are you sure? I thought Sean considered this a priority project."

"Was. Past tense." Victoria popped an antacid. "Besides, if Sean wants it so badly, he can assign it to one of his golden boys. I'm tired of being the studio's Holocaust expert because I once made a movie with Jewish characters." She waved her hand dismissively. "We'll find another historical drama. One without a protagonist who committed genocide."

"What about your lunch with Sean today? It's a quarterly check-in, right?"

Victoria grimaced. Lunch with Sean Lynch, Executive Vice President of Production, was already going to be painful enough without having to justify abandoning a project she'd been assigned.

"I'll tell him we're considering other options. Let someone else deal with Kennedy's revisionist history fantasies. God knows the studio has enough White male executives who could use a career-threatening disaster."

Lucy consulted her tablet again. "We're five million under the original budget approval. Kennedy's team insisted on the pay cut for the supporting cast to offset her quote."

"Are we seriously making a Hitler biopic with a slashed budget? What is this, 'Hitler on Ice'? *Springtime for Hitler*?"

Lucy looked up, brow furrowed. "Is that a reference to something?"

Victoria felt suddenly old. "Mel Brooks? *The Producers*? *Springtime for Hitler*? The musical within the musical?"

Lucy's blank expression said it all.

"Jesus, I keep forgetting you were born in the nineties." Victoria shook her head. "It's a famous satire. Two Broadway producers deliberately create a tasteless Hitler musical hoping it will flop so they can run off with investors' money. Of course, it becomes a hit because audiences think it's ironic."

"So... like our situation but backwards?"

"No, exactly like our situation. We're trying to make a serious film about evil, and it's turning into an accidental comedy." Victoria stared at the ceiling, counting the tiles to calm herself. "And we still don't have a Hitler, do we?"

"Well, about that. Finance hasn't approved a name with enough draw to justify the fee."

Victoria's gaze snapped back to Lucy. "So we have a star playing Eva Braun who's demanding script approval, refusing to sign her contract, a historian who just quit, a slashed budget, and no Hitler." She drummed her fingers on the desk. "Tell me again why I shouldn't let this project die?"

Lucy shifted uncomfortably. "I'll prepare the talking points for your lunch with Sean. Do you want the 'creative differences' angle or the 're-assessing our slate for maximum market impact' approach?"

"Go with 'strategic reallocation of resources.' It's corporate enough that no one will question it." Victoria turned back to her shelf, straightening an award that was already perfectly aligned. "That's the beauty of industry jargon. No one actually knows what it means, so they assume it's smart."

"I'll have it ready before your lunch," Lucy said, turning to leave.

"And Lucy?"

The assistant paused at the door.

"Tell Kennedy's team I'm reviewing her notes. In reality, I'll be reviewing how quickly we can disentangle ourselves from this mess."

"I'll phrase that more diplomatically."

"You always do." Victoria smiled thinly. "That's why I haven't fired you yet."

After Lucy left, Victoria stood alone in her office, staring at the collection of gold-plated validation. Each award represented a risk that paid off, a moment when her instincts had been right. But this Hitler project felt like throwing good money after bad. A project assigned to her because of who she was rather than what she could do with it.

She picked up her Outstanding Achievement in Storytelling award (ironically won for a documentary about Holocaust survivors) and studied its weight in her palm.

"Sometimes the bravest decision is walking away," she said to the empty room, setting the award back in its precise location.

Even if it meant admitting defeat.

Even if it meant giving up on what had once seemed like award bait.

Even if it meant her next round of shelf therapy would focus on reorganizing rather than adding.

It was time to let Hitler go.

***

The Polo Lounge at the Beverly Hills Hotel was Hollywood's longest-running power lunch theater. Its real product wasn't the overpriced McCarthy Salad but proximity: tables strategically positioned so industry players could pretend not to notice each other while obsessively calculating who got better placement. The pink-and-green patio was for studio heads and A-listers; the booths for serious negotiations; the indoor tables for those climbing the ladder. The food, consistently good but secondary to the scene, was merely the admission price to the daily industry drama.

Sean Lynch, EVP of Production at Pinnacle, had secured a prime center table. Of course he had. Victoria arrived precisely seven minutes late; enough to suggest she had more important things to do, but not enough to be genuinely rude.

Sean stood to greet her, his salt-and-pepper hair impeccably styled to suggest he was both distinguished and too busy to care how he looked. His handshake was firm but not aggressive; the practiced touch of a man who'd learned long ago that power displays are for the insecure. His booth position overlooked the patio but offered enough privacy for the kind of conversation that determined careers.

"Victoria," he said, smiling with exactly the right degree of warmth. "Always good to see you."

"Sean," she replied, sliding into her chair and placing her phone face-down on the table: the industry executive's equivalent of removing a gun from its holster and placing it on the bar.

"You look great. That awards shelf must be good for the skin."

Victoria arranged her napkin. "The shelf is fine. The shelf therapy bill, less so."

Sean laughed just loud enough for the neighboring tables to register his amusement. "We've all got our coping mechanisms. David. Fincher, I mean. He gets to set at five a.m. to meticulously check every detail before filming. I observed that discipline when I was on the *Mindhunter* set for a day."

Victoria nodded, resisting the urge to mention that "Almost Fincher" was how lower-level executives referred to Sean behind his back.

The waiter appeared with practiced timing.

"The branzino for me," Sean said without looking at the menu. "And sparkling water."

"I'll have the niçoise, no onions," Victoria said. "Still water."

As the waiter departed, Sean settled back in his chair. "So, quarterly check-in. How are things in your corner of the Pinnacle universe?"

"The Miramax retrospective is tracking well. Early buzz on the Rodriguez piece is strong. We've got three scripts in active development that I'm excited about."

Sean nodded, reaching for his water glass. "And the Hitler project?" He took a deliberate sip, holding her gaze over the rim.

Victoria kept her expression neutral, though her fingers tightened fractionally around her knife. "Challenging. Kennedy Oswald has some... creative interpretations of Eva Braun's historical role."

"I heard something about that." Sean set his glass down with precision. "The mustache thing?"

"Among others. She wants them to have met during Hitler's struggling artist phase."

"That timeline doesn't work, does it? Wasn't Eva still..."

"A toddler? Yes. But according to Kennedy, and I quote, 'Historical ages are flexible when emotional truth is more important.'"

Sean laughed, a sound like expensive tires on perfect asphalt. "God, I love actors. Never let facts interfere with character development."

Their salads arrived, arranged with the geometric precision of a tax form.

"Three historians have quit, no wait, I think the same historian has quit three times," Victoria added, spearing a piece of tuna with unnecessary force.

Sean chewed thoughtfully. "That's unfortunate. But you know what David always said about historical consultants..."

"Let me guess. 'They're there to make the filmmakers feel better, not the audience.'"

Sean's eyebrows rose slightly. "Actually, yes. That's exactly what he said during *Benjamin Button*." He paused. "I'm impressed you'd know that."

"Lucky guess." Victoria took a bite to hide her satisfaction.

Sean dabbed his mouth with his napkin. "The reason I'm asking about Hitler is that Goldman's been making noise."

Victoria's fork paused halfway to her mouth. "Marcus Goldman? The one who used to carry Michael Bay's protein shakes before he magically became a 'visionary producer'?"

"Yes, that Marcus Goldman." Sean smiled thinly. "The one who runs our Feature Division now. You two started out on that Michael Bay project, didn't you? Well, he's taken an interest in your Hitler project."

"Of course he has." Victoria's voice could have flash-frozen vodka. "Just like he took an interest in my Sarajevo script right before it won at Sundance."

"You're still holding onto that? It was five years ago."

"Four years, eight months, and approximately twenty-seven days. But who's counting?" She smiled tightly. "What does Marcus want with Hitler?"

Sean lifted his water glass again. "He's got some interesting ideas about the approach." He drank slowly, making her wait. "Apparently, he has a take that could minimize the Kennedy Oswald situation."

Victoria arranged her features into what she hoped was professional curiosity rather than mounting irritation. "Oh?"

"He's got contacts at Netflix. They're looking for prestige material, and he thinks a streaming play might make sense for this particular property."

"Netflix." Victoria nodded. "Where art goes to die between seasons of baking competitions."

Sean smiled thinly. "They've won Oscars."

"So has Al Pacino for *Scent of a Woman*. Not everything ages well."

Sean's attention shifted to his branzino, methodically separating flesh from bone with surgical precision. "Look, Victoria, I know this was your project. But sometimes we have to consider what's best for the studio."

"And Marcus Goldman is what's best for the studio?" Victoria's tone was carefully calibrated between question and statement.

"He's got a track record with difficult material." Sean looked up. "Sometimes projects need a different perspective."

Victoria's smile didn't reach her eyes. "Different how, exactly?"

Sean hesitated, perfectly timed. "You know I value your voice, Victoria. Your perspective brings something unique to our slate."

"My perspective."

"Your projects have a certain... cultural sensitivity that's invaluable."

Victoria set down her fork. "Are my eyes too diverse for a WWII epic, Sean?"

He laughed as if she'd made a joke. "Of course not. But you have to admit, the Hitler project doesn't play to your strengths. Your work on *Daughters of War* was exceptional; authentic, personal. Maybe there's another project that would better showcase your... unique viewpoint."

"My unique viewpoint." Victoria nodded slowly. "And what might that be?"

Sean reached for his water glass again. "We've acquired rights to a powerful slave narrative. Civil War era, female protagonist, strong awards potential." He drank, watching her over the rim. "I immediately thought of you."

Victoria's expression remained pleasant while her stomach acid achieved new pH levels. "How thoughtful."

"It's the kind of story that deserves your touch. The Hitler project is... well, it's Germany. It's Europe. It's..." He waved his fork vaguely.

"White?" Victoria supplied.

"Traditional," Sean countered smoothly. "The slave narrative has real cultural resonance. Real meaning."

Victoria dabbed her mouth with her napkin, buying time. This lunch had suddenly transformed from irritating to infuriating. She'd been ready to walk away from the Hitler project an hour ago. Now, surrendering it felt like conceding something far more important.

"When I was brought into Pinnacle," she said evenly, "I was told I'd have autonomy over my slate."

"Absolutely. And you do." Sean's smile was all teeth. "This is just a suggestion. A potential reallocation of resources."

"Resources like Hitler."

"Exactly." Sean nodded, pleased she understood. "Marcus already has some casting ideas that could address the budget issues."

Victoria's napkin crumpled slightly in her grip. "I'm curious: did you suggest Marcus take over my Rodriguez project too? That's Hispanic content, which is ostensibly 'my culture.'"

Sean's water glass paused halfway to his mouth. "The Rodriguez project is tracking beautifully. Why would we change anything?"

"So I'm qualified for Hispanic stories but not European ones? Just wondering where the line is between my 'unique perspective' and projects I'm supposedly not culturally equipped to handle."

"Victoria." Sean set down his glass with a soft clink. "Nobody is questioning your qualifications. This is about optimization. Using our strongest players where they'll have the most impact."

"And my impact is limited to stories about my own cultural background?"

"That's not what I..."

"Because I've got news for you, Sean. I know as much about slave narratives as I do about Hitler. Which is to say, I know how to make good movies regardless of subject matter."

Sean's smile flickered for just a moment before stabilizing. "No one doubts that."

"Then why is Marcus suddenly so interested in my problematic Hitler project?"

Sean took another sip of water, but this time it seemed less a power move than a need for hydration. "Marcus has been looking for a prestige play. He thinks he can make this work."

"Marcus Goldman wouldn't know prestige if it came with a gilt-edged invitation. What he wants is my project because it's mine."

"That's not fair, Victoria. He's got five nomination plaques on his wall."

"And not a single win. How many do I have?"

Sean studied her with newfound interest. "You seem surprisingly attached to a project you were complaining about ten minutes ago."

Victoria realized with irritation she'd taken his bait. She smoothed her napkin carefully. "I'm attached to the autonomy I was promised when I took this job. If I decide Hitler isn't worth the headache, that's my call, not Marcus Goldman's."

"Of course." Sean cut another perfect bite of fish. "Though I should mention the board is particularly interested in this project. The book option wasn't cheap, and we're up against a deadline."

"The board put me in charge of the project. I'll handle the board."

Sean popped the bite into his mouth, chewing thoughtfully. When he swallowed, he reached for his water again. "So you're saying you want to work with Hitler."

Victoria knew she'd been maneuvered into a corner. If she said no, Sean would hand the project to Goldman. If she said yes, she was committing to a disaster. The only winning move was not to play, but her pride refused to concede.

"I'm saying," she replied carefully, "that I'll make the decision that best serves Pinnacle's interests. But I won't have Marcus Goldman swooping in to 'save' a project he thinks I can't handle because it's too White."

"No one said anything about..."

"Of course not." Victoria's smile was polite and deadly. "Just like no one had to tell me why I was assigned a Native American documentary three years ago despite having no native heritage whatsoever. Apparently, one marginalized identity qualifies you to represent all of them."

Sean had the decency to look slightly uncomfortable. "That's not what this is about."

"Isn't it?" Victoria took a sip of her water. "Tell Marcus I appreciate his interest, but Hitler is still mine. If I want his perspective, I'll be sure to ask for it."

Something shifted in Sean's expression: a flicker of what might have been respect. "I'll pass that along."

"Please do."

They ate in silence for a moment, the tension cooling to a simmer.

"So," Sean said finally, "if you're keeping Hitler, how do you plan to handle Kennedy?"

Victoria surprised herself by smiling genuinely. "I have no idea. But I'm not giving her Eva Braun as a girlboss origin story, and I will find the awards bait here."

"The board will want to see movement soon. We're up against the option deadline."

"I'm aware." Victoria took another bite of her salad. "I'll figure it out."

Sean studied her with new interest. "You know, Victoria, that's what I've always appreciated about you. You're willing to take on projects no one else would touch."

She recognized the backhanded compliment for what it was but chose to take the win. "What can I say? I'm a glutton for punishment."

"Aren't we all? None of us would be in Hollywood if we didn't need some kind of validation."

"Speaking of validation," Victoria said, "how's your pursuit of the *Blood Meridian* rights coming along?"

Sean's expression flickered briefly before settling back into practiced affability. "We're making progress. McCarthy's estate is finally considering our approach. After thirty years in development hell, I think we might be the ones to finally crack it."

"I'm sure he remembers your visit to the *Mindhunter* set fondly."

"It was brief, but impactful. He told me, 'Perfectionism is a term thrown about by people who are lazy.' Changed my whole approach to production."

Victoria nodded with exaggerated interest. "Fascinating. I'm sure he says that to all the visiting executives."

Sean signaled for the check with the subtle efficiency of someone accustomed to having his needs anticipated. "Keep me posted on Hitler. If you need any support with Kennedy's team, let me know."

"I will." Victoria gathered her phone and purse. "And Sean? Thank you for the slave narrative offer, but I'll pass. I'm sure Marcus would bring a unique perspective to that project instead."

Sean's laugh was genuine this time. "Point taken. Hitler's yours until you decide otherwise."

"Exactly."

As Victoria walked back to her office, she wondered when exactly she'd decided to save a project she'd been ready to abandon an hour earlier. Pride, she thought, was a hell of a motivator. That, and the opportunity to spite Marcus Goldman.

Now she just needed to find someone to play Hitler.

And convince Kennedy Oswald that Eva Braun wasn't the feminist icon of the Third Reich.

And stop three more historians from quitting, or the same one, again.

And do it all before the option expired.

***

Chapter 2

Victoria stalked back into her office with the determined stride of someone who'd just remembered why they joined the industry in the first place: to prove people wrong.

Lucy glanced up from her laptop. "How was lunch?"

"Educational." Victoria tossed her bag onto her desk with calculated nonchalance. "Apparently Marcus Goldman feels uniquely qualified to rescue our Hitler project."

"Marcus Goldman? The guy who..."

"...tried to steal my Sarajevo script before Sundance? That's the one." Victoria kicked off her heels and retrieved her emergency flats from the bottom drawer. "But Sean's little power play backfired. We're keeping Hitler."

Lucy's fingers froze over her keyboard. "I thought you wanted to let the option lapse."

"I did. Past tense." Funny how spite could clarify one's priorities.

"Should I cancel the memo about strategic reallocation?"

"Delete it. We're pivoting to strategic reinvention." Victoria slipped on her flats and stood taller than seemed physically possible for someone in flat shoes. "Is everyone ready for the Zoom?"

"They're waiting in the conference room. André's team pulled together some preliminary marketing slides based on what we had before lunch."

"Perfect. Let's not keep Hitler waiting."

The conference room, unofficially named "Purgatory" for its windowless beige walls and the career-defining decisions made within them, contained a U-shaped table facing a wall-sized screen. Five people looked up as Victoria entered: Lucy slipped in behind her and took a seat in the corner, tablet at the ready.

"Sorry for the delay," Victoria announced, not sounding sorry at all. "Sean wanted to have an impromptu strategy discussion about our Hitler project."

André Reynolds, head of marketing, raised an eyebrow. "Strategy discussion? That's executive code for 'I'm taking your project,' isn't it?"

"Normally, yes." Victoria settled into the chair at the head of the table. "But not today."

Michelle Park, VP of Publicity and Digital Engagement, leaned forward. "So we're still green on Hitler? Last I heard, we were preparing exit strategies."

"Plans have changed." Victoria nodded to the tech sitting in the corner. "Let's get London on the line."

The massive screen flickered to life, revealing Aaron Weisman in what appeared to be a London hotel room, illuminated by soft amber light that made him look like he was being filmed for a Wes Anderson movie. He wore a rumpled button-down and had the bleary-eyed look of someone who'd been unexpectedly pulled from dinner.

"Aaron! How's the British weather?"

"Predictably British," Aaron replied, adjusting his glasses. "I thought we were shelving Hitler. My phone nearly exploded with notifications during dessert."

"Change of plans." Victoria smiled brightly. "We're making Hitler work. How quickly can you get back from vacation?"

Aaron stared into the camera. "This is a research trip, not a vacation. The Imperial War Museum has..."

"Fascinating. Can you be back by Friday?"

Aaron sighed. "I suppose my Churchill research can wait. Hitler takes precedence, historically speaking."

Victoria turned to the group. "All right, people. We have exactly thirty days before our option expires. Kennedy won't sign until she gets script approval, which we're not giving her, but we need to keep her attached. We have no Hitler, a slashed budget, and the risk of another historian quitting again."

David Katz, the screenwriter, slumped in his chair. "Dr. Friedman's gone? He was our historical ballast."

"He objected to Kennedy's Eva Braun empowerment arc," Lucy supplied from her corner perch.

"As would any historian with a functioning cerebral cortex," David muttered.

Victoria ignored this. "The point is, we're making this movie. And we're making it an awards contender."

André snorted. "A White historical drama about Hitler? In this awards climate?"

"Precisely why we need to rethink our approach." Victoria stood and began pacing, a habit she'd adopted after learning that male executives were judged as "dynamic" for the same behavior that got women labeled "anxious."

"The Academy's representation and inclusion standards are clear," she continued. "To qualify for Best Picture, we need to meet at least two of the four standards."

Lucy's fingers flew across her tablet as Victoria ticked off points on her fingers.

"Standard A: On-screen representation. Currently failing because our cast is as White as a Nordic ski team reunion."

A few chuckles around the table.

"Standard B: Creative leadership. We have some diversity here, but not enough." Victoria ticked off on her fingers. "I check two boxes: Hispanic and female. "

Michelle looked up from her phone. "I check two boxes as well, I guess, though I don't usually itemize them in budget meetings."

Victoria beamed. "Even better! That's four. See, folks? We're making progress already."

She turned to André. "You check a box too, right?"

André arched an eyebrow. "Black man in marketing? That's practically industry standard now."

"Do Jews count?" Aaron's voice crackled through the speakers.

Lucy glanced up from her tablet. "Not according to the Academy guidelines."

"Fascinating how we've quantified marginalization," Aaron muttered.

Victoria pressed on. "Standard C: Industry access. We can manage that with internships and training programs."

André made a note. "We already have the Pipeline Program. We can allocate some slots to this production. Though finding a diverse crew for location shooting in Germany might require flying people in. Not cheap."

"Budget concerns," Victoria said dismissively, waving her hand. "We'll worry about that later. Standard D: Audience development. Marketing and distribution for underrepresented audiences."

André gestured vaguely. "We can technically meet that, but it's a hard sell. 'Come see Hitler: now with more diverse marketing executives!'"

"So we need to focus on Standard A." Victoria stopped pacing and placed her hands on the table. "Which means our cast needs a significant overhaul."

David straightened in his chair. "We're not changing historical characters to..."

"We absolutely are," Victoria cut him off. "The history books have had their turn. Now it's our turn."

Aaron's voice came through the speakers. "Victoria, I brought you this project and agreed to direct because it was a serious historical drama about the human capacity for evil. Not a diversity exercise."

"And it still will be," Victoria assured him, her tone softening slightly. "But it will also be a film that can actually win something more significant than 'Best Sound Mixing in a Fascist Biopic.'"

Michelle leaned forward. "So what are you suggesting? Female generals? Black SS officers? Jewish Nazi sympathizers?"

Victoria's smile was sphinx-like. "I'm suggesting we start with Hitler."

The room went silent.

"Hitler," David repeated flatly.

"Hitler," Victoria confirmed. "We need a Hitler who brings something new to the role. Something unexpected. Something that makes people see the character, and history, from an entirely new angle."

Aaron's pixelated face contorted. "You want to race-bend Adolf Hitler?"

"I want to cast the best actor for the role," Victoria corrected. "In a mostly color-blind manner."

André began nodding slowly, a smile spreading across his face. "Oh, I see where this is going. It's genius. Completely batshit, but genius."

"The marketing angles alone..." Michelle murmured, already typing on her phone.

"We don't need another..." Victoria paused, carefully selecting her words. "...traditional interpretation. Let's do something completely different."

David looked pained. "So you want a Black Hitler? A Latino Hitler? An Asian Hitler?"

"I want the right Hitler," Victoria replied primly. "Someone who can carry this film, someone who can stand up to Kennedy's inevitable scene-stealing, and someone who will generate enough conversation that we can sell foreign rights before anyone realizes we've created a historical abomination."

Lucy's fingers had stopped moving entirely, her expression frozen in a mask of professional neutrality that couldn't quite conceal her alarm.

Aaron cleared his throat. "Victoria, may I have a word? Privately?"

"Of course." Victoria smiled at the team. "Start thinking outside the box, people. André, work up some preliminary marketing concepts. David, review the script for any changes we'd need to make if our lead is not... traditionally Hitler-esque. Michelle, draft a social strategy for how we position this. I want options by tomorrow morning."

As the team filed out, buzzing with a mixture of excitement and horror, Victoria turned back to the screen. "Lucy, can you set us up in my office?"

"Already done," Lucy replied, still looking slightly shell-shocked. "Aaron's waiting on your private link."

Victoria nodded. "And Lucy? This meeting never happened."

"What meeting?" Lucy replied automatically, the survival reflex of every assistant who'd lasted more than six months in Hollywood.

***

Back in her office, Victoria settled into her chair and clicked the video link. Aaron's face appeared on her screen, no longer softened by the conference room's video system. In high definition, his expression was a complex mixture of fascination and horror.

"Have you completely lost your mind?" he asked without preamble.

"Hello to you too, Aaron." Victoria leaned back, the picture of calm. "I take it you have concerns."

"Concerns? Victoria, you're talking about casting a non-White actor as Adolf Hitler. That's not a concern, that's a career suicide note."

"Is it, though?" She picked up a pen and twirled it between her fingers. "Or is it exactly the kind of bold choice that cuts through the noise?"

"This will be the noise!" Aaron ran a hand through his already disheveled hair. "This is not what I envisioned when I brought you this book. It was supposed to be a serious examination of how ordinary people become monsters, not... whatever this is becoming."

"The 'serious examination' approach has been done, Aaron. *Downfall, The Pianist, Schindler's List;* they've all explored the banality of evil. We need something less banal."

"New doesn't have to mean historically untethered." Aaron's voice had the weary tone of someone who'd had this argument before. "This is my grandfather's history we're talking about."

Victoria's expression softened. "I know. And that's precisely why it needs to be told in a way that makes people actually listen."

She set down the pen and leaned toward the camera. "Aaron, be honest. If we make a traditional Hitler biopic, what happens? Critics call it 'well-crafted but unnecessary.' It gets a limited release. PBS buys the rights for their documentary block. No one under forty or without a history degree sees it."

Aaron was silent, which Victoria took as tacit agreement.

"But if we cast against type? If we create something that makes people uncomfortable in a new way? Suddenly we're having conversations about representation, about how we portray historical villains, about who gets to tell these stories."

"I don't know if my grandfather's history should be a conversation starter," Aaron said quietly.

Victoria nodded, acknowledging the weight of his words. "I understand that. I really do. But Aaron, movies don't change minds by preaching to the converted. They can only change minds by getting people in the door first."

She pulled up a document on her computer. "Did you know that twenty-two percent of millennials aren't sure if they've heard of the Holocaust? Thirty-seven percent of Gen Z can't name a single concentration camp."

Aaron winced.

"Traditional historical dramas aren't reaching them," Victoria continued. "But you know what might? Something unexpected enough to cut through their TikTok feeds."

"By turning Hitler into a diversity hire?" Aaron's tone was skeptical, but less hostile.

"By using creative casting to highlight the absurdity of evil," Victoria corrected. "By making audiences question their assumptions about historical narrative. By creating something relevant to how people actually consume media now."

Aaron was quiet for a moment. "You sound like you actually believe this isn't just a cynical awards play."

"Maybe it started that way," Victoria admitted. "But I'm starting to see the potential here. This could be the kind of film that breaks through; not just commercially, but culturally."

"Or it could be a spectacular disaster."

"Those are often the same thing in retrospect." Victoria smiled. "Look at *The Producers.*"

Aaron's lip twitched despite himself. "Did you just compare our serious historical drama to *Springtime for Hitler*?"

"Life imitates art." She shrugged. "Especially in this town."

Aaron sighed deeply. "I still don't know if this is brilliant or insane."

"In my experience, the best projects are both." Victoria leaned forward. "Aaron, I know what this means to you. I wouldn't suggest it if I didn't think it could work."

"You've been wrong before."

"Yes, but I've been right more often." She paused. "And when I've been right, it's been spectacular."

Aaron removed his glasses and rubbed the bridge of his nose. "You know what really kills me? Part of me thinks this might actually work. What does that say about me?"

"That you understand today's media landscape better than you want to admit."

He laughed ruefully. "Hardly a comforting thought."

Victoria leaned forward. "Sometimes projects need a different perspective. And this one needs your unique perspective, Aaron. Your eyes on this material will bring something special to it."

Aaron's mouth quirked. "My 'unique perspective'? Is that code for 'Jewish'?"

Victoria shook her head. "No, it's about how you see film. You haven't forgotten why stories matter. You still believe in what movies can do beyond algorithms and focus groups."

"So not the 'diverse voice' thing, then."

"This industry is filled with people who forgot why they started making movies. You haven't. That's the perspective we need." Victoria's expression softened. "I don't want you to sacrifice your vision. I need you to find someone really, really good."

"And on budget."

"Yes, on budget, but really, really good."

"And of color."

"Ideally, yes, but really, really, really good." She emphasized each "really" with growing intensity.

"I'm sensing a pattern," Aaron said.

"The pattern is excellence." Victoria raised an eyebrow. "Excellence that happens to challenge conventional historical depictions."

Victoria decided it was time for her closer. "I know asking you to take this leap is a lot. Which is why I'm prepared to offer you something in return."

Aaron raised an eyebrow. "I'm listening."

"How long have you been trying to get your PGA mark?"

His posture shifted subtly. "Three years. Why?"

"This could be your ticket. You already have the director credit but now you'll also get a full producer credit. PGA-certified."

Aaron's expression remained neutral, but his eyes betrayed his interest. "You have that authority?"

"Sean just reaffirmed his complete confidence in my handling of this project." Victoria smiled. "So yes, I have that authority."

Aaron was quiet for a long moment. "You know, using my own ambition against my principles is a particularly elegant form of manipulation."

"I prefer to think of it as aligning incentives."

"You would." He sighed again. "I need some assurances."

"Name them."

"First, whoever we cast has to be exceptional. Not just good, not just interesting; truly extraordinary."

"Agreed."

"Second, the script maintains its integrity. No 'Eva Braun created the Third Reich' nonsense."

"I'll handle Kennedy."

"Third," Aaron leaned toward the camera, his expression deadly serious. "This can't become a circus. The subject matter deserves respect, even with... unconventional casting."

Victoria nodded solemnly. "I promise you, Aaron. This will be a film that matters."

He studied her face for a long moment. "You know, when you talk like that, with those Machiavellian eyes of yours, I almost believe you can pull this off."

"My 'Machiavellian eyes'?" Victoria repeated, amused. "Is that code for something?"

"It's code for 'you see angles no one else does.'" Aaron put his glasses back on. "Some would call it manipulative. I've always found it rather brilliant."

"High praise from the man who once called me 'Hollywood's most elegant shark.'"

"A compliment you promptly had printed on business cards."

Victoria laughed. "Only for special occasions."

Aaron's expression turned thoughtful. "You know, there was an actor I saw in London. Richard III at the Young Vic. He was... remarkable. Half-Black, I think. Classical training, but modern sensibility."

"Name?"

"James Wright. Or James something Wright, I think, formally. He kept his Nigerian middle name."

Victoria made a note. "I'm listening."

"He has this quality: he can make you understand monsters from the inside out. His Richard was both charming and terrifying. You understood why people followed him even as he led them to destruction."

"Sounds promising. Can he carry a film?"

"He hasn't had the chance yet. He's mostly done stage work and supporting roles in British television."

"So he's affordable."

Aaron smiled wryly. "I was focusing on his acting qualifications, but yes, he's likely within our budget."

"See? Your artistic instincts and my commercial ones make a perfect team." Victoria tapped her pen on the desk. "Can you send me his materials? And reach out to him directly?"

"I'll make some calls." Aaron paused. "Victoria, are we really doing this? Casting a Black actor as Hitler?"

"We're casting the best actor for the role," Victoria corrected. "If he happens to be Black, well... that's just our unique artistic vision."

"God help us all." Aaron shook his head, but he was smiling faintly. "I'll be back by Wednesday. Try not to completely reimagine world history before then."

"No promises." Victoria's smile was genuine now. "And Aaron? Thank you. I know this isn't easy."

"Nothing worth doing ever is." He adjusted his glasses. "Especially in this town."

She leaned back in her chair, fingers drumming a quiet rhythm on the armrest. The day had taken an unexpected turn. Twelve hours ago, Hitler was a problem to discard. Now, Hitler was her hill to die on or perhaps the mountain to plant her victory flag.

Victoria reached for her phone and pulled up her messages, scrolling to a thread labeled "Damage Control." Her thumb hovered over the screen before typing:

Need everything on James Wright, British stage actor, currently Richard III at the Young Vic. Theatre reviews, interviews, social media history. Especially anything mentioning politics, activism, identity. Budget parameters = "emerging talent tier." ASAP.

She hit send and placed the phone face-down on her desk. In Hollywood, even your screen saver could constitute insider trading.

Victoria stood and walked to her window, looking out at the Pinnacle lot. From her office, she could see six soundstages, each housing its own universe of creative egos, budget compromises, and craft services complaints. Somewhere on this lot, Paul Giamatti was probably arguing about the historical accuracy of a wig. Elsewhere, a first-time director was discovering that her "final cut" privileges had an asterisk the size of Texas attached.

And here she was, plotting to cast a Black actor as Hitler.

She found herself smiling. Not the practiced smile she deployed in executive meetings or the tight grimace she offered Sean Lynch over McCarthy salads. A genuine smile of someone who'd stumbled into an idea so absurd it might actually qualify as original.

Her intercom buzzed. Lucy's voice came through. "I have that information you requested about James Wright."

"Already? That was fast even for you."

"André's assistant owes me a favor. Plus, his UK agent had a package ready."

"Come in, then."

Lucy entered, tablet in hand, her expression suggesting she'd read something that unsettled her industry-calibrated sensibilities.

"So," Victoria said, returning to her desk. "what do we know about our potential Hitler?"

Lucy consulted her tablet. "James Olayinka Wright. British, thirty-two. Father is Professor Michael Wright, a White literature professor at Oxford. Mother is Dr. Folake Wright, née Olayinka, a Nigerian academic. Great-grandfather on the father's side was a WWII veteran."

"Interesting." Victoria leaned forward. "Professional background?"

"RADA trained. Primarily stage work, focusing on Shakespeare and classical theatre. Limited screen roles, mostly BBC period dramas in supporting parts." Lucy swiped through her notes. "Critics love him. 'Transformative presence,' 'psychological depth,' 'makes villains comprehensible without excusing them.'"

"Awards?"

"Olivier nomination for *Richard III*. Won the Evening Standard Award for Most Promising Newcomer three years ago."

"Controversies? Social media disasters? Secret OnlyFans account?"

Lucy almost smiled. "Remarkably clean, actually. Limited social media presence. Occasionally tweets about arts funding or refugee issues. Nothing that would alarm Legal."

"How refreshing. And disappointing." Victoria tapped her pen against her desk. "Representation?"

"Margaret Thorne at Spotlight Artists. She's an industry veteran, been representing British theatre actors for decades. According to André's source, she's 'carefully exploring opportunities for James in American productions.'"

"I bet they are." Victoria narrowed her eyes thoughtfully. "What's his quote likely to be?"

Lucy named a figure that made Victoria smile.

"Perfect. In our range, but not suspiciously low." She leaned back. "What else?"

Lucy hesitated. "There's one thing." She swiped again on her tablet. "In an interview with *The Guardian* last year, he talked about his approach to selecting roles."

"Meaning?"

"He said, and I quote: 'I'm drawn to characters with complexity and psychological depth, regardless of their background. I've been fortunate to work with directors and writers who see me as an actor first, not defined by my ethnicity. What matters to me is the humanity in the role, the opportunity to explore the full spectrum of human experience through my craft.'"

Victoria nodded thoughtfully. "Eloquent. And perfect for our purposes."

"He's certainly unexpected," Lucy agreed, her professional composure cracking slightly to reveal the absurdity of their situation.

"What about scheduling? Is he available?"

"Currently starring as *Richard III* at the Young Vic. The same production Aaron saw. Runs for another six weeks."

Victoria waved dismissively. "The escape clause. Every theater contract has one for film opportunities. It's practically a tradition; stage actors dropping out mid-run when Hollywood calls."

"There would be a buyout fee."

"Worth it. Is there an understudy?"

"Yes, and according to André's source, the understudy is 'eager for the opportunity.'" Lucy's tone suggested she was reading directly from a message.

"Of course he is. Understudies live for career-making illnesses and Hollywood poaching." Victoria tapped her pen against her desk. "So there's nothing stopping us from getting him in for a read immediately if Aaron can make the connection."

"Just the small matter of offering him Hitler," Lucy pointed out.

Victoria stood and walked back to her awards shelf, picking up her BAFTA and repositioning it slightly. "Lucy, what do you think of all this? Really."

Lucy blinked, startled by the personal question. In three years working together, Victoria had rarely solicited her genuine opinion.

"About casting a Black actor as Hitler?"

"Yes."

Lucy considered for a moment. "Professionally speaking, it's high-risk, high-reward. If it works, it's revolutionary. If it fails..."

"Career suicide," Victoria finished.

"For everyone involved," Lucy agreed.

"And personally speaking?"

Lucy hesitated again, weighing her response. "Personally... I think it's either brilliant satire or deeply problematic, and I'm not entirely sure which. I don't really know if the left or right will love or hate you more."

Victoria placed the BAFTA back in its precise location. "That's exactly the reaction we want. Uncertainty creates conversation. Conversation creates relevance." She turned to face her assistant. "And relevance wins awards."

Lucy nodded, still looking slightly uncomfortable. "Is there anything else you need before your next meeting?"

"Yes. Tell André I need concept posters by Friday. Nothing with actual faces yet; just tonal approaches. And get casting to get me other actors of this caliber who could play Hitler, as understudies. Oh, and have Legal start preparing an offer for Wright, contingent on a chemistry read with Kennedy."

"Chemistry read? For Hitler and Eva Braun?" Lucy couldn't hide her skepticism.

"Kennedy will demand it once she hears about the casting. We might as well get ahead of it." Victoria sat back at her desk. "And Lucy? All of this stays strictly confidential. If the trades get wind of this before we're ready, I'll know exactly where to look."

"Understood. Not a word." Lucy turned to leave, then paused. "Victoria? For what it's worth, I think Sean Lynch is wrong about you."

Victoria raised an eyebrow. "Oh?"

"A 'unique perspective' isn't just about checking boxes. After years of walking the tightrope between commerce and creativity, you're the only one who'd think of something this audacious and have the nerve to actually do it."

Before Victoria could respond, Lucy had slipped out of the office, leaving her with the unexpected sensation of being genuinely surprised; a rarity in an industry where predictability was the only reliable currency.

Victoria turned back to her awards shelf, studying the collection of gold-plated validation. Each award represented a risk that had paid off. Each risk had begun exactly like this: an idea too strange to ignore, too compelling to dismiss.

"Black Hitler," she said to her Oscar. "This might be your new best friend... or the end of all our careers."

The Oscar, like all good Hollywood players, kept its opinion to itself.

***

CHAPTER 3

Aaron Weisman had spent twenty years in the film industry witnessing actors pretend. He'd sat through countless auditions, endured innumerable rehearsals, and weathered more performances than he could count. Over time, he'd developed what he considered a healthy skepticism about the transformative power of acting: a necessary defense mechanism in an industry where hyperbole was the default currency and "revolutionary" performances were announced with the regularity of Marvel sequels.

Which is why, sitting in the fourth row of London's Young Vic, Aaron found himself profoundly unsettled by what was happening on stage.

James Olayinka Wright wasn't playing Richard III. He had become him.

The transformation was visceral, immediate, and disturbing. Wright's body contorted into Richard's famous hunch, his left arm withered against his chest, his gait a predatory limp across the minimalist stage. But it was his eyes, dark, intelligent, and terrifyingly alive, that held Aaron transfixed. They contained multitudes: the cunning of a natural tactician, the wounded pride of a man born different, and most disturbingly, the glee of someone who had discovered his talent for manipulation.

"Now is the winter of our discontent," Wright began, his voice a silken instrument that caressed each syllable of Shakespeare's text, "made glorious summer by this sun of York."

Aaron had heard the famous opening dozens of times, but never like this: as though Richard were sharing a delicious secret with the audience. Wright delivered the lines with the intimate satisfaction of a man unwrapping a gift he'd been anticipating for years.

Emily, seated beside him, squeezed his hand. The first time, weeks ago, she'd dragged him here to pry him away from his work dinners; tonight was his idea, last-minute tickets she'd charmed out of an old client, requested with an urgency he hadn't explained. "I need to see him again before I trust what I remember" was all he'd offered.

Aaron barely noticed. His attention remained locked on Wright, who was transforming the theater into his own psychological playground. When Wright's Richard shifted from soliloquy to dialogue, Aaron observed something remarkable: the actor maintained two distinct realities simultaneously. There was Richard's interior world, revealed to the audience through asides and expressions, and the careful persona he presented to the other characters. Wright navigated between these dimensions with frightening precision.

During the seduction of Lady Anne, Wright's Richard deployed charm like a weapon, his disability seemingly melting away as he approached her, only to return when he turned back to the audience with a triumphant smile. "Was ever woman in this humor wooed? Was ever woman in this humor won?" he asked, and a chill ran down Aaron's spine at the predatory satisfaction in Wright's voice.

As the play progressed, Wright's Richard accumulated power with the methodical precision of someone setting a complicated trap. Each betrayal, each manipulation, each murder was executed with such clear-eyed purpose that Aaron found himself understanding (not sympathizing with, but *understanding*) how a person could justify such acts to themselves.

By the time Richard ascended to the throne, Aaron wasn't watching a performance. He was witnessing a case study in how monsters are made: not born fully formed, but created through a thousand small choices, each one making the next atrocity easier.

The coronation scene struck Aaron with particular force. Wright sat on the throne, crown slightly askew, fingers drumming on the armrest in a gesture that somehow conveyed both triumph and immediate boredom. He had achieved his goal and found it instantly hollow; a man who could only find meaning in pursuit, not possession.

"What does he want now?" Emily whispered.

Aaron shook his head slightly.

In the play's final act, as Richard's power began to unravel, Wright revealed new layers. The confidence cracked, showing glimpses of the frightened, angry man beneath the monstrous exterior. The famous "My kingdom for a horse!" wasn't delivered as a desperate battlefield cry but as the petulant rage of a child whose toys were being taken away.

By the time Richard fell in battle, Aaron realized he had been holding his breath. The audience exploded into applause, but Aaron remained motionless, processing what he had witnessed.

Emily was on her feet, applauding with the rest of the audience. Aaron rose mechanically beside her, his mind already racing past appreciation to possibility.

This was what the Hitler project needed: not just technical skill, but this visceral understanding of how a human being becomes a monster while believing themselves the hero of their own story.

The cast took their bows, and when Wright stepped forward (now fully himself, the hunch gone, standing tall with a humility that seemed almost incongruous after his dominating performance) the theater erupted.

Someone threw flowers. A group of drama students in the balcony began stomping their feet in rhythmic appreciation.

Emily turned to Aaron, her face flushed with the peculiar high that comes from witnessing exceptional art. "Now *that* is what I call acting," she said, her voice raised above the continuing applause. "Worth watching a second time, don't you think?"

Aaron nodded, but his response wasn't about the play anymore. His thoughts had already jumped to Victoria's absurd Hitler proposal, and suddenly it didn't seem absurd at all. It seemed inevitable.

"I need to talk to him," Aaron said.

Emily raised an eyebrow. "Who? Wright? You can't be serious."

"Deadly serious. Can you get us backstage?"

Emily stared at him. "Aaron, I'm a literary agent, not a theater manager. I can't just..."

"You know people. You always know people." Aaron took her hands in his. "Em, this is important."

"Why?" Emily studied her husband's face. "Wait. This is about your Hitler project, isn't it?"

Aaron's silence was confirmation enough.

Emily's eyes widened. "Is that why you made me get these tickets so last minute? You can't possibly be thinking..."

"I am absolutely thinking."

"Aaron, that's insane. He's Black."

"Yes."

"And you want him to play Hitler?"

"Yes."

Emily blinked several times in rapid succession. "Have you been drinking?"

"Not nearly enough for this conversation." Aaron squeezed her hands. "Em, you saw what he just did up there. He made a monster human without excusing a single horrible act. That's exactly what our film needs."

"But Hitler? A Black Hitler?" Emily's voice lowered to an urgent whisper. "Honey, you'll be crucified. Both of you."

"Or it will be the most talked-about film of the year."

Emily stared at her husband as the audience began filtering toward the exits. After fifteen years of marriage to a filmmaker, she recognized the particular gleam in his eye: the intoxicating mix of artistic excitement and commercial calculation that preceded either his greatest triumphs or most spectacular failures.

"I know that look," she sighed. "Fine. I'll see what I can do. But when this blows up in your face, remember I warned you."

"If it blows up in my face, I'll dedicate my memoir to your foresight," Aaron promised. "But if it works..."

"It will still be completely insane." Emily pulled out her phone. "Let me text my contact at the theater."

***

The backstage area of the Young Vic hummed with post-performance energy: that peculiar mixture of exhaustion and exhilaration that follows creative adrenaline. Through Emily's connection, a former client who now worked in theater management, they'd secured access to the green room, where cast members were gradually appearing after removing costumes and makeup.

Aaron paced while Emily chatted with her contact, rehearsing his pitch in his head. How exactly does one approach an acclaimed Black British actor about playing Adolf Hitler? The absurdity of his mission hit him anew each time he completed a circuit of the room.

"He's coming," Emily whispered, returning to Aaron's side. "Apparently, he's always the last one out; takes his time transitioning back from character."

"Method?" Aaron asked.

"No, just thorough. Olivia says he's remarkably normal for someone with his talent. No drama, no ego trips."

"That'll change once he hits Hollywood," Aaron muttered.

Emily elbowed him. "Be nice. And please try not to sound completely deranged when you propose this."

Before Aaron could respond, James Wright entered the green room. In person, he was taller than he'd appeared on stage, his posture now straight and confident where Richard's had been twisted. With the bone structure of a classical statue and the presence of someone who'd never needed to raise his voice to command attention, Wright carried himself with the quiet assurance of genuinely talented actors who hadn't yet been corrupted by Hollywood's ego inflation system.

The stubble along his jaw was precisely maintained, not the calculated three-day growth of actors trying to look "approachable" for Vanity Fair, but the natural result of a man who'd been too focused on his craft to shave that morning.

He wore simple clothes: dark jeans and a gray Henley that revealed forearms corded with the lean muscle of someone who trained for stamina rather than magazine covers. Toweling his close-cropped hair dry after what must have been a quick shower, every trace of the tyrant king had vanished, replaced by a man who moved with the relaxed grace of someone comfortable in his own skin. Aaron immediately understood why casting directors would scramble to work with him: Wright possessed that rarest of screen qualities, something truly special. He was interesting to look at even when doing absolutely nothing.

Wright spotted Emily's contact and smiled, walking over to greet her warmly. After a brief exchange, she gestured toward Aaron and Emily. Wright nodded and approached them, hand extended.

"James Wright," he said, his voice now carrying the cadence of educated British English. "Olivia says you're interested in speaking with me."

Aaron took his hand, noting the firm grip. "Aaron Weisman. This is my wife, Emily Davidson-Weisman. Your performance was extraordinary."

"Thank you." Wright's smile was genuine but measured, the polite appreciation of someone who had heard similar compliments before but still valued them. "Always nice to hear, especially from industry professionals. Olivia mentioned you're a producer?"

"And director, yes, with Pinnacle Pictures in Los Angeles." Aaron gestured to Emily. "My wife is a literary agent with Creative Artists Partners."

"Ah, the real power in the relationship then," Wright said with a smile toward Emily.

Emily laughed. "I handle books. He handles egos. Different species of chaos."

Wright's laugh was warm and unguarded. "Fair enough. What brings you to our humble production? Just taking in London theater?"

Aaron exchanged a quick glance with Emily. "Actually, I'm here for work. I'm producing a historical drama, and after seeing your performance tonight, I'm convinced you'd be perfect for the lead."

Interest flickered in Wright's eyes. "That's very flattering. What's the project?"

"It's..." Aaron hesitated, suddenly aware of how the next words would sound. "It's a film about the rise of Adolf Hitler."

Wright's expression remained impressively neutral, but one eyebrow rose slightly. "I see. And you're interested in me for...?"

"Hitler," Aaron confirmed. "The lead role."

A beat of silence followed.

"Hitler," Wright repeated, his tone perfectly flat.

"Yes."

"Adolf Hitler."

"The very same."

Wright looked from Aaron to Emily and back again, seemingly checking if this was some elaborate joke. Finding only earnest intention, he gestured to a quiet corner of the room. "Perhaps we should sit down."

Once seated in the corner, away from the dwindling crowd of cast and crew, Wright leaned forward. "Mr. Weisman..."

"Aaron, please."

"Aaron. I appreciate your interest, and I'm flattered by your response to my performance. But I'm a bit confused about the... conceptual framework here."

Aaron nodded. "I understand your hesitation. Believe me, I had the same reaction when our executive first suggested it. I'm Jewish, and my grandfather survived Dachau, so this material is deeply personal for me."

"Which makes your interest in me even more perplexing," Wright said carefully.

"Not at all." Aaron leaned forward. "What I saw tonight was an actor who can inhabit moral complexity without simplifying it. You made Richard III simultaneously monstrous and human; exactly what this film needs. Hitler wasn't a cartoon villain; he was a human being who made monstrous choices, convinced others to follow him, and changed history through the force of his charisma and cruelty."

"While I appreciate that analysis," Wright said, "there's still the rather obvious issue of my appearance not aligning with historical reality."

Emily, who had been silent, interjected. "James, if I may: my husband tends to get carried away with the artistic merits before addressing the practical concerns. Perhaps you could explain the concept, Aaron?"

Aaron nodded gratefully. "We don't need another 'traditional' interpretation. We want to do something completely different. We've seen dozens of portrayals of Hitler that all follow the same visual and narrative patterns. This project needs your unique perspective. Your eyes on this material would bring something special to it."

Wright arched an eyebrow slightly. "My 'unique perspective'?"

"We need something completely new," Aaron continued, not acknowledging the question. "Something that forces audiences to confront their assumptions about how we depict historical figures, especially monsters."

Wright's expression remained skeptical. "So this is conceptual art, then? Political commentary?"

"It's serious drama that acknowledges we're making art, not a documentary," Aaron replied. "It's Shakespeare with Black actors playing European royalty. It's 'Hamilton' with multicultural founding fathers. It's using the tools of our art form to make audiences see familiar history with fresh eyes."

Emily shot her husband a quick, curious glance, noticing the shift in his language: the corporate cadence suddenly infiltrating his normally straightforward speech.

Wright studied Aaron with intelligent eyes. "I see. And who's directing this... conceptual approach to Hitler?"

"I am. I'd be with you every step of the way; I'm not just here to sign you up and run," Aaron said. "The project is being championed by Victoria Martinez, one of our top executives at Pinnacle. She's assembled an impressive team."

Wright nodded slowly. "And the script? Is it historically accurate apart from this casting approach?"

"Absolutely. We've had historians consulting at every stage." Which wasn't technically a lie; the historical consultant quit a lot, but he was there for every stage. "The film tracks Hitler's rise from obscurity to power, examining how a failed artist and dismissed political agitator managed to seize control of a nation and lead it toward atrocity."

"Hmm." Wright's fingers drummed once on his knee, a gesture Aaron recognized from his performance: a thinking tic that had transferred from actor to character rather than the reverse. "And who's playing Eva Braun? Another casting against historical type?"

Aaron hesitated. "Kennedy Oswald is attached."

"The romantic comedy actress?" Wright's surprise was evident. "That's... an interesting choice."

"She's looking to branch out," Aaron said diplomatically.

"I'm sure." Wright's tone suggested he understood exactly what that meant in industry terms. He looked thoughtful for a moment, then asked, "Why are you really doing this, Aaron? Beyond the artistic explanations and breaking new ground, why this approach with this subject?"

The directness of the question caught Aaron off guard. He glanced at Emily, who gave him a slight nod; a silent instruction to be honest.

Aaron sighed. "The truth? We've been making films about Hitler and Nazi Germany for decades. Some are excellent, some are exploitative, but most are forgettable because they follow the same visual and narrative template. Meanwhile, fewer and fewer people, especially young people, understand how fascism actually took root. A democratic society transformed into a genocidal regime not overnight, but through a series of choices that people rationalized to themselves. The term Nazi is losing its potency, and people are even starting to question whether the Holocaust was real."

He leaned forward. "But I saw your Richard III tonight. You showed us how a monster is made from the inside out; choice by choice, justification by justification. That's what I want for this film. Not another mustache-twirling villain, but a complex portrait of human evil that forces audiences to recognize the warning signs in our own time."

Wright studied him for a long moment. "That's a worthy aim. But there are less provocative ways to achieve it."

"Are there?" Aaron challenged. "When was the last time you saw a historical drama that genuinely surprised you? That made you see something familiar in a new light? Most people think they already know the Hitler story, which means they've stopped actually seeing it."

Wright didn't respond immediately. Instead, he looked to Emily. "Mrs. Weisman, you've been rather quiet. What's your perspective on this... unorthodox approach?"

Emily shot her husband a quick glance before answering. "Professionally? I think it's either brilliant or career suicide, likely both. Personally?" She paused. "I think art should provoke thought, not just comfort. But I also think context matters enormously with sensitive historical material."

Wright nodded appreciatively. "A diplomatic answer."

"I'm a literary agent," Emily replied with a smile. "Diplomacy pays the bills."

Wright laughed, then turned back to Aaron. "This isn't a decision I can make lightly. I'd need to read the script, speak with Ms. Martinez, understand the full creative vision."

"Of course," Aaron agreed quickly, trying to contain his excitement at what wasn't a "no."

"I'm also concerned about potential backlash," Wright continued. "Not just for me personally, though that's certainly a consideration, but for the historical significance. The Holocaust isn't abstract history for many people; it's family memory. Including my own family. I wouldn't want to participate in anything that trivializes that reality."

"I understand completely," Aaron said. "My grandfather..."

"Survived Dachau, yes," Wright finished for him. "Which is precisely why your involvement intrigues me. If you, with that personal connection, believe this approach has merit, it suggests you've thought deeply about the implications."

Aaron nodded, suddenly feeling the weight of his grandfather's history on his shoulders. Had he thought deeply enough about the implications? Or was he rationalizing an outrageous concept because it offered the path of least resistance to getting his PGA mark?

"I have thought about it," Aaron said finally. "And I believe that art sometimes needs to break convention to make people truly see. But I also believe we have an obligation to handle this material with appropriate gravity."

Wright seemed to appreciate the honesty, though a flicker of amusement crossed his face at Aaron's borrowed corporate phrasing. "My 'unique perspective,' you say. And what might that be, exactly?"

Aaron shifted slightly. "Your ability to bring humanity to monstrous characters without excusing their actions."

"Ah." Wright nodded, a knowing half-smile suggesting he recognized the verbal dodge. "For a moment I thought you meant something else entirely with that 'unique perspective' comment."

"What else would I mean?" Aaron asked with practiced innocence.

"Nothing, nothing." Wright's smile widened fractionally. "I've just heard similar phrasing in industry meetings before. Usually right before someone suggests I'd be 'perfect' for a role that happens to involve tribal drums or a Nigerian prince."

Emily coughed discreetly into her hand, unable to completely suppress her reaction.

"That's not..." Aaron began.

"I know," Wright cut him off, not unkindly. "Send me the script. And have Ms. Martinez call my agent: Margaret Thorne at Spotlight Artists. I'm not saying yes, but I'm willing to explore the conversation."

Aaron felt a surge of relief mixed with the distinct discomfort of having his borrowed language so neatly exposed. "Thank you. That's all we're asking for now. I'll have everything sent first thing tomorrow."

As they stood to leave, Wright fixed Aaron with a penetrating look. "One more question, if I may. What does Victoria Martinez envision for this project? Is this purely about provoking controversy, or does she have a deeper purpose?"

Aaron hesitated, remembering Victoria's mercurial blend of cynicism and unexpected idealism. "She's a complex person. Part of her sees the commercial and awards potential in doing something revolutionary. But another part genuinely believes in challenging how we tell historical stories, especially when those stories risk becoming so familiar we stop learning from them."

Wright nodded, seeming satisfied with the answer. "Well then. Let's see where this conversation leads."

As they exchanged contact information, Aaron felt a curious mixture of excitement and dread. He had come to London for background research, not to potentially cast the most controversial Hitler in cinema history. Yet here he was, setting in motion what could either be a revolutionary artistic statement or a spectacular career-ending disaster.

Emily's expression as they left the theater told him she was thinking the exact same thing.

"So," she said as they stepped into the cool London evening, "that went better than expected. He didn't laugh in your face or call security."

"He called me out on that 'unique perspective' line, though," Aaron admitted, wincing slightly.

"Yes, he did." Emily's tone was the verbal equivalent of a raised eyebrow. "Since when do you talk about 'unique perspectives' and 'different eyes on material'? You sound like you swallowed a corporate PR handbook."

Aaron shrugged. "Victoria used those exact phrases when she pitched me on this concept."

"And did you believe it when she said it to you?"

"Not really," Aaron admitted. "It felt like classic studio doubletalk."

"Yet here you are, passing it along verbatim." Emily's tone was more amused than accusatory. "Hollywood's version of telephone?"

"He's intrigued," Aaron replied, changing the subject. "Artists are always drawn to the unexpected."

"And you?" Emily linked her arm through his as they walked. "Are you really prepared for what happens if he says yes? If you actually make 'Black Hitler'?"

Aaron looked up at the London sky, searching for stars mostly hidden by city lights and gathering clouds. "I don't know," he admitted. "But I do know what I saw on that stage tonight. If anyone can make this work, it's him."

"Making it 'work' and surviving the aftermath are two different things," Emily pointed out.

"True." Aaron squeezed her arm gently. "But that's the price of making something that matters."

"Or the price of Hollywood absurdity reaching new heights," Emily countered, but her tone was affectionate. After a decade and a half with Aaron, she knew that the line between visionary and foolhardy was often invisible until after the fact.

"Either way," Aaron said, "Victoria's going to be thrilled."

"Victoria Martinez." Emily shook her head. "The woman who green-lit 'Daughters of War' and now wants to make 'Black Hitler.' She's either a genius or completely insane."

"In Hollywood," Aaron replied with a small smile, "those are often the same thing."

***

CHAPTER 4

Margaret Thorne's office in Soho occupied that sweet spot of London real estate that communicated success without ostentation. The entertainment industry equivalent of a firm handshake. Neither flashy Mayfair nor grimly practical Clerkenwell, it projected exactly what Margaret herself did: reliable professionalism with just enough style to be taken seriously.

James sat in one of her carefully selected visitor chairs, designed to be comfortable enough for clients to relax but not so comfortable they'd overstay. The walls displayed a carefully curated selection of production posters featuring her clients, prominent enough to impress visitors, but with enough space between to suggest selectivity.

Margaret sat behind her desk, reading glasses perched at the precise midpoint of her nose as she scrolled through her iPad. At sixty-two, she had the bearing of someone who had survived four decades of industry nonsense through the twin weapons of impeccable taste and tactical bluntness.

"So," she said, looking up from the screen, "Hitler."

James nodded. "Hitler."

"Well." She removed her glasses and set them on the desk with theatrical precision. "That's certainly... unexpected."

"That seems to be the point," James replied.

Margaret's lips twitched in what might have been amusement. "Aaron Weisman. Jewish producer/director with family Holocaust connections. Victoria Martinez. Latina executive with a reputation for calculated risks. And they want you," she gestured vaguely toward James, "to play Adolf Hitler."

"That's the proposition."

"And your thoughts?" Margaret's tone was carefully neutral, the cultivated blankness of an agent waiting to align with her client's position before revealing her own.

James considered for a moment. "I'm intrigued by the challenge. Getting inside the psychology of someone who perpetrated such evil while convincing others to follow him."

"Yes, the psychological aspect is fascinating," Margaret agreed smoothly, her eyes never leaving his face. "And the representation angle is... potent."

"Representation?" James repeated, one eyebrow lifting slightly.

"This is a barrier-breaking opportunity," Margaret said, shifting into what James recognized as her pitch voice. "Look at Jodie Turner-Smith. She played Anne Boleyn, a historically White Tudor queen, in that Channel 5 miniseries. Yes, there was controversy, but where is she now? Star Wars. Major Netflix projects. Cover of *British Vogue*."

James leaned back slightly. "Are you suggesting that controversy was good for her career?"

"I'm suggesting that breaking historical casting conventions created opportunities," Margaret replied with practiced precision. "She went from relatively unknown to a name on everyone's lips. From Channel 5 to Disney. And she became virtually untouchable to critics because she made history with that role."

"By playing someone from history."

"Exactly," Margaret said, missing or ignoring his dry tone. "Think about it: you'd be the first Black actor to portray Hitler in a major production. You'd be making history. Redefining how we approach historical figures. Challenging the entire concept of who gets to portray whom."

"I'm not particularly interested in being the first Black Hitler as a political statement," James said. "If I consider this, it would be for the psychological complexity of the role."

"Of course, of course," Margaret backpedaled with practiced ease. "The artistic challenge is paramount. I merely mention the groundbreaking nature as a... supplementary consideration."

James suppressed a smile. Margaret had represented him for seven years, ever since she'd spotted him in a student production at RADA. She had guided his career with a shrewd blend of artistic sensitivity and commercial instinct. But occasionally, her agenting instincts overwhelmed her understanding of his priorities.

"The script is actually quite good," Margaret continued, tapping her iPad. "Nuanced examination of Hitler's rise, the sociopolitical conditions that enabled him, the incremental normalization of extremism. Dramatically solid."

"And the inevitable backlash?" James asked. "Have you considered that?"

Margaret's expression shifted to what James thought of as her "concerned professional" face. Eyes softening while her posture remained impeccably upright.

"There will be noise," she admitted. "Conservative media will have opinions. Some Jewish organizations may express concerns. Twitter will do what Twitter does. But backlash creates conversation, and conversation creates opportunity."

"That sounds remarkably close to what Aaron Weisman said," James observed.

"Great minds," Margaret responded with a thin smile. "Look, James, this is the kind of powerful opportunity that could elevate your entire career trajectory. It's award bait if done right. The kind of role that demonstrates range and fearlessness."

James leaned back slightly. "And if it's perceived as a stunt?"

"Then we leverage the controversy itself." Margaret leaned forward, warming to her strategy. "You become the actor brave enough to tackle difficult material, to challenge conventional thinking about representation and historical portrayal. Either way, you win."

"I'm not sure I share your confidence in that win-win scenario."

Margaret tapped her pen against her desk, three precise taps, her signature thinking gesture. "Let me be candid, James. You're at a critical juncture in your career. You've established yourself in theater, you've done respectable BBC work, but breaking into American film requires something distinctive. Something that makes Hollywood actually pay attention."

"Playing Hitler certainly qualifies as distinctive," James said dryly.

"Precisely." Margaret set down her pen. "Additionally, this creates precedent. Once you've played Hitler, no one can credibly argue you aren't right for, say, Henry V or Hamlet on screen because you 'don't look the part.' You break the ceiling once, dramatically, and suddenly other doors open."

James considered this. It wasn't entirely without merit, though he suspected Margaret was oversimplifying the industry's complex relationship with race and casting.

"Have you thought about using James Olayinka, rather than James Olayinka Wright, for this project?" Margaret asked, her tone deliberately casual. "It would make a more bold statement about embracing your heritage while taking on this provocative role."

James felt a familiar tightening in his chest, the same sensation he experienced whenever someone tried to shape his identity to fit their narrative.

"I'm James Olayinka Wright," he said evenly. "That's my name."

"Of course," Margaret nodded quickly. "I just thought..."

"When I started out, I was told to go by James Wright because Olayinka would 'confuse' casting directors," James continued. "Now suddenly Olayinka should be front and center because it makes a better political statement? This is madness. I am who I am. One look at me tells people who I am. My acting should show them."

Margaret's expression shifted to genuine contrition. "I'm deeply sorry that anyone was ever so racist as to tell you to drop Olayinka. How erasing that must have been."

James studied her face, noting how quickly she'd pivoted from suggesting he emphasize Olayinka to expressing outrage that anyone had ever suggested he minimize it. The moral flexibility of agents never ceased to amaze him.

"I appreciate your concern," he said, letting her off the hook. "And I appreciated the mentor who advised me back then. They were wrong, but they thought they were helping. Just as you're trying to help now."

Margaret relaxed fractionally. "I only want what's best for your career."

"I know. But I will remain James Olayinka Wright, regardless of what role I'm playing."

"Understood." Margaret nodded briskly, moving past the awkward moment with professional efficiency. "So, about this Hitler opportunity..."

James gazed out the window at the London skyline for a moment, gathering his thoughts. The role presented genuine artistic challenges that intrigued him. The chance to explore the psychology of one of history's greatest monsters, to understand the human capacity for self-justification and evil. These were dramatically rich territories. But he wasn't naive about the industry machinations surrounding the project.

"I'm willing to be considered for the role," he said finally. "It's an intriguing challenge to get into the mind of Hitler, to understand how someone could commit such atrocities while convincing themselves and others of their righteousness."

Margaret's face lit up with carefully modulated enthusiasm. "Excellent. I'll inform Weisman and Martinez immediately. They'll want a chemistry read with Kennedy Oswald, of course."

"Kennedy Oswald," James repeated. "Eva Braun."

"Yes. Quite the casting coup for them. She has fifteen million Instagram followers."

"Essential for a Holocaust film," James said, his tone bone-dry.

Margaret chose to ignore the sarcasm. "She's transitioning from romantic comedies to more serious fare. Looking to demonstrate her range."

"Aren't we all," James murmured.

"The chemistry read would likely be remote initially," Margaret continued, already shifting into logistics mode. "They'll send sides, you'll do a self-tape. If that goes well, they might fly you to LA for an in-person read and discussions."

"And if I ultimately accept, what's their timeline?"

"Aggressive. They're up against an option deadline. Pre-production would begin within six weeks. They'd buy out your contract here at the Young Vic."

"What about Richard?" James asked. "I can't just abandon the production."

"Your understudy would step up. Standard practice when Hollywood calls." Margaret waved dismissively. "There'd be a fee, of course, but that's built into the contract."

James frowned slightly. "I made a commitment to that production. To the other actors."

"And they knew this was possible when they cast you," Margaret countered. "Your contract has the standard film/TV escape clause. Everyone understands how this works."

James nodded reluctantly. Theater actors dropping mid-run for screen opportunities was indeed an established tradition, if not one he particularly admired.

"Let's take it one step at a time," he said. "I'll do the chemistry read. We'll see where things go from there."

"Perfect." Margaret made a note on her iPad. "I'll coordinate with Pinnacle immediately."

As James stood to leave, Margaret looked up at him with an expression that seemed, for once, entirely genuine.

"James, whatever happens with this, whether it becomes a groundbreaking achievement or a fascinating footnote, know that I believe in your talent. Not your 'representation value' or your 'barrier-breaking potential.' Your talent."

James smiled slightly. "I know, Margaret, that's why you are my agent."

"Though the barrier-breaking potential is considerable," she added, unable to help herself.

James laughed. "And there she is. The Margaret Thorne I know and tolerate."

"Tolerate? I've made you more money than your last three productions combined."

"And reminded me of it more times than all my drama teachers combined," James countered good-naturedly.

Margaret smiled. "Somebody has to keep your feet on the ground while your head's in Hitler's psyche."

James paused at the door. "That may be the strangest sentence anyone has ever said to me."

"In this industry? I doubt it." Margaret was already turning back to her iPad. "Give it time. Especially if you take this role. I suspect 'strange' is just beginning."

***

The kettle whistled in the kitchen of the Wright family home in Hampstead, a Victorian terrace preserved with that very English mix of reverence for tradition and pragmatic modernization. The kitchen was warm, both in temperature and in spirit, with mismatched mugs collected over decades and bookshelves where cookbooks shared space with academic journals.

Professor Michael Wright moved with practiced efficiency, preparing tea for four with the muscle memory of countless Sunday afternoons. He added an extra spoonful of sugar to his father's cup (Thomas insisted his sweet tooth was the secret to his longevity) and arranged everything on the wooden tray his wife had brought back from Lagos thirty years earlier.

"Still can't believe my grandson's considering playing that bastard," Thomas Wright said from his armchair at the kitchen table, where he'd been stationed to supervise the tea-making. "Though I suppose if anyone could make sense of the madness, it'd be our James."

"Dad, for the tenth time, he hasn't accepted yet," Michael replied, placing the milk jug on the tray. "He's only read the script so far; he's just considering it."

"Well, considering or not, I say good on him. About time someone shook things up." Thomas adjusted his cardigan, a concession to the April chill that had settled over London. "These Americans think they've got it all sorted, don't they? Hollywood this, Hollywood that. Give 'em a proper English acting lesson, I say."

Michael smiled to himself. His father's pride in James had always been boundless, bordering on the ridiculous. When James had played Hamlet at the Adelphi, Thomas had informed every nurse, doctor, and fellow patient during his cataract surgery that his grandson was "redefining the Danish prince for the modern age."

"Let's go through," Michael said, lifting the tray. "They'll be deep into one of Folake's sociopolitical analyses by now, and James will need rescuing."

In the living room, Dr. Folake Wright was indeed mid-explanation, gesturing animatedly while James sat across from her, the book on Hitler's rise open on his lap. Framed family photos covered the walls and surfaces: James's graduation from RADA, Michael and Folake's wedding in Lagos, Thomas's father in RAF uniform beside a Spitfire he'd helped keep flying.

"...which means, of course, that your performative embodiment creates a dialectical tension with the historical record," Folake was saying, her Nigerian accent softened by four decades in British academia but still melodically present. "The audience must then confront their own preconceptions about... oh, brilliant! The tea's ready."

"Just in time," James mouthed to his father with a grateful smile.

"I've made it extra strong," Michael announced, setting down the tray. "I gathered from your mother's theoretical frameworks that we'd need the reinforcements."

Folake swatted her husband's arm affectionately. "You love my theoretical frameworks. You married them."

"I married you despite them," Michael countered with the comfortable teasing of thirty-five years together. "Though I'll admit they've grown on me, rather like an intellectual fungus."

"Charming," Folake said, rolling her eyes but smiling. "Tell that to the undergrads who queue outside my office hours to discuss my latest paper on post-colonial identity construction."

"They're trying to get better marks, love. I've seen the same faces outside my Victorian literature seminars, despite their obvious disinterest in Dickens."

Thomas accepted his tea with a nod of thanks. "Enough academic babble. I want to hear more about this Hitler business. Have you decided, James?"

James set aside the book (Dr. Benjamin Friedman's *The Rise of Tyranny: Hitler's Path to Power*) and accepted his tea. "I'm still thinking it through. The script is surprisingly good. Thoughtful exploration of how a failed artist became history's monster. How ordinary Germans embraced extremism step by step."

"And they want you to play him? A Black Hitler?" Thomas shook his head, though his eyes twinkled with amusement. "What next? Me playing the Queen?"

"You'd look smashing in a tiara, Grandad," James replied with a grin.

"Don't give your grandfather ideas," Michael warned. "He already tried to convince the nurses at his last check-up that he was related to the royal family."

"Fourth cousin twice removed," Thomas said with dignity. "Or so my mother always claimed."

Folake leaned forward, her academic intensity softening into maternal concern. "James, darling, have you thought about the potential backlash? The historical implications? The way certain political elements might weaponize this casting? Americans can be very political, you know."

"Every hour since I was approached," James admitted. "But there's something compelling about it too. The chance to humanize pure evil, not as a contradiction but as a warning. To show how a monster is made choice by choice, not born fully formed."

"It's the Richard III effect," Michael observed. "You made us understand him without sympathizing with him. That's a rare skill."

"The Nazi party constructed a racial hierarchy that positioned what they called 'Aryan' identity at its apex," Folake said, slipping unconsciously into lecture mode. "By casting a Black actor as Hitler, the production creates an inherent contradiction that forces the audience to confront..."

"Christ, Folake, he's not writing a dissertation," Thomas interrupted with an affectionate chuckle. "He's acting in a film."

"A film with significant sociopolitical implications," Folake insisted.

"Every bloody thing has 'significant sociopolitical implications' in your world," Thomas retorted. "Sometimes a story is just a story."

"Nothing is 'just' anything, Thomas," Folake countered. "Especially not a film about Hitler."

Michael caught James's eye over his teacup, their shared look conveying decades of loving exasperation at this familiar dynamic. Thomas and Folake had been having variations of this argument since James was a child: the pragmatic working-class English mechanic and the Nigerian academic theorist with fundamentally different ways of processing the world.

"I think what your mother is trying to say," Michael interjected diplomatically, "is that this role carries more weight than your usual performances."

"I'm well aware," James said. "That's part of what makes it interesting. But also terrifying."

Thomas made a dismissive sound. "You've got the chops for it, lad. Always have done. It's not all about race, you know. Our kid's got gravitas."

"Thank you, Grandad," James said with genuine warmth.

"Besides," Thomas continued, "my dad fought the real Hitler. Didn't come home from the war the same man, according to my mum. Hardly spoke about it. Just woke up shouting some nights." His weathered face grew momentarily distant. "I grew up in the rubble he left behind. Rationing until I was fifteen. Bombed-out buildings everywhere. Playing in craters on the way to school."

The room quieted, a moment of respect for memories rarely shared.

"What do you think Granddad would have made of his great-grandson playing Hitler?" Michael asked softly.

Thomas considered this, taking a long sip of his tea. "You know what? I reckon he'd have laughed himself silly. The idea of Hitler being played by exactly the sort of person he despised? Dad would've called that poetic justice."

James smiled. "I wish I'd known him."

"He'd have been proud as punch of you, same as I am," Thomas said. "Might've questioned your choice of profession, though. A proper actor in the family? We were factory and field people, not stage people."

"Until me," James said with a grin.

"Until you upended everything," Folake agreed with maternal pride. "First actor in either family."

"First potential Hitler too," James added dryly.

Michael chuckled. "There's always a pioneer in every generation."

"So you're leaning toward accepting?" Folake asked, studying her son's face.

James nodded slowly. "I think I am. There's something appealing about the challenge. And Aaron, the director seems to have a vision or at least enough connection to the material to make it seem plausible."

"What about this actress they've cast? The one playing Eva Braun?" Michael asked. "Will that be awkward? Given the, er, historical complexities?"

"Kennedy Oswald," James supplied.

Folake's eyes widened with unexpected recognition. "Kennedy Oswald? From *Summer in Santorini*? And *The Valentine Mix-Up*?"

James looked at his mother in surprise. "Don't tell me you watch romantic comedies, Mum?"

Folake straightened in her chair, adopting her dignified academic posture. "I occasionally engage with popular culture to better understand contemporary narrative constructions of gender and romance."

"She binges them when I'm at my chess club," Michael stage-whispered. "Has a whole list on Netflix."

"Michael!" Folake protested, but her embarrassment quickly transformed into a smile. "Fine. Yes. I enjoy a good romantic comedy. Kennedy Oswald has excellent timing and genuine charisma."

"Your mother's secret shame," Michael told James. "Along with her ABBA collection."

"Cultural touchstones," Folake insisted primly. "Not shame."

"You're playing opposite Kennedy Oswald? That blonde one with all the obsessive fans?" Thomas asked, impressed. "She's a stunner. Saw her in that Christmas film on the telly last year."

"*Mistletoe Mayhem*," Folake supplied, then caught herself. "Or so I've heard."

James couldn't help laughing. "The fact that you're all more impressed by Kennedy Oswald than concerned about me playing Hitler says something about our family priorities."

"We've raised a son who can handle Hitler," Michael said with quiet confidence. "Kennedy Oswald's celebrity empire is far more intimidating."

"Have you done the chemistry read yet?" Folake asked, a hint of girlish excitement breaking through her academic facade.

"Thursday," James confirmed. "Remote session over Zoom. If that goes well, they'll fly me to LA for final discussions."

"LA!" Thomas exclaimed. "Hollywood itself. Your great-grandddad would never believe it."

"What about *Richard III*?" Folake asked. "The production runs for another month."

James sighed. "That's the complicated part. They'd buy out my contract. My understudy would take over."

"Timothy would be thrilled," Michael noted. "He's been waiting for his chance."

"I know, but it still feels like abandoning ship," James admitted.

Thomas set down his cup with surprising force. "Nonsense. You've given that production everything. Timothy's been watching you every night, learning. The theater will survive. Opportunities like this don't come along twice."

"Your grandfather's right," Michael said. "Though I'm sure the Young Vic will be sorry to lose you."

Folake reached across to take her son's hand. "Whatever you decide, we support you. Even if it means playing history's greatest monster."

"Though if you do take it," Thomas added with a mischievous glint, "make sure they get his mustache right. Always thought it looked like he'd sneezed while someone was painting his upper lip."

The tension broke as everyone laughed, the sound filling the warm kitchen like it had throughout James's childhood: authentic, unguarded, and free from the calculated performances of the professional world.

"I've nearly finished the book," James said, indicating Dr. Friedman's tome. "The more I read about Hitler's rise, the more I see parallels to now: the weaponization of economic anxiety, the scapegoating of vulnerable groups, the cult of personality. Maybe there's value in retelling this story in a way that forces people to see it fresh."

"There's always value in good storytelling," Michael said. "Especially when it makes uncomfortable truths harder to ignore."

"And if anyone can find the human being inside the monster without excusing him, it's you," Folake added, her earlier academic tone replaced by simple maternal faith.

Thomas raised his teacup in a makeshift toast. "To my grandson, the actor. May you give Hitler the performance he deserves and would absolutely bloody hate."

They clinked cups, this unusual family united by love and a shared appreciation for life's absurdities. Outside, rain began to patter against the windows in that distinctly English way: not dramatic enough to be remarkable, but persistent enough to shape the mood of the day.

"More tea?" Michael offered, reaching for the pot.

"Please," James said. "And maybe some of those biscuits Grandad pretends not to hoard in the tin marked 'sewing supplies'?"

"Slander and lies," Thomas protested, but his eyes twinkled. "But since you're considering playing Hitler, I suppose you can have one. Maybe two."

"Your generosity knows no bounds, Grandad."

"Neither does my biscuit supply," Thomas replied with dignity. "A man needs his priorities."

As Michael disappeared to retrieve the biscuits, James felt the familiar comfort of being completely himself: neither the classical actor of the London stage nor the potential controversial Hitler of Hollywood, but simply James Olayinka Wright, grandson, son, and a young man still finding his way through an increasingly bizarre world.

***

CHapTer 5

Kennedy Oswald had perfected the art of looking compassionate while wearing two-thousand-dollar shoes.

On the makeshift stage of New York's Bowery Mission, she knelt beside an elderly homeless woman, careful to position herself at the camera-friendly three-quarters angle that her Instagram team had determined received 22% more engagement. Her blonde hair fell in artfully tousled waves that had required ninety minutes of styling to achieve that "I just care too much to worry about my appearance" aesthetic.

"Have you been coming to the mission long?" Kennedy asked, her voice pitched to that perfect register of concern; loud enough to be captured by the boom mic hovering just out of frame yet soft enough to seem intimate.

The woman, introduced moments earlier as Dorothy, clutched a donated blanket with gnarled fingers. "About three years, since my benefits got cut. They do good work here."

Kennedy squeezed her shoulder, holding the gesture long enough for her photographer, Javier, to capture several options. "That's what today is all about: recognizing the important work being done in our communities and amplifying these voices."

Behind them, a banner proclaimed: "HERSTORY HELPS: KENNEDY OSWALD FOUNDATION COMMUNITY OUT-REACH." A small army of assistants distributed care packages wrapped in recyclable paper bearing the same slogan.

"And cut!" called the director of Kennedy's documentary team. "Let's reset for the food service shots."

Kennedy's smile remained fixed as she rose gracefully, brushing her hand discreetly against her thigh (a gesture almost imperceptible to anyone not looking for it). Miguel, her personal assistant, immediately appeared at her side with hand sanitizer.

"Thanks, Miguel," she murmured, massaging the gel between her palms. "Is Zara here yet? She promised she'd make an appearance for the group shot."

"Her publicist texted that she's running fifteen minutes late." Miguel consulted his tablet, his fingers moving deftly across the screen. As her gay Latino assistant, Miguel featured prominently in Kennedy's "chosen family" Instagram stories, usually tagged with #RepresentationMatters. "Sasha and Lindsey are already here though, in the break room."

"Perfect." Kennedy turned to Dorothy, who was being gently guided away by a mission staff member. "Thank you so much for sharing your story, Diane."

"It's Dorothy," Miguel whispered.

"Dorothy, of course," Kennedy corrected. "Your courage is inspiring."

As Dorothy shuffled away, Kennedy turned to Javier. "Did you get enough options for the carousel post? I want to make sure we capture the authentic connection."

"Tons of great stuff," Javier confirmed. "The lighting was perfect; you both looked angelic."

"We'll need to be thoughtful about the edit," Kennedy mused. "Make sure it's about Dorothy's story, not me."

"Of course," Javier nodded, though they both knew the final carousel would feature five photos of Kennedy looking compassionate and perhaps one partial shot of Dorothy's hands.

Miguel steered Kennedy toward the staff break room where her actual friends waited. "Fifteen minutes until the food service segment. The mission director wants to know if you'll be comfortable serving the actual meals or if you'd prefer to just hand out bread rolls."

Kennedy considered this. "What did Angelina do when she visited that refugee camp last year?"

"Full meal service, but she brought her own organic hand sanitizer."

"Then I'll do the full service," Kennedy decided. "But have Dani post something about how we're highlighting food insecurity while being mindful of health safety for everyone involved."

"On it." Miguel typed rapidly on his phone.

As they entered the break room, Kennedy's entire demeanor shifted; the carefully calibrated compassion was replaced by genuine animation as she spotted her friends.

"Oh my god, you actually came!" she squealed, embracing Sasha Palmer, a Netflix series regular whose character had recently been killed off in a surprise mid-season twist. "I thought you'd still be in mourning over Cassandra's demise."

"Please," Sasha rolled her eyes. "I've been celebrating since I read the script. Now I can finally do feature work without being tied to that ridiculous contract."

Kennedy turned to Lindsey Moore, a former child star transitioning to adult roles with varying success. "And you! I thought you were still in Vancouver."

"Wrapped early," Lindsey shrugged. "The director got food poisoning, and we were already ten days over schedule, so the studio just called it."

"That means it's terrible," Sasha stage-whispered.

"Completely unwatchable," Lindsey confirmed cheerfully. "But I got paid, and they can fix it in post." She surveyed Kennedy with open admiration. "Meanwhile, look at you, feeding the homeless while looking like you just stepped off a Vogue shoot. How do you do it?"

Kennedy waved dismissively. "Please, I've been up since five. This foundation work is exhausting, but so rewarding. These people have such dignity despite their circumstances."

Miguel, standing discreetly by the door, maintained his professional poker face despite having witnessed Kennedy's twenty-minute meltdown when Dani had forgotten to bring her preferred brand of hand soap.

"So," Sasha leaned in conspiratorially. "What's happening with the Hitler movie? Cynthia told me you're playing Eva Braun?"

"Eve-uh Braun," Kennedy corrected automatically. "And yes, it's happening. It's actually a very complex, feminist take on how a woman's history has been relegated to footnote status. She was essentially caught in an impossible patriarchal system while trying to assert her own identity."

Miguel glanced up momentarily from his tablet at this creative historical interpretation but quickly returned to his professional neutrality.

"That sounds... historically dubious," Lindsey ventured.

"It's called artistic interpretation," Kennedy replied, a hint of defensiveness creeping into her voice. "The script really explores how Eva used what limited agency she had within an oppressive regime."

"So you're making Eva Braun a feminist icon?" Sasha raised an eyebrow. "Bold choice."

"It's about nuance," Kennedy insisted. "Complex female characters aren't just heroes or villains. They exist in gray areas."

"Pretty dark gray in Nazi Germany," Lindsey murmured.

Kennedy's phone buzzed with a text. She glanced at it, then frowned slightly. "Miguel, Victoria Martinez is trying to reach me. Can you set up a call after we finish here?"

"She flagged it as urgent," Miguel replied. "Studio priority."

Kennedy sighed. "Fine. I'll take it in the director's office after this segment. Tell her I'm in the middle of vital foundation work."

Miguel nodded, already composing the message.

"So," Sasha circled back, "who's playing Hitler? Please tell me it's not that method actor who made you cry in the Christmas movie."

"Bradley was intensely committed to his craft," Kennedy defended reflexively. "And we don't know yet. They're finalizing casting this week."

"I heard they're looking at non-traditional options," Lindsey said casually.

Kennedy's head snapped toward her. "What? From who?"

Lindsey shrugged. "My agent mentioned it. Said Pinnacle was exploring 'innovative interpretative approaches' or something."

"What does that mean?" Kennedy demanded, her composure slipping.

"No idea. Industry jargon for 'we can't afford a name actor' probably."

The documentary director appeared at the door. "Kennedy, we're ready for the food service segment."

"Coming!" Kennedy called, her professional smile reinstating itself instantly. She turned back to her friends. "Duty calls. Come watch me ladle soup looking fabulous yet humble."

As they exited the break room, Kennedy held Miguel back. "What exactly did Victoria's message say?"

"Just that she needs to discuss an urgent casting development regarding Hitler."

A flicker of worry crossed Kennedy's face. "Find out what you can. Text Dani to start researching 'innovative interpretative approaches' in historical dramas. And see what Bradley's availability is, just in case."

"On it," Miguel confirmed, already drafting multiple messages to Kennedy's Native American social media coordinator, the woman whose heritage Kennedy referenced in nearly every third post about "amplifying indigenous voices."

Kennedy squared her shoulders and glided toward the serving line, transitioning seamlessly back into America's Compassionate Sweetheart.

"Remember," she murmured to herself, "authentic connection, genuine warmth, three-quarter angle."

The cameras began rolling as she took her position behind the soup tureen, ladle poised gracefully in hand, ready to serve humanity while looking absolutely flawless doing it.

***

Victoria had redecorated the conference room for the occasion. The usual potted plants (sad affairs that always seemed one board meeting away from death) had been replaced with fresh orchids. The water pitchers contained actual lemon slices. Even the notepads were the good kind, with the Pinnacle logo embossed rather than printed.

"Trying to impress someone?" André Reynolds asked, sliding into his usual chair with a knowing smirk.

"Just creating a suitable atmosphere for selecting our Hitler," Victoria replied, straightening a folder with unnecessary precision. "Nothing says 'casting the most controversial role in recent cinema history' like proper hydration and quality stationery."

"The orchids are a nice touch," Michelle Park observed, entering with her tablet. "Very 'We're choosing Hitler, but make it classy.'"

Lucy arrived with a tray of coffee (actual French press, not the usual breakroom sludge) and began distributing cups according to each executive's known preferences. "Aaron just texted. He's on his way up with the final candidate videos."

Victoria nodded, feeling a flutter of anticipation she hadn't experienced since her first greenlight as an executive. "And Kennedy's team?"

"Still radio silent," Lucy reported. "Though her social media coordinator accidentally liked then unliked your latest insta post at 2 AM."

"Reconnaissance," André murmured. "Amateur hour."

The door opened, and Aaron entered, looking remarkably refreshed for someone who'd just returned from London. He carried his laptop under one arm and wore the quietly satisfied expression of a director who'd found exactly what the project needed.

"Welcome back to the cesspool of American filmmaking," Victoria greeted him. "How was the motherland of proper acting?"

"Rainy, expensive, and full of people who think Americans are culturally illiterate," Aaron replied, setting up his laptop. "So, exactly as expected."

David Katz slipped in last, clutching a dog-eared copy of the script like a talisman. "Sorry I'm late. I was trying to convince Dr. Friedman for the fourth time that we aren't completely desecrating history."

"Any luck?" Victoria asked.

"He called me a 'cinematic war criminal' but agreed to review the new pages," David reported. "So... progress?"

Victoria clapped her hands once. "Alright, people. We have twenty-seven days until our option expires. Kennedy Oswald still hasn't signed her contract. And we're about to cast Hitler. Just another Tuesday at Pinnacle Pictures."

"Actually, it's Wednesday," Lucy murmured from her corner perch.

"Time is a social construct when you're racing against an option deadline," Victoria declared. "Aaron, show us what you've got."

Aaron connected his laptop to the room's display system. "I've narrowed it down to five potential candidates, all of whom would bring something unique to the role."

"Unique," André echoed with a knowing smile. "There's that word again."

Aaron ignored him. "First up, Daniel Suarez. Thirty-four, Mexican-American. Strong theater background, limited screen work but critically acclaimed."

The screen displayed a solemn-faced Latino man with chiseled features and intense eyes, followed by clips from a regional theater production of "Death of a Salesman."

"He's got gravitas," Michelle acknowledged. "Very commanding presence."

"And the physicality is interesting," David added. "Not too traditionally handsome, which helps with Hitler."

André leaned forward, his fingers drumming thoughtfully on the table as he studied the image with marketing-calibrated eyes. "Hispanic Hitler. Interesting angle. We could potentially capture the Latino audience segment, which has been historically underserved in Holocaust narratives."

Victoria couldn't tell if he was joking.

"Next," Aaron continued, "Harsh Rao. British-Indian, RADA-trained. Primarily stage work, but had a supporting role in that BBC series about British colonialism in India."

The display showed a stern-looking man with elegant features delivering a monologue from "Macbeth" with impressive intensity.

"He's got that quiet menace," Michelle observed. "You can see the calculation behind his eyes."

"Indian Hitler," André mused. "That's a fresh take. We could position it as commentary on the historical connections between Nazism and Indian independence movements. There's actually fascinating material there about Bose and..."

"Let's stay focused on acting qualities," Victoria interrupted, sensing a potential tangent. "Who else, Aaron?"

"Ki-woo Park. Korean-American, Juilliard graduate. Been doing impressive work off-Broadway."

The clips showed a lean, intense performer with remarkable physical control, his movements precise and deliberate.

"Asian Hitler," André said. "Opens up the Eastern markets. The historical irony of Japan's alliance with Germany creates built-in marketing narratives."

"Are we casting Hitler or assembling a United Nations panel?" David asked dryly.

Aaron continued undeterred. "Next, Jordan Wilson. African American, early thirties. Primarily television work but recently broke out in an indie that did well at Sundance."

The screen displayed a handsome Black actor with a commanding screen presence, his performance in the clips showing impressive emotional range.

"Strong camera presence," Michelle noted. "Very photogenic."

"Too photogenic, maybe?" David suggested. "Hitler shouldn't be someone you want to look at."

André was already formulating angles. "He's got the right balance of attractiveness and intensity. Politically speaking, casting a Black American actor creates powerful symbolism about American racial history and..."

Aaron hesitated. "Well, I had a thought about going in a completely different direction. Taylor Rossi. Italian-American background, extraordinary stage presence."

The room fell silent as they watched clips of a performer with handsome dark features delivering a powerfully nuanced monologue.

"And how is this... bold?" Michelle finally asked, looking confused.

Aaron cleared his throat. "Taylor is gay. His interpretation brings a different layer of subversion to Hitler's hyper-masculine persona."

"I see," Victoria said, studying the screen thoughtfully. "And how exactly would audiences know that from looking at him?"

"Well, they wouldn't necessarily," Aaron admitted. "But once the press finds out..."

"Too subtle," Victoria replied firmly. "We're already pushing boundaries with non-traditional casting. The audience needs to see the subversion immediately."

"Plus," André added with blunt practicality, "how do we market that? The visual shorthand doesn't work. With Rossi, most viewers would just see a conventionally handsome, ambiguously ethnic Hitler, missing the entire point."

"I'm with Victoria," David agreed. "One revolutionary element at a time."

Aaron nodded, accepting their assessment without argument. "Fair enough. Those are our front runners based on preliminary readings and availability. But..." He paused for effect. "I've saved the best for last."

The screen changed to display James Olayinka Wright, his headshot revealing a face of remarkable charisma even in stillness.

"James Wright," Aaron announced. "Half-Nigerian, half-British. Royal Academy trained. Currently starring as Richard III at the Young Vic in London. Limited screen experience but extraordinary stage presence. And most importantly:" Aaron clicked to start the video. "he sent this self-tape yesterday."

The room fell quiet as Wright's audition began. He'd chosen the beer hall scene: Hitler's early days, testing his oratorical powers on small crowds. What was immediately apparent, even in the simple self-tape format, was Wright's complete physical transformation. His normally elegant posture had compressed into Hitler's characteristic tightly-wound stance. His gestures, while drawing on historically documented patterns, avoided caricature. Most remarkably, his eyes conveyed the dangerous mixture of wounded grievance and megalomaniacal ambition that defined Hitler's appeal.

When he spoke, the accent was flawless; Austrian-German inflected just enough to be historically accurate without becoming comedic. But it was the psychological truth of the performance that silenced the room. Wright showed how Hitler's famous rage wasn't just theatrical but emerged from genuine conviction, making his monstrosity all the more terrifying for its sincerity.

As the clip ended, no one spoke immediately. The cynical industry veterans, who typically discussed performances with the emotional investment of grocers evaluating produce, sat transfixed.

"Holy shit," André finally breathed.

"That's him," Victoria said simply. "That's our Hitler."

David nodded slowly. "He's transformed completely. Not a hint of parody or distance."

Michelle studied the frozen image on screen. "He's going to be a challenge for marketing. He's quite handsome, which complicates the messaging about Hitler's evil. But the performance quality is undeniable."

André was already calculating angles. "Actually, his appearance is perfect from a marketing perspective." He leaned forward, conspiratorially sharing his analysis. "Wright possesses that magical industry quality of being 'ethnically ambiguous enough' to appeal to multiple demographics while still being 'identifiably Black enough' to check diversity boxes. He has the kind of handsome features that test well with focus groups across all four quadrants; a face that could launch a thousand think pieces about representation without alienating midwestern conservative viewers."

He spread his hands wide, framing an imaginary billboard. "He's approachable-Black, not threatening-Black. The kind of Black that gets you on magazine covers and morning shows." André grinned broadly. "This is Black I can sell!"

Michelle winced slightly. "Maybe dial back the commodification of racial identity just a touch, André. Even if you're in on the joke."

"I'm just being honest," André replied unapologetically. "We need to cut the bull and get down to the nitty-gritty; it's how I keep some integrity when I throw away the rest."

"His looks do create an interesting tension," David observed, steering the conversation back to creative concerns. "Hitler's evil should be ordinary, not glamorous. We'll need to work with makeup and photography to ensure we're not accidentally creating 'Sexy Hitler.'"

"'Sexy Hitler' is definitely not on our approved marketing concepts list," Victoria agreed dryly.

Aaron closed his laptop with a decisive click. "So we're agreed? James Wright is our Hitler, pending a chemistry read with Kennedy?"

"Assuming Kennedy's still our Eva Braun," Victoria qualified. "She still hasn't signed, and now we need to tell her about this casting."

André grimaced. "That's going to be a delicate conversation. 'Congratulations, you're playing the girlfriend of history's greatest monster, and by the way, he's being played by a Black British actor.' Her social justice branding team is going to have an aneurysm trying to calculate the correct response."

"I'll handle Kennedy," Victoria declared. "Lucy, set up a call with her team for this afternoon. Position it as an exclusive first look at our groundbreaking casting approach."

"On it," Lucy confirmed, already typing.

"What about the chemistry read?" Michelle asked. "Kennedy's in New York this week for that sustainable fashion gala."

"We'll do it remotely," Victoria decided. "Aaron, can Wright be available for a Zoom session tomorrow?"

Aaron nodded. "His agent already confirmed his availability all week."

"Perfect." Victoria straightened her folders again, a habit that emerged whenever plans were coalescing. "André, I want preliminary marketing concepts that explore our approach without being exploitative. Michelle, prepare a social strategy for the announcement. David, look at the script for any dialogue that might need adjustment given our casting."

She stood, signaling the meeting's end. "This is happening, people. We're making Black Hitler. We're going to need to audience-test a few names, though."

As the team filed out, André lingered behind. "Victoria, a word? About the messaging strategy?"

She nodded, and once they were alone, André's professional mask slipped to reveal genuine concern.

"This is going to be a minefield," he said without preamble. "You know that, right? Jewish organizations will have questions. Black advocacy groups will have opinions. Conservative media will have a field day. Twitter will implode. I can't even predict if the left will be more angry or the right."

"I'm counting on it," Victoria replied. "Controversy creates conversation. Conversation creates relevance."

"And relevance wins awards," André finished, having heard her mantra before. "But this is different. This isn't just industry politics; it touches on deep historical wounds."

Victoria studied him with newfound respect. "I didn't realize you had such concern for historical sensitivity, André."

"I don't," he admitted frankly. "But I do have concern for you. This could end careers if it goes wrong. Including yours."

"It could also make careers if it goes right," Victoria countered. "Including James Wright's."

André nodded, conceding the point. "Just promise me one thing. When the storm hits, and it will hit, remember that marketing can spin a lot of things, but some reactions can't be managed or monetized. Some of it will just be genuine pain."

Victoria's expression softened slightly. "I know. That's why we need Wright. Did you see his performance? He understands the weight of this. He's not treating it as a stunt."

"And Kennedy?"

Victoria's smile turned sardonic. "Well, one authentic artist out of two isn't bad for Hollywood, is it?"

André chuckled despite himself. "I'll start drafting concepts. Brace yourself for the Kennedy call."

"Already braced," Victoria assured him. "I've been dealing with actors since you were crafting Instagram captions for direct-to-video releases."

"Ouch." André clutched his chest in mock pain. "The Latinx executive wounds me with her brutal accuracy."

Victoria laughed, the tension breaking. "Go make Black Hitler marketable without being offensive. That's your impossible task for the day."

"Just another Wednesday at Pinnacle," André replied with a grin, heading for the door.

Left alone, Victoria walked to the window, looking out at the sunny Pinnacle lot. In twenty-seven days, they'd either have a revolutionary project underway or a spectacular failure on their hands. And somewhere in London, a talented actor named James Olayinka Wright was preparing to step into the skin of history's greatest monster, unaware of the storm that awaited him.

Victoria smiled to herself. Hollywood had been built on just such audacious gambles.

Now they just needed to convince Kennedy Oswald that playing Eva Braun opposite a Black Hitler was the career-defining opportunity she'd been waiting for.

Easy.

***

Ten minutes later Kennedy Oswald's face filled Victoria's monitor with the high-definition clarity of someone who had invested significantly in professional lighting for Zoom calls. Her blonde hair fell in carefully tousled waves. Her expression combined practiced warmth with the vigilant alertness of someone perpetually aware they were being observed.

"Victoria! So lovely to connect," Kennedy exclaimed with the enthusiasm of a morning show host greeting a minor celebrity. "Miguel mentioned you had exciting casting news about our Hitler project."

Victoria noted the subtle ownership claim ("our Hitler project") despite Kennedy not having officially signed on. Behind Kennedy, Victoria could make out what appeared to be a hastily evacuated office space (the mission director's domain, temporarily commandeered for Kennedy's call). A "Bowery Mission" calendar hung visibly askew on the wall, the only hint that this was a place of actual charitable work.

"Kennedy, always a pleasure," Victoria replied, matching warmth with warmth. "How's New York treating you?"

"Oh, you know how it is: back-to-back meetings, catching up on my charity work, fittings for tomorrow's gala, squeezing in calls with my production team at HerStory." Kennedy's smile remained fixed, revealing nothing. "But I always make time for Pinnacle, especially for this project. It's become so important to me."

Victoria nodded, mentally translating: *I'm making sure you know how in-demand I am while emphasizing that working with you remains a priority for branding purposes.*

"We value your passion for the project," Victoria said. "Which is why I wanted you to be the first to know about our breakthrough with casting Hitler."

Kennedy leaned forward slightly, her interest seemingly genuine. "You've found someone? Anyone I know?"

"James Olayinka Wright," Victoria announced, watching carefully for Kennedy's reaction. "Phenomenal British stage actor currently starring as Richard III in London. Royal Academy trained. Critics call him transformative."

Kennedy's expression revealed nothing beyond polite interest. "I'm not familiar with him. Has he done any screen work?"

"Limited, but extraordinary quality," Victoria replied. "He's primarily a classical stage actor. Aaron Weisman discovered him in London and was blown away by his performance."

Kennedy nodded, still pleasant but noncommittal. "Wonderful. I'm always excited to work with new talent. Does he have a reel I could see?"

"Even better," Victoria said, positioning her mouse over the video file. "We have his self-tape audition. I think you'll be impressed."

"I'd love to see it," Kennedy replied, her expression still revealing nothing of her thoughts. "Just one quick question before you play it: is there anything... distinctive about Mr. Wright that I should know about?"

And there it was: the careful probe. Victoria paused, deciding to be direct rather than evasive.

"James is a British actor of mixed heritage; his father is white British, his mother is Nigerian. He's Black, Kennedy."

To Kennedy's credit, her expression shifted only fractionally, a slight widening of the eyes, a momentary tension around her perfect smile. Then, with the professional agility of someone who'd navigated countless public relations challenges, she nodded thoughtfully.

"How groundbreaking," she said after a precisely calibrated pause. "I assume this is a deliberate artistic choice rather than simply color-blind casting?"

Victoria admired the deft pivot. Kennedy was already framing her response in terms that would work on social media.

"Absolutely," Victoria confirmed. "We're taking a bold approach that challenges historical representation while delivering extraordinary performances. The film remains historically accurate in narrative and psychology, but visually recontextualizes these historical figures to create new resonance for modern audiences."

Kennedy nodded again, more enthusiastically now. Victoria could almost see her mentally drafting Instagram captions: *Thrilled to be part of this groundbreaking reimagining of history... Art that challenges conventions while honoring historical truth...*

"I'd love to see his audition," Kennedy said, her tone warm but professional.

Victoria shared her screen and played Wright's self-tape. As before, the power of his performance created immediate silence. Even through Zoom, Wright's transformation into Hitler was mesmerizing: the physicality, the psychological acuity, the dangerous charisma.

When the clip ended, Kennedy's expression had changed. Whatever she had been expecting, this clearly wasn't it. She looked genuinely affected.

"Oh," she said softly.

"Yes," Victoria agreed, recognizing the rare moment of authentic reaction. "Oh."

Kennedy composed herself quickly. "He's... quite extraordinary. The physical transformation is remarkable. And those eyes; he makes you understand how people could follow someone so..."

"Exactly," Victoria said, feeling a flash of genuine connection with Kennedy. "That's precisely what we need for this film to work."

Kennedy seemed lost in thought for a moment, then visibly switched back into professional mode. "I assume we'll need a chemistry read?"

"Yes, ideally tomorrow if your schedule permits. We're up against our option deadline, so moving quickly is essential."

"Miguel can make it work," Kennedy assured her. "Just send the sides to my team."

Victoria nodded. "We've selected the first meeting scene and the breakup-reconciliation from the bunker sequence."

"Perfect," Kennedy said, her business tone returning. "I should mention that my team still has some script concerns about Eva's character development, particularly in the middle section where..."

"Let's address those after the chemistry read," Victoria interrupted smoothly. "If you and James connect on screen, we can explore character refinements that serve both performances."

Kennedy smiled, recognizing the deflection but choosing not to push. "Of course. First things first."

Victoria prepared to wrap up the call. "We'll send everything to Miguel within the hour. Looking forward to tomorrow's read."

"One more question, Victoria." Kennedy's tone shifted slightly, becoming more intimate, as though they were girlfriends sharing secrets. "Off the record... how do you think people will react? To this casting choice?"

Victoria considered her answer carefully. "Honestly? There will be noise. Think pieces. Twitter debates. Fox News segments. New York Times coverage. But ultimately, extraordinary art creates conversations, sometimes uncomfortable ones. The performance will speak for itself."

Kennedy nodded slowly. "It's a brave choice."

"For all of us," Victoria agreed, recognizing the subtext: *What does this mean for my brand?*

"Well," Kennedy said, her smile returning full-force, "I've never been afraid of bold artistic choices. My followers appreciate authenticity and courage."

Translation: My social media team has already calculated that the progressive points outweigh the potential blowback.

"That's what makes you such a valuable creative partner," Victoria replied with practiced sincerity. "Your willingness to push boundaries."

"Send those sides over," Kennedy said, already shifting into preparation mode. "I'll make sure I'm fully prepared for tomorrow."

After the call ended, Victoria leaned back in her chair, analyzing the interaction. Kennedy hadn't fled in horror, which was a positive sign. Her immediate pivot to framing the casting as "groundbreaking" rather than "controversial" suggested her team would find a way to position this advantageously. And most surprisingly, she seemed genuinely impressed by Wright's performance, perhaps the first authentic reaction Victoria had witnessed from Kennedy since negotiations began.

Victoria's intercom buzzed. "Lucy, come in."

Lucy appeared, tablet in hand. "How did it go with Kennedy?"

"Better than expected," Victoria replied. "She's processing the implications, but Wright's performance spoke for itself. We're set for a chemistry read tomorrow."

"And her script demands?"

"Temporarily deflected, but they'll resurface." Victoria stood, stretching slightly. "Send the sides to both teams. And Lucy, make sure the lighting for tomorrow's Zoom is exceptional. We need this chemistry read to work."

"Already coordinating with IT," Lucy confirmed. "Also, André sent preliminary marketing concepts. He's exploring various approaches, from academic 'deconstructing historical representation' to more provocative 'history reimagined' angles."

"Tell him to keep working. We need options that walk the line between revolutionary and respectful." Victoria moved to her window, looking out at the studio lot bathed in afternoon sunlight. "Has the news leaked yet?"

"Nothing so far," Lucy reported. "Though Marcus Goldman's assistant asked our production coordinator if we'd made any 'interesting casting decisions' recently."

Victoria smiled thinly. "He's sniffing around. Good. Let him wonder."

"Should I prepare a response strategy for when it does leak?"

"Not yet," Victoria decided. "Let's get through the chemistry read first. If that works, we'll control the narrative with an official announcement. If it doesn't..." She shrugged. "We'll need a different strategy altogether."

Lucy nodded, making notes. "One more thing. Aaron asked if you want to observe tomorrow's read privately, or be visible on the call."

Victoria considered this. "Visible. I want Kennedy to feel the weight of executive attention, and I want Wright to know we're fully committed to this approach."

"Understood." Lucy moved toward the door, then paused. "Victoria? For what it's worth, I watched Wright's audition. He's remarkable."

"He is," Victoria agreed. "Almost makes you forget how absurd this whole situation is."

"Almost," Lucy echoed with a small smile before slipping out.

Alone again, Victoria returned to her desk and opened the folder containing Wright's headshot and resume. His face looked back at her: intelligent, composed, with eyes that suggested depth beyond his years. In twenty-four hours, they would know if this extraordinary actor and America's romantic comedy sweetheart could create believable chemistry as history's most notorious couple. If they did, Black Hitler would become reality. If they didn't...

Victoria closed the folder. There was no point contemplating failure. Not when they were so close to making history, or at least reimagining it in spectacular fashion.

***

CHAPTER 6

K ennedy Oswald had spent seventeen thousand dollars preparing for this chemistry read.

Not that anyone would know. The whole point of the emergency stylist, the vocal coach, the crash course with her method acting consultant, and the impromptu session with her therapist was to appear effortlessly authentic. Just Kennedy being Kennedy: a serious actress ready to tackle challenging material with the perfect balance of gravitas and charisma.

She sat in her hotel suite's makeshift studio setup, where her team had replaced the standard lamp with professional lighting that made her look simultaneously flawless and casually relatable. Her outfit, a cream cashmere sweater that probably cost more than some people's monthly rent, had been selected for its "thoughtful but not trying too hard" aesthetic. Her hair fell in what her stylist called "considered dishevelment."

Miguel hovered nearby, tablet in hand. "Five minutes until the call. Victoria and Aaron are already in the waiting room. David Katz just joined."

Kennedy nodded, attempting to project serene confidence while her stomach performed Olympic-level gymnastics. She wasn't supposed to get nervous. Kennedy Oswald didn't do nervous; she did "focused preparation" and "creative anticipation."

Yet here she was, one missed breath away from hyperventilating.

"Can we run through the talking points again?" she asked, smoothing an invisible wrinkle from her sweater.

"Of course." Miguel consulted his tablet. "You're 'honored to be part of such a revolutionary artistic vision.' You 'believe in challenging historical representation through thoughtful reinterpretation.' You're 'excited to explore Eva Braun as a complex woman navigating impossible circumstances.'"

Kennedy nodded, mentally filing each phrase. "And about James Wright?"

"You're 'thrilled to work with such extraordinary talent' and 'looking forward to the creative partnership.' If they ask directly about his race, you pivot to 'art that transcends conventional boundaries' and 'performances that capture emotional truth beyond physical appearance.'"

"Good." Kennedy took a sip from her specifically chosen mug, artisanal ceramic, not too perfect, suggesting a worldly appreciation for craftsmanship rather than mass-produced luxury. "And we prepared for all potential scenes?"

"Yes. Dani compiled a document on Eva Braun's mannerisms based on historical footage. Your dialect coach recorded pronunciation guides for the German phrases. And you've got physical blocking notes for both scenes."

Kennedy closed her eyes briefly. "I can do this."

"Of course you can," Miguel affirmed, though his tone carried the practiced encouragement of someone who had delivered similar reassurances before countless auditions, photo shoots, and talk show appearances.

Dani appeared from the adjoining room, phone in hand. "Kennedy? Are you... ready?"

Miguel checked his watch. "Three minutes until."

"It's fine," Kennedy said, waving him off. "What is it, Dani?"

Something in Dani's hesitant approach suggested she was treading carefully. "I've been reviewing recent interviews with James Wright. He seems... different from Bradley."

Kennedy's posture stiffened imperceptibly. "We don't talk about Bradley."

"I know," Dani said, eyes lowered in practiced deference. "I just meant this won't be like that. Wright seems... genuine in his interviews. No method actor power games."

"Bradley wasn't playing games," Kennedy said, surprising both Dani and herself with the sharp defense. "He was challenging me."

Dani took a small step back, recognizing the danger zone she'd entered. "Of course. I didn't mean to suggest otherwise."

"Good actors challenge each other," Kennedy continued, her voice taking on the quality of someone reciting a mantra they'd told themselves repeatedly. "That's how great performances happen."

A moment of uncomfortable silence hung between them. Dani had been with Kennedy longer than any other assistant, almost three years, precisely because she knew when to push and when to retreat.

"The preparation materials were helpful," Kennedy said finally, an olive branch of sorts. "Your research was... thorough."

"Thank you," Dani said, visibly relieved. Then, venturing cautiously: "It's a prestigious project. Historical drama with awards potential."

Kennedy glanced at her reflection in the nearby mirror, a flicker of something unreadable crossing her features. "My mother had a prestigious project once."

The words hung in the air, loaded with unspoken meaning. Kennedy didn't need to elaborate; Dani knew the story. How her mother had been hailed as "the next big thing" until suddenly, she wasn't. How she'd gone from magazine covers to "where are they now" features in the span of eighteen months. How she'd spent twenty years teaching Kennedy precisely how fickle Hollywood's love could be.

"This isn't..." Dani began, then stopped, recalibrating. "Your social reach alone ensures success."

"I know," Kennedy cut her off, the moment of vulnerability already being neatly packed away. "I have fifteen million followers. I have HerStory Films."

"And a foundation," Dani added helpfully.

"Named after me that feeds homeless people I can't remember the names of," Kennedy finished with a flicker of self-awareness that seemed to surprise even her.

Miguel cleared his throat. "One minute."

Kennedy straightened, the vulnerability vanishing as quickly as it had appeared. She adjusted her posture to hit what her media team had determined was her most photogenic angle. "How do I look?"

"Perfect," Miguel and Dani replied in unison.

"Great. Then let's make some revolutionary art, or whatever the fuck we're calling it." Kennedy took a deep breath and clicked to join the Zoom call.

Victoria Martinez's face appeared on screen, followed quickly by Aaron Weisman and David Katz. They were seated in what appeared to be a Pinnacle conference room, though Kennedy noted they'd upgraded the usual sad-looking plants with fresh orchids. Nice touch; subtle "we're taking this seriously" signaling.

"Kennedy!" Victoria greeted with what Kennedy recognized as executive-level warmth, just genuine enough to be convincing without crossing into unprofessional territory. "Thank you for making time in your schedule."

"Of course," Kennedy replied, activating her own carefully calibrated enthusiasm. "I've been looking forward to this all week."

"James should be joining us any moment," Aaron said, checking his watch. "He's calling in from London."

As if on cue, a fourth window appeared on screen, revealing James Olayinka Wright. Even through the digital interface, Kennedy was struck by his presence. Unlike her carefully constructed backdrop, his setting was simple; what appeared to be a modest apartment with bookshelves visible in the background. He wore a plain black t-shirt, his expression alert but relaxed in a way that suggested he hadn't spent hours preparing his "casual" appearance.

"Sorry if I'm late," he said, his British accent rich and precise. "Technical difficulties with the Wi-Fi."

"You're right on time," Victoria assured him.

Kennedy studied him with the practiced eye of someone who had spent a career evaluating co-stars for potential threats. His features were striking: the kind of face that would photograph well from any angle, not just the carefully determined ones her team had mapped out for her. But more concerning was the ease with which he inhabited the digital space, the lack of visible performance in his greeting. Either he wasn't trying, or more alarmingly, he was so good she couldn't see him trying.

"James," Victoria continued, "this is Kennedy Oswald, who will be playing Eva Braun."

"It's a pleasure," James said, his smile warm but not effusive. "I've enjoyed your work."

"Likewise," Kennedy replied automatically, though she had never seen him in anything. "I'm thrilled to explore this creative partnership."

Was that too formal? Too rehearsed? Kennedy felt a flicker of panic. She'd practiced sounding natural, but the practiced naturalness always sounded different in her head than when she actually said it.

"Let's get started," David said, taking control as the screenwriter. "We've selected two scenes that showcase the relationship dynamics. First, their initial meeting at the photography studio where Eva worked. Second, a more intimate scene from later in their relationship during the bunker period."

Kennedy nodded, mentally reviewing her notes. She'd spent three hours with her acting coach on just these scenes, breaking down every possible interpretation, every potential angle.

"James, would you like to begin?" Victoria asked.

"Of course," he replied.

And then, without any visible transition, he transformed.

Kennedy watched in astonishment as James's entire physicality shifted. His shoulders tightened, his posture became more rigid, his chin jutted forward slightly. But it was his eyes that underwent the most remarkable change: suddenly burning with an intensity that seemed to pierce through the screen.

"Fräulein Braun," he said, his voice now carrying the distinctive Austrian-German accent of Hitler without descending into caricature. "I understand you're Herr Hoffmann's assistant?"

Kennedy felt a jolt of panic. She'd prepared extensively, but watching James's seamless transformation made her acutely aware of the performance she was about to attempt. She took a breath, found her center, and slipped into Eva's character as best she could.

"Yes, Herr Hitler," she replied, adopting a slight German accent she'd practiced with her dialect coach. "I help with the developing and the cataloging."

As they moved through the scene, Kennedy found herself struggling to keep pace. James's Hitler wasn't the mustache-twirling villain of popular imagination, but a complex, charismatic figure whose intense focus made Eva's attraction to him comprehensible. His performance created a gravitational pull that Kennedy found herself responding to not as an actress playing a role, but as a character genuinely drawn into his orbit.

When they transitioned to the bunker scene, the dynamic shifted. James's Hitler now carried the weight of impending defeat, the charisma cracking in places, and Kennedy caught herself searching for the seams the way she'd search a rival's red-carpet smile. She couldn't find them. It was during their reconciliation dialogue that Kennedy found her footing, allowing Eva's desperate love to guide her performance rather than her prepared technical choices.

"You promised me," she said, genuine emotion breaking through her calculated delivery. "You promised we would have our life together."

"And we will," James replied, his Hitler conveying a complex mixture of manipulative charm and genuine affection. "In this life or the next, Eva. You are the only one who has never betrayed me."

When the scene ended, there was a moment of silence on the call. Kennedy searched the faces of Victoria, Aaron, and David for feedback, trying to gauge her performance against James's.

"Well," Victoria said finally, "I think it's clear we've found our Hitler and Eva."

Relief flooded through Kennedy, though it was tinged with a nagging doubt. Had she really matched James's performance, or was Victoria just saying what needed to be said to keep the project moving forward?

"That was remarkable, both of you," Aaron added, his expression suggesting genuine appreciation. "The chemistry is palpable."

"I'd like to adjust a few lines in the bunker scene," David said, scribbling notes. "There's an opportunity to heighten the contrast between Hitler's public and private personas that I think would serve both performances."

"Absolutely," Kennedy agreed eagerly. "I found myself wanting to explore Eva's complicity versus her genuine love. There's such complex psychology there."

She was babbling, she realized, falling back on rehearsed insights to mask her uncertainty about her own performance.

James nodded thoughtfully. "I'd be interested in that exploration as well. The historical record suggests their relationship had genuine moments of tenderness amidst the monstrous context."

His comment wasn't performance-focused but character-focused, Kennedy noted with a twinge of envy. He was thinking about Hitler, not about how he was playing Hitler.

"This is exactly the approach we need," Victoria said. "James, do you have any questions for us before we move forward?"

"Just one," he replied, reverting fully to himself now that the scene was complete. The transformation was so immediate, Kennedy almost expected to see physical evidence of the change, like a special effect in a film. "How are you planning to position this casting choice with the press and public? I ask because my family has connections to the history; my great-grandfather was a WWII veteran, and I want to ensure we're handling this material with appropriate gravity."

Victoria's expression shifted to what Kennedy recognized as her "thoughtfully prepared response" face. "We're developing a rollout strategy that emphasizes the artistic and intellectual foundations of our approach. This isn't stunt casting; it's a deliberate artistic choice to make audiences see familiar history with fresh eyes. Marketing will be finalizing our strategy very soon."

James nodded, seeming satisfied with the answer. "That aligns with my thinking as well. I wouldn't want to be involved in anything that trivializes the historical reality."

"Absolutely not," Kennedy jumped in, sensing an opportunity to demonstrate her own seriousness. "I'm thrilled to be part of such a groundbreaking reinterpretation that challenges how we view history while honoring its gravity."

She immediately regretted the rehearsed line, which sounded hollow next to James's genuine concern.

"Well, I think we have what we need," Victoria said. "James, we'll be in touch formally through your agent today, but consider this confirmation that we want you as our Hitler."

"Thank you," James replied with a simple dignity that made Kennedy's elaborate preparation seem suddenly excessive. "I look forward to working with all of you."

After brief goodbyes, the call ended. Kennedy sat motionless for a moment, processing what had just happened.

"That went well," Miguel offered cautiously.

"Did it?" Kennedy asked, a rare moment of genuine uncertainty breaking through. "He was... extraordinary."

"You held your own," Dani said, which wasn't exactly the ringing endorsement Kennedy had hoped for.

Kennedy turned to Dani. "Start drafting social media concepts for the announcement. Focus on 'artistic boundary-breaking' and 'challenging historical representation through diverse perspectives.' And get me everything you can on James Wright's previous work. I need to study him."

"On it," Dani replied, already typing on her phone.

Kennedy stared at her reflection in the now-dark computer screen. She had prepared meticulously, spent thousands, rehearsed every moment, and still felt like she had barely kept her head above water next to James Wright's effortless performance.

The realization was terrifying. And yet, somewhere beneath the fear was a flicker of something else: a kind of excitement she hadn't felt in years. The challenge of actually having to *act* rather than just looking pretty on camera while delivering lines. She smiled. Kennedy Oswald, serious actress, excited by creative challenges rather than threatened by them.

Aaron sat in his Pinnacle office, phone pressed to his ear, listening to the rhythmic ringing of an international call. The chemistry read had exceeded his expectations; not just in James's performance, which he had anticipated would be exceptional, but in the dynamic between him and Kennedy. There had been genuine moments amidst the technical execution, suggesting the possibility of a film that might transcend its own conceptual audacity.

The ringing stopped. "Margaret Thorne speaking," came the crisp British voice.

"Margaret, it's Aaron Weisman. Is James available?"

"He's expecting your call. One moment."

A brief silence, then James came on the line. "Aaron. That was quick."

"No point delaying good news," Aaron replied. "Consider this your official offer for the role of Adolf Hitler. Victoria was impressed; we all were."

"Thank you," James said, his tone measured. "Kennedy seems very... prepared."

Aaron chuckled at the diplomatic characterization. "She takes her craft seriously in her own way. Different path than yours, but she has qualities that work for Eva. The audience will understand her attraction to your Hitler."

"That's essential," James agreed. "Without that understanding, the relationship becomes cartoonish rather than tragic."

Aaron leaned back in his chair, struck again by James's focus on the work rather than the opportunity. Most actors would be asking about billing or trailer size at this point.

"James, before we move forward, I want to ask you something. During the read, you mentioned your great-grandfather was a WWII veteran. Is that why you're interested in this project?"

There was a pause on the line. "Partly," James admitted. "My grandfather, Thomas, grew up in the aftermath of his father's return and the war's end. He rarely spoke about it when my father was growing up, but he's talked to me about it some. He grew up in the rubble Hitler left behind. For him, Hitler wasn't a historical abstraction or an internet meme; he was the man who took away parts of his father and destroyed his family home."

Aaron felt a tightening in his chest. "My grandfather was in Dachau."

"I know," James said quietly. "You mentioned it when we met in London."

"Right." Aaron cleared his throat. "I guess what I'm asking is: are you sure about this? Taking on Hitler as a Black actor, it's going to provoke reactions from all sides. Some of them won't be pretty."

"I'm aware," James replied. "But if you're asking if I have the stomach for it, I do. This isn't just another role for me, Aaron. It's an opportunity to do something that matters."

There was something in James's tone that resonated with Aaron's own complicated feelings about the project; the mixture of artistic ambition and personal connection, the genuine belief that art could sometimes transcend its own absurdity to say something meaningful.

"That's exactly why you're the right person for this," Aaron said, surprised by the emotion in his own voice. "You're bringing unique perspective and extraordinary talent to material that deserves nothing less."

As soon as the words left his mouth, Aaron winced. "Unique perspective": he was parroting Victoria's corporate-speak again.

"My 'unique perspective'?" James repeated, a hint of amusement in his voice. "You're starting to sound like a studio executive, Aaron."

"God help me," Aaron groaned. "Next thing you know, I'll be talking about 'synergistic cross-platform audience engagement.'"

James laughed, the sound warm and genuine. "Save that for the marketing team."

"Speaking of which," Aaron continued, "be prepared for André Reynolds. He's our head of marketing, and he's already spinning concepts for how to position this. He's brilliant, but his methods can be... direct."

"I look forward to meeting him."

Aaron hesitated, then decided on honesty. "James, this project could be a win-win for all of us. Revolutionary art with commercial potential. Or it could blow up spectacularly in our faces."

"My agent said something similar," James admitted. "She seems to think either outcome would benefit my career."

"She might be right," Aaron acknowledged. "But I want you to know that whatever happens, I believe in what we're trying to do here. It's not just a stunt or a gimmick. At least, not anymore."

"I appreciate that," James said. "So, shall we make history? Or at least reinterpret it?"

Aaron smiled. "We start pre-production in four weeks. Your agent will have the formal paperwork today. We'll handle the Young Vic buyout. And James... thank you."

"For what?"

"For taking this seriously. For seeing the potential beneath the absurdity."

After they hung up, Aaron sat at his desk, contemplating what they were about to undertake. A Black actor playing Hitler. A rom-com star playing Eva Braun. A slashed budget and a looming option deadline.

It was either going to be the most meaningful project of his career or the most spectacular disaster.

Aaron reached for his phone again. "Lucy? It's Aaron. Please tell Victoria that James Wright is officially our Hitler. And maybe prepare some antacids. I have a feeling we're all going to need them."

***

André Reynolds liked to run his marketing meetings with what he called "surgical precision and controlled chaos." The surgical precision referred to his meticulously organized agenda, with exact time allocations for each topic. The controlled chaos referred to everything that happened once people actually started talking.

"All right, people," he announced, striding into Conference Room C with the confident gait of someone who knew exactly how much his Off-White Jordan 1s were worth. "We have exactly fifty-four minutes to determine how we're going to sell the world on Black Hitler. Let's not waste a single one."

The room contained his core team: Michelle Park, VP of Publicity and Digital Engagement; Ravi Mukerjee, Creative Director; Isa Davis, Michelle's intern, already stationed in the corner with a notebook; and two junior team members whose names André hadn't bothered to memorize yet because turnover in entry-level marketing positions at Pinnacle made learning names a poor ROI.

Michelle looked up from her tablet. "Did Victoria actually approve that name? 'Black Hitler'?"

"God, no," André laughed, setting his coffee on the table. "We're calling it 'Ascension' or 'Tyrant Rising' or some other focus-grouped bullshit. But let's be honest about what we're selling here: James Olayinka Wright as Adolf Hitler."

He turned to the whiteboard and wrote in large letters: CHALLENGES & OPPORTUNITIES.

"First things first," he continued, "let's acknowledge we're working with a slashed budget thanks to Kennedy's team negotiating everyone else's quotes into the ground. This means we need every penny to work triple-time. Controversy is our friend here, people."

"Are we leaning into the controversy or trying to contextualize it?" Ravi asked.

André gave him an appreciative nod. "Both. We need to engineer a very specific type of controversy: the kind that generates think pieces rather than boycotts. We want film critics arguing about artistic merit, not politicians using us as a talking point."

Michelle raised a hand. "I've been researching historical precedents: non-traditional casting in period pieces, racial boundary-breaking in theater, that kind of thing. There's a solid intellectual framework we can build on."

"Good," André said. "We need that intellectual cover. But let's be clear about our actual strategy: we're going to manipulate the conversation from both sides."

He turned back to the whiteboard, drawing a line down the middle and writing "LEFT" and "RIGHT" as headers.

"For progressive outlets, we position this as revolutionary representation that challenges White supremacist historical narratives. For conservative outlets, we emphasize the historical accuracy of the story itself while highlighting James's classical training and serious approach. And let's be honest, they'll like a Black man taking the heat for Hitler for once. And when the left have a problem with it, we point out that allowing Black actors to play complex characters is essential to fairness, Black people are not a monolith."

Ravi looked skeptical. "You really think we can control the narrative that precisely?"

André grinned. "No. But we can start fires in specific places and then sell ourselves as the reasonable middle ground." He gestured to the junior team members. "That's why you two are going to be creating burner accounts to plant specific talking points in targeted online communities. We need to seed the conversation before it seeds itself."

The two exchanged uncomfortable glances.

"Isn't that a bit... unethical?" one of them asked.

André laughed. "Welcome to Hollywood marketing, kid. We operate at the intersection of art and commerce, which is located in a moral gray area somewhere between 'creative storytelling' and 'strategic misrepresentation.'"

Michelle rolled her eyes. "We don't need to corrupt the children quite so quickly, André."

"They're in marketing. Consider it professional development." André turned back to the whiteboard. "Now, let's talk about James Olayinka Wright. Thoughts on how we position him?"

"He's genuinely talented," Michelle offered. "I watched some clips from his Richard III. We should emphasize his classical training: Royal Academy, Shakespeare, all that prestige stuff."

"Exactly," André nodded. "We're selling him as an actor's actor who happens to be Black, not as a Black actor playing Hitler. Subtle but crucial difference. Like the next Idris Elba."

He wrote "PRESTIGE" on the board, then paused, tapping the marker against his chin thoughtfully. "I wonder if we could convince him to go by just 'Olayinka' for this project. Single name, like Zendaya or Colman. Creates intrigue, emphasizes his Nigerian heritage, gives us an extra cultural angle to work with."

"I think that might be crossing a line," Michelle said carefully.

"The line is way behind us at this point," André replied. "We're casting a Black actor as Hitler. We've not only crossed the line, we've erased it and redrawn it in another county."

He checked his watch. "Forty-one minutes remaining. Let's talk movie titles. We need something that's vague enough to avoid immediate controversy but compelling enough to generate interest."

The room erupted with suggestions:

"Rise of Evil?"

"The Dictator's Path?"

"Ascension of Hate?"

"The People's Monster?"

André wrote them all down, then stepped back to survey the list. "Not bad, but we're still in generic historical drama territory. We need something that hints at our approach without being explicit."

Michelle had been quiet, scrolling through her tablet. Now she looked up. "What about simply 'Adolf'? Clean, direct, creates immediate recognition while leaving room for interpretation."

André considered this. "I like it. Put it on the testing list." He wrote it on the board, then continued: "We should also test titles that incorporate our approach more subtly. 'The Mirror of History.' 'The Face of Evil.' Something that plays on appearance versus reality."

"Speaking of appearance," Ravi interjected, "what's our approach to the marketing materials? Are we showing James as Hitler right away, or holding back?"

"Teaser campaign," André said decisively. "We release abstract materials first: shadowy profiles, partial images, evocative quotes. Build anticipation and curiosity. Then we control the reveal on our terms."

He turned to Michelle. "What kind of social media strategy are we looking at?"

Michelle set down her tablet. "I've been developing concepts for a multi-phase rollout. We start with intellectual groundwork: interviews with historians about how we perceive historical figures, discussions about representation in historical drama. Then we introduce James as an acclaimed classical actor taking on a challenging role. Only after establishing both contexts do we reveal the full concept."

"Smart," André nodded. "And Kennedy? How do we position her?"

"Serious actress taking on challenging material," Michelle replied. "We emphasize her commitment to complex female roles and her courage in tackling controversial subject matter."

"Perfect," André said. "She'll love that. Her team is probably already drafting Instagram captions about 'artistic bravery' and 'challenging historical representations of women.'"

He checked his watch again. "Thirty minutes left. Let's talk focus groups. We need to test key scenes to make sure the audience is processing this concept the way we intend."

Isa flipped to a new page in her notebook as Michelle asked, "What demographics are we targeting for the focus groups?"

"I want a wide range," André replied. "Art house regulars, mainstream moviegoers, history buffs, diverse racial backgrounds. We need to understand how different audiences react to seeing James as Hitler."

He paused, tapping the marker against the whiteboard. "But here's what's really interesting about this project: we don't actually need everyone to like it. In fact, some negative reaction is valuable. Every outraged tweet, every angry Facebook post, every YouTube rant is free marketing. As long as they're talking about us, we're winning."

Michelle looked up from her notes. "Is that really our metric for success now? Engagement regardless of sentiment?"

"Welcome to entertainment in 2024," André replied. "Parrot Analytics doesn't distinguish between love and hate when measuring demand. According to their metrics, a show that everyone despises but can't stop talking about is more 'successful' than a show everyone quietly enjoys."

He grinned. "Ten thousand hate-watching hate-posters generates more engagement than a million quiet fans. I could buy a bot network for less than ten grand that would make this movie 'popular' by industry standard metrics even if no one actually watches it."

Ravi laughed. "Let's not give Victoria any ideas. She's desperate enough for this to work that she might actually try it."

"I'm just saying," André continued, "controversy isn't a bug in our marketing plan; it's a feature. This industry has evolved to monetize outrage as effectively as appreciation."

Michelle sighed. "I actually love World War II historical dramas. I specifically asked to be on this project because I thought we were making a serious film about the rise of fascism. Does anyone care about the actual story anymore?"

André patted her shoulder condescendingly. "Oh, sweet summer child. The story is whatever gets people in seats or generates streams. Remember the Cleopatra controversy? Or the Velma disaster? Or that Roland Emmerich Shakespeare movie where they made him a fraud? Nobody remembers if those were any good. They remember the conversation."

He turned back to the board. "And that's our real job here. Not to make a good movie; that's Victoria and Aaron's problem. Our job is to make sure people never stop talking about it."

"That's cynical, even for you, André," Michelle said.

"That's why they pay me the big bucks," he replied with a grin. "I keep it real in the room so we can sell fantasy to the world."

He checked his watch. "Twenty minutes left. Let's nail down our initial press strategy. Exclusive with *The Hollywood Reporter*? Thoughtful interview in *The Atlantic*? Maybe both simultaneously to target different segments?"

As the team debated outlet strategies, André stepped back and surveyed the whiteboard covered in notes, strategies, and angles. Black Hitler. It was either going to be the most talked-about film of the year or the most notorious disaster in Pinnacle's history.

Either way, André Reynolds intended to market the hell out of it.

"All right, people," he announced, clapping his hands for attention. "Let's bring it home. By the time we're done, the whole world will be talking about James Olayinka Wright as Adolf Hitler; not because they're outraged, but because they can't look away."

Michelle gave him a searching look. "Do you actually believe in this project, André? Beyond the marketing challenge?"

André's perpetual grin faded momentarily, replaced by something more contemplative. "I believe that art should provoke reaction. I believe that casting a Black man as Hitler creates an inherent tension that forces people to examine their assumptions. And I believe in a media landscape driven by algorithmic engagement; anything that makes people feel something, anything, is better than content that makes them feel nothing."

He shrugged, the grin returning. "Also, the whole thing is so fucking absurd, it might actually work. And I love being part of history, even if it's the wrong kind."

Michelle nodded, seemingly satisfied with his honesty, if not his perspective.

"Now," André continued, "let's get back to figuring out how to sell a Black Hitler to a world that didn't know it wanted one."

*****

CHAPTER 7

On the day Pinnacle Pictures officially announced James Olayinka Wright as the new Hitler, Victoria Martinez's phone began vibrating at 5:43 a.m. and didn't stop for the next seventy-two hours.

She lay in bed, watching the notifications cascade across her screen with the serene satisfaction of someone who had just lit a match and tossed it into a pool of gasoline. The initial exclusive with *The Hollywood Reporter* had gone live at five-thirty a.m. Pacific; strategically timed to catch the East Coast morning media cycle while giving European outlets enough time to pick up the story for their evening news.

Victoria had insisted on the accompanying photo: James Wright in partial shadow, his face illuminated just enough to be recognizable, with a hint of the iconic side part but no mustache yet. The caption read simply: "James Olayinka Wright will portray Adolf Hitler in Pinnacle's upcoming historical drama *The Dictator's Shadow*." André's team had finally settled on the title after focus-testing seventeen alternatives, rejecting "Adolf" as "too on-the-nose" and "The Dark Rise" as "sounding like a Batman movie."

Now, watching her phone light up like Times Square on New Year's Eve, Victoria allowed herself a small, satisfied smile. *The Hollywood Reporter* headline was appropriately measured: "Groundbreaking Casting: James Wright to Play Hitler in Pinnacle Drama." Vulture had already gone with "Pinnacle Pictures Reimagines Hitler with Revolutionary Casting Choice." TMZ, predictably, had opted for "BLACK HITLER?! Hollywood's Most Shocking Casting Yet!"

Victoria's private phone, whose number only twelve people in the industry had, rang. Lucy.

"Are you seeing this?" Lucy asked sans prelude.

"I'm watching the notifications," Victoria replied, sitting up in bed. "What's the temperature?"

"Total chaos," Lucy reported with the clinical precision of someone who had spent the past hour cataloging digital outrage. "Fox News already has a segment scheduled for tonight called 'Hollywood's War on History.' CNN is assembling a panel of historians. Twitter is trending six different hashtags, ranging from #BlackHitler to #BoycottPinnacle to #JamesWrightDeservesAnOscar."

"And none of those people have even seen the movie," Victoria said, unable to keep the satisfaction from her voice. "The beauty of controversy: everyone has an opinion before they have information."

"André's team is monitoring across platforms. The response is exactly what he predicted: absolute confusion about whether this is progressive or offensive. No one knows whether to be outraged or impressed."

"Perfect," Victoria said, swinging her legs out of bed. "Is Kennedy breathing into a paper bag yet?"

"Her publicist released a statement at six-fifteen. Hold on, I'll read it: 'Kennedy is honored to be part of this revolutionary artistic vision that challenges traditional historical representation through thoughtful reinterpretation. As an actress committed to complex female roles, she looks

forward to exploring Eva Braun as a woman navigating impossible circu
mstances.'"

Victoria snorted. "That sounds exactly like something Kennedy would say if Kennedy had a PhD in media studies instead of an Instagram strategy team."

"Should I send André's first analytics report to your email or would you prefer to review it in the office?"

"Email it. I want to see the full spectrum of reactions." Victoria padded toward her kitchen. "And Lucy? Tell Sean I'll be late. I don't want to appear too eager when he inevitably calls to either congratulate me or fire me."

"He's already called twice," Lucy confirmed. "I told his assistant you were in an emergency meeting with legal about the announcement."

"That should terrify him appropriately," Victoria said, pleased. "I'll be in by ten."

After hanging up, Victoria opened Twitter and searched #BlackHitler. The results did not disappoint.

Conservative commentators were predictably apoplectic: "Hollywood's war on history reaches new heights of absurdity! What's next? Beyoncé as Queen Victoria?"

Progressive film critics were performing intellectual gymnastics to con-textualize the casting: "Wright's casting creates a meta-textual dialogue be-tween historical power structures and contemporary representation poli-tics that forces viewers to confront their own complicity in..."

Black Twitter seemed divided between those celebrating the barri-er-breaking casting and those questioning the wisdom of fighting for the right to play Hitler: "Me: We need more diverse roles for Black actors. Hollywood: How about Hitler? Me: That's not what I..."

Kennedy Oswald was trending separately, with reactions split between those praising her "bravery" and those questioning her judgment. Victoria scrolled through several posts before finding one that made her laugh out loud: "Eva Braun is finally getting her girlboss origin story! #StrongFemale-Leads #FemaleNazis #WaitWhat"

Her doorbell rang. Victoria glanced at the security camera feed on her phone to see a delivery person with her Alfred coffee. Lucy had anticipated her needs again. She made a mental note to discuss a raise for her assistant; the woman was practically psychic at this point.

This, Victoria reflected as she retrieved her oat milk cortado with a half-pump of lavender syrup, was what they'd been aiming for: total chaos, maximum conversation, complete uncertainty about how to process the casting choice. It wasn't just breaking the internet; it was breaking the algorithms that predicted how people would react.

She sipped her coffee and smiled. Somewhere in London, James Olayin-ka Wright was either celebrating his sudden fame or wondering what fresh hell he had signed up for. But he was signed; no backing out now. Mean-while, at an absurdly expensive New York hotel, Kennedy Oswald was undoubtedly gathering her team for emergency brand management.

Her phone buzzed with a text from Lucy: "You need to see this. TJ Jackson just posted."

Victoria raised an eyebrow. TJ Jackson, the self-styled "historical truth-teller" whose dramatized TikTok history lessons had gained him millions of followers through a just-asking-questions brand of conspiracy theory, was trending. She clicked the link Lucy had sent.

The video opened with TJ Jackson's signature look: dramatic light-ing, professorial glasses, and the intense expression of someone who was about to reveal that the moon landing was staged by Elvis. Dramatic music swelled as he leaned toward the camera.

"So Hollywood finally caught up to what I've been telling y'all for YEARS," he began, his voice dropping to a theatrical whisper. "The casting of James Wright as Hitler isn't just 'creative' or 'groundbreaking'; it's his-torically ACCURATE."

He paused for dramatic effect, eyebrows raised meaningfully.

"That's right. The facial recognition AI that originally analyzed Hitler's features found African ancestry markers before they 'fixed' the algorithm. Interesting timing that Pinnacle Pictures makes this casting announcement right after my video on Hitler's hidden heritage went viral, isn't it? [thinking-face emoji] They're not ready for the FULL truth, but this is a start. #HiddenHistory #TruthReveal #IWasTellingYouAll"

The video ended with TJ's catchphrase: "History doesn't lie, but historians do."

Victoria burst out laughing. The video already had 2.3 million views and counting.

She texted Lucy back: "This is gold. We're making a historically inaccurate film and this guy thinks we're finally telling the truth."

Lucy responded immediately: "Should I reach out to his team? He has a huge following."

Victoria paused, considering the absurdity of adding a conspiracy theorist to their already controversial project. Then again, this was Hollywood, where absurdity was just another workday.

"Get his contact information," she texted back. "We might need a 'historical consultant' if things get ugly. His kind of pseudohistory could be our perfect smokescreen."

She added, "But obviously don't actually contact him yet," followed by a cry-laughing emoji.

Lucy's response came instantly: "Obviously. Though I think he'd have a heart attack from excitement if he thought Pinnacle was validating his theories."

Victoria was in a good mood as she opened her laptop and clicked on André's email. The subject line read simply: "We have ignition."

***

"This is a fucking disaster," Kennedy hissed, pacing her hotel suite in Louboutins that made her feel in control, an overpriced security blanket. "Or a triumph. I honestly can't tell anymore."

Miguel and Dani sat on the sofa, tablets in hand, monitoring the real-time response across platforms. They exchanged a quick glance, the silent communication of assistants who had weathered Kennedy storms before.

"The overall sentiment analysis is actually positive," Dani offered cautiously. "Sixty-four percent of mentions are supportive or intrigued rather than critical."

"But what about *my* mentions?" Kennedy demanded, stopping her pacing to stare at Dani. "What are they saying about *me*?"

Dani hesitated, which was answer enough.

Miguel, ever the diplomat, intervened. "The conversation is primarily focused on James Wright and the concept itself. You're being mentioned as part of the project, but not as the main focus."

Kennedy's face went through a complex series of expressions, finally settling on something between outrage and panic. "I'm not the main focus? I have fifteen million followers! I founded HerStory Films! I'm playing Eva-fucking-Braun!"

She gestured frantically between Miguel and Dani, who maintained their practiced neutral expressions. "We're literally the most diverse team in the business. Miguel, how many times have I featured you on my Instagram?"

Miguel cleared his throat. "Seventeen posts this quarter."

"Seventeen!" She jabbed a finger in the air like she was puncturing the argument. "And Dani, didn't I just do that whole series on amplifying indigenous voices where I let you explain your grandmother's traditional recipes?"

"You did," Dani confirmed, her voice carefully modulated to reveal nothing. "It got excellent engagement."

"Exactly! I've been doing the work. I've been showing up!" Kennedy snatched her phone and began scrolling furiously through her photos. "I have pictures with every marginalized group at every award show. How can James be getting more attention? I'm the one who made this project inclusive!"

"Yes, but James Wright is playing Hitler," Miguel pointed out gently. "And he's... Black. That's naturally going to dominate the conversation initially."

Kennedy collapsed dramatically onto an armchair. "Show me. Show me everything. I want to see exactly what they're saying."

Miguel handed her his tablet, open to a carefully curated selection of social media responses that mentioned Kennedy specifically. She scrolled rapidly, her expression darkening with each swipe.

"'Kennedy Oswald continues her journey from rom-com queen to serious actress with this boundary-pushing project,'" she read aloud. "That's... fine, I guess."

She continued scrolling. "'Is Kennedy Oswald really trying to make Eva Braun a feminist icon? Girl, read a history book.' How dare they? I never said..."

"Actually, the HerStory Films press release did mention 'reclaiming Eva's narrative through a contemporary feminist lens,'" Dani reminded her.

"That's different," Kennedy snapped. "That's about showing her complexity as a woman trapped in a patriarchal system."

"A patriarchal system she enthusiastically supported," Miguel murmured, then immediately regretted it when Kennedy's head snapped up.

"What was that?"

"Nothing," Miguel backpedaled swiftly. "Just noting that the historical context creates narrative challenges."

Kennedy returned to the tablet, her frown deepening. "'Kennedy Oswald playing Eva Braun opposite a Black Hitler is either the most progressive or most offensive thing I've ever heard. Possibly both.' What does that even mean? How am I supposed to respond to that?"

"That's actually the reaction we want," Dani said, sounding more confident now. "Confusion creates conversation. Conversation creates relevance."

"And relevance wins awards," Kennedy finished automatically, echoing the mantra Victoria had repeated during their calls. "But what about my brand? HerStory is built on clear feminist messaging. This... ambiguity doesn't align with our values statement."

Miguel and Dani exchanged another glance.

"Your followers are waiting for your personal statement," Miguel said carefully. "The studio release mentioned you, but people want to hear your authentic voice on this."

"My authentic voice," Kennedy repeated, staring at the ceiling. "What exactly is my authentic voice saying about playing the girlfriend of Hitler when Hitler is being played by a Black man?"

The room fell silent as all three contemplated this genuinely novel public relations challenge.

"Show me what else people are saying," Kennedy demanded, extending her hand for Dani's tablet.

Dani hesitated before handing it over. "There's a lot of noise right now; maybe we should focus on crafting your statement first."

"No, I need to see everything. All sides. I need the full picture to properly contextualize my artistic approach." Kennedy's voice had the rehearsed quality of someone who had recently attended a media training seminar.

Reluctantly, Dani handed over her tablet. Kennedy began scrolling, her expression shifting between concern, confusion, and occasional flickers of genuine curiosity.

"Who's this TJ Jackson person? His video about our movie has nine million views already."

Miguel and Dani exchanged a quick, concerned glance.

"He's a... social media historian," Miguel explained carefully. "He has quite a following for his historical takes, especially his 'hidden history' series."

"Play it," Kennedy commanded, passing the tablet back.

Dani tapped the video, and TJ Jackson's dramatically lit face filled the screen. He wore professorial glasses and had positioned himself in front of bookshelves that somehow looked both impressive and hastily assembled. Four minutes followed: the destroyed records from his father's birth region, the facial structure analysis mainstream historians kept dismissing, the "corrected" algorithm, all delivered through a mixture of cherry-picked footnotes, misrepresented studies, and significant pauses followed by raised eyebrows. He ended with his signature move: leaning back, removing his glasses, and delivering his catchphrase with practiced gravitas. "History doesn't lie, but historians do."

The video ended, and Kennedy stared at the screen in stunned silence.

"His combined videos have almost a billion views," Dani said quietly. "His book *Hidden in Plain Sight: The African Origins of Everything* is currently number three on Amazon."

Kennedy's expression shifted from confusion to calculation.

"Is he... credible?" she asked, in the tone of someone who already knew the answer but was searching for a reason to pretend otherwise.

"No reputable historian supports his theories," Miguel said firmly.

Kennedy nodded slowly. "But a billion views... That's more engagement than my entire HerStory Films channel."

"Kennedy," Miguel began cautiously, "his theories are completely..."

"Did his book get reviewed in the *New York Times*?" Kennedy interrupted.

"Actually, yes," Dani admitted. "They called it 'dangerous pseudohistory dressed in academic language.'"

"But they reviewed it," Kennedy pointed out, her eyes taking on the gleam of someone discovering a marketing opportunity. "Which means he's part of the conversation."

She stood up and began pacing, the click-clack of the Louboutins the only soundtrack to her strategic thinking visibly activating. "We need to reach out to him. Not to endorse his theories, obviously, but to... engage with the discourse he's creating."

"That seems risky," Miguel ventured. "The studio would probably want to distance the project from conspiracy theories."

Kennedy waved this concern away. "The studio wants attention. That's the entire point of casting a Black actor as Hitler. They've already crossed the line from historical accuracy to artistic interpretation; this just adds another layer to the conversation. Possibly legitimization."

She stopped pacing, struck by a new thought. "Besides, what if he's right? What if there actually is some evidence that Hitler had African ancestry? That would completely change how my performance as Eva needs to be approached."

The absurdity of this statement hung in the air, but neither Miguel nor Dani dared challenge it directly.

"Should I draft a response to his video?" Dani asked instead. "Something acknowledging the conversation without endorsing specific theories?"

"Not yet," Kennedy decided. "Order his book first. I want to see what he's actually saying before we engage. And see if he's available for a private consultation. Not formally connected to the production, just... a background conversation about historical context."

As Dani made notes, Kennedy returned to the window, her mind clearly racing with the possibilities. "This could actually be perfect," she murmured. "It creates a whole new framework for the project. We're not being historically inaccurate; we're exploring alternative historical narratives that challenge conventional Western historical orthodoxy."

Miguel suppressed a sigh. Kennedy had found a way to reframe the conversation in terms that made her performance seem not just creatively daring but intellectually courageous. The fact that it required entertaining fringe conspiracy theories was apparently a minor detail.

"We've drafted three options," Dani finally said, retrieving her own tablet. "Option one emphasizes artistic boundary-breaking: 'Art should challenge us to see history through new lenses...'"

"Too academic," Kennedy interrupted. "I don't want to sound like I'm lecturing."

"Option two focuses on your partnership with James: 'I'm honored to work alongside the extraordinarily talented James Wright as we explore these complex historical figures...'"

"Better, but it sounds like I'm riding his coattails."

"Option three takes a personal approach: 'Throughout my career, I've sought roles that stretch me as an artist and contribute to meaningful conversations...'"

Kennedy turned away from the window to look at Dani. "That one. Start with that, then add something about being 'humbled by the opportunity to participate in this groundbreaking artistic vision.' Add that it's my goal that the 'best person gets the job'. It doesn't have to say anything about this project, just make sure they know I've always been race-blind."

As Dani began typing, Kennedy's phone rang. The screen displayed "Mother" with a photo of a woman whose resemblance to Kennedy was both striking and somehow melancholy. The same features but aged by disappointment rather than just time.

Kennedy stared at the phone as if it might explode. "She never calls in the morning."

"Do you want me to..." Miguel began.

"No, I'll take it." Kennedy stood and walked to the window, answering with forced brightness. "Mom! What a surprise!"

Miguel and Dani pretended to focus on their tablets while surreptitiously watching Kennedy's reflection in the glass. Her expression shifted from false cheer to defensive to something more vulnerable as she listened.

"It's not a stunt, Mom... No, I'm not trying to be controversial... Because it's a serious historical drama with award potential... Yes, Hitler is being played by a Black actor... No, I didn't suggest it... Because it's a creative choice that challenges historical..."

She paused, listening.

"Mom, I'm not twenty-two anymore. I know what I'm doing... This isn't like your situation with *The Widowmaker*. The industry has changed..."

Another pause, longer this time.

"That's not fair. That's..." Kennedy stopped, staring at her phone. "She hung up on me," she said, sounding genuinely shocked.

Miguel and Dani exchanged concerned looks.

"Your mother is just worried," Miguel offered. "The announcement is very fresh, and she's from a different generation of the industry."

Kennedy turned from the window, her expression no longer the practiced mask of perfect composure but something rawer. "She said I'm making myself a punchline. That I'll 'never be taken seriously after this.'"

"She doesn't understand the contemporary media landscape," Dani said firmly. "This kind of boundary-pushing is exactly how you transition from commercial success to critical recognition."

Kennedy nodded, but her confidence seemed shaken. "What if she's right? What if this is Halle Berry doing *Catwoman* instead of Cate Blanchett doing *Elizabeth*?"

The question hung in the air, a rare moment of genuine self-doubt from someone who had built a career on projecting unwavering self-assurance.

Miguel stood and approached Kennedy, dropping the professional assistant demeanor for a moment of genuine connection. "Kennedy, I've watched every performance you've ever given. You're more talented than people give you credit for. This role could show everyone what we already know: that there's real depth beneath the perfect Instagram aesthetic."

Kennedy blinked, surprised by both the comment and the sincerity. Then, just as quickly as it had appeared, the vulnerability vanished, replaced by her usual determined poise.

"You're right," she said, straightening her shoulders. "This is my chance to prove them all wrong. To prove my mother wrong." She turned to Dani. "Finish that statement and add something about 'the courage to confront difficult historical realities through art.' Then schedule a call with my acting coach. I need to dig deeper into Eva's psychology."

As Kennedy strode toward her bedroom, projecting renewed purpose, Miguel and Dani shared a final knowing look.

"Find me everything James Wright has ever said in interviews about his process," Kennedy called over her shoulder. "If he's going full Method for Hitler, I need to know the method now so I can prepare."

"Right away," Miguel responded automatically, already typing in the search terms, wondering if Kennedy had any idea how much more complex this project had become for her.

***

André Reynolds' condo in West Hollywood featured the aesthetic of someone who made too much money too quickly and hired a decorator who used phrases like "curated minimalism" and "statement pieces." The open-concept living area contained furniture that looked better than it felt and art selected for investment potential rather than emotional resonance.

The only spaces that truly reflected André himself were his home office (a chaos of movie memorabilia, marketing books, and framed advertisements he'd created) and the kitchen, where he now stood preparing breakfast while his wife, Nadia, sat at the island finishing her coffee before her shift at Cedars-Sinai.

"Dad! Have you completely lost your mind?"

Zoe Reynolds, their fourteen-year-old daughter, stormed into the kitchen waving her phone. She wore the navy blazer and plaid skirt of her private school uniform, but had accessorized with multiple ear piercings that walked the line between school regulations and rebellion.

"Good morning to you too, sunshine," André replied, flipping a perfect omelette with a practiced flick of his wrist. "I see you've been catching up on entertainment news."

"Entertainment news? You made Hitler BLACK!" Zoe exclaimed, dropping her backpack on the floor. "Do you know what that's going to be like for me at school today? Mackenzie's dad is a film professor at USC; he's probably writing a think piece about this right now."

Nadia hid her smile behind her coffee cup. "Eat your breakfast, Zoe. Your dad doesn't make casting decisions. He just..."

"...sells whatever decisions other people make," Nadia and Zoe finished in unison, clearly a well-worn family phrase.

"Exactly," André said, sliding the omelette onto a plate and placing it in front of his daughter. "I don't choose the product. I just create the packaging."

"You know we don't have to take the blame for this, right?" Zoe asked, reluctantly picking up her fork. "Black people didn't ask for Black Hitler."

André laughed. "No one's asking you to claim him, Zo. Though the actor, James Wright, is extraordinary. This isn't a stunt cast; the man can actually act."

"That's what makes it worse," Zoe muttered through a mouthful of eggs. "If he was terrible, we could all just dismiss it."

Nadia checked her watch, a practical, non-designer timepiece of someone who worked with her hands. "Luka will be here soon; more eating, Sweetie. He's picking you up today. I've got the late shift."

"Fine, but tell him not to wear his Pinnacle Pictures jacket. I don't want to be associated with Dad's Hitler project." Zoe said after a gulp of orange juice.

"It's not 'Dad's Hitler project,'" André corrected. "It's the Black Hitler project." He smiled at her. "Just another project I'm marketing."

"Same difference," Zoe retorted, but her tone lacked real heat. This was familiar territory: the good-natured family teasing about André's often absurd profession.

"Seriously, though. If anyone gives you a hard time about this at school, remember..."

"...Hollywood isn't reality, and Dad just sells the dreams," Zoe finished. "I know, Dad. But this one's going to be rough. Maya texted me ten times already asking if you've lost your mind."

André sat down across from her. "Tell Maya that André Reynolds does not make casting decisions. André Reynolds creates cultural conversations." He grinned. "And this conversation is going to pay for your college tuition."

Zoe rolled her eyes, but smiled despite herself. "You're impossible."

"Impossibly good at my job," André corrected, standing to make his own breakfast. "Now finish eating or you'll be late. Luka will be here in fifteen minutes."

"Fine." Zoe scrolled through her phone as she ate. "Oh God. TJ Jackson is already making videos claiming your movie proves his theory that Hitler was actually Black. Do you know about this guy?"

"The conspiracy historian? Unfortunately, yes." André cracked eggs into a bowl. "He's been on our radar since his first viral video about facial recognition AI supposedly finding African features in Hitler's face."

"We're inviting conspiracy historians into Hollywood now? And people actually believe this stuff?" Nadia asked, truly impressed at the new levels of audacity.

"He has like a billion views," Zoe responded, as if that was the answer.

"People believe what makes them feel something: outrage, vindication, superiority, whatever." André shrugged. "Welcome to media literacy in 2024. Remember, you want to do this job someday too; it's your chance to be a nepo baby."

Zoe rolled her eyes as she gathered her plate and placed it in the dishwasher. "Maybe I'll just become a nurse like Mom. I'm not claiming Hitler for Black people. That's a whole new level of cultural appropriation we didn't ask for."

André laughed. "That's actually a pretty good take. Write that down; it could be your college essay."

A car horn beeped outside.

"That's Luka." Zoe grabbed her backpack and hugged her father and mother quickly. "Try not to cause a cultural meltdown before I get home, okay? I've got a reputation to manage."

"No promises." André kissed the top of her head. "Love you, Zo."

"Love you too, marketing monster."

With that, she dashed out the door, leaving André and Nadia alone in the suddenly quieter kitchen.

"You've officially broken the internet," Nadia announced, returning her attention to her screens. "My mother just texted, and she thinks Twitter is a bird-watching app."

"It's beautiful, isn't it? Complete chaos. No one knows whether to be outraged or impressed," André said, cracking more eggs for his own breakfast.

"The conservative takes are exactly what you predicted," Nadia reported, gesturing to a laptop displaying Fox News. "They're running with 'Hollywood's War on History' and 'Woke Revisionism Gone Too Far.'"

"Predictable," André said, whisking eggs with practiced efficiency. "What about Black media? That's where the interesting tension is."

Nadia switched to another screen. "All over the map. The Root published 'Why the Casting of James Wright as Hitler Matters' supporting it as a barrier-breaking moment. But Black Twitter is divided. Some are celebrating Wright getting a major role, others are questioning why this is the role Black actors have to fight for."

André nodded, pouring the eggs into the pan. "And the film community?"

"Film Twitter is having an absolute meltdown trying to figure out if this is progressive or problematic. Half of them are writing thread analyses about 'the semiotics of racialized historical representation' and the other half are making popcorn memes waiting for the fighting to start."

André grinned, expertly flipping his omelette. "It's playing out exactly as I mapped it. Everyone's talking, no one knows what to think, and every hot take generates more conversation."

"The kid from UCLA uploaded his reaction video," Nadia said, clicking on a YouTube clip from the channel "I See LA." "The one you said would be critical."

They watched as a young Black film student with a growing following appeared on screen, his expression thoughtful.

"Welcome back to 'I See LA.' Everyone's blowing up my mentions asking what I think about James Wright playing Hitler," he began. "And honestly? I've been sitting with this for hours trying to figure out how I feel."

He paused, gesturing with his hands as he found his words.

"On one level, yes, it's wild that we're still fighting for basic representation in mainstream films, and suddenly there's a Black Hitler. Like, that's not exactly what folks meant by 'we want more diverse roles,' you know?"

André nodded along, having predicted this exact criticism.

"But here's the thing," the YouTuber continued, "I watched Wright as Richard III last year when the Royal Shakespeare Company streamed it. The man is a force of nature. He doesn't just act roles; he inhabits them. And if you think about it, there's something genuinely subversive about a Black man portraying the most iconic White supremacist in history."

"And there it is," André said triumphantly. "The perfect take that legitimizes our approach."

"He's not done," Nadia warned.

"The question isn't whether Wright can play Hitler," the YouTuber continued. "He absolutely can, probably better than anyone. The question is whether this is actually revolutionary or just provocative for provocation's sake. And we won't know until we see the film itself. Is this genuine artistic boundary-breaking, or is it just Hollywood using racial politics for publicity? I'm reserving judgment, but watching very closely."

André nodded appreciatively as the video ended. "That's exactly the kind of thoughtful skepticism we need. Validates the artistic potential while maintaining critical distance. Perfect."

His phone buzzed with several email notifications in quick succession. He glanced down, scanning the preview texts.

"The press requests are already coming in," he announced, scrolling through his inbox. "MSNBC is asking if we can provide a spokesperson for their panel on 'Representation in Historical Drama' next week. CNN wants to book Victoria for an interview. They're trying the cultural correspondent angle, which is smart."

"That was fast," Nadia said, sipping her coffee.

"Twitter moves faster than traditional media, but the bookers aren't far behind," André replied. "Their job is to chase the conversation. Right now, we're the conversation."

He opened another email, his eyebrows raising slightly. "Interesting. *The View* is requesting Kennedy for next Thursday's show. That would actually be perfect timing: right as we're transitioning from announcement buzz to production updates."

"Would Kennedy be good for that?" Nadia asked. "Talk shows can be unpredictable."

"Kennedy will be perfect for *The View*," André said, typing a quick note to his assistant. "She'll talk about artistic courage while looking supremely photogenic. The perfect gateway to the middlebrow audience." He glanced up. "But Victoria will want to approve everything first. No one from this production talks to press without coordination. It's too volatile."

"Speaking of Kennedy," Nadia said, holding up her phone, "her statement just dropped on Instagram. Want to hear it?"

"Hit me."

"'Throughout my career, I've sought roles that stretch me as an artist and contribute to meaningful conversations,'" Nadia read. "'I'm humbled by the opportunity to participate in this groundbreaking artistic vision alongside the extraordinary James Wright. Eva Braun has historically been reduced to a footnote, but her story offers a window into the complex reality of women who aligned themselves with power, even when that power was monstrous. Art requires courage: the courage to confront difficult historical realities and challenge our understanding of the past. I'm grateful to Pinnacle Pictures for taking this bold artistic approach. #TheArtistAsChallenger #HistoryReexamined #JamesWrightForTheWin'"

André snorted. "The hashtags are a bit much, but the content is solid. Her team earned their retainer this morning."

Nadia set down her phone, studying her husband with newfound curiosity. "Beneath all the marketing calculation, do you actually believe in this project? Or is it just an elaborate publicity exercise to you?"

André paused, fork halfway to his mouth, considering the question seriously. "Both," he finally admitted. "Part of me sees it as the ultimate marketing challenge: selling something that defies easy categorization. But another part genuinely believes there's something powerful in forcing people to see Hitler through a different visual lens."

He set down his fork, uncharacteristically reflective. "Think about it. By casting a Black actor as Hitler, we're creating an immediate visual disconnect that prevents audiences from slipping into the comfortable patterns of how they've seen Hitler portrayed before. They can't relax into familiar imagery. They have to actively engage with the performance, with the history, with their own reactions."

"That's... surprisingly profound," Nadia admitted.

"I contain multitudes, some only you get to see," André replied with a grin, his momentary seriousness evaporating. "Also, the memes are going to be incredible. Have you seen the one where they've photoshopped Wright's face onto the Hitler 'Downfall' meme? It already has two million views."

Nadia rolled her eyes affectionately. "And we're back to André the cynical marketing guru."

"Hey, I can believe in artistic merit and still appreciate a good meme," André protested, checking his own phone as it buzzed with new notifications. "Oh shit."

"What?"

"The American Historical Association just released a statement expressing 'profound concern about the casualization of Nazi imagery in popular culture.' And the Anti-Defamation League is 'monitoring the situation closely.'"

Nadia frowned. "That's not good."

"Actually, it's perfect," André countered, already typing a response. "It means we need to pivot slightly in our messaging. Less 'revolutionary casting' and more 'serious artistic approach that challenges how we visualize evil.' I'm texting Victoria now."

"What about James Wright? How's he handling all this?"

André paused, realizing he hadn't actually considered the human at the center of the storm they'd created. "I... don't know. His agent is handling his press for now. We're keeping him mostly quiet until the initial wave passes."

"Smart," Nadia agreed. "Let everyone else fight it out while he stays above the fray."

André's phone rang: Victoria's direct line.

"The queen herself," he announced, answering with his professional voice. "Victoria! I was just about to call you. Have you seen the AHA statement?"

As he listened, his expression shifted from concern to calculation to delight. "Brilliant approach. Yes, we pivot to 'historical gravity through new perspective.' I love it. And James? Keeping a dignified silence? Perfect."

He hung up, turning to Nadia with renewed excitement. "Victoria wants to accelerate production. Get cameras rolling before the controversy can crystallize into organized opposition. We start principal photography in three weeks."

"Can you actually be ready that quickly?"

André grinned, the manic energy that had made him Hollywood's most effective marketing strategist fully activated now. "We don't have a choice. The conversation has a half-life. We need to capitalize on the chaos before people settle into fixed positions."

He grabbed his tablet, already shifting into work mode despite being dressed in sweatpants and a vintage Wu-Tang Clan t-shirt. "I need to reorganize the entire marketing calendar. The window just moved up by a month."

Nadia checked her watch. "I need to go. Early rounds today." She stood and kissed André quickly. "Have a good day breaking the internet. Try not to cause an international incident while I'm saving lives, or our daughter might never forgive us."

"No promises," André replied, already deep in his marketing plans. "The best incidents are international."

As Nadia left for her shift, André opened his laptop and began rapidly reshuffling his marketing strategy. Outside their window, the Los Angeles morning unfolded in perfect sunshine, oblivious to the digital storm that had transformed "Black Hitler" from an absurd Hollywood concept into the most talked-about film project in the world, all before a single frame had been shot.

In offices, coffee shops, and social media feeds across the globe, everyone was talking about James Olayinka Wright as Adolf Hitler, each conversation feeding the algorithmic beast that turned controversy into currency. The only person not publicly commenting was Wright himself, whose dignified silence only added to the mystique.

Three weeks to cameras rolling. Three weeks to transform chaos into controlled narrative.

André Reynolds couldn't wait.

***

CHAPTER 8

"In what can only be described as the inevitable conclusion of Hollywood's war on Western history, Pinnacle's upcoming film will feature a Black actor as Adolf Hitler. You read that correctly."

Lucy speed-walked beside Victoria, tablet clutched to her chest like a medieval shield as they navigated Pinnacle's hallways. She continued reading from the screen, struggling to keep pace with her boss's determined stride.

"Not content with race-swapping fictional characters, gender-bending historical figures, and rewriting every narrative to fit their agenda, Hollywood has now moved to its logical end point: erasing the visual reality of history's most recognizable villain..."

"Let me guess," Victoria interrupted, not breaking stride. "*The Daily Wire*?"

"Yes. Brandon Witt's latest. He goes on to say your casting isn't 'brave' or 'challenging' but a 'deliberate provocation, a calculated move to generate publicity through outrage'..."

"Okay, so he's onto us, but he's still talking about us," Victoria muttered. "What else?"

"He asks if we would approve casting a White actor as Malcolm X or Martin Luther King Jr., saying the double standard reveals our 'true agenda.'"

Victoria snorted. "Typical. They always jump to MLK, as if we haven't had White actors playing Cleopatra, Moses, and Jesus for decades." She stopped abruptly, causing Lucy to nearly collide with her. "Actually, send that quote to André. It might be useful for our 'thoughtful discourse' marketing angle."

"You want to use criticism from *The Daily Wire* in our marketing?"

"Not directly. But we can use their outrage as proof we're challenging entrenched perspectives." Victoria resumed walking. "What's the overall temperature out there?"

Lucy consulted her tablet, swiping through meticulously organized sections. "Social media remains chaotic. TJ Jackson's conspiracy videos claiming Hitler had African ancestry have collectively hit eighty million views. Historians are publishing rebuttals, which he's spinning as 'the establishment trying to silence the truth.'"

"Of course he is. Glad to give him a ratings boost; hopefully he returns the favor."

"Film Twitter is divided. Many Black critics are questioning why this is the 'barrier-breaking' role being celebrated, while others are praising our truly race-blind casting."

"And Kennedy's statement?"

"Performing well. Over two million likes on Instagram. Her 'art requires courage' line is getting traction. Though there's a subsection of users pointing out the irony of her speaking about courage while posting from what appears to be a $12,000-per-night suite at The Four Seasons."

Victoria smiled thinly. "Social media: where authenticity is both demanded and immediately dissected."

They reached the door of the conference room, unaffectionately called "Purgatory", where Lucy handed Victoria a small paper cup containing two antacid tablets. Victoria accepted them with silent gratitude, swallowing them dry.

"Any word from the non-digital world?" Victoria asked.

"Three major Jewish organizations have requested meetings. The German Film Institute issued a statement expressing 'concern about potential historical trivializations.' Oh, and Marcus Goldman left a voicemail congratulating you on 'creating the industry's most expensive publicity stunt.'"

Victoria's smile turned predatory. "Make a note of that for my year-end performance review."

"As a positive or negative?"

"Both."

Lucy nodded, making a note. "One last thing: Sean Lynch wants an update on production timeline. He mentioned something about the board getting nervous."

"The board isn't nervous. They're excited. They just don't know it yet." Victoria adjusted her custom-tailored blazer, the armor of female executives everywhere. "Tell Sean I'll call him after this meeting with an accelerated production schedule that will make him look like a visionary to his bosses."

"Got it. Good luck in there."

"Luck is for amateurs and indie directors," Victoria replied. "We're making history. Or at least making it commercially viable."

With that, she pushed open the door to Purgatory.

The room had undergone a transformation in the three days since the casting announcement broke. Gone were the carefully arranged orchids and premium notepads of the pre-announcement meetings. The walls now displayed production schedules, casting grids, and marketing mock-ups; all bearing iterations of what they were still internally calling "Black Hitler."

Aaron Weisman stood at the far end, deep in conversation with David Katz. They broke off as Victoria entered, their expressions a study in contrasting stress responses: Aaron's methodical concern versus David's barely contained panic.

"Victoria," Aaron greeted her. "We were just discussing the impossible timeline you're about to propose."

"Clairvoyant as well as talented," Victoria replied smoothly, setting her folder on the table. "Where's André?"

"Finishing a press release responding to the Anti-Defamation League's statement," Michelle Park supplied from her seat at the table. "He's trying to thread the needle between 'we hear your concerns' and 'we're doing it anyway.'"

"And Dr. Friedman?"

David winced. "He's quit. Again. Permanently this time, he claims."

"Is that the fourth or fifth time?" Victoria asked, settling into her chair.

"Fifth. But he means it this time. He sent back his consultant fee with a note saying he can't in good conscience be associated with what he calls," David checked his notes, "'the cinematic equivalent of historical graffiti.'" He looked up. "I don't think he's going to renew or extend the option if it lapses."

"His loss," Victoria shrugged. "His name's still in the credits, whether he likes it or not. And now we have a clear deadline."

The door burst open and André Reynolds entered with the controlled chaos that seemed to follow him everywhere, a wake of energy carrying folders, coffee, and two assistants who looked simultaneously exhausted and exhilarated.

"The internet remains buzzing," he announced. "We're currently trending in fourteen countries. *The Daily Mail* just published an article titled

'Hitler Race Row Divides Hollywood.' And Kennedy's post reached more users than her last three sponsored content campaigns combined."

"So exactly as planned," Victoria said.

"Better than planned," André corrected, settling into his chair. "The confusion about whether this is progressive or problematic is generating exactly the kind of intellectual uncertainty that keeps people talking. No one knows what to think, which means everyone's thinking about us."

"Excellent," Victoria said, addressing the room. "Now we need to capitalize on this moment before it crystallizes into predictable camps. As of this morning, we have exactly twenty-three days before our option expires. And from what I've been told, Dr. Friedman isn't enthusiastic about renewing. Kennedy has a hard out date of August 15 for her next project. It's currently April 7."

She paused for effect. "Ladies and gentlemen, we need to begin principal photography within three weeks and complete it by early August."

The room fell silent. Aaron exchanged glances with David, whose expression suggested someone had just proposed they film on the actual moon.

"That's impossible," David finally said.

"No, that's necessary," Victoria corrected. "The option expires at the end of April. If we don't have cameras rolling by then, we lose the rights. And once this announcement buzz settles, the money people will start getting nervous."

"Three weeks to pre-production and twelve weeks to shoot?" Aaron shook his head. "Victoria, even with a conventional film, that would be aggressive. With this material, the sensitivities involved..."

"We don't have a choice," Victoria cut in. "We need to maintain momentum. Right now, we're riding the wave of controversy. If we let that energy dissipate, we're just another historical drama with a slashed budget. This is our moment."

She turned to the whiteboard, writing "PRODUCTION TIMELINE" in crisp letters. "Aaron, I need you to assemble your team immediately. Location scouting, production design, costume; everything has to happen simultaneously."

"Most of my first-choice crew is already committed to other projects," Aaron pointed out. "With this accelerated timeline..."

"Then we go with second choices," Victoria said firmly. "Or third. We make this work with whoever's available."

David raised his hand like a hesitant student. "Um, slight problem. The script isn't actually finished."

"You've had months," Victoria's voice took on a dangerous edge.

"Yes, but we keep changing fundamental elements," David protested. "First it was Kennedy wanting Eva to be a feminist icon. Then it was casting a Black actor as Hitler, which requires script adjustments to make sense of..."

"The script doesn't need to acknowledge the casting," Victoria interrupted. "We're not making an alternative history where Hitler was actually Black. We're making a serious historical drama with a Black actor playing Hitler."

"But that creates cognitive dissonance..."

"Exactly," André chimed in. "That's the whole point. The dissonance forces audiences to engage with the material in a new way. It's meta-cinematic commentary on historical representation."

"It's going to be really hard to write and direct that distinction," Aaron said carefully.

Victoria waved away these concerns. "Look, we can't afford elaborate period sets anyway. Our budget was slashed, remember? So we lean into that limitation. Make it more intimate, psychological. A claustrophobic character study of evil."

"A talkie," Aaron translated. "Lots of interior locations. Brooding Hitler."

"Exactly," Victoria smiled. "And André, I need you to reserve a significant portion of the marketing budget for awards season. We finish principal photography, head into post immediately, and target the festival circuit by fall."

André looked up from his tablet. "So we're going full-steam ahead on the 'serious prestige film that happens to have a Black Hitler' approach? Not embracing the controversy?"

"We acknowledge the conversation but rise above it," Victoria clarified. "Let the YouTubers and TikTokers talk and tie themselves in knots with careful guidance. Keep interviews with friendly publications and press, people who will listen to our talking points. Lean into the historic nature and 'best man for the job' narrative. Remind all of them how truly talented Wright is."

Michelle raised her hand. "Speaking of Wright, when does he arrive? We should prepare a press strategy for his first appearance on set."

"He lands Sunday," Aaron supplied. "We're keeping it very low-key. No airport photos, straight to a private residence. We need him focused, not dealing with paparazzi shouting Hitler questions. He'll need to be prepped on our talking points too."

"Good." Victoria nodded. "Now, for locations: I think our best bet right now is to shoot here in Los Angeles."

Aaron frowned. "It's going to be hard to make LA look like 1930s Germany."

"We use minimal exteriors," Victoria countered. "Focus on interiors, close-ups, psychological spaces. Besides, shooting here meets another Academy inclusion criterion: employing a diverse local crew. It's LA." Victoria gestured around the table. "The most diverse city on Earth. David and Aaron here are our token White guys."

Aaron's eyebrow shot up. "I'm Jewish."

"Which makes you our most appropriate token White guy for this project," Victoria replied. "Now, what other elements need immediate attention?"

David raised his hand again. "Kennedy isn't available for the first two weeks of shooting. There's a clothing line launch she's contracted for."

Victoria pressed her lips together. "Fine. We start with Hitler's early political scenes. Beer halls, street speeches, whatever doesn't require Eva."

"May I remind everyone that I still need to write those scenes. If we're moving toward a talkie, that's extensive rewrites," David interjected.

"So rewrite," Victoria replied sharply. "You have three weeks."

She checked her watch. "Let's take fifteen minutes. When we return, we'll finalize the accelerated pre-production schedule and discuss remaining casting."

As everyone filed out, Victoria caught Aaron's eye and gestured for him to stay behind. When they were alone, she closed the door and turned to face him.

"You think I'm pushing too hard," she said. It wasn't a question.

Aaron sighed, removing his glasses to rub the bridge of his nose. "I think you're asking for the impossible."

"I'm asking for the extraordinary," Victoria corrected. "There's a difference."

"Victoria, even if we somehow manage this accelerated pre-production, that leaves us maybe nine months for post. For a historical drama that will require careful editing, scoring, effects work..."

"I know it's a lot," Victoria acknowledged, her tone softening slightly. "But consider the upside. If we pull this off..."

"My PGA mark," Aaron finished.

"Exactly." Victoria stepped closer. "This project is already making industry history with the casting. Why not make production history too? The film that went from controversy to cameras in three weeks. And if we pull it off, we're looking at festivals and awards, I'll make sure of it."

"And if we fail spectacularly?"

"Then we fail trying something revolutionary," Victoria said simply. "Better than failing at something safe."

Aaron smiled despite himself. "You should have been a director. You know exactly how to get performances out of reluctant actors."

"I direct executives, which is considerably harder," Victoria replied. "So are you with me on this timeline?"

Aaron put his glasses back on, resignation mixing with determination in his expression. "Kennedy's only available for ten weeks, not twelve. We'll have to backload her scenes, shoot out of sequence, and probably work weekends."

"So we will," Victoria said. "I'll handle Kennedy. You focus on making this film something extraordinary, which only you can."

"With a Black Hitler."

"With a Black Hitler," Victoria agreed. "Who, I might add, is the most talented actor in this entire project."

Aaron nodded slowly. "That's what keeps me going through this insanity. Whenever I start questioning this whole concept, I remember his audition. He's... phenomenal."

"Then let's make sure the production lives up to his talent," Victoria said, patting Aaron's shoulder. "Now go call in some favors and find us a crew crazy enough to make this work."

Aaron headed for the door, then paused. "Victoria? When this is over, either way it goes, I'm going back on my vacation. A long vacation."

"I'll approve it personally," Victoria promised. "Now go make history."

Fifteen minutes later, everyone was back and the meeting's focus shifted to completing the cast. Joining them was Melissa Lewis, Pinnacle's head of casting, a diminutive woman whose calm exterior masked a legendary tenacity in securing talent.

"We've filled most of the supporting roles," Melissa reported, distributing casting sheets. "Many of the smaller parts were easy; the controversy is actually attracting actors who want to be associated with a boundary-pushing project."

"Any notable challenges?" Victoria asked.

"Several German historical organizations have contacted actors of German descent, urging them to decline roles," Melissa admitted. "Though interestingly, we've had more interest from German actors than expected. They see it as confronting historical demons through art."

Victoria flipped through the casting sheets. "These all look solid. What about Goebbels? That's our last major role."

Melissa exchanged glances with Aaron, a silent communication that suggested previous discussions. "We have several options, but Aaron has suggested Andrew Kline."

The name sent a ripple through the room. Michelle Park sat up straighter. "Andrew Kline? *The* Andrew Kline?"

"Yes," Aaron confirmed. "I worked with him years ago, before his... difficulties."

"Difficulties?" Victoria repeated. "That's a generous euphemism for a racist tirade at a Golden Globes afterparty, followed by a plantation-themed wedding, topped off with a drunk driving arrest while wearing a Confederate flag t-shirt."

"He's had some issues, mostly alcoholism," Aaron acknowledged. "But he's also a two-time Oscar winner who's been effectively blacklisted for the past twelve years. He's attempting a comeback, and his quote is now a fraction of what it once was."

"He's also one of the most talented actors of his generation," Melissa added. "And physically perfect for Goebbels."

Michelle looked skeptical. "His social media history is problematic, to put it mildly. And given our already controversial casting of Hitler..."

"That's precisely why it works," André interjected, looking up from his tablet with sudden interest. "It creates another layer of meta-commentary. The controversial White actor playing the Nazi propagandist opposite the Black actor playing Hitler? The think pieces practically write themselves... with my help."

Victoria considered this. "What's his current status? Is he still drinking?"

"Supposedly clean for two years," Melissa reported. "His new agent swears he's reformed, focused on rebuilding his career."

"He's been doing serious theater in Chicago," Aaron added. "Small venues, challenging material. By all accounts, he's humbled and hungry for a second chance."

Victoria turned to Michelle. "What's your take? You'd be handling him as the unit publicist."

Michelle hesitated. "It's high-risk. If he behaves, it's a casting coup; Oscar-winning talent at a bargain price. If he doesn't, it's another controversy on top of an already controversial project." She paused. "Though I did specifically request this project because I wanted to work on meaningful historical material."

"Not just for the Holocaust content?" André quipped.

Michelle shot him a withering look. "Some of us actually care about the subject matter beyond its marketing potential."

"Say it isn't so!" André grinned.

"Back to Kline," Victoria redirected. "Aaron, you'd be directing him daily. Can you handle him?"

Aaron nodded. "He's intense, method to a fault, but he respects craft. If I can convince him this is serious artistic work, not a stunt, I believe I can manage him."

"And Kennedy?" Victoria asked. "She'll have scenes with him as Goebbels. She's not exactly known for handling difficult co-stars gracefully."

"That's an understatement," Michelle muttered. "Her last director told me she threatened to call her 'connections at *Vogue*' when her co-star kept improvising lines. She's a leaky ship when unhappy."

"We'll need to be hands-on with both of them," Aaron admitted. "But Kennedy responds well to flattery, and Andrew responds to intellectual challenges. Different approaches, same goal: keeping them focused on the work."

Victoria drummed her fingers on the table, weighing options. "Michelle, if we go with Kline, you'd need to manage him carefully. Are you up for that?"

"I've handled difficult talent before," Michelle replied. "And I'm particularly invested in making sure this project is treated with appropriate gravity. If that means babysitting a recovering problematic actor, so be it."

Victoria nodded. "One last question: does James Wright know about Kline's history?"

A moment of awkward silence followed.

"I haven't specifically discussed it with him," Aaron admitted. "But he's a professional. I'm sure he can separate the actor from the person."

"A Black actor playing Hitler opposite a possibly racist actor playing Goebbels," André mused. "This production keeps getting more meta by the minute."

"Offer the role to Kline," Victoria decided. "But with strict behavioral clauses in his contract. One inappropriate comment, one drunken night, and he's out, Oscar or no Oscar."

"Understood," Melissa said, making notes. "I'll have legal draw up the specifics."

"Good." Victoria stood, signaling the meeting's conclusion. "Three weeks, people. Three weeks until cameras roll. We need to shoot something, anything, with James as Hitler to secure the option. Even if it's just Hitler petting his dog. I don't care. We need physical evidence of production."

"Blondi," David said suddenly.

"What?" Victoria frowned.

"Hitler's dog was named Blondi," David explained. "We could actually shoot a simple scene with Hitler and his dog. It's historically accurate and requires minimal production design or scripting."

"Hitler loved that dog more than people," Aaron added, warming to the idea. "There's something unsettling about seeing a monster show tenderness to an animal while planning genocide. It would be a powerful character moment."

"Do it," Victoria ordered. "Find a German Shepherd, a minimalist set, and shoot Hitler loving his dog. Consider it our official start of production."

As the meeting broke up, Victoria caught André before he could leave. "Make sure the press gets carefully controlled glimpses of our first day of shooting. I want just enough to fuel conversation without revealing too much."

"Already planning it," André confirmed. "Shadowy profile shots, perhaps a hint of the iconic haircut, definitely the dog. Domestic Hitler is even more unsettling than ranting Hitler."

"Perfect." Victoria nodded. "We show just enough humanity to make the monster more disturbing."

"That's what Wright brings to the role," André said. "The terrifying reminder that Hitler wasn't an alien or a demon; he was human. That's what makes it truly frightening."

"Exactly," Victoria agreed. "Now go sell that to a world that's simultaneously outraged and fascinated by our Black Hitler. And workshop some new titles before our internal name gets out..." She shuddered.

As the last of her team filtered out, Victoria remained alone in Purgatory, surrounded by the ephemera of their impossible project: production schedules, casting grids, marketing concepts. They had twenty-three days to start filming, a controversial cast, an unfinished script, and a budget that was optimistic at best.

But they also had James Wright, whose talent transcended the conceptual absurdity of their approach. They had chaos working in their favor, with no one able to dismiss the project outright because no one knew exactly where they stood on it. And they had momentum, that rarest of Hollywood currencies that couldn't be bought, only captured and channeled.

Victoria gathered her notes, mentally preparing for her call with Sean Lynch. She would tell him they were accelerating production to capitalize on the buzz. She would position it as strategic responsiveness rather than desperate scrambling. And she would conveniently omit mentioning that their historical consultant had quit for the fifth time or that they were casting a possibly racist actor as their Nazi propagandist.

***

PRODUCTION

P roduction started, as identity crises often do in Hollywood, with not enough money, not enough time, and twenty million mentions on social media.

CHapTer 9

Aaron Weisman's alarm blared at 3:47 a.m., a time he considered an abomination against nature and basic human dignity. He silenced it with the precision of a man who had spent decades waking up too early for too little money, only to spend his days begging millionaires to remember their lines.

"First day," he mumbled to the ceiling.

Emily stirred beside him. "Is it that ungodly hour already?"

"Three weeks of prep compressed into twenty-one sleepless days," Aaron confirmed, swinging his legs off the bed. "Today we either start rolling or go back to the drawing board, possibly both."

Emily propped herself up on an elbow, her dirty blonde hair charmingly disheveled. "At least they're paying you for the dual honor."

"If this falls apart, the PGA mark was just Victoria dangling a carrot to get me to direct a nightmare," Aaron muttered, shuffling toward the bathroom. "If we somehow pull it off, she'll claim it was her brilliant plan all along."

"That's why they call it show business, not show friendship." Emily's voice followed him. "Break a leg, darling. Try not to break Hitler."

Aaron snorted, then caught sight of himself in the bathroom mirror. The shadowed eyes stared back, a man who'd spent three weeks assembling a crew from whoever was desperate, available, or curious enough to join a production that industry insiders now referred to as "Stunning and Stupid."

His phone buzzed on the counter. A text from Victoria: *First day! Cameras = option secured. Don't fuck it up.*

He texted back: *Your confidence is touching. Going back to bed.*

Her response came immediately: *Funny. Send me footage by noon or I unleash Sean Lynch on your set.*

Aaron groaned. Victoria's ability to motivate through strategic threats remained unparalleled in Hollywood.

Ninety minutes later, his Range Rover pulled into the studio lot. They weren't shooting on location, no time, no money, no German-looking exteriors in Los Angeles that hadn't already appeared in a hundred other films. Instead, they'd leased a small soundstage at Valley Studios, a charmingly dilapidated facility whose main selling point was availability on short notice. This would be their home for the week before the Pinnacle studio they needed was available.

"Good morning, Aaron!" Lucy Chen chirped as he approached the entrance, looking improbably alert for someone who had likely been awake even longer than he had. "Victoria sent me to observe and report back."

"You mean spy," Aaron translated, accepting the coffee she offered.

"I prefer 'executive liaison,'" Lucy smiled. "She wants hourly updates. I convinced her we could manage with three throughout the day."

"You're a saint among assistants," Aaron muttered, taking a grateful sip. "Tell me something good."

"Craft services arrived on time, the German Shepherd passed his behavior assessment, and the set dressing looks surprisingly period-appropriate given our time constraints."

"And the bad news?"

Lucy's professional mask slipped momentarily. "Dr. Friedman has been in heated discussion with David for the past forty minutes. I believe the phrase 'intellectual vandalism' was used. Several times."

"Perfect," Aaron sighed. "What else could possibly make this day more industry-standard?"

"Kennedy's team called at midnight to request script changes for scenes she's not even in today. Her publicist followed up at two a.m. wanting to know the 'social hashtag strategy' for her first day on set next week."

Aaron nodded sagely. "The universe remains in perfect, terrible balance."

Inside, the soundstage hummed with the controlled chaos of a film set on the first day. Crew members scurried about making final adjustments. The minimalist set featured a period-appropriate sitting room, sparsely decorated but with just enough Nazi-era German touches to establish time and place. A custom banner bearing a swastika hung partially visible in the background, carefully positioned to be recognizable but not so prominent as to dominate the frame.

Across the room, David Katz and Dr. Benjamin Friedman were engaged in what could generously be called a spirited intellectual exchange but more accurately resembled two academics on the verge of a cafeteria food fight.

"That's absolute historical nonsense!" Dr. Friedman was saying, his white hair standing at attention as if electrified by his indignation. At seventy-three, the distinguished historian carried himself with the rigid posture of someone who had spent decades correcting undergraduate essays and had the spinal fortitude to prove it.

"It's a character moment, Ben," David replied, his patience clearly hanging by a thread. "It doesn't change your thesis about Hitler's rise to power."

"It most certainly does! Placing this scene in 1943 rather than 1941 fundamentally alters the psychological progression. By '43, the Eastern Front was collapsing. His relationship with Blondi takes on entirely different symbolic weight."

"We're shooting this scene because we need to start principal photography for contractual reasons," David explained for what was evidently not the first time. "Whether it appears in the final film at all is beside the point."

"Irrelevant?" Dr. Friedman's eyebrows shot up so dramatically they threatened to leave his face entirely. "The integrity of historical narrative is irrelevant? This is precisely the kind of intellectual casualness that;"

"Good morning, gentlemen," Aaron interrupted, approaching with a carefully neutral expression. "I see we're having a productive historical debate before our six a.m. call time."

Dr. Friedman turned, his academic indignation finding a new target. "Aaron! Perhaps you can explain why we're filming a scene that may not even make the final cut, using a historical moment that's been chronologically displaced for what David calls 'emotional resonance.'"

"Because we need to start shooting something, anything, by today or we lose the rights to your book," Aaron replied bluntly. "A book which, may I remind you, you've quit this production over five times now."

"Six," David muttered. "He quit again last night via email."

"That was a strongly worded expression of concern, not a resignation," Dr. Friedman corrected primly.

Aaron took another fortifying sip of coffee. "Benjamin, we doubled your consulting fee. We promised to keep Kennedy's 'feminist reframing' of Eva Braun to a minimum. David has rewritten the script seventeen times to accommodate your historical notes. Short of building a time machine and preventing Hitler from existing altogether, what more can we do?"

Dr. Friedman's expression softened slightly, the righteous anger of a historian giving way to the weary resignation of someone who'd spent too long in Hollywood's reality-distortion field.

"You could stop that woman from turning my carefully researched historical analysis into what she called..." He consulted a small notebook. "'A she-ro journey of a woman trapped in patriarchal power structures.'"

David winced. "That was actually one of her more restrained notes."

"Benjamin," Aaron said, placing a hand on the historian's shoulder, "I promise you that without your continued involvement, Kennedy would have even more influence over the historical content. You're our academic shield. Our footnoted fortress against absurdity."

"Your Maginot Line of historical integrity?" Dr. Friedman suggested dryly.

"Exactly," Aaron agreed, choosing to ignore the implication that, like the Maginot Line, this defense might prove tragically ineffective.

A production assistant approached carrying a tablet. "Guys? There's something you might want to see."

She held up the screen, which displayed a YouTube video already in progress. The title read "Ella Jones on Black Hitler Project: Hell No, White People. You Can KEEP Hitler!"

On screen, Ella Jones, a former character actor turned cultural commentator with a BET News segment and three million YouTube subscribers, was mid-rant.

"...of all the historical figures you could finally let a Black man play, you choose HITLER?" Jones exclaimed, her perfectly tailored blazer stretching as she threw her hands up. "Hitler?! We're still waiting for proper Black historical figures to get their due on screen, but sure, let's make Hitler Black. That makes sense."

The production values were slick and professional; this wasn't amateur outrage but commercially packaged indignation designed for maximum engagement.

"Let's be real for a minute," Jones continued, the camera pushing in dramatically on her face. "Hitler's whole thing, his WHOLE IDEOLOGY, was White supremacy taken to its most extreme, violent conclusion. Making him Black doesn't subvert anything; it just creates this weird historical confusion where the architect of the Holocaust somehow doesn't believe in his own inferiority?"

David ran a hand through his already disheveled hair. "And this is why I drink before noon."

"She makes valid points," Dr. Friedman observed, nodding along.

"Not helping, Benjamin," Aaron cut in. "Victoria will be thrilled though. A former SAG Award nominee is talking about us on a platform with millions of viewers. She'd frame this clip if she could." He turned to the PA. "How many views?"

"Eight million since yesterday," she replied. "And climbing."

"Fantastic," Aaron muttered.

The PA hesitated. "There's more. TJ Jackson posted a new video claiming there's 'documented evidence' that Hitler's grandmother worked for a Jewish family with North African connections."

"Oh for..." Dr. Friedman sputtered. "That's complete pseudo-historical garbage! That man has no credential. There's no credible evidence whatsoever."

"And it has twelve million views," the PA added.

Aaron pinched the bridge of his nose and sighed. "Welcome to filmmaking, where historical accuracy competes with conspiracy theories and loses by four million views."

David was scrolling through his phone. "It gets better. Kennedy just posted that she's 'eager to explore Eva Braun's journey as a woman whose perspective history has systematically erased.' She tagged TJ Jackson with 'perspective matters.' He responded with 'truth-tellers unite.'"

Friedman looked physically pained. "Can we revoke her library card? Does she even have one?"

"That would require her to have entered a library," David replied.

Aaron checked his watch. "All right, enough internet drama. We have a movie to shoot. Or at least, a scene of Hitler petting his dog to secure our option."

"Speaking of which," David said, lowering his voice slightly, "I should probably warn you; Kennedy is refusing to sign her contract."

Aaron froze. "What?"

"Her agent called at four a.m. Apparently, she's unhappy with the latest draft. Says it doesn't make Eva central enough. She's especially upset about how much screen time Goebbels has compared to her."

"We've cut three of his scenes already!" Aaron protested.

"Four," David corrected. "And added two Eva monologues that never happened historically."

"She wants to be the face of the Nazi party," Dr. Friedman muttered. "Why doesn't she just play Hitler? Wouldn't that be more 'revolutionary' for you Hollywood types?"

"That might be too revolutionary for us," David said. "Or not enough since she's still White... I don't know."

The three men fell into momentary silence, contemplating the reality of their situation. The compromises they'd already made were staggering, no German locations, a slashed budget, historical accuracy sacrificed on the altar of studio politics, and now their Eva Braun was holding out for more screen time.

"At least there's one silver lining," David offered. "With filming in LA instead of Germany, we actually have an excuse to minimize the rally scenes. That means Eva won't be making speeches to the adoring masses, as Kennedy suggested."

"Small mercies," Dr. Friedman said. "Though I still don't understand why she refuses to read my book."

"She says she wants to bring 'fresh eyes' to the role," Aaron answered.

"What does that mean, 'fresh eyes'?" Dr. Friedman asked.

"Fresh eyes uncontaminated by historical knowledge?" David guessed dryly.

"What about James?" David added. "Has he met her beyond the chemistry read?"

"Not yet," Aaron replied. "He's only been in LA for a few days, should be heading to makeup soon for his transformation. Don't tell him about Kennedy's contract issues. He's got enough to worry about. And meeting Andrew Kline on set tomorrow."

"Speaking of Andrew Kline," Dr. Friedman said, changing subjects with academic abruptness, "I saw his Churchill at the Goodman Theatre in Chicago last year. Brilliant performance. I'm pleased you managed to secure him for Goebbels, despite his... personal controversies."

"Do you know him?" Aaron asked, surprised.

"We corresponded briefly when he was researching Churchill's wartime speeches," Dr. Friedman replied. "He's quite thorough in his historical preparation, though a bit... intense. Not unlike many method actors I've consulted with."

"Intense is one word for it," Aaron muttered. "His contract has more behavioral clauses than Kennedy's has social media requirements. One outburst, one racist comment, one liquor-fueled tirade, and we can legally terminate him."

Their conversation was interrupted by the arrival of a tall handsome man in a simple dark jacket and jeans. Aaron immediately recognized James, looking nothing like the dictator he was about to portray. Instead, he carried himself with the quiet, composed dignity of a Royal Shakespeare Company veteran, observing the chaos of the American film set with the bemused expression of an anthropologist who'd stumbled upon a particularly fascinating tribal ritual.

"Aaron?" he said, extending his hand. His British accent carried the precise crispness of classical training. "I hope I'm not interrupting."

"James!" Aaron broke into a genuine smile, taking his hand. "Perfect timing. We were just discussing historical implications, creative liberties, and the impending collapse of Western civilization. The usual pre-shoot conversation."

"Sounds delightful," James replied with a hint of dry humor. "Should I come back when you've solved the major philosophical quandaries?"

"If we waited for that, we'd never roll camera," Aaron said. "Let me introduce you. This is David Katz, our screenwriter and resident optimist."

"A pleasure," James said, shaking David's hand. "I've thoroughly enjoyed the script. The beer hall scene particularly captures Hitler's calculated approach to audience manipulation."

David looked momentarily stunned at receiving actual praise from an actor. "Thank you. That's... exactly what I was aiming for."

"And this," Aaron continued, "is Dr. Benjamin Friedman, author of the book we're adapting and our historical consultant."

"Dr. Friedman." James extended his hand with noticeable respect. "It's an honor to meet you, sir. Your book was instrumental in my preparation."

Friedman seemed momentarily speechless, a condition Aaron suspected was rare for the professor. He finally shook James's hand. "A pleasure, Mr. Wright. I... admit I had concerns about the casting approach, but I appreciate you taking the time to read the material."

"Understandable concerns." James nodded. "I shared them initially. But I believe there's value in destabilizing how audiences perceive this historical figure, forcing them to see the man beneath the monster rather than the comfortable archetype they think they know."

Friedman's eyebrows lifted in surprise. "That's... a remarkably thoughtful perspective."

James reached into his jacket pocket and pulled out a well-worn copy of Friedman's book, its pages bristling with colored sticky notes. "Your analysis of Hitler's psychological progression from failed artist to genocidal dictator provided crucial insights. I particularly appreciated your chapter on his manipulation of collective grievance."

Friedman's face transformed, academic delight breaking through his crusty exterior like sun through storm clouds. "You've really read it!"

"Several times," James confirmed. "My parents are both academics, my father teaches English literature at Oxford, my mother African literature at UCL. They instilled a certain research rigor."

"Unlike some cast members who shall remain nameless," David muttered, though he promptly named them anyway.

James turned to David. "Mr. Katz, I should mention, your screenplay brilliantly translates Dr. Friedman's academic analysis into dramatic narrative."

David looked stunned once more, then deeply pleased. "Thank you. That's exactly what I was aiming for." He glanced at Friedman with a hint of vindication. "See? Some people appreciate the dramatic necessities."

Aaron was watching this exchange with growing amusement and relief. Whatever concerns he'd had about James's commitment to the role were evaporating rapidly.

"I understand we're shooting the Blondi scene today?" James asked. "A simple setup, minimal dialogue to establish Hitler's paradoxical humanity."

"Exactly." Aaron nodded. "We needed something we could film quickly to secure our option rights."

"I have a question about that," James said, turning back to Friedman. "Your book mentions Hitler's peculiar ability to emotionally segregate, showing genuine warmth to his inner circle and pets while orchestrating mass murder. Was this cognitive dissonance conscious or unconscious, in your analysis?"

Friedman practically glowed with academic validation. "Excellent question! The evidence suggests that Hitler maintained distinct psychological compartments. His tenderness toward Blondi wasn't performative; it was genuinely felt. This makes his monstrous actions toward certain humans all the more disturbing because it confirms his capacity for empathy was intact but selectively applied."

James nodded thoughtfully. "So the scene serves to underscore that his evil wasn't from an inability to feel, he wasn't a sociopath, but from a warped moral framework that dehumanized certain groups while maintaining normal emotional connections to others."

"Precisely!" Friedman exclaimed, looking as though he might hug James. "The banality of evil isn't about emotional flatness but about moral compartmentalization."

Aaron checked his watch. "I hate to interrupt this academic love fest, but we need to get James to makeup ASAP if we want to get cameras rolling by noon."

"Just one more question, if I may," James said. "Dr. Friedman, your chapter on Hitler's private spaces versus his public persona;"

"James," Aaron interrupted, more firmly this time. "The sun is up, Victoria is undoubtedly already texting Lucy for updates, and we need footage of you with a dog by noon or we all start updating our resumes."

James nodded, instantly professional. "Understood. Where's my four-legged co-star?"

"The animal wrangler has her ready," Aaron confirmed. "Beautiful German Shepherd named Sadie who'll be playing Blondi."

"Has everyone met Kennedy yet?" James asked casually. "I haven't seen her since our chemistry read."

A loaded silence fell over the group.

"She's not needed until next week," Aaron replied carefully.

"Fortunate timing," Dr. Friedman muttered.

"She's very... dedicated to her interpretation," Aaron added diplomatically.

"She believes Eva Braun was a 'girlboss babe trapped in patriarchal constraints,'" David said, holding up air quotes, missing the memo.

James looked up, brow furrowed. "A what?"

"A term from contemporary female empowerment language," David translated. "It suggests Eva was secretly a powerful woman constrained by societal expectations rather than a willing participant in the Nazi inner circle."

"Which is revisionist nonsense," Dr. Friedman added. "Eva Braun was politically uninterested but socially ambitious. What one might call a gold digger. She wasn't trapped; she was exactly where she wanted to be, adjacent to power."

"I see," James said slowly. "That seems at odds with the historical record."

"Everything about this production is at odds with the historical record," Dr. Friedman replied. "Starting with, well..." He gestured vaguely toward James himself.

"Fair point," James acknowledged with surprising good humor. "Though I'd argue the visual dissonance might actually help audiences engage more critically with the material."

"That's what I keep telling him," Aaron said. "Now, we really need to get you to makeup." He flagged down a PA. "James needs to get to makeup immediately. Tell Sarah she has exactly two hours to transform our star into history's greatest monster."

"On it." The PA nodded, gesturing for James to follow.

James turned to Dr. Friedman with genuine respect. "I look forward to continuing our conversation, Doctor. Perhaps during lunch break? I'd value your insights on Hitler's rhetorical techniques."

"I'd be delighted," Dr. Friedman replied, looking slightly dazed at having encountered an actor who actually cared about historical accuracy.

As James was whisked away to the makeup trailer, Aaron turned back to find both David and Dr. Friedman staring after him with identical expressions of stunned appreciation.

"Well," Dr. Friedman said finally, "he's certainly not what I expected."

"He actually read my script," David marveled. "The whole thing. Not just his scenes."

"And my book," Dr. Friedman added. "With annotations."

Aaron couldn't help smiling. "Told you he was the real deal. Now if we can just get him into makeup, shoot this scene, and deliver footage to Victoria before she unleashes corporate hell, we might actually survive day one."

His phone buzzed again, a text from Victoria: *Update? Hitler ready? Cameras rolling?*

He typed back: *Hitler meeting makeup. Dog standing by. Midnight footage delivery still on track.*

Her response came seconds later: *Make it noon or I release Sean Lynch.*

Aaron pocketed his phone. "Gentlemen, I suggest we take advantage of these few hours while James is transforming to prepare the set, finalize the blocking, and perhaps engage in a quick prayer circle for divine intervention."

"I'm Protestant," David pointed out.

"I'm an atheist," Dr. Friedman added.

"Perfect," Aaron nodded. "Between the three of us, we should have all theological bases covered."

As he hurried off to check on the set preparations, Aaron felt the peculiar mixture of dread and excitement that accompanied every production, amplified tenfold by the sheer audacity of their undertaking. They were about to put a Black British actor on screen as Adolf Hitler, with a rom-com darling playing Eva Braun, a possibly racist Oscar winner as Goebbels, and a historian who'd quit six times providing historical oversight.

And he had approximately four hours to call "action," or they'd all be updating their LinkedIn profiles by dinner.

***

CHAPTER 10

The makeup trailer smelled of spirit gum, foundation, and the peculiar mix of anxiety and creativity that permeated every film set. Sarah Abramowitz, head of makeup, was hunched over her phone when James entered; her laughter echoed in the cramped space.

"Oh my God, this one's even better," she was saying to her assistant. "Look, they photoshopped James's face onto that Hitler *Downfall* meme."

The assistant peered over her shoulder. "The subtitle translation is hilarious. 'When you've been preaching Aryan supremacy but your casting director is woke.'"

Sarah looked up, noticing James standing in the doorway with the PA who'd escorted him. Her laughter cut off abruptly, replaced by professional composure that couldn't quite hide her momentary embarrassment.

"Mr. Wright! I'm so sorry, I didn't;"

"Please, it's James." He smiled, extending his hand. "And don't apologize. I'd rather people laugh than burn effigies."

Sarah relaxed visibly, shaking his hand. "Sarah Abramowitz. This is my assistant, Tina. We're actually running a bit behind schedule, thanks to some last-minute prosthetic adjustments."

"Is there time for coffee before we start?" James asked. "I'm still adjusting to the time difference."

"Absolutely. Tina, could you grab Mr. Wright, sorry, James, some coffee while I set up?"

As Tina scurried out, Sarah gestured to the makeup chair. "Have a seat. Fair warning: transforming you will take about two hours, give or take Hitler's mustache precision."

James settled into the chair, studying Sarah's workspace, meticulously organized makeup palettes, reference photos of Hitler from various periods, and detailed sketches of the transformation process.

"You've done your research," he observed.

"When you're Jewish, Hitler's face is unfortunately burned into your cultural memory," Sarah replied, then winced. "Sorry; that came out darker than intended."

"No, I appreciate the honesty," James said. "Actually, if you don't mind my asking, how do you feel about this project? The concept, I mean."

Sarah considered the question as she draped a cape around his shoulders.

"Honestly? When I first heard 'Black Hitler,' I thought someone had lost their mind. Then I saw your audition tape." She met his eyes in the mirror. "It was... disturbing. Not in a bad way, but in the way art should disturb, making familiar things unfamiliar."

"That's precisely what drew me to it," James said, watching as she began organizing her tools. "Though I admit, the online discourse has been rather overwhelming."

Sarah laughed, pulling up a stool. "Oh, have you seen the one with the White supremacist guy? He's wearing a swastika armband, holding *Mein*

Kampf, then he sees a poster for our movie and looks completely bewildered. The caption is 'When did White supremacy become inclusive?'"

James chuckled despite himself. "I haven't seen that one. The discourse seems quite polarized."

"That's the internet; if you aren't polarizing, it feels like you don't exist," Sarah agreed, beginning to apply a base layer to his skin. "My mother called me yesterday asking if I'd lost my mind working on this. Her mother survived Treblinka, came to America in the fifties."

"What did you tell her?"

"That it's complicated." She paused, brush in hand. "She wasn't convinced, but she did say, 'At least make him look like shit,' which is funny if you knew her; she doesn't use toilet language."

James laughed. "I'll do my best to honor her request with my performance."

"My real concern," Sarah admitted, "is whether audiences will see past the 'Black Hitler' headlines to actually watch the movie. I don't think holocaust stories really sell out theaters anymore. If it's not a dopamine rush, does anyone watch? Controversy is only good if it gets butts in seats, right?"

"That's my worry as well," James said. "I want people to look at this story and think about what Nazism or Hitler means. The words are thrown at everything now, and it's slowly eroding their force."

Sarah began the delicate work of applying the first prosthetic, subtle alterations to James's nose and chin to echo Hitler's features without descending into caricature.

"I think it depends on the execution," she said thoughtfully. "In less capable hands, this could be a disaster. I guess I've become cynical and jaded, but people are engaging in unexpected ways. Some think you are the perfect Hitler, no offense. But also maybe there's something powerful about having Hitler portrayed by someone he would have considered sub-human, because fuck him."

"My grandfather said something similar," James laughed, careful not to move as she worked. "He grew up in post-war Britain. His father served in the war and came back changed. When I told him about this role, he said there was a certain poetic justice in Hitler being played by 'exactly the sort of person he despised.'"

"Smart man, your grandfather," Sarah murmured, focused on her work. "That's what I told my mother: there's something almost... I don't know, karmically satisfying about it."

"Assuming I don't butcher the performance," James added.

"From what I've seen? I have some faith." Sarah stepped back to assess her progress. "Now, I need you to hold very still for this next bit. Hitler's distinctive hairline requires precision work."

As Sarah continued the transformation, they fell into comfortable conversation. Despite the bizarre circumstances (or perhaps because of them), a genuine rapport developed between the actor and the makeup artist, both professionals navigating the surreal territory of creating a Black Hitler for mainstream consumption.

"The real question," Sarah said as she began work on the infamous mustache, "is whether audiences will grasp the nuance we're aiming for. The world isn't exactly known for its nuanced take on complex subjects these days."

"That's the risk," James agreed. "I've promised myself, and my family, that whatever happens, I'll ensure he remains hate-filled and cruel. The historical truth of Hitler's monstrosity isn't up for reinterpretation, even if his visual representation is."

"That's the challenge, isn't it? Maintaining historical truth while creating visual disruption." Sarah applied the final touches to the mustache with surgical precision. "But perhaps that's exactly why this approach might work. By making Hitler look different from how we expect, maybe people will actually pay attention to the history again, rather than dismissing it as familiar territory they already know. Kind of like saying it could be anyone."

"That's my hope," James said. "It's what convinced me to take the role, despite the obvious risks."

Sarah stepped back, studying her work with professional scrutiny. "Almost there. We just need the final hair coloring, and Herr Hitler will be ready for his close-up."

James examined his reflection. The transformation was already remarkable. His features had been subtly reshaped to echo Hitler's distinctive appearance, and the mustache was flawlessly applied. But the face looking back was still unmistakably his own, a Black actor in the process of becoming history's most famous White supremacist.

"It's... unsettling," he admitted.

"Good," Sarah said firmly. "It should be. If it were comfortable, we'd be doing something wrong."

The door to the trailer opened, and Tina returned with coffee. She stopped short, seeing James's partial transformation.

"Wow," she breathed. "That's... incredible and terrifying."

"Exactly the reaction we want," Sarah nodded, accepting the coffee from her assistant. "Now, James, drink this before it gets cold. Hitler runs on caffeine today, and we still have hair to complete."

As they continued the transformation, James felt the weight of what they were creating, not just a role or a performance, but a deliberate disruption of historical imagery designed to give history back its power, not erase it. Whether it would be received as profound artistic statement or dismissed as provocative stunt casting remained to be seen.

But in the hands of Sarah Abramowitz, at least, Hitler's face was being reconstructed with the perfect balance of historical accuracy and artistic subversion, one careful brushstroke at a time.

***

Michelle Park arrived at Valley Studios precisely at 10:43 a.m., having timed her entrance to coincide with what production schedules optimistically projected as "mid-morning momentum," that sweet spot when things were supposedly running smoothly but before the inevitable midday crisis.

Reality, as usual, had different plans.

"What do you mean 'Eva Braun's nose fell off'?" she heard a PA shouting into a walkie-talkie as she approached the soundstage. "We need to roll camera in twenty minutes!"

Michelle suppressed a smile. Just another day in Hollywood, where sentences like "Eva Braun's nose fell off" were met with professional concern rather than historical confusion.

Her intern, Isa, hurried to keep pace with her determined stride, while Danny, the social media photographer André had insisted accompany them, trailed behind clutching his camera equipment. Ravi Mukerjee completed the procession at an unhurried stroll, phone out and already recording: André had decreed that no transformation imagery left the lot without his Creative Director capturing it personally, and Ravi had found it simpler to never stop filming at all.

"Okay, team," Michelle turned to address them both. "Day one documentation needs to strike the perfect balance, enough behind-the-scenes content to feed the publicity machine but nothing that could be taken out of context as, well..."

"As promoting Nazism?" Isa supplied helpfully.

"Exactly. We want 'historical drama in production,' not 'Pinnacle Pictures endorses the Third Reich.'"

Danny nodded seriously. "André sent very specific instructions. He wants artfully shadowed profile shots of James, nothing full-face until the official poster reveal. Oh, and plenty of the dog."

"The dog?" Michelle asked.

"Apparently the internet loves dogs, even Nazi dogs. Especially Nazi dogs?" Danny looked confused by his own statement. "André says a cute German Shepherd humanizes the production without legitimizing Hitler."

"The marketing logic of André Reynolds continues to defy conventional understanding," Michelle sighed. "All right, check out the set, scout good angles, then we'll reconvene for the official first shot documentation."

As Danny and Isa scurried off, Michelle headed for the makeup trailer, Ravi at her shoulder, phone still recording. She'd worked with Sarah Abramowitz on three previous Pinnacle productions, developing the kind of shorthand that made the publicity-creative relationship bearable for both sides.

She knocked briefly before entering, finding Sarah putting the finishing touches on what could only be described as the most surreal transformation in recent cinema history. James Wright, the handsome British actor she'd met during pre-production, had been transformed into an unmistakable Adolf Hitler, albeit one whose overabundance of melanin created an immediate visual disruption of expectations.

"Michelle!" Sarah greeted her without looking away from her work. "Perfect timing. I'm about to create cinematic history, or career suicide, depending on tomorrow's Twitter trends."

"The line between those outcomes grows thinner every year," Michelle replied, then turned to James. "We haven't properly met in person. Michelle Park, Unit Publicist and designated damage controller."

"I'd shake your hand," James replied with a warm smile that looked bizarrely incongruous beneath Hitler's severe haircut and mustache, "but Sarah has threatened dismemberment if I disturb her final touches."

"I'd settle for professional disgrace and eternal shame," Sarah corrected, carefully applying what appeared to be the final dabs of color to Hitler's signature hairstyle. "But physical violence remains an option."

Michelle laughed. "I'd never risk the wrath of the makeup department. They know too many ways to make me look terrible in press photos."

"So," Michelle said, borrowing one of Sarah's brushes to fix a gap in her own foundation, the kind of slip she'd never have missed on a normal day, "how are you feeling about your first day as Hitler?"

"Surreal," James admitted. "Though Sarah's artistry makes it feel more grounded. There's something about physically transforming that helps center the performance."

"He's being modest," Sarah interjected. "He came in fully prepared, research notes, historical references, psychological analysis. My job was just decorative. He does the heavy lifting."

"Hold still," Sarah commanded, working on a final detail. "Perfect. Ladies and gentlemen, I present Adolf Hitler, updated for modern audiences!"

She spun the chair so James could see the completed transformation. The effect was remarkable: Hitler's distinctive features had been carefully recreated, from the severe side-parted hair to the infamous mustache.

"It's extraordinary work, Sarah," James said quietly, studying his reflection.

"It certainly is," Michelle agreed, already mentally drafting how to position this for press. "The perfect balance of historical recognition and artistic disruption."

Ravi circled the chair once, phone raised, documenting the transformation with the reverence of a man archiving evidence. "André is going to weep," he said. "Embargoed until the poster drops, but he will weep."

The door burst open as Isa rushed in, looking flustered. "Michelle, we have a situation."

"Eva Braun's nose falling off? I heard."

"No, worse. Well, different." Isa lowered her voice, though in the small trailer everyone could hear perfectly. "The set is... problematic for photography. Danny can't figure out how to shoot anything without... you know."

"Without what?" Michelle asked.

"Swastikas," Isa whispered, as though the word itself might be contagious. "They're everywhere. Period-appropriate Nazi imagery. Impossible to get a clean shot for socials without capturing symbols that would absolutely get us flagged on every platform."

Michelle closed her eyes briefly, summoning patience. "It's a movie about Hitler, Isa. Did we expect Buddhist imagery?"

"Technically," Ravi said, lowering his phone, "swastikas are Buddhist imagery. And Hindu, and Jain. There's one painted on my grandmother's doorstep in Kolkata, and on every wedding invitation in my family going back generations. It meant good fortune for three thousand years until one Austrian tilted it forty-five degrees, and somehow he's the one who gets to keep it. Him and the hippies."

"The hippies?" Michelle asked.

"They took yoga, they took incense, they took om. The swastika they returned, and only because Hitler got to it first. We noticed."

Michelle stared at him for a moment. Then the publicist in her visibly rebooted. "How big is the box office in the Indian subcontinent these days?"

"A billion and a half people who already know the symbol isn't his," Ravi replied.

"I'll handle it." Michelle turned back to James and Sarah. "Duty calls. James, break a leg out there, metaphorically, of course. Sarah, magnificent work as always."

"I'd kiss you goodbye," Michelle told James with mock seriousness, "but Sarah would murder me for disturbing her masterpiece."

"Murder is such an ugly word," Sarah replied cheerfully. "I prefer 'justified homicide for makeup sabotage.'"

Michelle hurried out, Isa and Ravi close behind, leaving James to get into costume before facing cameras as history's most notorious dictator, reimagined for an era where nothing, not even Hitler, remained uncontested cultural territory.

The set of *The Dictator's Shadow* (a title Michelle still found too generic but which had tested well with focus groups) was indeed adorned with period-appropriate Nazi imagery. Banners bearing swastikas hung in carefully positioned backgrounds; props tables displayed replica medals, documents, and smaller flags, all featuring the infamous symbol.

Michelle found Aaron deep in conversation with a large Black man she recognized as Marcus "Big Marc" Johnson, the lighting director whose reputation for technical brilliance was matched only by his booming laugh and colorful commentary.

"We need more shadow on stage right," Marc was saying. "Hitler should emerge from darkness, both literally and metaphorically. Visual storytelling 101."

"Aaron," Michelle interrupted. "We need to talk."

Aaron turned, recognizing her tone as the universal harbinger of publicity concerns. "Michelle. Welcome to day one chaos. Have you met Big Marc?"

"Not officially." Michelle shook the man's enormous hand. "Michelle Park. I've admired your work on several projects."

"Likewise," Marc rumbled. "Though I gotta say, this one takes the cake for industry insanity. Twenty years lighting films, and I never thought I'd be asking, 'Does this shadow make Black Hitler look appropriately menacing?'"

His deep laugh rolled across the set like thunder. "This business keeps finding new ways to surprise me."

"Marc, can you give us a minute?" Aaron asked. "Lighting, check the dog's position for the close-up?"

"Sure thing. But remember what I said: Hitler from darkness, dog in light. Visual metaphor for his compartmentalized humanity." Marc moved away, still chuckling to himself.

Michelle waited until he was out of earshot. "We have a problem. A swastika problem."

"You mean the Nazi symbols in our Nazi movie about the leader of the Nazi party?" Aaron asked dryly. "How unexpected."

"I'm serious, Aaron. We need to implement some kind of Swastika Sensitivity Protocol immediately."

Aaron stared at her. "A what?"

"A system for hiding or removing Nazi imagery when we're not actually filming. When press is on set, when social documentation is happening, during breaks, anytime cameras aren't rolling for the actual movie, when any of the crew could take a selfie!"

"Michelle, we're making a film about Hitler. The swastika is rather central to the visual language."

"I'm not suggesting we remove them from the film," Michelle clarified with practiced patience. "I'm saying that in today's media environment, with social platforms algorithmically flagging Nazi imagery, with press photographers potentially capturing contextless images, we need to be extremely careful about optics."

"Optics," Aaron repeated. "Of our Hitler movie."

From a few feet away, Marc's laugh boomed again. "She's got a point, Aaron. My sixteen-year-old daughter already asked if her daddy's lighting 'the racist movie.' Context gets lost quickly these days."

Michelle nodded gratefully toward Marc. "Exactly. In an environment where everyone calls everyone else Hitler already, actual Hitler imagery without careful contextual framing is guaranteed to create problems."

"So what are you suggesting?" Aaron asked. "Nazi symbol wranglers?"

"Precisely," Michelle said, seizing on the term. "A dedicated team responsible for covering or removing Nazi imagery between takes. We can frame it as a sensitivity measure for cast and crew comfort."

"The left will eat that shit up," Marc contributed helpfully. "Worker protection from harmful imagery? That's grade-A BS for PR right there."

Aaron looked between them. "Let me get this straight. You want me to assign crew members to be 'Nazi wranglers' who cover swastikas between takes, not because anyone has actually complained about Nazi imagery in a Hitler film, but because it might photograph badly for social media?"

"Yes," Michelle confirmed without hesitation. "That's exactly what I'm saying."

"This is absurd."

"That's modern publicity," Michelle replied unapologetically. "If the camera sees it, the internet will react to it without context. If we want the conversation to be about our artistic intentions rather than 'Pinnacle Fills Set with Nazi Imagery,' we need to control what's visible when."

Marc was openly enjoying the exchange, his deep laugh punctuating the conversation. "Man, I love Hollywood. No other business would have meetings about how to make a Hitler movie without people seeing Hitler stuff."

Aaron ran a hand through his hair. "Fine. I'll assign PAs to cover the larger symbols between takes. But I draw the line at removing Hitler's mustache for Instagram."

"That would defeat the entire premise," Michelle agreed seriously.

She pulled out her phone and quickly texted André: *Implementing Swastika Sensitivity Protocol on set. Dedicated crew handling Nazi imagery visibility between takes.*

His response came almost instantly: *BRILLIANT. Sensitivity theater + real protection. Press will eat it up. Make sure to document our "responsible approach to difficult historical imagery." Lots of photos, maybe interview a crew member. Already drafting press release.*

Michelle pocketed her phone, smiling. "André approves. He's already turning it into a marketing angle."

"Of course he is," Aaron muttered. "That man could market a funeral as a 'life celebration opportunity with guaranteed audience engagement.'"

Marc's laugh rolled across the set again. "This shit just keeps getting better! Wait till I tell my crew they're officially 'Nazi wranglers' now. Bet that wasn't in the job description." He clapped Aaron on the shoulder. "Don't worry, man. This movie might be industry insanity, but at least it ain't boring."

As if summoned by the rising absurdity, a PA appeared at Aaron's elbow. "Sir? Hitler is ready, but the dog is having anxiety issues. Animal wrangler says she needs ten minutes to calm her down."

Aaron closed his eyes briefly. "Tell Hitler to stand by. And find some crew members who can act as," he glanced at Michelle, "'Nazi wranglers' for between takes."

"Nazi what?" the confused PA asked.

"Michelle will explain," Aaron said, already moving toward the animal wrangler. "I need to go solve a canine anxiety crisis before we can shoot our Nazi pet therapy scene."

As Aaron walked away, Marc shook his head in amused disbelief. "Day one, and we already got Black Hitler, anxious dogs, and Nazi wranglers. This movie better win all the awards!"

Michelle couldn't help but agree as she began explaining the nuances of swastika management to the bewildered PA. Hollywood had always specialized in managing the gap between public perception and behind-the-scenes reality, but "Black Hitler" was pushing that gap to unprecedented and possibly unbridgeable extremes.

The trailer door opened, and James emerged in full Hitler regalia.

The set fell silent.

It wasn't merely the visual contradiction, though that was certainly striking. It was the complete transformation of James's physicality. His normally fluid, graceful movements had been replaced by Hitler's distinctive stiffness. His shoulders, slightly hunched; his left arm, held rigid against his side; his right hand, ready to gesture emphatically.

Aaron, returning from a hushed conference with the dog handler, stopped mid-stride. "Jesus," he whispered.

Even Marc, who had been cracking jokes all morning, fell quiet, his professional eye assessing the lighting challenges presented by James's brown skin against the stark black and red of the Nazi uniform.

"Places, everyone," Aaron called, his voice cutting through the silence. "First team on set."

The spell broken, crew members scrambled to their positions. Two PAs hurriedly adjusted a swastika banner that had partially fallen, while the script supervisor made last-minute notes. The cameras, those impassive mechanical eyes, were positioned and checked one final time.

From his director's chair, Aaron surveyed the scene, his vision finally taking physical form after months of preparation, controversy, and compromise. Whatever mixed motivations had brought them all to this point, whatever careers hung in the balance, the moment of truth had arrived.

Behind the camera, Dr. Friedman watched with the intensity of a man who'd spent his career analyzing the very figure now being recreated before his eyes. David Katz stood beside him, script clutched like a security blanket, whispering what sounded like small prayers to whatever deity oversees historical adaptation.

"Sound speed!" called the sound engineer.

"Camera speed!" responded the camera operator.

Aaron took a deep breath, his eyes locked with James's in a moment of silent communication. Whatever happened next, triumph or disaster, they were committed now.

"And... action!"

***

CHAPTER 11

André Reynolds leaned back in his chair at PSB Insights' Los Angeles office, tapping his Concord 11s against the polished floor. The private observation room had the corporate blandness that made it feel simultaneously expensive and forgettable: neutral walls, ergonomic furniture, and the obligatory two-way mirror that separated them from the empty focus group room next door.

"Remind me again why we're doing this at nine-fifty in the morning?" André asked, accepting a coffee from the PSB staff member who'd just entered. "Focus groups should be illegal before noon. People aren't properly judgmental until after lunch."

Ravi Mukerjee, Creative Director, glanced up from his tablet. "Because this was the only time slot available on short notice. Victoria wants us to nail down a name and gauge audience reactions for our PR response by tomorrow's executive meeting."

"Of course," André sighed. "I think 'Black Hitler' has a simple ring that would sell tickets, but I suppose the execs aren't going to like that."

Michelle Park arranged her notes with methodical precision, her intern Isa wedged in beside her balancing a laptop and the team's coffee orders. "Better to know what we're dealing with now than be blindsided later. Social sentiment is... complex."

"Complex as a heart attack," André snorted. "We have both progressives and conservatives yelling at us for entirely different reasons. It's beautiful, actually."

The PSB facilitator, a tall woman with the practiced neutral expression of someone professionally trained to have no visible opinions, popped her head in. "We're set to begin at ten. The participants are in the reception area completing their intake forms. Coffee preferences?"

"Already taken care of, thanks," André replied, raising his cup in acknowledgment. "Quick question: how strictly did we adhere to the demographic breakdown I requested?"

"Precisely as specified," she assured him. "Twelve participants total. Politically, we have five left-leaning, four centrists, and three right-leaning individuals. Demographically, four Black participants, five White, two Latino, and one East Asian. Age range 25-55, with emphasis on regular moviegoers who consume historical dramas."

"Perfect." André nodded. "Run a tight ship in there. We need raw, unfiltered reactions."

As the woman left, Michelle looked up from her notes. "Are we sure about this? Testing a concept this volatile through a focus group feels... risky."

"That's exactly why we need it," André replied, leaning forward. "We're navigating uncharted territory here. We need real human reactions, not just social media metrics and algorithmic sentiment analysis."

"Speaking of social media," Ravi said, his tone shifting from casual to concerned, "there's something you need to see. A TikTok that's gaining serious traction."

He handed his tablet to André, who accepted it with a raised eyebrow. "Please tell me it's not another Hitler dance challenge."

"Worse." Ravi grimaced. "It's gone viral in the last seventy-two hours. Eight million views and climbing exponentially."

André pressed play, watching as a young woman with pink hair and a septum piercing appeared on screen, applying winged eyeliner with practiced precision. The username "@LiftieInLipstick" and display name "Jade," flanked by raised-fist and rainbow-flag emojis, hovered in the corner, alongside her follower count of 834.5K.

Text overlaid the video: "Getting ready while explaining why Black Hitler is NOT the representation we asked for." Part 1/4 appeared in the corner.

"Okay so APPARENTLY we're all just supposed to celebrate Pinnacle casting a Black actor as LITERAL HITLER?" the creator began, her voice carrying the performative outrage that characterized viral TikTok commentary. "And I'm over here like... am I the ONLY ONE who sees what's happening?!"

André watched with increasing disbelief as she continued, applying eyeliner with one hand while gesturing emphatically with the other.

"This isn't representation. This is a right-wing PSYOP, and I'm gonna explain why while I finish this wing."

"A what now?" André muttered.

The TikTok continued, the creator's theory growing more elaborate with each stroke of eyeliner. "For YEARS the right has been FURIOUS that we call out their fascist behavior. When we say 'this politician is acting like Hitler' or 'these policies are Nazi-adjacent,' they LOSE THEIR MINDS."

She leaned back, examining her handiwork. "So what's their solution? Make Hitler Black! This way, when we compare right-wing politicians to

Hitler, they can be like 'oh, so you're comparing them to a Black man? That's racist!' See what they did there?"

Isa's mouth dropped open as the creator continued.

"It's the ultimate gaslight. They're literally trying to REBRAND NAZI IMAGERY to neutralize one of our most powerful political tools for calling out fascism for what it is!"

"Oh my God," André whispered, his expression caught between horror and fascination.

"Making Hitler Black doesn't challenge White supremacy; it OBSCURES it!" Jade declared with flourish. "It's like their new version of 'I have Black friends'... except now it's 'even our Hitler is Black!'"

She finished with a dramatic final statement: "Hitler stays White because HISTORICAL ACCURACY MATTERS when we're talking about THE ARCHITECT OF WHITE SUPREMACIST GENOCIDE!"

The video ended with a perfect eyeliner wing and a promise of part two, where she'd "break down the studio's right-wing connections while testing out my new foundation kit!"

André stared at the black screen for a long moment, then burst into incredulous laughter. "This has to be performance art. The mental gymnastics required to frame our diversity casting as a right-wing conspiracy... I'm worried she's going to throw her back out."

"Eight million views, André," Ravi emphasized. "And it's spreading. People are making response videos, stitches, duets, there are already threads on Reddit trying to uncover the supposed 'right-wing connections' to our production."

"Wait, wait, wait," André shook his head, still processing. "So the woke left, who usually demand diverse casting, are now upset that we cast a Black actor because it's somehow a conservative plot to neutralize Hitler as a political comparison?"

"That appears to be the theory, yes," Isa confirmed, scrolling through her own phone. "The hashtag #HitlerStaysWhite is trending in multiple regions."

"I can't decide if this is brilliant or terrifying," André marveled. "Hollywoke, as the right loves to call us, is suddenly a right-wing conspiracy? After all the DEI initiatives, the inclusion riders, the sensitivity readers, and after all the purity rituals we've performed?"

André's laugh deepened. "We're bringing people together! Isn't that what movies are supposed to do? Create common ground? We're just doing it in our own unique way!"

"Should we respond?" Michelle asked, ever the practical voice. "We could seed some contextual counterpoints through friendly outlets, maybe have a progressive thought leader address the conspiracy angle head-on."

André shook his head, a calculating gleam in his eye. "No, no. Let these creators enjoy their viral fame for a bit. Let the conversation evolve organically. Just keep an eye out for parts two through four, I'm dying to know what right-wing donors I've supposedly been meeting with."

"She's scheduled to drop part two tomorrow," Ravi confirmed. "Something about a huge studio secret."

"I can't wait," André said with genuine enthusiasm. "This is exactly the kind of bonkers discourse that keeps people talking. Eight million views of someone discussing our movie, even just to call it a fascist plot? That's free marketing, baby. And Kennedy's count is up three million since the announcement. A third of them are bots, but bots don't buy tickets. They buy credibility."

The door opened as the PSB facilitator returned. "We're ready to begin whenever you are. The participants are all seated."

André glanced through the two-way mirror at the focus group room, where twelve carefully selected individuals were settling into their chairs around a large table. Name placards and notepads had been positioned with precision in front of each participant.

"Look at them," André murmured. "Twelve ordinary people who have no idea they're about to weigh in on one of the most controversial casting choices in recent cinema history."

Ravi scanned the participants critically. "I see we only got one Asian participant, and he appears to be Chinese. That's going to make it difficult to gauge broader Asian audience response."

"We'll make a note to diversify more next time." André nodded. "Though honestly, the Asian demographic might be too small a segment for our marketing priorities on this film."

He clapped Ravi on the shoulder with a grin. "Besides, you're here! You can represent a billion people if you're up for it."

Ravi laughed despite himself. "Sure, let me speak for an eighth of the world's population. No pressure."

Through the glass, they watched as the moderator entered, a large African American woman with a clipboard and the practiced smile of someone who'd facilitated hundreds of such sessions.

"Hmm," André frowned slightly. "Make a note: next time, let's not have a Black moderator for this topic. We need participants to be completely honest about their reactions to our Black Hitler, and having a Black woman asking the questions might complicate that dynamic."

"Does it matter if some of them have racist responses?" Isa asked quietly, not looking up from her laptop.

"For our purposes? Absolutely," André replied without hesitation. "We need the unfiltered pulse of every demographic segment to maximize our marketing strategy, even the uncomfortable ones. Especially the uncomfortable ones. We're not here to judge their reactions; we're here to understand and leverage them."

"Cynical," Ravi acknowledged.

André nodded in agreement. "But effective."

The moderator was introducing herself to the participants, explaining the format and ground rules with practiced ease.

"Here we go," André said, settling back in his chair with the gleeful anticipation of a scientist about to witness a particularly volatile chemical reaction. "Twelve average Americans about to tell us whether 'Black Hitler' is revolutionary art or the end of Western civilization."

He took a sip of his coffee. "Either way, at least it'll be enlightening."

***

Victoria's office at 11:47 p.m. resembled the aftermath of a controlled explosion: papers scattered across her desk, half-empty coffee cups marking the passage of time like archaeological artifacts, and her awards shelf looking suspiciously rearranged (possible evidence of her stress-response).

Aaron sat across from her, his normally tidy appearance betraying the day's chaos: tie loosened, brown hair disheveled, the haunted expression of someone who'd spent fourteen hours wrangling both actual Nazis and the Hollywood variety.

"So," Victoria said, pouring a generous amount of bourbon into two glasses, "tell me about the Kline incident."

Aaron accepted the drink gratefully. "Surprisingly anticlimactic. He arrived precisely on time, sober, prepared, and called James 'sir' twice during their first scene together."

"Are we talking about the same Andrew Kline? Six-foot-two, Oscar winner, once told Steven Spielberg his blocking was 'pedestrian'?"

"The very same," Aaron confirmed. "Though this version appears to have had a personality transplant. He was almost... deferential."

Victoria raised an eyebrow. "To you?"

"To James," Aaron clarified. "That's the strange part: the notoriously difficult, possibly racist actor is treating our Black Hitler with the reverence usually reserved for Anthony Hopkins on his birthday."

"Fascinating," Victoria murmured. "And the crew?"

"Terrified. Smiling nervously, maintaining safe distance, ready to dive for cover at the first problematic remark." Aaron took a sip of bourbon. "It was like watching wildlife photographers approach a sleeping lion."

"But he behaved?"

"Impeccably. Knew his lines, hit his marks, offered thoughtful character insights. Almost disappointingly professional." Aaron leaned forward. "I think he's genuinely desperate for this comeback. He knows one slip, one drunken tirade, and he's done."

"Good," Victoria nodded. "Let fear be the better part of valor. Now, what about our other potential crisis?"

Aaron's expression darkened. "Kennedy still hasn't signed her contract. Her agent called after wrap with an expanded list of demands that would make Cleopatra blush."

"Barry Hickson? Oh yes, he's a peach. Three decades of being an agent from less civilized times when agents had to be the biggest bastard in the room to get anything done, or so he thinks."

"Another ego to look forward to, I guess," Aaron muttered.

"What are their demands? Let me guess, more Eva scenes, fewer Hitler scenes, and a personal 'emotional support' peacock on set?"

"Worse." Aaron grimaced. "She wants access badges for her entire entourage, eleven people minimum on regular shooting days."

Victoria nearly choked on her bourbon. "Eleven? For Eva Braun? Hitler's girlfriend had fewer people in her actual entourage during the actual Third Reich."

"Here's the breakdown," Aaron said, pulling out his phone to read the list. "One for Kennedy herself, obviously. Two for her assistants: the Latino one and the Native American one she features in her Instagram posts about 'amplifying voices.'"

"Miguel and..." Victoria snapped her fingers, searching for the name.

"Dani," Aaron supplied. "Then there's her publicist, her agent, two to three stylists depending on the day's 'aesthetic requirements,' two to three bodyguards because apparently Eva Braun faces significant security threats in 2025, and, my personal favorite, her masseuse."

"Her masseuse," Victoria repeated flatly. "To massage what, exactly? Her ego?"

"Apparently maintaining 'physical alignment' is essential to her process," Aaron said, using air quotes. "Oh, and she also requested a badge for her mother."

Victoria burst out laughing. "Her mother? Isn't that the woman who had one decent supporting role in the 90s and never lets anyone forget it?"

"That's her, though Kennedy's team assures us that's merely a formality. Her mother 'rarely leaves Malibu these days' but apparently needs the 'option of access.'"

"Of course she does," Victoria muttered. "What else?"

"Phone access is the big one," Aaron continued. "Normally we'd restrict personal devices on set, especially during sensitive scenes with potential for leaks,"

"Like anything involving Nazism," Victoria interjected.

"Exactly. But Kennedy's agent, that shark from WME, said, and I quote, he would 'rather be set on fire' than lose access to his phone."

Victoria rolled her eyes. "Barry Hickson and his dramatic ultimatums. I once saw him threaten to 'eat his own Rolex' if his client didn't get a better trailer. Though to be fair, he actually started unscrewing the back when the line producer called his bluff."

"He wants top-level phone access for himself, Kennedy's publicist, and both assistants," Aaron continued. "Unlimited texting, calls, and, this is rich, social media documentation privileges."

"So they want to live-tweet our historically sensitive, potentially explosive production?" Victoria clarified. "What could possibly go wrong?"

"She did graciously offer to reduce her entourage to seven people on 'closed set days,'" Aaron added. "As if that's some kind of meaningful concession. She's also requesting script approval, final cut privileges, and..." He winced. "A producer credit."

"For a mid-budget historical drama? What happened to 'I just want to tell important stories' Kennedy from the pitch meeting?" Victoria drummed her fingers on her desk, the rhythm of strategic calculation. "What's your assessment? Is she trying to torpedo the production, or just flexing?"

Aaron considered this. "Neither, actually. I think she's creating leverage. There's something specific she wants, and these absurd demands are smokescreens."

"Smart." Victoria nodded. "What's the real play?"

Aaron took a deep breath. "She wants to bring TJ Jackson on as a 'sensitivity consultant.'"

The silence that followed had weight and density; it was the kind of silence that film composers spend careers trying to orchestrate.

"TJ Jackson," Victoria finally said. "The conspiracy TikToker who claims Hitler had African ancestry."

"The very same," Aaron confirmed. "Though Kennedy's team has carefully rebranded him as a 'sensitivity consultant' rather than a 'historical consultant.' Specifically, she cited our 'admirable Swastika Sensitivity Protocol' and suggested Jackson would 'add to the feeling of safety and sensitivity on set for the diverse crew.'"

Victoria stared at Aaron for a long moment, then burst into laughter. The deep, genuine kind rarely heard in executive offices. "Oh, that's brilliant. Absolutely brilliant. She's weaponized our own corporate sensitivity theater against us."

"There's more," Aaron continued. "She also wants a therapist on set for anyone who 'feels triggered by the difficult historical material.' She's suggested a Brazilian-Italian Latina practitioner who specializes in critical race theory and demands to be addressed as a doctor."

"Let me guess, this therapist happens to be a personal friend of hers who charges $500 an hour?"

"$750 actually," Aaron corrected. "Kennedy's team helpfully included her CV: Camilla Russo, counselor with certification in 'trauma-informed historical processing' and 1.2 million followers."

Victoria laughed again. "Fascinating. She's building herself a perfect shield. If we refuse these 'sensitivity' measures, we look like we're disregarding the wellbeing of our diverse cast and crew. If we accept them, she gets TJ Jackson on set to legitimize her pet conspiracy theory."

Aaron nodded grimly. "Her team mentioned that having both Jackson and this therapist would provide 'excellent coverage' for potentially controversial elements like having Andrew Kline on set."

"She's not wrong," Victoria admitted. "Having a Latina therapist specializing in microaggressions does create convenient optics for our possibly racist Goebbels."

"So what do we do?" Aaron asked. "I genuinely can't tell if Kennedy is a strategic genius playing twelve-dimensional chess or a privileged celebrity who's accidentally stumbled into a perfect power move."

Victoria leaned back, studying the ceiling thoughtfully. "Tell me, what was your impression of this TJ Jackson character?"

Aaron's expression soured. "A cynical pseudo-historian capitalizing on algorithm-friendly conspiracy theories to build a personal brand. A grifter selling historical fanfiction to people who find actual history too complex or inconvenient; Dr. Friedman's worst nightmare."

"So you're not a fan," Victoria observed dryly.

"You could say that," Aaron confirmed. "The man is peddling completely unsupported theories about Hitler's ancestry based on misreading facial recognition AI studies and cherry-picked anecdotes."

"And yet," Victoria noted, "his content has hundreds of millions of views. His book is climbing bestseller lists. He's being discussed in mainstream media outlets. They're even inviting him to panels. If enough social proof surrounds him, he's not far from legitimacy."

"Popularity doesn't equal legitimacy."

"In the modern day, it absolutely does," Victoria countered. "Aaron, we're millions in the hole on this production. Cameras are rolling. Kennedy deliberately waited until now to make these demands because she knows we can't replace her without imploding the entire project. We're past the point of no return."

"So," Victoria ticked off Kennedy's demands on her fingers, the lamp light catching on her understated Patek Philippe Nautilus, "Kennedy wants unlimited set access for her entourage, script approval possibly informed by TJ Jackson's 'historical research,' her own producer credit, and a therapist on set for the cast and crew's 'emotional well-being.'"

Aaron rubbed his temples. "Is that all? No pony rides and ice cream socials?"

"The ice cream social is actually scheduled for next Thursday," Victoria deadpanned. "Production morale initiative."

"Hilarious," Aaron muttered. "So what exactly are we giving her?"

Victoria leaned forward, all business now. "Seven badges maximum, including Kennedy herself."

"Seven?" Aaron's eyebrows shot up. "That's a small village."

"It's fewer than the eleven she asked for," Victoria countered. "Her agent gets phone privileges,"

"Christ."

",but only during designated breaks and in specific areas away from set."

Aaron poured himself another finger of bourbon from the crystal decanter that Victoria kept hidden in her credenza for "crisis management"; this definitely qualified.

"The therapist is approved on a limited schedule," Victoria continued. "Twice a week for anyone who actually wants it, which will be exactly nobody except Kennedy and whoever she bullies into going."

"Generous," Aaron said, swirling his drink.

"She gets the producer credit,"

"You can't be serious."

",during the end credits only, not the opening, and she gets one representative during editing."

Aaron's expression darkened. "One representative? In the editing room? Victoria, that's out of the question."

"So she feels involved," Victoria cut in smoothly, "but we're not contractually obliged to take her ideas. It's optics, Aaron. Kennedy just wants to tell her followers that she's 'helping shape the narrative.'"

"And TJ Jackson?" Aaron asked, his voice tightening.

"Three supervised set visits. Not daily consultant access like she wanted. Zero script say, and absolutely no phone privileges anywhere near the set."

Aaron sighed heavily. "So we just... give in? Let a conspiracy theorist onto our set, potentially undermining the historical integrity we've fought to maintain?"

"We negotiate," Victoria corrected, flicking an invisible piece of lint from her sleeve. "It's not giving in; it's strategic concession."

"Dr. Friedman will quit again when he finds out," Aaron warned. "Possibly for real this time."

"Let me handle Benjamin," Victoria said with the confidence of someone who'd talked numerous academics off numerous ledges. "I'll explain that having Jackson on set gives us the perfect opportunity to demonstrate the contrast between actual historical scholarship and TikTok conspiracy theories. Feed his academic ego a bit."

Aaron considered this, grudgingly impressed. "It might work." He paused. "Though I still don't understand why Kennedy is so invested in Jackson's theories. She's never shown interest in historical accuracy before, quite the opposite."

Victoria's lips curved into a knowing smile. "Because it creates a narrative where her Black Hitler isn't 'controversial' or 'historically inaccurate'; it's 'brave truth-telling.' If Hitler actually had African ancestry, then our casting isn't provocative art, it's historical justice. And Kennedy gets to position herself as a courageous ally rather than an actress in a potentially problematic production."

Aaron's eyes widened in realization. "That's... actually brilliant."

"Told you," Victoria smiled, leaning back in her ergonomic chair that cost more than Aaron's monthly rent. "If Kennedy Oswald ever learned how to play chess, she might actually be formidable. Fortunately, she's more of a 'pretty Instagram photos and strategic tantrums' tactician."

"So we're really doing this?" Aaron asked, setting his glass down with a definitive clink. "Allowing a conspiracy theorist onto our set and potentially validating his absurd theories just to keep Kennedy happy?"

"We're allowing a popular online personality limited access to generate additional buzz while maintaining strict controls over the narrative," Victoria corrected. "And yes, we're doing it to keep Kennedy happy because until day one of shooting her scenes, she has us over a barrel."

Aaron drained the last of his bourbon. "This business is insane."

"No," Victoria said with surprising seriousness. "This business is transactional. Everyone has something they want: Kennedy wants legitimacy as a serious actress, Jackson wants mainstream validation, you want your PGA mark, and I want a successful film that gives me leverage for contract renegotiation next year."

"And what does James want?" Aaron asked quietly.

Victoria's expression softened slightly, a momentary crack in her executive armor. "Based on what I've seen so far, he wants to create something meaningful. Which makes him either the most naive or the most authentic person in this entire project."

"Maybe both," Aaron agreed, staring into his empty glass like it might contain the answer to how he ended up in this situation.

Victoria glanced at her watch. "It's after midnight. Go home, get some sleep. Tomorrow we're shooting Hitler's first speech, right?"

"Yes. One of the scenes Dr. Friedman actually approves of, historically speaking."

"Small mercies," Victoria said. "Oh, and Aaron? Good work today. James looked... disturbingly convincing in the dailies."

Aaron stood, collecting his jacket. "That's what worries me. He's not just playing Hitler; he's finding the human there. Which is exactly what we wanted artistically, but..."

"But it makes for uncomfortable viewing," Victoria finished. "Good. Comfortable art rarely changes anything."

Victoria leaned back in her chair, swirling the remainder of her bourbon. "Before you go, André ran a focus group today."

Aaron paused at the door, hand on the knob. "Ah, yes. The ritual sacrifice of artistic vision on the altar of audience testing. What's the verdict? Are we doomed, or merely in serious trouble?"

"Actually," Victoria's lips curved into a rare genuine smile, "they've settled on the perfect title."

"Really?" Aaron turned back, curiosity piqued despite his exhaustion. "Let me guess, something suitably provocative? 'Dictator's Paradox'? 'The Black Führer'? 'Hitler Reimagined'?"

"Simpler," Victoria shook her head. "One word."

"'Downfall' is already taken," Aaron quipped. "'Monstrous'? 'Humanity'? 'Descent'?"

Victoria set down her glass with a decisive click. "'Gravity.'"

The word hung in the air between them. Aaron blinked, considering it from multiple angles.

"'Gravity,'" he repeated slowly, testing how it felt. "Hmm."

"Think about it," Victoria continued, her voice taking on the quality it always did when she was genuinely excited about something. "Clean, elegant, single word, which works beautifully for poster design and awards consideration."

"It evokes the serious weight of the subject matter," Aaron nodded, warming to the concept. "The gravity of the historical events..."

"Exactly. But it also suggests Hitler's charismatic pull, how he drew people into his orbit, the gravitational force of his personality that bent an entire nation to his will."

"There's already an Oscar-winning *Gravity*," Aaron pointed out.

"André said the same thing." Victoria waved it away with her glass. "Then he said, and I quote, 'Good. That'll help our lean marketing budget.'"

Aaron's tired expression gave way to thoughtful consideration. "It's... actually perfect. Subtle enough to be taken seriously by critics, provocative enough to generate conversation, abstract enough to avoid direct historical controversy."

"André said the room responded immediately. Even the participants who hated the concept of our casting choice found themselves nodding at the title."

"'Gravity,'" Aaron said again, this time with conviction. "James Wright is Adolf Hitler in *Gravity*. I can see the poster already."

"So can André," Victoria confirmed with a laugh. "He's already mapping out a minimalist black design with just the title and James's silhouette. No mustache required."

Aaron reached for the door again, but his posture had changed: shoulders slightly straighter, the burden of the day's chaos momentarily lightened by this small creative victory.

"'Gravity,'" he said one final time. "It's actually brilliant. Not that I'll tell André that, his ego barely fits through standard doorways as it is."

"Your secret's safe with me," Victoria promised. "Go home and kiss Emily."

As Aaron left, Victoria turned to her shelf to move her Golden Globe to a more artistic skew. She tested the word on her own lips: "Gravity." It felt right, substantial yet elegant, exactly what their audacious project needed.

They'd found one perfect element.

One word that might just anchor their explosive project firmly enough to survive the storm coming their way.

***

CHAPTER 12

Michelle Park arrived at the Pinnacle Lot at the unholy hour of 5:17 a.m., clutching her second espresso and mentally rehearsing the day's disaster containment strategies. Eva Braun was coming to set, and with her came a hurricane of complications in the form of an entourage that rivaled an actual dictator's.

The parking lot was suspiciously full for this early hour. Michelle recognized Aaron's Range Rover, André's impractically expensive Tesla, and several production vehicles already positioned for what promised to be the most logistically overcomplicated day of filming yet.

Inside, the soundstage hummed with the energy of people trying to prepare for a catastrophe they couldn't fully anticipate. PAs scurried about with greater urgency than usual. The "Nazi wranglers" (a designation that had somehow stuck despite Michelle's attempts to reframe it as "historical imagery management team") were meticulously checking every swastika, ensuring they could be quickly covered between takes.

Aaron stood near the monitor, deep in conversation with his first AD. Both men had the hollow-eyed look of professionals who'd accepted their fate but weren't happy about it.

"Good morning," Michelle greeted, handing Aaron a coffee from the cardboard tray she carried. "Or as good as it can be on Kennedy Oswald Day."

"Is that what we're calling it now?" Aaron accepted the coffee gratefully. "I've been referring to it as 'D-Day,' but with a different D word."

"The troops are assembled," Michelle gestured around the set. "Nazi wranglers at the ready, PAs briefed on no-phone protocols, and Dr. Friedman has been given both a sedative and a reminder that his book deal for the sequel depends on his continued cooperation."

Aaron smiled despite his exhaustion. "You're terrifyingly efficient."

"Survival mechanism," Michelle shrugged. "I've handled publicity for four different Kardashian product launches. After that, even Hitler and Eva seem manageable."

Her phone buzzed. André's name flashed on the screen, accompanied by a text: *Welcome to Armageddon Day! Check your email IMMEDIATELY. TikTok Part 2 just dropped. 11 MILLION VIEWS IN 8 HOURS. It's... creative.*

Michelle opened her email with growing dread, finding André's message with a video attachment and the subject line: "We're officially a right-wing conspiracy!!!"

"Apparently LiftieInLipstick has released the sequel to her 'Black Hitler is a Right-Wing Psyop' masterpiece," Michelle told Aaron. "And according to André, it's already at eleven million views in just eight hours."

"What's the conspiracy this time?" Aaron sighed. "That we're secretly funded by lizard people?"

Before Michelle could respond, Big Marc approached, his massive frame drawing attention as he spotted her phone.

"Is that the LiftieInLipstick video?" he asked, his voice carrying across the soundstage. "Oh, you gotta play that on loud. This girl is connecting dots that don't even exist in the same universe!"

A small crowd began to form as Michelle reluctantly increased her phone's volume. The sound of a young woman's voice filled the space, carrying the cadence of practiced outrage that had become TikTok's default setting for delivering conspiracy theories.

Text overlaid the video: *"CONNECTING THE DOTS on Black Hitler's ACTUAL creators."* Part 2/4 appeared in the corner.

"So after my last video blew up, people were asking WHO is actually behind this Black Hitler movie?" Jade's voice blared from the phone's speakers. "And girlies, it's EVEN WORSE than I thought. [detective emoji]"

The growing crowd around Big Marc's phone included gaffers, PAs, and several members of the lighting crew, all watching with expressions ranging from baffled amusement to genuine concern.

"Let's start with Marcus Goldstein, the Pinnacle exec who fought to get the rights for this book," Jade continued, pushing pink hair back and applying foundation with practiced strokes. "He's notoriously pro-Israel, which is code for supporting a literal apartheid state. Coincidence? I think NOT."

Aaron's eyes widened. "Marcus Goldman, not Goldstein. And he fought to take the project away from Victoria, not to secure it."

"Shh." Big Marc grinned. "Don't interrupt the conspiracy with facts."

"And the main producer/director?" Jade's voice continued, crescendo-ing with dramatic flair. "Aaron Weisberg, ANOTHER pro-Israel figure in Hollywood. Are we seeing a pattern yet? They're using a Black actor as COVER while pushing their own agenda!"

"Weisberg?" Aaron spluttered. "She can't even get my name right!"

"But wait... it gets JUICIER," Jade announced with a dramatic pause, staring directly into the camera. "They hired Andrew Kline to play Goebbels, a man who was LITERALLY CANCELLED for having a PLANTATION WEDDING and wearing Confederate flag merch! He's from Arkansas and was photographed in a Confederate t-shirt! Tell me he's not an actual Nazi sympathizer! I'll wait! [nail-polish emoji]"

Big Marc's booming laugh echoed through the soundstage. "At least she got one name right! That's a solid thirty-three percent accuracy rate."

"This is the same studio that gave us those two slavery movies with the most CRINGE White savior narratives," Jade continued, blending foundation along her jawline. "Remember how they completely sidelined the actual Black characters to focus on the 'good White people'? SAME ENERGY."

"What slavery movies?" a PA asked, genuinely confused. "Did Pinnacle make slavery movies?"

"Not in the last decade," Michelle confirmed, her PR training allowing her to maintain composure despite the absurdity unfolding on screen.

"This isn't representation," Jade declared with absolute conviction. "This is a calculated move by right-wing Hollywood executives to neutralize our ability to call out ACTUAL Nazis by confusing the imagery."

She capped her beauty blender with dramatic finality. "The more I dig, the more obvious it becomes. Black Hitler isn't progressive, it's a shield for the people ACTUALLY pushing Nazi-adjacent ideologies right now!"

The video ended with a final dramatic look at the camera. "Follow for part three where I break down the script leaks and show you how they're planning to HUMANIZE Hitler while demonizing his victims! Contour tutorial included! #BlackHitlerIsARightWingPsyop #PinnacleNaziConnections #HollywoodExposed #RightWingMediaTakeover."

A moment of stunned silence followed. Then Big Marc burst into renewed laughter, clutching his sides.

"Eleven million views!" he wheezed. "This girl is making up whole damn universes, and eleven million people are nodding along! I can't even be mad; it's too beautiful!"

"I can be mad," Aaron muttered. "She got my name wrong and invented a conspiracy connecting me to an executive who isn't even involved in this project. There are actual issues with this production worth discussing, but none of them involve whatever fever dream she's describing; these are insane theories."

"Eleven million views, though," Michelle said, her publicist's brain automatically calculating the engagement metrics. "That's more exposure than our official press release got."

Shanice, one of the lighting techs, a young African American woman with close-cropped hair and thoughtful eyes, glanced up from her light board.

"All this talk about 'representation' and 'right-wing plots' is missing the point," she said, her voice cutting through Big Marc's laughter. "This isn't what representation is supposed to be about, is it? I mean, representation is supposed to give us positive role models, right? I don't want my kids looking up to Black Hitler."

The crew quieted, turning toward her with sudden interest.

"That's a valid concern," Michelle said, stepping closer. "But isn't representation also about allowing actors of color access to complex, challenging roles? Not just limiting them to playing heroes and saints?"

"Sure, complex roles," Shanice agreed, adjusting a lighting preset without looking up. "But there's complex, and then there's actual Hitler. We've spent decades fighting to see ourselves as more than criminals and thugs on screen, and now we're celebrating casting a Black man as history's biggest war criminal?"

"All I know," Big Marc interjected, "is that if James Wright wins an Oscar for playing Hitler, every drama school in America is gonna have Black dudes practicing that little mustache in the mirror the next morning. For better or worse, success will change the conversation."

This prompted a ripple of laughter, breaking the tension.

"Also you have got to see TJ Jackson's latest theory," Big Marc grinned, nodding toward Michelle's phone. "Shanice, you are gonna get all the representation you can handle."

Michelle pulled up another video. On the screen, TJ Jackson sat in his familiar professorial pose, glasses perched precisely at the midpoint of his nose and carefully arranged bookshelves visible behind him.

"Y'all ready for some real history?" TJ began, his voice taking on the smooth cadence of a practiced storyteller. "The kind they don't want you to know? [thinking-face emoji]"

The dramatic music swelled in the background as he leaned toward the camera. "Let's talk about the BIGGEST cover-up in human history. Bigger than any conspiracy you've heard. Ready?"

He paused for effect. "Every single person on Earth started out Black."

He let that sit, then gestured at the carefully arranged bookshelves behind him. "They hid Beethoven from you. They hid Queen Charlotte, a literal Black queen of England, and trust me, that video is COMING. So when I tell you what they've been hiding about Hitler, you'll be ready."

Michelle paused the video, looking up at Aaron with a pained expression. "This is the 'historian' Kennedy is bringing to set today?"

"Unfortunately, yes," Aaron confirmed. "Victoria managed to negotiate his role down from 'historical consultant' to 'three supervised set visits,' but today is definitely one of those visits."

"Oh, this gon' be good," Big Marc laughed. "Dr. Friedman's gonna have a stroke when he hears this man's theories."

"Which is why," Michelle said firmly, "we need to ensure that TJ Jackson doesn't have his phone on set. No recordings, no photos, no live-streaming his 'validated theories' to his millions of followers."

"You think he's gonna hand over his phone?" Big Marc asked skeptically. "That man's phone is basically his identity at this point."

"His phone will be secured in a Faraday-caged lockbox and he's signed an ironclad NDA," Michelle replied, her tone making it clear this wasn't a request. "Kennedy agreed to those terms. It's non-negotiable."

Aaron's phone buzzed, a text from security. "Well, we're about to test Kennedy's commitment to agreements. Her team just arrived at the gate."

Michelle checked her watch. "Already? They're not supposed to be here for another hour."

"Apparently Kennedy believes in punctuality when it suits her," Aaron said, already moving toward the entrance. "Though I suspect this is more about establishing dominance than professional courtesy."

"Party time, people!" Big Marc called out, turning back to his crew with a theatrical flourish. "Eva Braun approaches with her army of sycophants and a TikTok historian. Let the games begin!"

Outside, a small convoy of vehicles had arrived. A black Escalade led the procession, followed by two luxury SUVs and a vintage red Mercedes that had been modernized with contemporary safety features; Kennedy's preferred transport when she wanted to make "a subtle statement."

Security personnel emerged first, scanning the area with the excessive vigilance of men who'd watched too many bodyguard movies. Behind them came Miguel, Kennedy's assistant, clutching both a tablet and what appeared to be a monogrammed water bottle with specific liquid requirements.

Kennedy emerged next, looking impeccably styled for six a.m. Her outfit carefully calculated to suggest both artistic credibility and Instagram-readiness. Behind her came Dani, her social media coordinator, followed by TJ Jackson himself, looking smaller in person than his online presence suggested but with the unmistakable confidence of someone who'd built a career on creativity rather than credentials.

Behind them came Barry Hickson, marching with the brisk efficiency of a man who viewed time as a resource more precious than uranium. He was Kennedy's agent and the human embodiment of a great white shark in a Loro Piana suit. At fifty-eight, Hickson had the precisely maintained tan of someone who scheduled his UV exposure with the same ruthless efficiency as his client negotiations. His silver hair was cut with military precision, and he spoke exclusively in two volumes: boardroom quiet and litigious threat.

"Kennedy!" Aaron greeted with professional warmth. "Welcome to our production. We weren't expecting you quite so early."

"I believe in respecting the process," Kennedy replied, somehow making punctuality sound like a revolutionary artistic choice. "Eva deserves my full preparation time."

"Aaron Weisman," Barry cut in, extending a hand with the swift assurance of someone who'd closed deals during actual heart attacks, both his and others'. "We spoke on the phone. Barry Hickson, WME."

"Of course." Aaron nodded, accepting the handshake, which proved to be exactly as aggressive as industry protocol dictated, firm enough to establish dominance without triggering a workers' comp claim.

"So where's the fucking cucumber water?" Barry asked without preamble, his voice carrying the rasp of someone who'd spent decades shouting into phones before texting was invented. "Kennedy's rider specifically states Icelandic cucumber water, not fucking tap water with a slice in it."

"I'm... sure we can arrange that," Aaron replied, slightly thrown by the abrupt pivot.

"And the dressing room situation," Barry continued, scrolling through his phone with determined focus. "I was promised fresh orchids. White Phalaenopsis, not those purple monstrosities you typically get from supermarkets and perfectly sectioned grapefruit. Not just sliced, sectioned. There's a fucking difference."

"I'll make sure everything's taken care of," Michelle interjected smoothly, stepping forward with the practiced smile of someone who'd faced far more unhinged demands. "We're thrilled to have Kennedy joining us today."

"Thrilled is what you'll be when she delivers an awards-worthy performance despite the conditions," Barry replied, his tone suggesting he was personally offended by every molecule of air on the soundstage. "We cut you a break on the quote, but that doesn't mean cutting corners on the requirements."

Kennedy placed a gentle hand on her agent's arm. "Barry's just making sure everything's perfect for my process. Eva Braun deserves my full commitment."

"And Eva Braun's commitment deserves proper remuneration," Barry added. "Speaking of which, let's discuss that backend participation clause."

"Perhaps we should continue these discussions after Kennedy has had a chance to settle in?" Michelle suggested diplomatically.

Barry's eyes narrowed, but he nodded curtly. "Fine. But I'll be here all day. Every day. Kennedy's contract guarantees me full set access throughout production and post."

"You're... planning to be on set during the entire production?" Aaron asked, failing to hide his horror.

"Someone's gotta make sure Kennedy's artistic vision is respected and her needs are appropriately met," Barry replied. "I'll be your shadow until this picture wraps; then I'll be your conjoined twin through post. Consider me the guardian angel of Kennedy's narrative integrity."

Kennedy beamed, apparently viewing this arrangement as perfectly reasonable. "Barry has been instrumental in helping me transition to more serious dramatic work. His industry experience is invaluable."

Across the lot, Michelle was midway through sarcastically reading one of TJ's tweets aloud to a nearby PA: "'Every time someone tries to tell this truth, they get called "controversial" or "unscientific." But notice how they never actually address the evidence...'"

TJ's face lit up with recognition as he approached. "That's my thread on decolonizing historical narratives! You're familiar with my work!"

Michelle froze, caught in the awkward position of being discovered essentially trash-talking someone to their face. Her PR training kicked in instantly. "I was just familiarizing myself with your perspective before your visit today."

"She was reading it out loud to prepare the team," Aaron added smoothly. "We want everyone to understand the... perspectives that inform our production."

TJ beamed, either missing or ignoring the sarcasm. "I appreciate the thoroughness! Most productions don't do the research. They're content to perpetuate colonial narratives without questioning the underlying power structures."

"We're all about questioning here," Michelle replied, her smile fixed in place.

"Speaking of questioning," Barry interjected, eyeing Michelle's phone, "I trust there won't be any unauthorized recording devices on set? Kennedy has strict image control requirements."

"Absolutely," Michelle confirmed. "In fact, we'll be collecting all phones, including TJ's, before anyone enters the set."

Barry's eyebrows rose fractionally, the equivalent of a normal human's jaw dropping. "You're confiscating Kennedy Oswald's team's phones? Do you have any idea what her social media schedule looks like?"

"It's standard protocol for this production," Michelle explained, not backing down. "Given the sensitive historical imagery;"

"Given the 'sensitive historical imagery,'" Barry mimicked with air quotes, "her fans expect behind-the-scenes content. Eighteen million followers don't feed themselves, honey."

"We've negotiated designated photography periods," Michelle replied. "Your team agreed to these terms, Mr. Hickson."

Barry's eyes narrowed dangerously. "We'll discuss this later. At length."

Dr. Friedman and David Katz arrived almost simultaneously, both carrying the haggard expressions of men who'd already fought several battles before sunrise. Their faces fell in perfect unison when they spotted TJ Jackson.

"Dr. Friedman!" Kennedy called out with practiced enthusiasm. "And David! Perfect timing. I was hoping to discuss some of Eva's motivations before I head to makeup. TJ has some fascinating insights about Eva's likely awareness of Hitler's heritage."

Dr. Friedman stopped walking so abruptly he nearly toppled forward. "His... heritage?"

"The African connection," TJ supplied helpfully, stepping forward with his hand extended. "Dr. Jackson, historical researcher. I've documented substantial evidence suggesting Hitler's grandmother had North African origins, which explains his obsession with 'racial purity', classic self-hatred projected outward."

Dr. Friedman's face underwent a remarkable transformation, cycling through confusion, outrage, and finally settling on a kind of fascinated horror, like a biologist discovering a previously unknown species of toxic fungus.

"Dr... Jackson, is it?" he finally managed. "I wasn't aware you held a doctorate. In what field, may I ask?"

"Life experience and independent research," TJ replied without hesitation. "I find traditional academic structures too limiting for truly revolutionary historical work. It's always the systems that perpetuate, isn't it?"

David Katz made a small choking sound that he quickly disguised as a cough.

"And your evidence for Hitler's supposed African heritage?" Dr. Friedman asked, his tone achieving a remarkable blend of politeness and incredulity.

"Multiple strands," TJ began, warming to his topic. "Destroyed records from his paternal grandmother's region, facial recognition AI that initially identified African features before being 'corrected' by establishment programmers, his distinctive mustache style originating in Black communities, plus the psychological pattern of self-hatred driving his obsession with 'racial purity.' The evidence is overwhelming once you break free of colonial academic frameworks. I'll have to get you a copy of my book; I am very thorough."

Shanice, who had approached to adjust a nearby light, looked up with unexpected interest. "Wait, that mustache thing is actually true. That style was popular in Black barbershops before Hitler adopted it."

TJ turned to her with delight. "Exactly! One of many details that traditional historians conveniently ignore!"

"Although," Shanice continued thoughtfully, "that doesn't necessarily mean Hitler had African ancestry. Cultural appropriation has always been a thing."

"Or convergent fashion evolution," Dr. Friedman muttered, looking like a man desperately trying not to have an aneurysm.

"These details support a larger pattern," TJ insisted. "When viewed holistically rather than in isolation."

"Perhaps we should continue this fascinating historical discussion after Kennedy has been through makeup?" Aaron interrupted smoothly. "We're on a tight schedule today."

"Of course," Kennedy agreed. "I respect the production timeline. Eva was always punctual, another of her underappreciated qualities."

As Kennedy allowed herself to be escorted to the makeup trailer, her security team maintaining a perimeter around her like Secret Service agents guarding a president, Michelle sidled up to Aaron.

"That went... exactly as terribly as expected," she murmured.

"We're making a serious historical drama with a rom-com star who believes Hitler was secretly Black and a conspiracy theorist who thinks he has a doctorate in 'life experience,'" Aaron replied under his breath. "I'm starting to think Marcus Goldman was right. This is the most expensive publicity stunt in Pinnacle's history."

The soundstage door opened and James Wright emerged. Even without his Hitler makeup, there was something in his carriage that suggested he was already partly in character, a certain stillness, a focused intensity.

"Good morning," he greeted Aaron and Michelle. "I heard Kennedy's team arrived early. I thought I'd come say hello before heading to makeup."

"Brace yourself," Michelle warned quietly. "TJ Jackson is with her."

Kennedy spotted James and immediately broke away from her makeup escort, moving toward him with the practiced grace of someone who knew cameras might be watching, even when they weren't.

"James!" she exclaimed, embracing him with the familiarity of an old friend rather than a co-star she'd met exactly once during the chemistry read. "I'm so excited for our first day together. This is going to be revolutionary."

James accepted the embrace with polite professionalism. "Kennedy. Welcome to the set. I hope your journey was comfortable."

"Absolutely. And I've brought someone I'm dying for you to meet." She turned, gesturing for TJ to join them. "TJ Jackson, the historical researcher whose work has been so instrumental in contextualizing our project."

TJ stepped forward, visibly starstruck. "Mr. Wright. An honor. Your courage in taking this role, bringing truth to a history that's been white-washed for decades, is genuinely inspiring."

James shook his hand with diplomatic neutrality. "Thank you. Though I should clarify that my approach to Hitler is based on Dr. Friedman's scholarly work and historical documentation, not on theories about his ancestry."

"Of course, of course," TJ nodded, undeterred. "The establishment version has its place. But consider this an opportunity to bring multiple perspectives together: the academic and the suppressed."

"We're all ultimately seeking truth," James replied carefully.

"Exactly!" Kennedy beamed. "That's why this project is so important. It's us against the establishment narrative, isn't it? Like Hitler and Eva against the world. Except, you know, for good reasons rather than genocidal ones." She laughed at her own comparison, apparently oblivious to its jarring inappropriateness.

"I should probably get to makeup," James said, skillfully sidestepping both the analogy and Kennedy's attempt to create a united front. "Sarah needs extra time for the transformation."

"Of course." Kennedy nodded. "I'll be there soon myself. Eva requires her own kind of transformation, from historical footnote to fully realized woman."

As James departed with a polite nod, Kennedy watched him go, her smile slipping slightly.

"He doesn't seem very... appreciative," she observed to her inner circle once James was out of earshot. "I mean, I'm putting my reputation on the line to support this casting, bringing TJ's research to legitimize the choice, protecting the production from controversy, you'd think he'd be a little more grateful."

"He's probably just focused on his performance," Miguel suggested diplomatically. "From what I've heard, he's quite serious about his craft."

"As am I! Still," Kennedy frowned. "We're partners in this. The two leads. Hitler and Eva. If I can embrace this revolutionary approach despite the potential professional implications, he could at least acknowledge my allyship."

Dani and Miguel exchanged a quick glance, the silent communication of long-term assistants who'd witnessed many such moments.

"Perhaps he's just not fully aware of all you're doing behind the scenes," Dani offered carefully. "The contract negotiations, bringing TJ on board ..."

"Exactly!" TJ agreed enthusiastically. "Artists often don't understand the political dimensions of their work. They're focused on craft while others manage the larger implications. This is what struck me about you immediately: you are artist and patron, the system and the reckoning."

Kennedy nodded, mollified. "That must be it. He's caught up in the artistic challenge while I'm handling the cultural context." She turned to TJ with renewed purpose. "Which is why your perspective is so essential. You give this project historical legitimacy beyond mere 'artistic choice.'"

Dani caught Miguel's eye again, a flicker of concern passing between them. Unlike TJ, who had joined Kennedy's team just days ago, they had witnessed her evolving fixation on the "Hitler's African ancestry" theory, a theory she'd initially dismissed as "fringe nonsense" before recognizing its strategic value.

"Miss Oswald?" A PA approached cautiously. "Makeup is ready for you now."

"Perfect timing." Kennedy smiled, instantly switching back to her professional mode. "Eva awaits. TJ, we'll continue our historical discussion later? I'd love your thoughts on how Eva might have supported Hitler through his identity struggles."

"Absolutely," TJ beamed. "I've actually been developing a theory about Eva's possible role as identity protector that would make a fascinating addition to her characterization."

As Kennedy glided toward makeup, flanked by her security detail like a head of state, David sidled up to Aaron, script pages still clutched in his white-knuckled grip.

"Please tell me we're not actually incorporating TJ's 'theories' into the script," he whispered urgently.

"Over my dead body," Aaron assured him. "Though at this rate, that might be a realistic outcome for this production."

"Changing the script or your dead body?"

"First one, then the other swiftly after."

From across the soundstage, Michelle watched the unfolding drama with the practiced eye of a publicist who'd seen many disasters (yet somehow never this specific configuration of absurdity).

She made a mental note to double the studio's crisis PR budget, get André to increase manpower on set, and possibly update her resume.

***

CHAPTER 13

Camilla Russo arrived at Pinnacle Pictures at precisely 11:23 a.m., a time she had calculated using principles of "chronological energy alignment" that she frequently explained to clients but never quite in the same way twice. And because it would be close to a break, allowing her to demonstrate her usefulness immediately.

She wore the meticulously casual uniform of high-end wellness professionals: perfectly ironed linen pants, handcrafted leather sandals from an "ethical cooperative" in Peru, and a flowing silk blouse in a shade her Instagram followers knew as #AuthenticEarthTone but everyone else would call beige. She wore an Hermès scarf wrapped around her head, a Brazilian pattern she had in every color to authentically call back to her mother's roots.

The security guard at the entrance examined her credentials with the skeptical expression of someone who'd seen too many varieties of Hollywood charlatans to be impressed by another.

"You're the... therapist?" he asked, squinting at her badge.

"Holistic psychological wellness facilitator," Camilla corrected, her accent an elegant blend of wealthy American and mildly South American that somehow made even nonsense sound authoritative. "I create safe spaces for emotional authenticity in high-stress environments."

The guard nodded vaguely, having clearly fielded stranger job titles on this production. "Lot 3, Soundstage B. Follow the signs that say 'Hitler Production.' Can't miss it."

"Thank you for holding space for my journey," Camilla replied, offering a namaste gesture that the guard did not return.

As she approached the soundstage, she noted with professional interest the unusual energy of the production: crew members hurrying with greater urgency than typical film sets, hushed conversations that halted abruptly when others approached, and most peculiarly, several people scrambling to cover wall decorations whenever cameras weren't rolling.

A young woman with a tablet and the harried expression of someone perpetually behind schedule approached her. "Ms. Russo? I'm Isa, Michelle Park's intern. I'm supposed to get you set up."

"It's Dr. Russo, but please, just Camilla," she replied, smiling warmly. "Hierarchical titles create barriers to authentic connection."

"Um, sure," Isa replied, already turning to lead her into the building. "Michelle asked me to review some protocols with you before you begin your... services."

"I prefer to call them 'healing dialogues,'" Camilla corrected gently. "Services sounds so transactional."

Isa nodded without slowing her pace. "Right. So first thing: phones. All devices need to be surrendered before entering the set. No exceptions."

Camilla stopped walking. "Excuse me?"

"It's standard protocol for sensitive historical material. It was part of your NDA," Isa explained, gesturing to a table where a security guard sat beside what appeared to be a high-tech lockbox. "Everyone complies, even Kennedy's team."

"But that's deeply problematic," Camilla frowned. "Apart from the fact that everyone here has full confidentiality from my practice, many people use technology as a coping mechanism. Electronic claustrophobia is a recognized trauma response in my practice. Have you considered the psychological implications of forced digital disconnection?"

Isa's expression suggested she had not, in fact, considered these implications, nor did she much want to start now. "I'm just following Michelle's instructions. All phones get secured in the Faraday cage."

"A Faraday cage?" Camilla's eyebrows rose dramatically. "That's practically technological incarceration."

"It's studio policy," Isa replied implacably. "Especially with the historical imagery on set."

Before Camilla could further expound on the psychological harm of phone separation, Michelle herself appeared, extending her hand with the practiced smile of someone who had explained things to difficult people many times before.

"Dr. Russo, welcome. I see Isa is reviewing our security protocols. I hope you understand the sensitive nature of our production necessitates certain precautions."

"Of course." Camilla nodded, shifting to a more collegial tone. "Though I should probably discuss alternative accommodations for those with technology-dependent coping mechanisms. Perhaps a medical exemption process?"

Michelle's smile tightened almost imperceptibly. "I've read your impressive résumé, Ms. Russo. USC psychology undergraduate, life coaching certification from the International Coaching Federation, and your work with several high-profile clients is certainly notable."

"I prefer Dr. Russo, but thank you for acknowledging my journey."

"However," Michelle continued smoothly, "I noticed your credentials don't include an M.D. or psychiatric certification, so you wouldn't be qualified to make medical exemptions."

Camilla's smile remained fixed as she recalibrated. "I am a qualified psyche healer and certified counselor. My approach integrates traditional therapeutic modalities with holistic wellness practices, many beyond traditional western medicine, developed through working with CEOs and thought leaders."

"Absolutely." Michelle nodded. "So you understand the importance of adhering to our established protocols. Your phone, please?"

With reluctance that bordered on physical pain, Camilla surrendered her rose gold iPhone Pro to the security guard, who placed it in the Faraday cage with ceremonial solemnity.

"It feels ungrounded to be separated from my digital extension," Camilla murmured, mostly to herself. "But I suppose it creates space for more authentic presence."

"Exactly," Michelle agreed, already moving them toward the soundstage entrance. "Now, we've prepared a quiet corner where you can meet with any cast or crew members who request your services. We've announced your availability via the call sheet this morning."

As they entered the main area, Camilla immediately noticed Kennedy Oswald in full Eva Braun costume: a period-appropriate ensemble that somehow managed to look like it had been designed for an Instagram photoshoot rather than historical accuracy. She was in mid-scene with James Wright, whose transformation into Hitler was so complete it momentarily gave even Camilla pause.

"I cannot continue to ignore you, Adolf!" Kennedy was saying, her German accent wavering somewhere between Berlin and Brooklyn. "I have sacrificed everything for you. EVERYTHING!"

James, fully inhabiting Hitler's physicality, turned with a stiff, controlled movement. "The German people are my priority, Eva. Personal considerations must wait."

"CUT!" called Aaron from behind the monitors. "Kennedy, remember Eva wouldn't have challenged Hitler so directly. The historical record suggests she was deferential, especially in the Berghof period."

"But that doesn't serve the character's emotional arc," Kennedy objected, dropping the accent entirely. "Eva needs to show agency or her eventual decision to die with him lacks motivation."

Dr. Friedman, standing nearby with an expression of pained resignation, took a staggered breath. "Historical accuracy is the motivation. She was devoted to him despite his neglect. That's the tragedy."

Kennedy spotted Camilla and immediately lit up, waving enthusiastically. "Camilla! You're here! Everyone, this is Dr. Camilla Russo, the most incredible healing facilitator I've ever worked with."

She rushed over, embracing Camilla with the practiced warmth of someone who had perfected the art of performed intimacy. "She literally saved my life during the *Summer Solstice* press tour. My inner child was practically in the ICU until Camilla helped me reconnect with my authentic vulnerability."

"You're too kind." Camilla smiled, returning the embrace with equal performance. "You did the work. I merely held space for your journey."

"And opened my eyes to my own privilege," Kennedy added earnestly. "I never realized how being rich, White, and conventionally attractive in Hollywood was affecting my spiritual alignment."

From nearby, Shanice, wearing a boom operator's headphones, muttered, "Your eyes didn't see those thousand-dollar rose-tinted glasses on your face?"

Kennedy either didn't hear or chose to ignore the comment, continuing to extol Camilla's healing virtues while crew members exchanged glances that ranged from skeptical to openly amused.

Meanwhile, Camilla observed the set with growing concern. Several crew members, the ones she'd noticed earlier covering wall decorations, were frantically adjusting sheets over what appeared to be Nazi imagery whenever cameras weren't rolling.

"Are those people okay?" she asked Michelle quietly. "The ones rushing around with the sheets?"

"The Nazi wranglers?" Michelle replied. "They're fine. That's their job: covering historical imagery between takes to maintain set sensitivity."

"Nazi wranglers," Camilla repeated, testing the phrase. "The psychic burden of that role must be enormous. I should hold a special struggle session for them specifically."

Before Michelle could respond, James approached, still in full Hitler regalia but with his natural speech patterns restored. "I understand you're our new psychological support specialist? James Wright. It's a pleasure to meet you."

"I'm Camilla. The energy you're bringing to this difficult historical figure is remarkable," Camilla said, studying him with professional interest. "How are you processing the grief inherent in embodying such darkness?"

James smiled politely. "I've developed my own methods over years of classical training. But thank you for your concern. If you'll excuse me, I need to consult with Dr. Friedman and David about the next scene."

As James walked away, Camilla turned to Aaron, who was reviewing footage on a nearby monitor. "As a Jewish director guiding a Black actor playing Hitler, you must experience profound internal dissonance. Perhaps we could explore that tension through a guided meditation?"

Aaron glanced up with the expression of someone being offered a complicated dessert while actively experiencing food poisoning. "That's... quite an offer. Unfortunately, I'm a bit busy making sure our production doesn't implode before lunch. Another time, perhaps?"

He caught Michelle's eye with a silent plea for intervention.

"Camilla," Michelle said smoothly, "why don't I show you to your designated space? The crew needs to reset for the next scene."

As they moved through the soundstage, they passed TJ Jackson deep in animated conversation with a production assistant who looked increasingly confused.

"Dr. Russo!" TJ called out, breaking off his discourse on Hitler's grandmother. "A pleasure to finally meet you. Kennedy speaks highly of your work."

"The pleasure is mine," Camilla replied, genuinely excited to meet the social media phenomenon. "Your decolonization of historical narratives resonates deeply with my approach to deconstructing emotional barriers."

TJ nodded enthusiastically. "Exactly! Traditional frameworks constrain both historical truth and personal healing. We're both doing the same work, just in different domains."

"These poor people," Camilla said, lowering her voice dramatically while gesturing around the set. "They must be so frightened by this environment that they cannot speak freely. The historical trauma being recreated here requires specialized holding."

"That's why Kennedy insisted on your presence," TJ agreed. "She understands the importance of emotional safety when challenging established narratives."

They exchanged phone numbers, or would have, if Camilla's phone hadn't been imprisoned in the Faraday cage. Instead, she memorized his number with practiced efficiency.

"I'm struggling to scale my impact," she confided. "1.2 million on Instagram, 500K on YouTube, but only three million on TikTok. I can't seem to gain proper traction."

TJ's expression turned professorial. "Algorithm optimization requires pattern disruption. Try contrasting soothing voice with controversial claims; this creates cognitive dissonance that increases engagement. Also, use the phrases 'they don't want you to know' and 'hidden truth' in your first fifteen seconds. Triggers curiosity algorithms."

"Fascinating," Camilla murmured, mentally taking notes. "I'll have to implement that."

She broke off as Andrew Kline walked past, his Goebbels costume creating an unsettling silhouette. Camilla immediately pivoted toward him.

"Mr. Kline! I'd love to make sure your sobriety remains supported in this potentially triggering environment. Perhaps we could discuss coping strategies for historical reenactment trauma?"

Kline stopped, his expression shifting from surprise to barely contained irritation. "With all due respect, I need to get to makeup. Also, my sobriety is managed through established channels that don't include impromptu therapy sessions on set."

As he walked away, Camilla turned to Michelle. "Resistance often indicates the deepest need for intervention. His defensive energy suggests significant unprocessed trauma."

"Or a busy actor on a tight schedule," Michelle suggested diplomatically.

Camilla's attention had already shifted to a large Black man directing the lighting crew with booming authority and easy laughter. "Who is that?"

"Marcus Johnson. Everyone calls him Big Marc. He's our lighting director."

"The emotional labor of a Black professional in this environment must be extraordinary," Camilla observed. "His jovial exterior likely masks profound pain. I should help him process his internalized responses to this historical material."

Michelle's expression shifted to alarm. "I wouldn't recommend that."

But Camilla was already moving toward Big Marc with the confident stride of someone who had charged wealthy executives $750 an hour to tell them they needed to cry more.

"Mr. Johnson? I'm Dr. Camilla Russo, the production's psychological wellness facilitator. I'd love to create a safe space for you to process your experience on this challenging set."

Big Marc turned, his imposing frame making Camilla look almost comically small in comparison. "Process my what now?"

"Your experience as a Black professional surrounded by Nazi imagery while participating in a production that recasts Hitler. The cognitive dissonance alone must be exhausting."

Big Marc looked down at her with genuine confusion. "Lady, I'm lighting a movie. That's what I do. Been doing it for twenty years."

"Exactly." Camilla nodded empathetically. "And how does that make you feel?"

"Feels like I'm getting paid to do my job," he replied simply.

"Your emotional guardedness is a natural response to historical oppression," Camilla continued smoothly. "Many find it difficult to vocalize their authentic pain in professional settings."

By now, several crew members had paused their work to watch the interaction, including Shanice, Big Marc's crew, and several PAs trying to conceal their amusement.

Big Marc's expression remained bemused. "No offense, Doc, but I'm not guarding anything. I'm here to make Hitler look appropriately evil through subtle side-lighting and dramatic shadow work. It's actually kind of fun, technically speaking."

"The normalization of proximity to symbols of genocide is a trauma response in itself," Camilla pressed on, undeterred. "Your psyche creates distance as self-protection."

"Or maybe I just like solving lighting puzzles," Big Marc suggested. "Last month I lit a romantic comedy. A few months before that, a superhero movie. This one's got Nazis. Next one might have aliens. It's all just creating the right mood with light."

Andrew Kline had returned from makeup now fully transformed into Goebbels, and paused to observe the increasingly amusing standoff. The corner of his mouth twitched in what might have been the beginning of a smile.

Camilla, sensing her approach wasn't working, tried a different angle. "Perhaps the presence of Mr. Kline on set creates additional tension? Given his historically documented problematic behavior? After all, he's been photographed wearing symbols of oppression for your people."

Big Marc glanced at Kline, then back at Camilla. "You mean the Confederate t-shirt thing? Lady, I'm from Mississippi. That's nothing. Folks at my church picnic wore worse."

This unexpected response caught everyone by surprise, including Kline himself, whose carefully neutral expression shifted to something more genuine.

"I don't think you're allowing yourself to acknowledge the full spectrum of your emotional response," Camilla insisted. "Perhaps a guided meditation would help you access your suppressed trauma?"

"The only trauma I'm experiencing is trying to figure out how to light a scene with sixteen Nazi wranglers running around covering up half my key light sources," Big Marc laughed, his deep voice resonating through the soundstage.

Even Kline couldn't suppress a chuckle at this point, causing Camilla to turn to him with renewed therapeutic determination. Before she could launch into another attempt, however, Aaron's voice called out for everyone to return to their positions.

"We'll have to continue this healing dialogue another time," Camilla said, not quite willing to admit defeat. "I'll be available regularly for sessions. You can sign up in advance."

As the crew dispersed to their positions, Kline approached Big Marc with unexpected openness.

"I appreciate that response," he said quietly. "People have been walking on eggshells around me since I arrived. It's... refreshing to be treated normally."

"Man, I've been lighting films for two decades," Big Marc replied. "Worked with all types. People are people. Some are assholes, some aren't. I figure everyone deserves the benefit of the doubt until proven otherwise."

"That's a generous philosophy," Kline said. "I wish I had your mental fortitude. The tabloids haven't exactly been kind over the years."

"That's just us Mississippi folk," Big Marc shrugged. "We learn to take things as they come."

Kline looked genuinely surprised. "Mississippi? I wouldn't have guessed. I'm from a small town in Arkansas myself, right near the border."

"No shit?" Big Marc's eyebrows shot up. "Wouldn't have pegged you for a Delta boy. Where about?"

"Little place called Osceola. Doubt you've heard of it."

"Get out!" Big Marc's face split into a wide grin. "My cousin married a girl from Osceola. Small world!"

As they walked toward the set together, finding unexpected common ground, Camilla watched with the slightly bewildered expression of a therapist whose carefully constructed narrative had just collapsed. Michelle appeared at her side, diplomatically avoiding any hint of "I told you so" in her expression.

"Perhaps we should review which crew members have actually requested your services?" Michelle suggested gently. "A more targeted approach might be more... effective."

"Yes," Camilla agreed, recovering her professional composure. "The healing journey reveals itself in unexpected ways. Resistance often precedes the deepest breakthroughs."

"Of course it does." Michelle nodded, guiding her away from the set. "Let's just make sure those breakthroughs don't interfere with our shooting schedule."

***

Victoria's office weeks into filming had taken on the ambiance of a war room, if wars were fought with publicity strategies and TikTok counter-measures. Maps had been replaced by social media analytics displayed on multiple screens. Battle plans had given way to PR calendars color-coded by controversy type. At nine p.m., the bourbon had been upgraded to the "good stuff": the bottle Victoria kept hidden behind her Emmy for emergencies and existential crises.

André paced energetically, tablet in hand, his White Cement 3s squeaking slightly against the polished floor as Aaron slouched in an armchair looking like he'd aged a decade in the past few weeks.

"First looks are set for tomorrow," André announced, swiping through his presentation with the enthusiasm of a general planning an invasion. "Three carefully vetted entertainment outlets, tightly controlled access, fifteen minutes each. Just enough to generate buzz without risking a full-blown disaster."

"Define 'carefully vetted,'" Aaron muttered.

"Publications with enough credibility to be taken seriously but enough industry dependence that they won't risk burning bridges by misrepresenting us," André replied. "The sweet spot in the journalistic integrity spectrum: compromised but not completely sold out."

Victoria nodded approvingly. "Perfect. What about our Nazi wrangler situation? Michelle mentioned we might need reinforcements."

"Already handled. Four additional wranglers start tomorrow, all signed to enhanced NDAs." André's grin widened. "But that's not the exciting news. You have got to see this Substack piece that's been making the rounds. It's being shared by every left-leaning film site from *Slate* to *The Mary Sue*."

He handed Victoria his tablet, displaying an article with the bold headline: "THE MISSED OPPORTUNITY: Why 'Black Hitler' Should Have Gone Even Further."

Victoria skimmed the first paragraph, one eyebrow rising incrementally. "Imani Biira-Clarkson? The Ugandan film critic with the critical race theory PhD?"

"That's her," André confirmed. "She thinks our approach is, and I quote 'another half-measure masquerading as revolution. Another corporate risk carefully calibrated to generate just enough controversy to fill theater seats without fundamentally challenging anything.'"

Aaron leaned forward. "Let me guess: we're not diverse enough?"

"Oh, it's so much better than that," André laughed, taking back the tablet and finding his favorite part. "Listen to this gem: 'Black Hitler should have followed the *Hamilton* blueprint. Not with a single provocative casting choice surrounded by conventional historical trappings, but with a complete inversion of the power dynamics. Every Nazi officer, every SS guard, every supporter of the regime should have been portrayed by actors of color, while keeping the victims historically accurate.'"

Victoria choked on her bourbon. "She wants an all-BIPOC Third Reich?"

"It gets better," André continued gleefully. "'Picture it: James Wright's Hitler surrounded by an entirely BIPOC inner circle. Eva Braun played by an Indigenous actress. Goebbels portrayed by a dark-skinned Latino. Göring by a South Asian actor. Himmler by an East Asian performer.'"

Aaron ran a hand through his hair. "So according to this critique, our mistake wasn't casting a Black actor as Hitler; it was not casting enough actors of color as... Nazis?"

"Exactly," André nodded.

Victoria studied the article with renewed interest. "You know, she actually has a point. Can you imagine the optics of something like this? It might be a guaranteed award right there! The Academy would collectively orgasm at the conceptual audacity."

"If we added Lin-Manuel Miranda's music," Aaron added dryly, "wouldn't it just be an all-BIPOC *Springtime for Hitler*?"

André burst into laughter. "The horseshoe theory of representation in action! Some think we've gone too far with diversity, others think we haven't gone nearly far enough. We've created the perfect controversy: absolute confusion about what position anyone should take."

"Read the part about our 'timid gestures,'" Victoria prompted, refilling her glass.

André scrolled down, clearing his throat dramatically. "'They cast a Black Hitler but kept him in the same visual language, the same narrative framework, the same cinematic tradition as every White Hitler before him. They surrounded him with a largely White supporting cast, maintained traditional period aesthetics, and approached the material with unearned solemnity.'"

"Unearned solemnity," Aaron repeated, shaking his head. "As opposed to what? A Hitler musical with choreographed SS dance numbers?"

"Careful," Victoria warned with a smile. "She might hear you and write a follow-up piece demanding exactly that."

André set the tablet down, shifting gears. "In other news, we've successfully arranged for TJ Jackson to be elsewhere during tomorrow's media visits. He's been booked as an 'expert panelist' on representation for a local news channel that gets roughly the same viewership as a high school morning announcement broadcast."

"Perfect," Victoria nodded. "The last thing we need is his 'Hitler had African ancestry' theories coloring the coverage."

"Speaking of coverage," André continued, "we need to finalize who's authorized to speak on the record. Kennedy's a given: her media training is impeccable, and her team has already provided pre-approved talking points about 'artistic courage' and 'reframing historical narratives.'"

"What about Kline?" Aaron asked.

André and Victoria exchanged glances.

"Absolutely not," Victoria said firmly. "One unscripted comment about 'historical authenticity' or 'traditional casting approaches' and we're looking at a social media firestorm."

"What about James?" Aaron pressed. "He's the centerpiece of this entire project."

André hesitated. "That's... complicated. He speaks beautifully, but he's very nuanced and educated. Might not help us."

"These outlets want sound bites, not actual insights," Victoria added. "They're looking for controversy and quotes they can misconstrue. James is too thoughtful; he'd give them context and complexity. That's the last thing viral content needs."

Aaron looked incredulous. "So our Hitler is too articulate to discuss our Hitler movie?"

"That's entertainment journalism." André shrugged. "If we can't provide them with simplistic takes they can weaponize for clicks, they'll create them through selective editing."

"Which is why," Victoria interjected, "we've added a clause to the media agreements stating that all recordings remain property of Pinnacle until approved. If the interviews go sideways, they never see the light of day."

"So tomorrow's carefully orchestrated media circus will feature Kennedy waxing poetic about her 'brave artistic journey' while our actual Hitler remains silent?" Aaron summed up, reaching for Victoria's bourbon.

"Precisely," Victoria nodded. "For once, Kennedy will be a great boon. You'll handle the directorial vision questions, of course."

Aaron choked slightly on his drink. "My what? This thing isn't my vision; it's a circus."

"And isn't that all movie sets?" Victoria countered with a wry smile. "High-budget circuses trying to grab the attention of increasingly distracted audiences?"

André snorted. "Some just have more clowns than others."

Victoria leaned back, swirling her bourbon. "Speaking of clowns, how's our TikTok historian behaving? Any new developments in the TJ Jackson saga?"

"For a conspiracy theorist, he's been surprisingly professional," André admitted. "Though Dr. Friedman might disagree. TJ keeps engaging him in what he calls 'academic discourse' but what increasingly looks like deliberate harassment."

"He's started a new video series," Aaron added. "'Watch Me Destroy the System's History Keepers.' It's basically him taking Friedman's points from their on-set arguments and dismantling them through careful caricature and straw-man counterarguments."

"Does Friedman know about this?" Victoria asked.

"Not yet," Aaron replied. "And I'd prefer to keep it that way. We're hanging onto our historical consultant by a thread as it is."

Victoria leaned back in her chair, contemplating the situation. "You know, these videos are generating remarkable engagement. Six million views across all his socials in the past week. #HitlerWasBlack is trending."

Aaron's expression darkened. "That's exactly the problem. This pseudo-historian is turning our serious film into some kind of conspiracy validation."

"A pseudo-historian with a new book deal," André interjected, checking his phone. "Apparently Regency Press offered him mid-six figures for *Hitler's Hidden Heritage: The Conspiracy to Whitewash History.*"

"You've got to be kidding me," Aaron groaned.

"The publishing industry knows engagement when they see it," André shrugged. "His follower count has doubled since he started posting about our movie."

Victoria studied Aaron with calculating eyes. "When Dr. Friedman inevitably discovers these videos, and let's face it, that's a matter of when, not if, what do you think his reaction will be?"

"Nuclear," Aaron said flatly. "Friedman has spent his entire academic career maintaining historical accuracy about this period. TJ is basically spitting in the face of everything he stands for."

"And you're concerned that if Friedman quits again;"

"When, not if," Aaron corrected.

"That we won't be able to get him back this time," Victoria finished.

"Precisely." Aaron nodded. "And we need him, Victoria. His knowledge has been invaluable, especially with Kennedy constantly trying to reinvent Eva Braun as some kind of feminist icon trapped in the patriarchy."

Victoria took a deliberate sip of her bourbon. "Do we, though? Need him, I mean."

Aaron stared at her, genuinely shocked. "Of course we do. He's our historical conscience, our academic foundation. Without him, I don't know what we'd do."

"Without him, we still have his book, his research notes, and all his previous script contributions," Victoria interrupted. "What exactly is he contributing at this point that isn't already baked into the material?"

"Integrity," Aaron said simply. "Authenticity. The ability to tell Kennedy that her 'Eva Braun came up with the iconic mustache' theory is complete nonsense."

André snorted at this, though he quickly composed himself when Aaron shot him a look.

"TJ Jackson is becoming our most effective marketing asset," Victoria countered. "His videos have generated more engagement than our entire official promotional budget."

Aaron leaned forward, his expression hardening. "So what exactly are you suggesting? That we just… let Friedman go when he inevitably objects to TJ's conspiracy theories about our movie?"

Victoria's expression remained calculatingly neutral. "I'm suggesting we be strategic. TJ's theories are driving conversation about our film across demographics we'd never reach otherwise. Academic circles are producing response videos debunking him, which only generates more interest in our project. Other historians are coming out in support of him."

"And what about historical accuracy?" Aaron pressed. "The entire premise of this film was to examine how fascism takes root through manipulation of truth. Now we're just going to embrace actual manipulation of historical truth for marketing purposes?"

Victoria's eyes narrowed slightly. "We're not 'embracing' anything. We're simply not publicly refuting an independent content creator's interpretation of our film."

"That's a hell of a semantic dance," Aaron replied.

"That's Hollywood," Victoria said dryly. "Land of the carefully worded non-statement."

Aaron shook his head, genuine moral discomfort evident in his posture. "So when Friedman discovers these videos and threatens to quit, again, you're fine with that? Just let him walk?"

"Look," Victoria said with diplomatic precision, "do what you can to manage Friedman. Flatter his academic ego, appeal to his sense of artistic responsibility; whatever works. But TJ stays. Those videos are marketing gold, and quite frankly, Kennedy has it in her contract anyway."

She reached for the bottle, pouring herself another finger of bourbon as if to physically mark the end of the discussion. The silence between them stretched just long enough to be uncomfortable before she pivoted with practiced executive efficiency.

"And speaking of Kennedy's contractual requirements, how's our therapist working out?" Victoria inquired, her tone deliberately lightening, though Aaron's frown made it clear he recognized the tactic for what it was: strategic topic changing with Hollywood precision.

"Camilla?" Aaron grimaced, choosing to let the Friedman issue rest for now, though his expression suggested it was far from settled. "She's been remarkably unkind to Kline; keeps trying to ambush him with sobriety interventions and process his 'unexamined historical complicity.' She's also insisting that we tone down the Nazi imagery for 'mental wellness consid erations.'"

"Michelle's been handling it masterfully," André noted. "But at some point, we might need to hire her an actual therapist to get through this."

"Add it to the budget." Victoria waved dismissively. "Speaking of online disasters, has anyone seen part three of the LiftieinLipstick series? Do we need to worry about script leaks?"

André grabbed his tablet again, pulling up the TikTok. "I don't think so, but it's even more deranged than her previous installments. She claims to have 'industry insiders' sending her confidential information."

"She has no sources," Aaron stated flatly. "The details she's citing don't even exist in our script. She claims we've 'glossed over the Beer Hall Putsch'; we have two full scenes dedicated to it. And Dr. Friedman insisted we emphasize the antisemitism more prominently than earlier drafts, not less."

André played the video, the three of them watching as a pink-haired woman applied contour while making increasingly outlandish claims about their production.

"SO! My DMs have been FLOODED with industry insiders after my last two videos," Jade declared, carefully blending along her cheekbone. "People who actually WORK at Pinnacle are risking their careers to show me what's really happening. Whistleblowers, basically."

"The script focuses on Hitler's relationship with his dog, trying to make us SYMPATHIZE with him," she continued. "Classic fascist propaganda technique: humanize the monster so people forget what they actually DID."

Aaron looked genuinely baffled. "We shot ONE scene with the dog to secure our option. It's not even clear if it will make the final cut."

"The most CHILLING part?" Jade's voice rose dramatically as she applied more contour. "My sources say there's a scene where Hitler talks about 'protecting German culture' that uses IDENTICAL LANGUAGE to what Trump supporters use about 'protecting American values.'"

Victoria paused the video. "I think we should remind the crew about the NDA consequences. Not because I believe anyone's actually leaking to a TikTok makeup influencer, but because this illustrates how easily completely fabricated narratives gain traction."

"Thirteen million views and counting," André noted. "With essentially zero factual content. This series really increased her virality."

"To the attention economy," Victoria toasted. "Where truth is whatever gets the most engagement. May we get enough to pull this over the finish line."

She stood, moving to the window that overlooked the lot. "Tomorrow's first look is crucial. We need to establish enough of our own narrative to counterbalance these conspiracy theories and misrepresentations."

"And if we can't?" Aaron asked quietly.

Victoria turned, her expression hardening slightly. "Then we embrace the chaos. As André keeps reminding us, all publicity ultimately serves our purposes. If people are arguing about whether our Hitler movie is too diverse or not diverse enough, that's still people talking about our Hitler movie."

"The ultimate irony," Aaron mused, "is that James is creating a genuinely remarkable performance that might actually achieve what we originally intended: a disturbing, humanizing portrait that makes audiences understand how a monster is made, and the calculated cruelty he unleashed on the world."

"And no one will notice because they're too busy debating whether we should have cast an Indigenous actress as Eva Braun," André added.

Victoria raised her glass in a mock toast. "To Hollywood, where the discourse about art has become more entertaining than the art itself."

As they clinked glasses, the absurdity of their situation hung in the air like expensive bourbon fumes: intoxicating, disorienting, and impossible to ignore.

***

CHapter 14

"There's a ten-foot Nazi flag behind Interview Station B and we're already thirty minutes behind schedule," Michelle hissed, clutching her tablet like it might provide divine intervention. "Someone please explain how none of us knew about this very visually problematic set piece until literally right now?"

Sarah, head of makeup, stood beside her friend in the corner of soundstage B, both of them staring at the enormous swastika banner that production assistants were frantically attempting to fold while maintaining some semblance of dignity.

"Apparently it's for Hitler's hallucination sequence," Sarah explained, wincing as one PA tripped, nearly face-planting into the offending symbol. "James walks through it in slow motion while his hand starts trembling; this foreshadows his eventual suicide. Very artistic, completely unexpected, and absolutely terrible timing."

"It takes six people to move it," Michelle noted with growing horror. "Six. People. And we've got entertainment journalists arriving in," she checked her watch, "forty-three minutes."

"May I make a possibly unpopular suggestion?" Sarah offered, watching another PA join the increasingly chaotic flag-folding operation. "Could we just... burn it? Say it was a technical malfunction? I'm Jewish; I'll take full responsibility."

"Tempting, but it's a $14,000 custom piece with integrated lighting effects," Michelle sighed. "Victoria would murder us both and hide our bodies in the Faraday cage with everyone's phones."

The soundstage door burst open as André entered with his characteristically controlled chaos energy, trailed by Ravi and an entourage of marketing assistants who seemed to multiply daily. He stopped to survey the scene with the calculating gaze of a field general.

"Morning, ladies!" André called out, approaching with a suspiciously cheerful smile. "How's our first press day?" His voice died as he spotted the enormous swastika. "Well, that's certainly not making it into the media package."

"It's for the hallucination sequence," Michelle and Sarah replied in unison.

"Of course it is," André murmured, watching the PAs struggle to fold the massive banner. "Because nothing says 'tasteful historical drama' like a Nazi flag you could use as a parachute."

He turned to Michelle. "New plan. We move all interviews outside to the lot. Set up in front of the generic beige wall by soundstage C. We'll tell the journalists it's to 'minimize spoilers.' Problem solved."

"Outside interviews weren't in the approval process," Michelle protested. "We promised controlled lighting, controlled sound, controlled conditions."

"That was before we discovered the world's largest swastika was going to photobomb our carefully managed press event," André cut in. "Unless you'd prefer explaining to *The Hollywood Reporter* why their exclusive first look includes what appears to be a Nazi rally backdrop?"

Michelle conceded with a nod. "I'll have the team pivot. Isa!" she called to her intern. "Text facilities: we need three director's chairs, lighting equipment, and a backdrop outside soundstage C in thirty minutes! Get a few of the other interns to move the snacks & waters outside too."

Ravi leaned toward André. "What about the talent? James is already in makeup."

André's expression shifted to strategic calculation. "Sarah, how extensive is James's Hitler transformation today?"

Sarah crossed her arms defensively. "Full protocol: hair, subtle prosthetics, mustache, the works. We can't half-ass Hitler."

"Can we... tone it down a bit? Maybe lose the mustache for the interviews?"

Sarah looked genuinely offended. "André, have you seen James Wright? The man is ridiculously handsome. Without the prosthetics and makeup, he's not Hitler; he's a Black model in a period suit. He'll end up having suburban housewives creating a cult to him thinking they can change him."

Big Marc passed by, clipboard in hand, and caught the tail end of the conversation. "I hate to break it to you, but I'm pretty sure the ugly White Hitler already has a female cult. Nazi fangirls, definitely a thing on the dark web."

"Not helping, Marc," Michelle murmured.

André ran a hand through his hair. "Fine, keep the mustache, but let's minimize the rest. These interviews are audio recorded for written pieces; just approved photos, we can focus on Eva and we can release the first day photos. Just get him recognizable without giving these writers horror-fuel for their nightmares or their keyboards."

Aaron approached, looking like he hadn't slept more than four consecutive hours in weeks. "André, a word?" His voice carried the edge of someone holding onto their patience by the thinnest of threads.

"Can it wait? We're in the middle of a Nazi flag emergency."

"No, it can't wait," Aaron replied. "I heard you're asking Sarah to alter James's makeup for the interviews. This is a Hitler movie. You can't keep trying to erase Hitler from the Hitler movie."

"We're not erasing Hitler," André countered smoothly. "We're managing the optics of our historically sensitive production in a media landscape that sacrifices nuance for outrage and context for clicks."

"It's a movie," Aaron insisted. "Not a marketing exercise."

"It's both," André replied. "And right now, the marketing needs to ensure your movie has an audience. Unless you'd prefer to create your artistic masterpiece exclusively for film historians and curious squirrels when it's released directly to the Pinnacle archives?"

Before Aaron could respond, a commotion erupted from the direction of Kennedy's dressing room. A series of expletives grew louder and more colorful until Barry Hickson emerged, his perfectly coiffed silver hair seeming to bristle with rage.

"Where the FUCK is Park?" he bellowed, scanning the room until his gaze locked onto Michelle. "You! The publicist with the so-called attention to detail!"

Michelle stepped forward with professional calm. "Good morning, Mr. Hickson. Is there an issue I can help with?"

"Is there an issue?" Barry's voice reached a dangerously controlled volume. "Kennedy specifically requested pink peonies, her mother's favorite flowers, to help her stay centered during interviews. What do I find instead? Fucking *carnations*. CARNATIONS! Do you have any idea what carnations represent in Kennedy's emotional landscape?"

"I wasn't aware."

"Of course you weren't aware," Barry cut in, his voice dripping with sardonic venom. "Because no one in this three-ring circus of a production bothers to read the eighteen-page rider that we helpfully provided detailing Kennedy's specific requirements for emotional stability during press events!"

Michelle maintained her composure. "I'll handle it immediately. Isa!"

The harried intern materialized at her side. "Already calling the flower service. They claim the peonies were out of season, but I've located three florists within a twenty-mile radius with pink peonies in stock. Priority delivery in process."

"See?" Michelle turned back to Barry. "We're resolving this."

"You're not resolving shit until those second-rate funeral flowers are removed from her sight line," Barry snapped. "Kennedy is in her bathroom doing breathing exercises to counteract the emotional distress of botanical betrayal. Every minute she spends hyperventilating over inappropriate flora is a minute she's not preparing to discuss her groundbreaking performance as Eva fucking Braun."

Michelle signaled frantically to a PA, who scurried toward Kennedy's dressing room with the desperate energy of someone whose career depended on flower removal.

"Mr. Hickson," she said calmly, "I understand your frustration. We want Kennedy at her absolute best for these interviews. The correct flowers will be here within the hour. In the meantime, we're relocating the press setup outside for better lighting."

Barry's eyes narrowed suspiciously. "Outside? That wasn't in the agreement. Kennedy's hair has specific humidity requirements for optimal photographic representation."

"It's a print interview, no new photos," Michelle reminded him. "And our weather report shows ideal conditions: seventy-two degrees, thirty percent humidity."

"Fine," Barry conceded grudgingly. "But I want it in writing that this deviation from agreed-upon protocols is entirely your production's failure, not Kennedy's team being difficult."

"Of course," Michelle agreed, making a note on her tablet. "I'll have legal draft the addendum immediately."

As Barry stalked back to Kennedy's dressing room, Michelle exhaled slowly, turning to find Aaron and André watching her with something between amusement and respect.

"And that," André said appreciatively, "is why we pay her the big bucks."

"We don't pay her the big bucks," Aaron corrected.

"Well, we should," André replied. "That man has made studio executives cry during negotiations. I once saw him reduce Paramount's head of production to stress-eating an entire cheesecake during a contract dispute."

Their moment of solidarity was interrupted by Dr. Friedman barreling toward them with uncharacteristic speed, his usually meticulously combed white hair standing at frantic attention. His iPad was clutched in one trembling hand, his expression oscillating between academic outrage and personal betrayal.

"Aaron!" he called, voice cracking slightly. "I demand that charlatan be removed from this production immediately! This is beyond academic disagreement; this is calculated character assassination!"

Aaron stepped forward, concern evident. "Benjamin, what's happened?"

"That... that... internet hustler you've allowed on set!" Dr. Friedman thrust his iPad forward. "He's been recording our conversations and distorting them for his so-called content! Six million views of him making me look like a conspiracy-hiding fool!"

Aaron took the iPad with trepidation. The screen displayed TJ Jackson's latest TikTok series, "Watch Me Destroy the System's History Keepers." The view counter showed an alarming 5.7 million and climbing.

"May I?" André asked, gently taking the iPad from Aaron's hands. He pressed play, watching with professional interest as TJ's performance unfolded: the dramatic music, the calculated pauses, the scribbled notes supposedly documenting their conversations.

"'Ask yourself: who benefits from missing records? The same institutions that write our 'official' history books,'" TJ's voice declared from the iPad. "'Drop a magnifying-glass emoji if you're ready for more conversations with our 'official' historians. The truth is coming out, one missing record at a time.'"

"I never said records were 'conveniently' lost!" Dr. Friedman sputtered. "I explained the well-documented destruction of civil administration buildings during Allied bombing raids! He's completely misrepresenting my words."

"Oh, there's more," André said, scrolling to the next video. "He's made an entire series. This one's called 'When the Academic Mask Slips.'"

They watched in collective horror as TJ systematically twisted Dr. Friedman's explanations about facial recognition technology into supposed "admissions" of historical conspiracy.

"This is... not ideal," Aaron sheepishly admitted.

"Not ideal?" Dr. Friedman's voice rose dangerously. "He's gotten three so-called 'independent historians', all internet personalities with their own dubious platforms and questionable credentials, to back his theories! They're citing ME as a source for their absurd claims!"

David approached, casting a concerned look at the gathering. "What's happening now?"

"TJ Jackson has turned his conversations with Dr. Friedman into viral content," Aaron explained, running a hand through his hair. "He's presenting Benjamin's academic explanations as 'proof' of historical cover-ups."

"I want him gone," Dr. Friedman demanded. "Immediately. Today. This is the final straw. Either he leaves, or I do."

"Benjamin," Aaron began cautiously, "I completely understand your position."

"Dr. Friedman," André interrupted smoothly, "I share your outrage. What TJ is doing is intellectually dishonest and professionally disrespectful." He placed a sympathetic hand on the historian's shoulder. "Unfortunately, removing him would create significant complications. Kennedy's contract specifies his presence three days a week during filming. If we breach that clause, we risk losing our Eva Braun."

"I don't care if we lose our Hitler, our Eva, and the entire Third Reich!" Dr. Friedman exploded. "This is academic malpractice! I've dedicated my life to rigorous historical scholarship, and now my reputation is being undermined by a man whose credentials consist of dramatic music and badly-edited jump cuts!"

David gently guided Dr. Friedman toward the coffee station. "Let's get some air and discuss this privately. I promise we'll address the situation, but maybe not minutes before our first press interviews?"

Aaron watched them go, turning to André with a pained expression. "This is a disaster."

"Actually," André replied, still studying the TikTok metrics, "Victoria is right, TJ has been remarkably effective from a marketing perspective. His videos have generated more engagement than our official channels by a factor of ten. His conspiracy theories about Hitler have created an unexpected halo effect for our production."

"You can't be serious."

"Completely serious," André confirmed. "Parrot Analytics reports show tremendous demand for this film: much of it driven by the 'discourse' around Black Hitler, across the political spectrum, enraged or engaged, doesn't seem to matter. We've secured solid foreign distribution deals based partly on the controversy being generated."

"So we're sacrificing historical accuracy, Dr. Friedman's mental health, and possibly Dr. Friedman for marketing metrics?" Aaron asked incredulously.

"I understand your concern," Michelle interjected, rejoining them after resolving the flower crisis. "And I share your discomfort with the situation. But the unfortunate reality is that all of these laymen takes from TJ Jackson to @LiftieInLipstick have created more public interest in this film than Dr. Friedman's meticulous scholarship ever could."

"That's... profoundly depressing," Aaron muttered.

"That's entertainment in 2025." André smiled without warmth. "Where being factually wrong but passionately persistent is more valuable than being right and reasonable."

He checked his watch. "The first journalist arrives in twenty minutes. Where are James and Kennedy?"

"Kennedy's still recovering from her floral trauma," Michelle replied. "James is finishing makeup. Is our outdoor setup ready?"

"Almost," Isa confirmed, appearing with her tablet. "Lighting is adjusted for natural conditions, sound checks complete. Now we just need to make sure our Hitler and Eva are prepped."

Ten minutes later, Kennedy emerged from her dressing room looking immaculately composed: her Eva Braun costume tailored to suggest historical accuracy while maintaining photo-friendly aesthetics. Her blonde hair fell in period-appropriate waves that somehow managed to look thoroughly modern, and her expression carried the practiced serenity of someone who had centered their energy through premium flower arrangements and controlled breathing exercises.

James appeared moments later, his transformation into Hitler both subtle and striking. Sarah had indeed toned down certain elements, the sallow skin coloring was less pronounced, the prosthetic alterations minimal, but the iconic hair and mustache remained, creating the unsettling juxta-position that had made their project both controversial and compelling.

"You both look perfect," Michelle assured them. "The interview's primary focus will be on the artistic approach: your preparation, your emotional journey with these complex characters, the experience of bringing them to life."

"Where's Andrew?" James asked, looking around for his co-star. "I thought he was joining us."

Michelle and André exchanged glances.

"We decided it would be best to focus on you and Kennedy for these first interviews," Michelle explained diplomatically. "Andrew's presence might... complicate the narrative we're establishing."

"Bad optics," André added bluntly. "A possibly racist actor playing Goebbels opposite a Black Hitler creates too many potential landmines for a fifteen-minute interview."

"That seems unfair." James frowned. "Apart from his smoking habit, he's been nothing but professional and supportive on set."

"Another time," Michelle promised. "These initial interviews need careful management."

"James," André added, stepping closer, "a word of advice for these journalists? Don't be too academic. They'll try to make you speak for all Black actors or turn this into a broader statement about representation. Keep your answers focused, positive, and light on nuance."

"Light on nuance?" James repeated skeptically.

"These aren't scholarly publications," André explained. "They want sound bites they can shape into narratives. 'Grateful for the opportunity,' 'groundbreaking approach,' 'challenging but rewarding experience'; that kind of thing. The more complex your actual thoughts, the more likely they'll be misrepresented."

James nodded with reluctant understanding. "I see."

"Short phrases, clear statements, gracious demeanor," André continued. "We'll be monitoring, ready to intervene if questions get offensive or baiting. Remember, most of their readers haven't seen a frame of this film; first impressions matter."

"I'm ready," Kennedy announced, adjusting her period-appropriate bracelet. "Barry and I have prepared comprehensive talking points about Eva's emotional journey and my approach to humanizing historically marginalized women."

"Perfect," Michelle replied, resisting the urge to point out that Eva Braun, willing companion to history's greatest monster, was perhaps not the poster child for "historically marginalized women."

Barry appeared at Kennedy's side, smartphone clutched in his manicured hand. "The peonies arrived. Kennedy's energy is aligned. We're prepared to discuss her brilliant approach to Eva Braun's psychological complexity for exactly fifteen minutes per outlet. Not a second more."

"Understood." Michelle nodded. "James, Kennedy, if you'll follow me to the interview area? The first journalist has arrived."

As they headed toward the exit, André surveyed the controlled chaos of the production: the Nazi wranglers still struggling with the enormous flag, Dr. Friedman gesticulating wildly to David in a far corner, crew members hurrying to prepare for the day's actual filming while navigating the added complication of press presence.

He adjusted his designer tie and headed outside to watch history's greatest monster and his girlfriend charm the entertainment press, all while making sure no one mentioned the ten-foot Nazi flag being hastily stuffed into storage just yards away.

***

The outdoor interview area had been transformed with impressive efficiency: three director's chairs arranged in front of a neutral beige backdrop that suggested nothing more controversial than corporate blandness. Portable lighting equipment softened the natural sunlight, creating what photographers called "the golden hour at any hour" effect, designed to make everyone look approximately thirteen percent more attractive.

Michelle approached the waiting journalists with professional warmth. "Thank you all for your patience with the location change. We're excited to give you this exclusive first look at our groundbreaking production."

The three entertainment reporters, Olivia Kit from *The Hollywood Reporter*, Justin Garner from *Deadline*, and Lauren Wang from *Entertainment Weekly*, smiled with identical expressions of polite interest masking predatory anticipation.

"We apologize that Andrew Kline couldn't join us," Michelle continued smoothly. "He's currently filming a pivotal scene, and as you know, production schedules wait for no one, not even the press."

The journalists exchanged knowing glances. Olivia Kit's eyebrow lifted almost imperceptibly. Justin Garner suppressed a smirk. Lauren Wang nodded with practiced understanding.

"Of course," Wang replied. "Production schedules are sacrosanct."

Translation: *We all know you're hiding the controversial racist from us.*

"James and Kennedy will be with us shortly," Michelle continued. "We're allocating fifteen minutes per outlet: enough time for substantive conversation without disrupting our filming schedule."

"Very generous." Garner nodded.

Translation: *Barely enough time to get them to say something career-ending.*

From the sidelines, André and Ravi watched with the careful attention of bomb disposal experts. André leaned toward his colleague. "Wang's wearing her 'I'm about to ask something inappropriate' earrings. She only wears those hoops when she's planning an ambush."

"Garner is typing notes on his phone," Ravi observed. "Setting up his gotcha questions. He thinks we can't see because of the glare."

"Amateur hour," André scoffed. "If you're planning to torpedo someone's career, at least have the decency to memorize your attack plan."

Kennedy appeared first, gliding into the interview area with the confident grace of someone who had been professionally photographed since childhood. She greeted each journalist by name, with personalized references to their recent work: a masterclass in media relationship management.

"Lauren! Your piece on women directors breaking barriers was brilliant. I shared it with my entire HerStory team."

"Justin, that profile on Asian-American screenwriters was exactly the conversation the industry needs."

"Olivia, your festival coverage is always so insightful. You find gems others miss."

James followed moments later, his transformation into Hitler creating a momentary cognitive dissonance that the journalists poorly disguised. His British-Nigerian heritage combined with the iconic Hitler hairstyle and mustache produced exactly the visual disruption the production had intended: familiar yet utterly new, historically recognizable yet conceptually revolutionary.

He greeted the journalists with dignified politeness, his handshake firm, his smile genuine despite the absurdity of being in Hitler costume for a press junket.

"Thank you for your interest in our film," he said simply. "It's a challenging project with serious historical weight, and we appreciate thoughtful coverage."

The journalists nodded, their expressions shifting subtly as they recalibrated their planned questions. James's quiet dignity and educated British accent had already disrupted their expectations of how this interview might go.

Once the recording was on, the questions came rapid-fire, like artillery shells in a carefully planned assault:

"James, as a Black man, do you feel guilty portraying history's most notorious White supremacist?" Kit opened with all the subtlety of a sledgehammer.

"I approach Hitler as an actor, not primarily as a Black actor," James replied with measured patience. "My job is to reveal the human mechanisms that allow monstrosity to develop."

"Would you say playing Hitler is your way of getting revenge on White people?" Garner followed immediately.

James's eyebrow lifted fractionally, the British equivalent of an eye roll. "That interpretation fundamentally misunderstands the purpose of acting. My goal isn't revenge but revelation."

The questions continued in the same vein, each more absurd than the last:

"If you can play Hitler, should White actors be allowed to play Malcolm X?"

"Is this just another example of 'woke Hollywood' going too far?"

"You kept your Nigerian middle name professionally. Is playing Hitler a deliberate provocation given your heritage?"

"Are you worried children might see a Black Hitler as a role model?"

"Do you agree with TJ Jackson that Hitler actually had African ancestry?"

James fielded each question with increasingly strained patience, his answers growing more concise as the absurdity escalated. His responses remained thoughtful but briefer, a man recognizing the futility of nuance in an industry that trafficked in outrage.

When the journalists finally turned to Kennedy, their approach shifted dramatically: less confrontational, more inviting of her carefully packaged insights.

"Kennedy, isn't it problematic to portray Eva Braun as anything other than complicit in the Nazi regime?"

Kennedy leaned forward with practiced intensity, her expression serious but camera-ready.

"That's exactly the nuanced conversation this film invites us to have," she replied with perfectly calibrated passion. "Eva existed in an impossible system where women had limited agency. I'm not whitewashing her choices; I'm examining how power structures shape human decisions. History often reduces women to footnotes in men's stories."

Her answer continued for exactly forty-five seconds: long enough to seem substantial, short enough for social media clips, and perfectly struc tured for pull quotes.

The pattern repeated itself throughout the interviews: James received questions about race, revenge, and controversy; Kennedy fielded softballs about her "artistic journey" and "courage" in tackling difficult material. Where his responses were extracted with verbal forceps, hers flowed like a well-rehearsed TED Talk.

"James Wright approaches his craft very differently from you," Wang observed for Kennedy's final question. "Has that created tension on set?"

Kennedy's smile turned warm and generous, like someone who'd prac ticed "authentic" expressions in the mirror until they became second na ture.

"James is absolutely extraordinary," she gushed. "What I love about cre ative collaborations is how different approaches produce magical results! James brings this incredible Shakespearean technique, while I've developed my process through years in front of the camera." She launched into a perfectly structured sound bite about their "different paths to the same destination."

From the sidelines, André whispered to Ravi, "That answer will be on her Instagram within the hour, guaranteed. Hashtag CreativePartnership, hashtag ArtisticJourney, hashtag BlessedToWorkWithJames."

"With a carefully staged black and white behind-the-scenes photo they haven't even taken yet," Ravi agreed.

When the interviews concluded, the contrast between the two stars couldn't have been more stark: Kennedy energized by another successful media performance, James visibly drained by the relentless focus on everything except his actual work.

"They asked me almost exclusively about race," James observed quietly once the journalists had departed. "Not a single question about character psychology or artistic approach."

"Welcome to entertainment journalism," André replied with sympathetic cynicism. "Where substance is the enemy of clicks."

"I thought the questions were fascinating," Kennedy interjected. "They allowed us to highlight both the artistic integrity and cultural significance of our approach."

James regarded her with polite skepticism. "Did they? All I heard were attempts to generate racial controversy or validate conspiracy theories."

"That's why media training is so essential," Kennedy explained with practiced modesty. "It's about redirecting the conversation to your preferred narrative. I'd be happy to share some techniques if you'd find them helpful."

"Thank you, but I'd prefer to speak authentically, even if it's less algorithmic." The understated British shade in James's reply wasn't lost on anyone within earshot.

As James departed for makeup, André turned to Kennedy with genuine admiration. "That was a master class in media management. Every potential landmine transformed into a branding opportunity."

Kennedy's smile carried the perfect blend of humility and confidence. "Experience. I've been answering loaded questions since I was twelve. It's all about reframing: turning their agenda into yours without them noticing the redirection."

After Kennedy glided away, André found Michelle staring at her tablet with a mixture of amusement and horror.

"What?" he asked.

"Kit's already filed her first draft," Michelle replied, showing him the screen. "The headline is 'Black Hitler Star Refuses to Make Hitler "About Race" Despite Groundbreaking Casting.'"

"James was talking about the role, not actual Hitler," André frowned.

"Modern journalism, I guess," Michelle said, scrolling further. "Where context goes to die and answers are spun to drive maximum engagement."

"And Kennedy?"

"'Kennedy Oswald Bravely Confronts Female Complicity in Fascist Regimes,'" Michelle read. "Followed by three paragraphs of quotes presented exactly as she delivered them."

André snorted. "Of course. The Black actor giving thoughtful responses gets twisted into controversy. The White actress with rehearsed talking points gets quoted verbatim."

"The system works exactly as designed," Michelle replied dryly. "For some definitions of 'works.'"

They watched the journalists depart, already transforming the nuanced conversation they'd witnessed into whatever narratives would generate the most clicks.

"*The Hollywood Reporter* will focus on racial controversy," André predicted. "*Deadline* will push the 'dangerous precedent' angle. *Entertainment Weekly* will go with meta-commentary on representation."

"And none will capture what James was actually trying to express," Michelle added.

"Of course not," André replied with professional resignation. "That would require treating this like art rather than content. And in my department, art becomes discourse, discourse becomes controversy, and controversy extends our marketing budget."

He clapped his hands with sudden enthusiasm. "Now, shall we see if they've managed to fold that giant Nazi flag, or should we prepare for Holocaust Memorial organizations to start calling?"

***

CHAPTER 15

T he *Gravity* wrap party unfolded at the Terrace Pool Deck at the Sunset Tower Hotel, that perfect blend of old Hollywood glamour and contemporary LA swagger. The open-air space offered panoramic views of the city's twinkling grid, a shimmering backdrop that made even the most jaded industry veterans pause mid-networking to admire it. The venue struck that calculated balance between "exclusive enough for executives to feel superior" and "trendy enough for creatives to post without irony," with lighting designed by someone who clearly understood that the right amber glow could add forty points to Rotten Tomatoes scores and ten years to studio relationships.

Near the edge of the pool, close enough to suggest danger but far enough to prevent actual liability claims, André held court with Ravi and Big Marc, all three crowded around André's phone as if it contained nuclear launch codes instead of just the finale of @LiftieInLipstick's viral TikTok series. Their laughter punctuated the hotel's carefully curated playlist, engineered to signal cultural currency without triggering any generational anxiety. It was the sonic equivalent of a film described as "universally appealing."

"Shh, shh, this is the best part," André instructed, turning up the volume as Jade's face filled the screen, her highlighter brush waving dramatically for emphasis.

"*THIS IS IT, besties. The finale you've been waiting for,*" Jade declared with rehearsed intensity, tapping her highlighter brush against her cheek with theatrical precision. "*Let's follow the MONEY behind Black Hitler and see where it leads!* [money-with-wings emoji]"

Big Marc's booming laugh threatened to drown out the audio. "Please tell me she found our secret Nazi gold stash."

"*I got invited to a private screening of* Patriots Rising *last year,*" Jade continued, applying highlighter to her brow bone with the intensity of someone diffusing a bomb. "*That military propaganda film that basically glorified war crimes? Guess who was at the afterparty? MARCUS GOLD- STEIN and THREE Pinnacle executives! And they were LOVING IT.*"

"Marcus who?" Ravi snorted. "She can't even get the man's name right. It's Goldman, not Goldstein."

"Details are the enemy of engagement, my friend," André replied with professional admiration. "Goldman, Goldstein; what matters is the Jewish-sounding name paired with right-wing conspiracy. Classic algorithm fodder."

On screen, Jade's eyes widened dramatically as she leaned toward her ring light. "*And their CEO Raymond Fletcher has donated over $2 million to Republican campaigns! Don't tell me they didn't know where that money came from. PLEASE!* [eye-roll emoji]"

"Raymond Fletcher?" Big Marc wheezed. "Our parent company's CEO is Alicia Roberts. Has been for eight years. Who the hell is Raymond Fletcher?"

"An impressive fabrication," André said appreciatively. "Creates a villain with a wealthy White male name: perfect for the narrative. Using a real person would risk legal issues. Very savvy."

Jade examined her highlighting work in a mirror before turning back to the camera with militant seriousness. *"And the biggest bombshell? Pinnacle tried to buy the rights to Elon Musk's biography in 2023. The SAME Elon Musk who later threw actual Nazi salutes at rallies! The SAME Elon Musk who's bankrolling fascist politicians!"*

She struck a final dramatic pose with her highlighter brush held aloft like Lady Liberty's torch. *"They're using a Black actor as COVER while their money LITERALLY funds the right-wing pipeline! They're trying to defang our ability to recognize fascism by confusing the visual language we use to identify it!"*

"Damn," Ravi whispered with genuine awe. "She connected casting a Black Hitler to defending actual fascism. That's like Olympic-level mental gymnastics."

"It's the perfect storm of online discourse," André agreed. "Progressive-sounding language deployed to argue that diversity is actually secretly right-wing. It's so circular it's beautiful."

The video continued as Jade leaned in, lowering her voice to a conspiratorial whisper. *"Don't let them get away with it. Share this series everywhere. They're already trying to shadow-ban me; this video will probably disappear. Save it now."*

"Ah, the classic 'they're trying to silence me' move," André nodded appreciatively. "Creates urgency, drives shares, and preemptively discredits any response as 'censorship.' Tactical brilliance."

"Thanks for following this journey," Jade concluded with jarring perkiness. *"Highlight tutorial coming tomorrow for my regular beauty content! #FollowTheMoney #BlackHitlerExposed #RightWingPropaganda #FascismHasAFace"*

Ravi leaned in, squinting at the metrics. "Holy shit, this series got her over five hundred thousand new subscribers. She's monetizing our controversy better than we are."

"Good for her," André said with unexpected sincerity. "She's figured out the algorithm warfare better than most studios. Create outrage, present 'evidence' nobody can easily verify, wrap it all in a beauty tutorial so it technically doesn't violate community guidelines, and finish with a call to action that triggers both sharing and protective instincts."

Big Marc shook his head, laughing again. "So according to this girl, we're secretly right-wing extremists using a Black actor as cover to normalize fascism? Do I have that right?"

"That's the simplified version," Ravi confirmed. "The extended cut includes shadowy funding networks, mysterious private screenings, and apparently dead-wrong employee names. If we were this organized at actual evil, we'd probably run a more efficient production."

"Facts don't generate engagement, my friend," André replied with the weary wisdom of a digital prophet. "Righteous indignation does. And nothing generates righteous indignation like the perfect blend of plausible elements arranged in improbable ways."

André's phone buzzed with a notification. He glanced down, eyebrows rising with interest. "Speaking of engagement: our counter-content strategy is working. The fact-checking video we seeded through that film historian channel has hit two million views in twelve hours."

"How much did we pay them to 'independently' debunk her claims?" Big Marc asked.

"Twenty grand through three shell companies," André replied without hesitation. "Worth every penny. Their audience skews older, more educated; perfect demo to create counter-narrative weight."

"And our analytics?" Ravi inquired, reaching for his gin and tonic.

André's smile widened as he pulled up another screen. "Spectacular. Pre-awareness metrics are through the roof. Unaided recall at eighty-two percent among target demos. Social mentions up four hundred thousand percent month-over-month. Media coverage triple our annual average."

"All thanks to pink-haired Jade and her conspiracy theories," Big Marc chuckled.

"Not just her," André corrected. "Her wild claims spawned thirty-seven response videos, each with their own audience. Film Twitter has spent approximately nine million words debating our casting choice. YouTubers have created three-hour deep dives analyzing footage from our other movies."

Big Marc whistled, impressed. "All this noise about a movie that's not even out yet."

"The best marketing campaigns are the ones where the audience does the work for you," André said, pocketing his phone. "People are fighting about 'Black Hitler' in corners of the internet I didn't even know existed. Reddit threads, Discord servers, TikTok comment sections; they're all doing our promotion for free. It really works for our budget."

"And all we had to do was cast a Black actor as Hitler and wait for the internet to implode," Ravi added.

"Technically, we also had to survive a production involving Kennedy's entourage, TJ's conspiracy theories, and Camilla's therapeutic interventions," André amended. "Which reminds me: where is our beautiful disaster of a therapist tonight?"

"Kennedy didn't invite her," Ravi revealed. "Apparently Camilla made the mistake of suggesting Kennedy's connection to Eva Braun might be 'unhealthily narcissistic' during their final session."

"A professional assessment Kennedy did not appreciate," André guessed.

"Kennedy had her removed from set within the hour," Ravi confirmed. "Called her a 'toxically negative presence' who was 'disrupting her artistic alignment.'"

"This business," André said, raising his glass. "Never a dull moment."

"Speaking of moments." Big Marc nodded toward the bar. "Check out the unlikely trio."

***

At the bar, an elegant marble affair that screamed "we paid extra for this stone to look expensive in every photo", James, Andrew, and Aaron sat in a row like the setup to a joke no one had yet delivered. James, fully himself again after months of Hitler transformations, nursed a whiskey neat. Aaron hunched slightly over a craft beer with an insufferably clever name that had grown warm from neglect. And Andrew Kline, once Hollywood's most notorious bad boy, held what appeared to be a virgin margarita, complete with salt rim and a tiny umbrella that seemed comically incongruous against his weathered gravitas.

"What actually is that?" James asked, eyeing the colorful concoction with amused curiosity.

"Virgin strawberry margarita," Andrew replied unapologetically. "Back in my drinking days, I would've never gone near one of these. Too worried about looking soft. Real men drink bourbon straight, right?" He snorted. "What bullshit. Turns out when you're not looking for the fastest way to get smashed, taste actually matters. And girls' drinks without the alcohol are ridiculously good."

"I'll take your word for it." James smiled, lifting his whiskey in a small toast.

"Three years sober next month," Andrew added, his expression a complex mixture of pride and something more vulnerable. "Never thought I'd make it this far."

"Congratulations," Aaron said with genuine warmth. "That's truly impressive."

Andrew stirred his drink. "Best thing I ever did. Well, that and this movie, weirdly enough. Never thought I'd get a second shot at a decent role after everything."

A comfortable silence settled between them: three men who had navigated the bizarre intensity of the *Gravity* production and somehow emerged with mutual respect intact. For a moment, they were just colleagues sharing a drink at the end of a challenging project, the absurdity of their situation temporarily set aside.

James broke the silence, voicing a question that had clearly been on his mind for some time. "Andrew, something I've been wondering... why haven't you ever told your side of the story? All these controversies they blame you for, the Confederate shirt, the plantation wedding, lack so much context." He hesitated, then pressed on. "The more I've gotten to know you, the more I realize how much the public narrative about you is missing."

Andrew's expression shifted to something more guarded. "What would be the point? Nobody wants the complicated version of anything anymore."

"Still, it might help people understand."

"Understand what?" Andrew cut in, not unkindly. "That I grew up dirt poor in rural Arkansas where Confederate flags were as common as pickup trucks? That my wedding was at that plantation because when I lived in the trailer park it looked like the home of the gods? That I was blackout drunk when I put on that shirt someone handed me at a party? Hollywood loves context for characters but hates it for actors. Makes for cleaner headlines." He shook his head. "Actors are commodities, James. Valuable when we're rising, disposable when we fall. When I was making studios money, they overlooked my 'eccentricities.' When I became a liability, they discarded me."

"That's cynical." Aaron frowned.

"That's accurate," Andrew countered without heat. "Look, I'm not claiming to be a saint. At my worst, I was self-destructive, unreliable, and a nightmare on set. I earned a lot of that backlash. But the industry didn't care about my behavior until I stopped being profitable."

He took a sip of his virgin margarita. "Anyway, I'm grateful for this second chance. Getting to work with talented people again, doing what I love." He turned to James with unexpected sincerity. "Especially you. I wasn't sure what to expect, but you're the real deal. No bullshit, no ego tricks, just solid craft."

James smiled. "Coming from a two-time Oscar winner, I'll take that as high praise."

"Speaking of which," Aaron said, raising his glass. "To complex villains."

"To complex villains," James and Andrew echoed, clinking glasses.

"And to the rare occasion when Hollywood accidentally makes something meaningful while trying to make money," Andrew added. "Like finding a diamond while mining for social media content."

"Your Richard III was what made me want to work with you," Andrew revealed. "When Aaron showed me the recording, I recognized something I've always tried to do in my own work: finding the person under the madness and presenting them to the world in their reality."

"That's precisely what drew me to your performance in *Cold Harbor,*" James replied. "Your serial killer was terrifying precisely because you made him comprehensible."

Aaron looked between them, shaking his head with amused disbelief. "Who would have thought? A posh Nigerian-British Shakespeare veteran and a reformed bad boy from Arkansas becoming the best of friends. If the public could see you two now..."

"They'd take pictures of my drink and start a countdown to my next bender," Andrew laughed without bitterness.

"Twitter analysts would have a field day," James agreed. "'Sources close to the production say Kline's sobriety is a publicity stunt.'"

"'Body language experts analyze tense exchange between controversial co-stars,'" Aaron added, mimicking a headline.

Their laughter drew attention from nearby partygoers, including Michelle and Sarah, who approached with the slight unsteadiness of people several drinks into their evening.

"What's so funny?" Michelle asked, sliding onto the stool next to Aaron. "Share with the class."

"Just imagining how the media would interpret three guys having a pleasant conversation at a bar," Aaron explained.

"With at least six hidden agendas and a secret power struggle," Sarah added, signaling the bartender. "Because heaven forbid people just get along."

"I should probably head out," Andrew said, finishing his drink. "It's already past my old-man bedtime."

"You're leaving already?" Sarah protested. "It's only," she checked her watch and seemed surprised by the result, "ten fifteen? When did that happen?"

"Some of us need our ten hours," Andrew explained, standing. "James, Aaron, it's been a pleasure working with you both. I look forward to reuniting for the release."

After exchanging genuine handshakes, Andrew departed with the quiet dignity of a man who had learned the hard way to leave parties while they were still enjoyable.

"I still can't believe how well that worked out," Michelle said once Andrew was gone. "When Victoria told me we'd cast him, I ordered industrial-strength aspirin in bulk."

"You weren't the only one with concerns," Aaron admitted. "But he was a complete professional. Never late, always prepared, sober as a judge."

"Speaking of sober," Sarah interjected, "I am decidedly not, and I need someone to drive me home later."

"The studio's providing car service for everyone," Aaron assured her. "Drink responsibly but without transportation anxiety."

"My hero," Sarah declared, dramatically patting his cheek.

Michelle laughed, the sound slightly looser than her usual carefully modulated public relations tone. "I can always handle my alcohol. Even when I was a boy, I could drink the other guys under the table."

A split second of silence followed as Michelle's eyes widened, registering what she'd just said.

"I mean," she began, then stopped, looking at the surprised faces around her. "Oh. Well. That wasn't how I planned to bring that up."

"Five drinks in is rarely the optimal disclosure strategy," Sarah said gently.

James looked between them, processing this new information with calm consideration.

"You don't seem shocked," Michelle said to him.

"Aaron, Sarah, and I were just talking about how outward appearances rarely tell the complete story," James replied with a warm smile. "Also, my father's name is Michael, so that might have been confusing anyway."

The tension broke as Michelle laughed with genuine relief. "Probably for the best then."

"Besides," Sarah added, "we're sitting here with a man who spent six months as 'Black Hitler.' I think we're well past the point of being shocked by identity complexities."

"Fair point," Michelle conceded. "Though I'm never sure which is more surprising to people: that I'm trans or that I work in a high-stress PR job voluntarily."

"Definitely the PR job," Aaron deadpanned. "No sane person would choose that career."

Their laughter drew André's attention from across the room. He approached with his characteristic swagger, Ravi close behind.

"What's happening at the cool kids' table?" André asked, sliding into the conversation with the practiced ease of a man whose LinkedIn profile probably listed "seamless social integration" as a professional skill.

"We're discussing the fundamental absurdity of the entertainment industry," Aaron replied. "You know, our collective decision to spend millions of dollars making pretend for a living while convincing ourselves it's both art and commerce."

"My favorite subject!" André declared, pulling up a chair. "After creating a film about history's greatest evil with a cast including a Black British actor, a rom-com star who wants Eva Braun to be a feminist icon, and a controversial Oscar winner making his comeback, I've concluded that this business is beyond satire."

"You forgot the conspiracy historian who thinks Hitler had African ancestry," Michelle added.

"And the therapist who doesn't have a psychology degree," Sarah contributed.

"And the executive who greenlit the whole thing to spite a colleague," Aaron finished.

André raised his glass. "To the lunatic asylum that is Hollywood, where we somehow turned 'Black Hitler' from an industry joke into *Gravity*. I think we might have accidentally created art while trying to win an internet argument."

"Victoria will be insufferable if this works," Aaron groaned. "She'll have that smug 'I deliberately cast a Black Hitler and won' expression in every meeting for the next decade."

"Victoria is already insufferable," Michelle countered. "But if we pull this off, she'll be insufferable with a new production deal and executive power.

She'll put 'disruptor of historical narratives' in her email signature and get a profile in *Vanity Fair* about her 'brave approach to representation.'"

"Speaking of unexpected success stories," André said, turning to James, "you've become quite the industry darling. Three agencies fighting to sign you, two major directors pursuing you for projects, and Kennedy keeps tagging you in Instagram tributes to your 'artistic brilliance' that somehow feature more photos of her than you."

"Kennedy's campaign to appear artistically elevated through association continues unabated," Michelle translated. "She's curating a narrative where she bravely embraced your 'controversial casting' while 'elevating the female narrative in Hitler's circle.' I believe yesterday's post featured the hashtag 'BreakingBarriersWithJames' next to a photo where you're barely visible behind her perfectly contoured cheekbones."

Sarah raised her glass. "To surviving the madness with our spirits and careers intact. And to bringing actual artistry to a project that began as an elaborate industry chess move."

"And to all of you," James replied with sincere warmth, "for making this bizarre experience something I'll actually miss."

The night continued, the city lights twinkling beyond the pool deck like earthbound stars bearing witness to that rarest of Hollywood phenomena: genuine connection amid strategic networking.

Tomorrow would bring new projects, new controversies, new algorithm-optimized outrage cycles. But tonight, they were simply colleagues who had survived the production of "Black Hitler" and lived to tell the tale, a little piece of industry myth-making already taking shape in the retelling.

And in Hollywood, that counted for something like magic.

***

POST-PRODUCTION

Post-production began, as artistic compromise often does in Hollywood, with too many cooks, not enough kitchen, and a hundred different recipes for the same meal.

CHAPTER 16

Aaron's temple throbbed with the pain that only came from conversations with pretentious composers. He ended the call with Gabriel "Gabe" Trent mid-tirade, having absorbed the morning's demands: the Vienna Philharmonic flown to Los Angeles, because the musicians "breathe the same cultural air that shaped the era"; a composer budget already fifty percent over its original allocation; and something called a glass armonica, which Aaron had briefly mistaken for an exorcism requirement. There were, Gabe had informed him, no alternatives to authentic art.

A message alert flashed on Aaron's phone screen: Lucy, reminding him about the editing session starting in fifteen minutes, no doubt at Victoria's demand.

He quickened his pace through Pinnacle's corridors, heading toward the editing suites. As he rounded the corner, he spotted André and Ravi near the coffee station, both laughing hysterically at something on André's phone.

"You two look happy," Aaron observed, sliding his phone into his pocket. "I could use a laugh."

André looked up, his grin widening. "Aaron! Perfect timing. Have you seen PatriotZach1776's latest masterpiece? This kid has single-handedly created the fresh controversy we needed to kick off post-production."

"Another outrage merchant?" Aaron asked wearily.

Ravi turned the phone so Aaron could see: A red-faced teenager in a gaming chair, American flag mounted behind him, gesticulating wildly. The title read: "HOLLYWOOD'S LATEST AFRICAN WARLORD MOVIE NOBODY ASKED FOR!"

Aaron's brow furrowed. "Is he... is he talking about our movie? About Hitler?"

"He's confusing it with some kind of African dictator film," André confirmed, barely containing his glee. "The kid has never even watched our trailer. He saw a brief clip of James in uniform and jumped to conclusions. His entire rant is about how 'Hollywood is obsessed with African warlords' and how 'nobody asked for this.'"

"It's completely incoherent," Ravi added. "But it's generating millions of views. The comment section is a goldmine of people arguing, none of whom have seen the actual film. He's actively sending people to our teaser trailer!"

André's eyes sparkled with the joy of a marketing executive witnessing accidental viral content. "A few more controversies like this, and we might actually have extra money for Victoria to allocate toward awards season." He paused. "Not that I would ever suggest such a thing."

Aaron checked his watch. "I need to get to editing. First day with Cris St. Claire."

"Ah, the 'Oscar Whisperer.'" André nodded appreciatively. "Getting him was a coup. Though he's certainly earned his reputation for believing editors are more important than directors or actors."

"Thanks for the reminder," Aaron muttered.

"Is Barry going to be there?" André asked innocently. "What was her contractual requirement again? One representative during editing?"

"Yeah, Barry Hickson," Aaron confirmed grimly. "Her agent. He's supposed to arrive at ten."

André winced. "Good luck with that. I'll bring you a whiskey in a coffee cup midday if you'd like."

"I might take you up on that," Aaron said, already dreading the combination of Cris's renowned perfectionism and Barry's aggressive agent tactics.

As Aaron approached the editing suite, he could already hear raised voices. His pace slowed, a survival instinct kicking in as he identified Barry's sharp tone cutting across Cris's deeper rumble.

"Absolute hell will fucking freeze over before I allow some agent to dictate artistic choices in my editing bay!" Cris was shouting.

"My client's contract clearly states observer status with commentary rights during editing," Barry fired back. "You can take your artistic integrity elsewhere."

Aaron pushed open the door, forcing his face into a neutral expression. "Good morning! I see you two have already met."

Cris, a barrel-chested man with a silver ponytail and the intensity of someone who viewed each frame as a matter of life and death, turned to Aaron with barely contained fury. "Get him out of here. Now."

Barry straightened his Zegna suit, smartphone clutched like a weapon. "I have a contractually guaranteed right to be here. Kennedy's input needs representation."

"I don't give a rat's ass about Kennedy's input," Cris snapped. "I've cut films for Scorsese. For Spielberg. For Nolan. None of them had their actor's agent hovering over my shoulder like a vulture."

"Gentlemen," Aaron interjected, closing the door behind him. "Let's take a breath. Barry, you do have contractual observation rights."

"Observation," Cris emphasized. "Not participation."

"And Cris, you remain our lead editor with final creative control, subject to my approval as director," Aaron continued smoothly. "Now, can we proceed like professionals trying to make the best film possible?"

Barry's eyes narrowed, but he took a step back. "Fine. But Kennedy has specific concerns about Eva's screen time and character development."

"I'm sure she does," Cris muttered.

"Let's start with the first assembly," Aaron suggested, desperate to move past the confrontation. "Barry can observe, take notes for Kennedy, and we can address specific concerns at appropriate intervals."

Cris grumbled but returned to his workstation, hands moving over the controls with practiced efficiency. As the editor immersed himself in his craft, Barry pulled Aaron aside, his voice lowered to a dangerous whisper.

"What's being done about PatriotZach1776?" Barry demanded. "That little Twitch twit is dragging our film through the mud."

Aaron blinked. "Marketing is handling it. The appropriate response is generally silence; engaging directly would just amplify his reach."

"No response?" Barry looked incredulous. "This idiot is telling millions of followers our film is some kind of African dictator propaganda piece. The studio needs to set the record straight and protect Kennedy's image."

"His audience is mostly teenage gamers," Aaron pointed out. "They're not exactly Kennedy's demographic of left-leaning White women aged nineteen to forty-five."

"His clips are being shared across platforms," Barry insisted. "This morning alone, three entertainment blogs picked up the story. The studio needs to respond publicly, put this shit in his place, and stand by their brave artistic choices."

Barry's phone buzzed. He glanced at it, then back at Aaron. "We'll continue this discussion later. Kennedy needs me to handle something."

As Barry stepped outside to take the call, Aaron exchanged a look with Cris, who rolled his eyes dramatically.

"I should have become a dentist like my mother wanted," Aaron sighed.

"Dentistry has its own headaches," Cris replied grimly. "But at least teeth don't have agents."

***

Victoria adjusted her elegant suit jacket as her driver navigated the evening traffic toward Nobu Los Angeles. She touched the leather folio beside her for the fourth time, her armor for the upcoming battle. She checked her reflection in her compact mirror: not vanity but strategy. In this industry, appearances weren't superficial; they were ammunition.

Her phone buzzed with a text from André, containing a link to a Tik-Tok video. *New reverse psyop series just dropped. TruthHunterRyan claims LiftieInLipstick is our PLANT to discredit legitimate criticism. The snake is eating its own tail now.*

Victoria tapped the link, watching with growing amusement as a woman with short blonde hair and conspiracy-board aesthetics explained how Jade from LiftieInLipstick was actually a studio plant designed to make criticism of Black Hitler seem absurd.

"Follow the money!" TruthHunterRyan whispered dramatically. "Jade's sponsored by OrganiLife Cosmetics. Who owns OrganiLife? Sunburst Media Group. Who sits on Sunburst's board? THREE former executives from the SAME STUDIO making Black Hitler!"

Victoria couldn't help but laugh. Pinnacle had no connection to Sunburst Media Group or OrganiLife Cosmetics, but the conspiracy was delicious in its elaborate fabrication. This was even better than they could have orchestrated themselves: the internet doing their marketing for them, spinning ever more complex webs of outrage and counter-outrage.

She texted André back: *Let's see if I can't get Sean to help fund our Hollywood psyop. Perfect timing for my awards budget discussion.*

The car pulled up to Nobu, where the sleek minimalist interior served as both sanctuary and stage for Hollywood's power players. Unlike its Malibu sibling, this location lacked ocean views, offering instead the carefully curated spectacle of industry elite engaged in the performance of casual dining. At any given table, one could spot studio executives finalizing deals, stars avoiding paparazzi in discreet corners, and agents whispering career-altering promises over plates of pristine sashimi that cost more than most people's utility bills.

Sean Lynch was already seated at a prime table, strategically positioned to see and be seen by anyone who mattered, while maintaining just enough distance from tourists to prevent unwanted interruptions.

"Victoria," he greeted, rising partially from his chair in that peculiar half-stand of male executives acknowledging female colleagues. "You're looking dangerous with that folio. Must be budget season."

"Sean." She smiled, taking her seat. "Always a pleasure to watch you pretend this isn't a meeting about money."

Victoria deliberately placed her sleek Italian leather portfolio on the table rather than pulling out a tablet: physical materials conveyed gravitas in a digital age, and she needed every psychological advantage for this conversation.

A waiter materialized to take their drink orders: Sean's usual Japanese whisky, Victoria's martini, extra dry. The ritual of expensive alcohol serving as social lubricant for even more expensive requests.

"So," Sean began once the waiter departed, "I've been following the online discourse around your Hitler project. Or *Gravity*, I should say." He made air quotes around the title. "I have to admit, your approach has generated remarkable engagement. The left thinks it's either revolutionary or offensive, the right can't decide if they're more upset about historical revision or excited about a Black man being associated with evil. It's quite the Rorschach test."

"That's the beauty of it," Victoria replied. "When no one knows what position to take, everyone keeps talking while they figure it out."

"The teaser looks great. And James Wright." Sean shook his head. "The man is extraordinary. I watched some dailies; I haven't seen acting that compelling since Day-Lewis in *There Will Be Blood*."

"Which is precisely why I'm here," Victoria said, smoothly transitioning to her agenda as their drinks arrived. She opened her portfolio, revealing meticulously printed analytics reports rather than the expected digital presentation. "We need to lock in our festival budget now. Cannes submissions close in March, which gives us about six months to position this film correctly."

She flipped to a separate page: a name printed in elegant typeface surrounded by an impressive list of awards campaigns. "I also want to secure Cynthia Teback as our awards strategist."

Sean nearly choked on his whisky. "Teback? 'The Statue-Maker' herself? Victoria, be reasonable. She's famously selective about her projects, and her retainer starts quite high."

"Forty thousand monthly, escalating to two-hundred during peak season," Victoria finished for him. "With her special 'Alchemist' package clocking in at one-point-eight million for the full campaign."

"Precisely," Sean said. "That's a significant chunk of any awards budget before we've even locked picture."

"In this climate, that's exactly when you need to lock down Teback," Victoria countered. "Her availability for the festival-to-awards pipeline is already limited, and you know that everyone will be pursuing her by then.

I'd rather not compete for her attention in three months when we could secure her exclusive focus now."

Sean sipped his whisky, eyebrows rising as he glimpsed the figure at the bottom of the first page. "Three million? Victoria, this isn't *The English Patient*. It's a controversial historical drama with a concept that half of America already hates."

"Exactly why we need Teback's unparalleled ability to transform controversy into prestige," Victoria countered, sliding forward a print-out of social media analytics. "We've generated more pre-release conversation than any Pinnacle film in the last decade. But here's the industry truth: controversial films need prestigious launchers. Without Cannes validation, we're just a provocative concept. With a Palme d'Or nomination, we're revolutionary cinema."

She flipped to the next page: a carefully constructed festival strategy with precise budget allocations. "This covers creation of festival-specific promotional materials, press representatives in key European markets, talent travel and accommodations, private screenings for selection committees, and 'cultural exchange events' with influencers."

"Cultural exchange events," Sean repeated dryly. "You mean bribing film bloggers with fancy dinners."

"I prefer to think of it as 'contextualizing our artistic vision through interpersonal dialogue,'" Victoria replied evenly. "It's an investment, not an expense."

Sean leaned back, studying her with newfound interest. "You're sure Teback would even take this on? The woman who refused to represent Scorsese's last film because it 'lacked transformation potential'?"

"I'll convince her," Victoria said with quiet confidence. "But I need budget authorization first. Teback doesn't even take meetings without a guaranteed retainer."

"We're two weeks into post, Victoria." Sean swirled his whisky thoughtfully. "Don't you think you're getting ahead of yourself?"

"In today's landscape? Not at all." Victoria flipped to another page in her portfolio, revealing a carefully plotted timeline. "Festival submissions for next spring are due in six months. If we want Cannes, and we do, we need to start generating the right buzz with the selection committee by December. That means private screenings of early cuts, strategic leaks to European critics, and the right narrative framing. And nobody frames narratives like Cynthia Teback."

"And how much would the full awards campaign cost, hypothetically speaking?" Sean asked, though his tone suggested he already knew the answer wouldn't be small.

"For a proper, competitive FYC campaign with Teback at the helm? Eight million minimum," Victoria said without blinking. "But we can approve that in phases. Right now, I'm just asking for the three million festival budget, which includes Teback's initial engagement."

Sean's glass stopped halfway to his mouth. "Eight million for awards when the time comes? Marcus Goldman is also requesting awards consideration for his refugee immigration project."

"*Journey's End*," Victoria supplied. "The heartwarming tale of African refugees trekking across continents to reach America. The one I passed on; how convenient that it landed with Marcus."

"Its trailer tested extremely well with critics," Sean noted. "Early screenings are generating serious buzz."

"Among how many people? Forty academic types and film festival programmers in controlled environments?" Victoria challenged. "We're tracking real-world engagement here. André's team has documented a thirty-five hundred percent spike in online conversation about James playing Hitler in the past week alone. Our teaser hit five million views in twenty-four hours, breaking our internal record."

Sean leaned forward slightly. "And the like-to-dislike ratio?"

"An exceptional thirty percent negative," Victoria said triumphantly. "For a movie about Black Hitler, that's practically universal approval."

Sean's expression remained carefully neutral as he weighed the financial equations in his head. "Two million for now," he finally said. "Enough to cover the essential festival strategy and Teback's initial retainer. If she signs on and Cannes bites, we can discuss the additional funding for expanded festival presence and early awards positioning."

Victoria hid her disappointment. "Teback will need certainty."

"Teback will understand how studio financing works," Sean finished. "Two million is generous for a film that hasn't even got a rough cut. Remember, if the studio has limited resources, they'll be choosing between your project and Goldman's. And *Journey's End* has all the traditional awards elements without the inherent controversy."

"No one's even heard of it," Victoria countered. "Apart from internal memos and a small *New York Times* mention."

"It doesn't matter," Sean replied. "It checks all the boxes that make critics and awards voters feel good about themselves without challenging them. Sometimes that's enough."

Victoria took a deliberate sip of her martini, recalculating. "Thanks for getting us Cris St. Claire. I know he's a personal friend."

"He's a genius," Sean replied. "And accepting his standard retainer was a significant favor to the studio."

"I'm sure," Victoria said, her tone neutral. "I heard Goldman got Allen Lee for *Journey's End*. Was that a favor too?"

Sean's expression shifted to something more genuine. "Yes, actually. David Fincher connected us personally. We got very lucky there."

The rest of dinner proceeded with the familiar rhythm of industry smalltalk: which executives were rumored to be leaving which studios, which stars were difficult on set, which upcoming slate announcements would reshape the competitive landscape. But Victoria's mind remained focused on her next move. Two million wasn't enough for the comprehensive strategy she'd envisioned, and she knew Sean wasn't being entirely forthcoming about the competition for awards resources.

As her car took her home later that evening, Victoria pulled up PatriotZach1776's latest video on her phone: the teenager now fully committed to his misinterpretation of their movie as "another African dictator film nobody asked for."

"WAKE UP PATRIOTS!" he shouted, red-faced and animated. "Next they're gonna make a movie about some African guy inventing electricity or computers or some made-up BS!"

Victoria smiled to herself. The outrage machine was operating at peak efficiency. When actual White supremacists were attacking your film for all the wrong reasons, the conversation inevitably shifted in your favor. Perhaps there was an opportunity here that Sean wasn't seeing: a narrative to leverage for both publicity and festival positioning.

She texted André: *Have you seen the responses to PatriotZach1776? What if we positioned them as vindication of our approach? "The film White nationalists don't want you to see" has a certain compelling ring to it. Might help with our Cannes narrative.*

His response came almost immediately: *Always ten steps ahead. Already drafted press strategy leveraging right-wing outrage as proof of our artistic relevance. Will share tomorrow. European festival programmers love nothing more than feeling they're championing something American conservatives hate.*

Victoria leaned back, satisfied. The festival budget battle wasn't over; it was just entering its next phase. And if there was one thing she'd learned in this industry, it was that controversy, properly channeled, could be converted directly into gold statuettes.

In Hollywood's upside-down economy, even racist teenage gamers who completely misunderstood your movie could become unlikely allies in the campaign for prestige. The absurdity was perfect, the circularity complete.

Two million down, nine to go. And now she just needed to convince Cynthia Teback,the woman who'd once told Steven Spielberg his Holocaust film was "too expected", that *Gravity* was worthy of her legendary narrative alchemy.

***

CHAPTER 17

André Reynolds was dreaming about an algorithm that could predict Academy Award winners with perfect accuracy when his phone's ringtone shattered the illusion. He fumbled in the darkness, knocking over a glass of water before his fingers closed around the vibrating device.

"This better be about Hitler," he mumbled, squinting at the screen that read *Michelle Park - 5:43 a.m.*

Beside him, Nadia groaned and pulled a pillow over her head. "It's not even six. Tell whoever it is that normal humans require sleep."

André slipped out of bed, phone still ringing, and padded barefoot toward the hallway. "It's Michelle; must be important."

"I'm on double shifts this week," Nadia reminded him, voice muffled by the pillow. "Get out of here with your marketing emergency."

André stepped into the hallway, closing the bedroom door behind him, and answered with the combination of alertness and irritation that long-time executives perfected for pre-dawn crisis calls.

"Please tell me James Wright hasn't been arrested for actual war crimes," he said by way of greeting.

Michelle's voice came through tight and clipped. "Kennedy posted a response to PatriotZach1776 last night. Without consulting anyone."

André's foggy brain cleared instantly. "She did what? Those assistants of hers should confiscate her phone at bedtime. Post-midnight social media is like drunk dialing an ex; nothing good ever comes from it." He started toward his home office. "What's the damage?"

"It's... extensive," Michelle replied. "She's gone full White savior while attempting to defend James against racism. There are references to African dictators being less evil than White European leaders, claims about colonialism, and a bizarre tangent about 'real film fans' that's being torn apart online."

"Sounds like Tuesday in Hollywood," André muttered, booting up his laptop. "Hold on, let me pull it up."

He navigated to Kennedy's Instagram while Michelle continued.

"The worst part is her team clearly tried to stop her. There's literally a line where she says, 'My team advised against it,' right before launching into this train wreck."

André found the post and scanned it quickly, his expression shifting from professional concern to something resembling awe at the sheer magnitude of the miscalculation.

"'No African dictator has EVER approached the scale of systematic evil that White European leaders have inflicted upon this world,'" he read aloud. "Well, I'm sure the survivors of Rwanda, Uganda, and the Democratic Republic of Congo will be relieved to hear their suffering wasn't quite evil enough to qualify."

"Do you think she genuinely doesn't see how tone-deaf this is?" Michelle asked. "She's speaking for James, lecturing about racism, and making wildly inaccurate historical claims. All while positioning herself as the brave woman standing up against bullies."

André scrolled through the comments, his marketing brain already calculating the damage. "Look at her comments. Her primary audience: progressive White women with disposable income and Netflix accounts. They're eating this up. 'Queen speaking truth to power,' 'This is what real activism looks like.'" He scrolled further. "Though the comments from actual film industry people and BIPOC accounts are considerably less enthusiastic."

"That's putting it mildly," Michelle said. "BIPOCFilmCollective basically told her to stop white-splaining racism."

"Kennedy's done exactly what she wants," André observed. "Made a loud statement that sounds brave while doing absolutely nothing, positioned herself as an ally while speaking over the people she claims to support, and let everyone in Hollywood see her 'standing up' to a nineteen-year-old gamer with 2.3 million followers."

"About that," Michelle sighed. "PatriotZach1776 already posted an apology video yesterday evening. Hours before Kennedy's post. She's re sponding to something he already semi-walked back."

"You're kidding me." André pulled up YouTube and quickly found the video titled "MY RESPONSE TO THE HATERS."

He watched as the teenager, still red-faced but now with the distinct discomfort of someone being forced to apologize by parental figures, stumbled through a half-hearted retraction.

"So yeah, I guess it's not an African dictator movie," the kid mumbled, adjusting his oversized gaming headphones. "It's about Hitler or whatever. Still looks stupid and woke though. Why can't they just make normal movies with normal Hitler? Anyway, sorry if you got triggered or whatever. Make sure to smash that subscribe button and check out my Twitch stream!"

André leaned back in his chair, processing. "This is... workable. Not ideal, but workable. The kid's 'apology' is such a classic sorry-not-sorry that

Kennedy's overreaction still feels somewhat proportional to the general public."

"So what's our move?" Michelle asked.

"We issue a carefully worded press release to select media outlets," André decided, fingers already typing notes. "We express support for our creative team without specifically mentioning the controversy or the kid. Something like 'Pinnacle Pictures stands behind our exceptional cast and values their voices. We trust our talented team to engage with important conversations surrounding art and representation.'"

"Generic enough to mean absolutely nothing while sounding supportive," Michelle noted approvingly.

"Exactly. It makes us look like we value Kennedy's 'brave stand' without directly endorsing anything specific she said." André continued typing. "Then you need to reach out to Kennedy's team; preferably to Dani, not Miguel. Miguel's too scared of Kennedy, but Dani seems to have some sense of hierarchy. Make it clear that all movie-related social posts need to be run by us going forward."

"And James?"

"Maintain his dignified radio silence at all costs," André said firmly. "Even if he's currently fantasizing about strangling his new 'ally.'"

A soft knock on the office door interrupted him. Zoe stood in the doorway, pajama-clad and squinting against the hallway light.

"Dad? It's not even six a.m."

"Sorry, sweetheart," André said, covering the phone. "Work emergency. Did we wake you?"

"Kind of hard to sleep through 'African dictators' and 'systematic evil' discussions," she yawned, leaning against the doorframe. "More Hitler drama?"

André nodded, then returned to Michelle. "Let me call you back in fifteen. Start drafting that press release and I'll review it before we send."

He hung up and turned to his daughter. "Sorry about that. Kennedy Oswald decided to play activist on Instagram without consulting anyone."

"I saw." Zoe nodded. "It's all over my TikTok feed already. People are making these dramatic reading videos of her post with the emotional piano music in the background."

André sighed. "Of course they are."

Zoe studied him for a moment. "I don't think I've seen you in like three days."

"Has it been that long?" André frowned, genuinely surprised. "I've been practically living at the office since the teaser dropped."

"So... is it worth it?" Zoe asked, the question carrying the weight of genuine curiosity rather than teenage accusation. "All this stress and early morning calls and barely being home?"

André considered this for a moment, then gestured for her to follow him to the kitchen. "Let me make you some hot chocolate."

"Dad, I'm fourteen, not six," she protested, though she followed him anyway.

"Age is irrelevant when it comes to hot chocolate diplomacy," André replied, pulling out milk and cocoa powder. "This was how we had our best conversations when you were little, remember?"

As he worked, warming milk on the stove the way his mother had taught him, no microwaved shortcuts, he considered his daughter's question.

"When you find what you love, you'll know it," he said finally. "The stress, the ridiculous hours, the constant chaos. It's worth it when you feel that connection to the work."

"Even when you're dealing with tone-deaf actresses at six in the morning?"

André laughed. "Especially then. You know, the industry has changed so much in my twenty-plus years. When I started, we were just figuring out internet marketing. Social media barely existed."

"How did people even know about movies?" Zoe asked, accepting the steaming mug he handed her.

"We had to tell them," André said with mock seriousness. "Face to face. One human at a time. Can you imagine? Utterly inefficient."

"Sounds impossible," Zoe deadpanned. "How did you even live?"

"We didn't. We were all just waiting to be born into the social media age," André replied, taking a sip of his own cocoa.

Zoe smiled, cradling her mug. "I saw the teaser. Well, actually I saw the trailer because of that stupid PatriotZach video. But it looks... real. Like a real movie, not just a controversy with cameras."

André felt an unexpected swell of pride. His daughter had seen enough of the industry's machinery to be justifiably cynical, but her assessment hit on something important.

"That's what we're trying for," he said. "Beneath all the marketing stunts and social media controversies, Aaron and James and the team have made something with actual substance. Something that might outlast the noise."

"And Kennedy?" Zoe asked with the precision of someone who already knew the answer.

André sighed dramatically. "Kennedy is... contributing in her own special way."

Zoe laughed, a sound that reminded André why all the pre-dawn emergencies were indeed worth it.

"Things should calm down a bit once we're deeper into post-production," he promised. "The movie's in the hands of an overly egotistical surgeon, your Uncle Aaron, and a shark named Barry."

"Sounds like the setup to a joke."

"The entire industry is the setup to a joke," André replied. "We're just waiting for the punchline."

He glanced at his watch. "I need to call Michelle back. But thanks for the chat. It's a good reminder of why I do this. So I can afford your private school tuition. And you keep getting those A's in Geometry."

"Very funny," Zoe said, rolling her eyes. "But seriously, Dad? The trailer looks good. Like it might actually say something worth hearing."

As Zoe headed back to bed, André found himself genuinely touched by his daughter's assessment. In an industry built on appearance rather than substance, recognition of actual quality was the rarest currency of all.

He picked up his phone to call Michelle back. There was a fire to contain, a press release to craft, and an actress's ill-advised activism to reframe as courageously on-brand. But for a moment, he allowed himself to acknowledge that beneath all the marketing machinations, they might have actually made something real.

Then he dialed Michelle's number, sliding back into crisis management mode with practiced ease.

"Okay, so here's the plan," he said the moment she answered. "We distance ourselves from the specific claims while embracing the general sentiment. The hashtag 'StandWithJames' is actually perfect, so we'll subtly encourage that without mentioning Kennedy's post directly..."

Outside his window, Los Angeles was just beginning to wake up, unaware that its entertainment overlords had been managing perceptions, crafting narratives, and spinning controversies since before dawn; the invisible machinery behind the dream factory, operating with methodical precision regardless of the hour.

***

Victoria Martinez's office had undergone a subtle transformation over the preceding weeks. Alongside her meticulously arranged awards shelf, last adjusted during an especially frustrating call with the film's composer, a new wall featured an intricate timeline of festival submission deadlines, printed in oversized format with color-coded markers indicating priority events. The art prints,selected to convey the right amount of personality and appreciation for modern art, that once adorned her walls had been replaced with framed preliminary *Gravity* poster concepts. Shadowy, artistic renderings of James Wright in profile, the iconic haircut visible but the face obscured.

Lucy entered carrying two cups of coffee: the expensive kind from the artisanal place three blocks away, not the burned studio sludge that fueled most of Pinnacle's workforce. She'd learned early in their relationship that Victoria's caffeine preferences escalated in direct proportion to her stress levels.

"Sean sent over the paperwork for two million," Lucy announced, setting down Victoria's oat milk cortado with a half-pump of lavender syrup. "Though his assistant made a point of emphasizing it's a 'significant concession in challenging fiscal circumstances.'"

Victoria snorted, not looking up from her spreadsheet. "Translation: he's giving Marcus money too, and wants me to feel grateful for my crumbs."

"At least it's something," Lucy offered. "Two million for festivals is hardly crumbs."

"It's a million shy of what we need," Victoria countered, finally looking up. "We have until March to secure the rest if we want any shot at proper positioning." She tapped her pen against the timeline on the wall. "Cannes submissions close in six months. Venice and Toronto shortly after. Without the right narrative framework established beforehand, we're just 'that controversial Hitler movie' instead of 'this year's most boundary-breaking artistic achievement.'"

Lucy settled into the chair across from Victoria's desk. "I still can't believe Sean gave Marcus Allen Lee. He hasn't cut anything less than Oscar bait in five years."

"Oh, I believe it," Victoria's expression darkened. "Sean's deliberately pitting us against each other. Probably amuses him to watch us fight over awards resources like seagulls over a discarded sandwich. Either way, he wins."

"Do you think..." Lucy hesitated, then pressed on. "Do you think he secretly wanted you to keep the Hitler project?"

Victoria looked momentarily thrown by the suggestion, then her eyes narrowed in consideration. "That would be diabolically clever, even for Sean. Pretend to want to take it away so I'd fight to keep it, securing commitment to an impossible project..."

"You do work better with something to prove," Lucy observed carefully.

"Who cares?" Victoria waved away the thought. "Marcus isn't going to steal another Oscar from me. Not this time. We're technically on the 'same team'," she made air quotes around the phrase, "but we'll find a way to outspend him."

She stood and moved to the timeline wall, studying it with the intensity of a general planning a military campaign. "I want Best Picture. There will be dozens more movies like Marcus's well-intentioned refugee drama, but there is only one Black Hitler. This won't be done again."

"So what do we need to show Sean and the board to get the additional budget?" Lucy asked, pulling out her tablet to take notes.

"Results," Victoria replied simply. "Early critic response, festival selection committee interest, and most importantly, industry buzz that extends beyond the controversy. We need to convince him this is genuinely award-worthy, not just algorithmically optimized for social media engagement."

Lucy nodded, typing rapidly. "We'll need to start the festival campaign in December for March entry. Critical screenings for key European critics, quiet dinners with selection committee members, strategic leaks to prestigious publications."

"Precisely. And for that, we need the full three million I asked for, minimum."

"We could cut costs in some areas," Lucy suggested, scrolling through the budget spreadsheet. "Maybe reduce the private reception budget at Cannes? Or scale back the talent travel accommodations?"

Victoria's expression suggested Lucy had proposed selling one of her kidneys. "Absolutely not. Those private receptions are where half the selection decisions actually happen. And Kennedy would have a social media meltdown if she didn't get a suite with Mediterranean views. We'd be fielding posts about 'the patriarchal budget constraints of female-led films' for weeks."

"What about the critic dinners at Sketch?" Lucy tried again. "That's nearly $150,000 for one evening."

"Those British critics are the gateway to BAFTA, and BAFTA momentum directly feeds Oscar voting patterns," Victoria countered. "I need those stuffy Brits tipsy on overpriced wine and three-Michelin-star food while James Wright charms them in person."

Lucy sighed, setting down her tablet. "So we're not actually looking to cut anything."

"Correct," Victoria confirmed unapologetically. "We're going to get the full budget by convincing the board this is our best shot at major awards. I refuse to let Goldman outspend us into relevance." She picked up her coffee, taking a contemplative sip. "This movie is literally called *Gravity*. It's begging for awards consideration based on our name and casting choice alone."

Lucy's phone buzzed. She glanced at it, then looked up with barely suppressed amusement. "Speaking of social media controversies, have you seen TruthHunterRyan's second video? 'Exposing Hollywood's Psyop Behind Hitler Stays White'?"

Victoria's expression brightened with genuine interest. "No. Is it as absurd as the first one?"

Lucy turned her tablet toward Victoria and pressed play. The screen filled with a serious-looking woman in her thirties wearing what appeared to be a tactical vest over a t-shirt, gesturing dramatically at a laptop.

"The response to part one has been INSANE," the woman declared, leaning intensely toward the camera. "Their bots are mass-reporting me, which proves I'm over the target!"

Victoria settled back in her chair, already enjoying the spectacle. "Ah yes, the classic 'persecution means I'm right' defense. A timeless classic."

"Now for the smoking gun," Ryan continued, her expression growing conspiratorial. "LiftieInLipstick claims to be a makeup artist from Portland. But look at this!" The screen showed a blurry Instagram post. "This is Jade at the Sunburst Media holiday party SEVEN MONTHS AGO! Why would a 'small Portland makeup artist' be at an LA industry party? MAKE IT MAKE SENSE!"

"Is that even the same person?" Lucy squinted at the screen. "That could be literally any White woman with pink hair."

"Details destroy conspiracy theories," Victoria replied, waving away the question. "Don't interrupt our entertainment with logic."

The video continued, growing increasingly unhinged as Ryan outlined an elaborate theory involving fake septum piercings, industry plants, and corporate psyops designed to discredit legitimate criticism.

"Here's what's really happening," Ryan whispered urgently. "They KNEW this movie would face criticism from both sides. So they created their OWN criticism they could control!"

Victoria burst out laughing. "I wish we were that organized! If we could orchestrate conspiracies this elaborate, we wouldn't need to fight for budget increases."

"They're trying to make ALL criticism look unhinged," Ryan continued, pointing aggressively at the camera, "by having this 'leftist creator' make bad arguments that distract from the REAL issues; for example, how this movie whitewashes American imperialism!"

Lucy paused the video, looking genuinely confused. "How does a movie about Hitler whitewash American imperialism? That doesn't even make sense."

"It doesn't have to make sense," Victoria explained with the weariness of someone who'd spent too long in the content trenches. "It just has to sound vaguely intellectual while being outraged. That's the perfect algorithm fuel: just specific enough to seem credible, just vague enough that no one can definitively prove it wrong."

She shook her head, still smiling.

Lucy unpaused the video for its dramatic conclusion.

"Oh, and that septum piercing? FAKE," Ryan whispered. "I have a friend in VFX who analyzed the footage. It GLITCHES in frame 372! Wake up!"

The screen filled with text: "They're getting NERVOUS! Part three coming if I don't get [banned]!"

Victoria leaned back, expression shifting to something more contemplative. "Send this to André. He'll want to track the engagement metrics. If it crosses a certain threshold of views, it might be worth including in our presentation to the board."

"You want to show the board conspiracy videos about our movie?" Lucy asked, surprised.

"I want to show them evidence that our film has penetrated the cultural conversation to such a degree that people are creating elaborate theories about it before it's even released," Victoria clarified. "In Hollywood's twisted economics, that kind of engagement has monetary value."

She stood and moved to her window, gazing out at the Pinnacle lot, the illusion factory where fantasies were manufactured with military precision. "The conspiracy theorists, the outraged gamers, the Twitter academics with their fifteen-part threads deconstructing our trailer; they're all doing unpaid marketing work for us. The more they talk, the more people want to see what the fuss is about."

Lucy made a note on her tablet. "So for the board presentation, we emphasize the cultural impact metrics over traditional marketing reach?"

"Exactly. We don't just have a controversial movie. We have a cultural event." Victoria turned back, expression hardening with renewed determination. "Track all engagement, positive and negative. Collect every think piece, every reaction video, every viral theory. Quantify the conversation in dollars and cents. That's how we get our extra million."

She glanced at her watch. "I need to call Sean. Make up some pretense about an urgent production matter."

"Why?" Lucy asked.

"To see if I can get him to reveal anything about Marcus's presentation strategy," Victoria replied as if it were obvious. "Know your competition."

Lucy stood to leave, then paused. "Victoria? For what it's worth, I think James's performance really is extraordinary. Beyond the controversy, beyond the marketing angles; there's something remarkable there."

Victoria's expression softened momentarily. "I know. The irony of this is that beneath all the social media noise, we might have accidentally made something with actual artistic merit." She smiled with unexpected sincerity. "Don't tell anyone I said that; it would ruin my reputation as a cynical, calculating executive."

"Your secret capacity for genuine artistic appreciation is safe with me," Lucy promised with a smile, heading toward the door.

"And Lucy?" Victoria called after her. "Get me everything you can on Allen Lee's editing schedule for *Journey's End*. I want to know exactly how much time Marcus's 'prestigious editor' is actually spending on his precious refugee drama."

Lucy nodded, unsurprised by the rapid return to competitive strategy. "Already on it."

Left alone, Victoria turned back to her spreadsheet, fingers dancing across the keyboard as she adjusted budget allocations. The numbers represented the strange alchemy of modern filmmaking: transforming controversy into conversation, conversation into prestige, and prestige into gold statuettes that would eventually necessitate rearranging her awards shelf yet again.

She had twelve weeks to secure another million dollars for a film about a Black actor playing Hitler. A sentence that would have seemed like absurdist fiction just a year ago, but now represented the peculiar reality of an industry where the boundary between art and commerce had long since dissolved into something more akin to performance art with profit margins.

And Victoria Martinez intended to win, whatever "winning" meant in this context. After all, in Hollywood's funhouse mirror version of reality, sometimes the most absurd premises yielded the most genuine results.

***

CHAPTER 18

A aron Weisman was experiencing a headache that no legally available medication could touch. The throbbing pain had graduated from mere discomfort to something with personality and possibly citizenship rights. He'd named it Kennedy, after the actress who continued to haunt his professional existence even in absence.

"This sequence is absolutely essential to understanding Eva's psychological journey," Barry insisted, jabbing his manicured finger at the monitor where Kennedy Oswald sat at a vintage dressing table, staring wistfully at her reflection with the practiced melancholy of someone who'd studied "thoughtful gazing" at drama school. "It's the perfect visual metaphor for her internal imprisonment in the gilded cage of the Third Reich."

"It's the perfect visual metaphor for narcissism," Cris countered, not bothering to hide his disdain. "Three minutes of an actress staring at herself while pretending to have profound thoughts? It's indulgent garbage that belongs in her video diary, not in my edit."

"Your edit?" Barry's eyebrows shot up with such speed they threatened to leave his forehead entirely. "I wasn't aware we'd renamed the film 'Cris

St. Claire's *Gravity*.' Kennedy's contract stipulates minimum screen time requirements that this scene helps fulfill."

"Kennedy's contract can stipulate she gets carried around set on a golden palanquin by shirtless Vikings; that doesn't make it good filmmaking," Cris retorted, his silver ponytail swinging as he gesticulated toward the monitor. "This scene contributes nothing to the narrative."

Aaron rubbed his temples, watching the two men square off across the editing bay. Three months into post-production, the Sisyphean task of bringing *Gravity* to its first rough cut had reduced him to a diplomatic middleman caught between clashing egos, all fighting for control over a film that had long since escaped anyone's individual vision.

Behind them, sprawled on the leather sofa with the casual disregard of someone whose talents apparently exempted him from basic spatial courtesy, Gabe hummed softly to himself while manipulating something on his iPad. The composer's disheveled appearance (expensive linen shirt wrinkled as if he'd slept in it for weeks, designer glasses perpetually sliding down his nose) belied his reputation as one of Hollywood's most sought-after musical geniuses.

"I remain unconvinced about the Hitler hallucination sequence," Gabe announced suddenly, as if continuing a conversation no one else had been having. "The glass armonica we used simply lacks the necessary spectral resonance."

Aaron turned wearily toward this new front in his multi-dimensional battle. "Gabe, we've discussed this. We already spent fifteen thousand dollars on that glass armonica recording. It's now the most expensive minute of music in the entire movie."

"Yes, but it's a modern instrument!" Gabe protested, leaping to his feet with unexpected agility. "I've found something revolutionary: an original Finkenbeiner glass armonica built in 1782, played by Franz Mesmer himself during his controversial hypnotherapy sessions. It's available for rental, but only for three days next week."

Barry looked completely lost. "Glass what now?"

"Armonica," Gabe corrected with the condescension reserved for those he considered musically illiterate. "The instrument Benjamin Franklin invented. Rotating glass bowls played with wet fingers to create an ethereal, almost otherworldly sound. The one we used is a crude modern replica."

"The original was banned in several German towns," Gabe continued, warming to his subject, "because people believed its harmonic resonance caused madness and hysteria. What could be more thematically perfect for Hitler's psychological collapse?"

"We already have one," Aaron began.

"A pale imitation," Gabe declared with theatrical disdain. "The Mesmer instrument produces overtones in the 4-6 kilohertz range that stimulate the limbic system in ways our current recording simply cannot. The psychological discomfort is palpable."

"And this historically authentic madness-inducing instrument costs...?" Aaron asked, already knowing the answer would be painful.

"Only twelve thousand additional dollars per day," Gabe replied, eyes gleaming with the madness Aaron had come to recognize as the look of a creative professional about to die on an extremely specific artistic hill. "A bargain at twice the price for transcendent authenticity."

"Twelve thousand more dollars for someone to run their wet fingers over slightly different glorified wine glasses?" Barry scoffed. "Meanwhile, Kennedy's pivotal mirror scene, which cost considerably more to shoot, faces the editorial guillotine."

"Because it's redundant garbage!" Cris exploded, spinning in his chair. "We already have FOURTEEN scenes establishing Eva's emotional conflict! Do we need a fifteenth where she literally stares at herself while a single elegant tear, which took seventeen takes to get right, by the way, rolls down her professionally contoured cheek?"

Aaron's phone buzzed with a text from Victoria: *Where the hell are you? Focus group starts in 45 minutes. Don't make me send André to find you.*

"Gentlemen," Aaron said, summoning the last reserves of his diplomatic energy, "we need to make some decisions quickly. I have to get this cut to the screening room for the focus group at seven."

"A focus group? Tonight?" Barry's expression shifted to alarm. "Kennedy wasn't informed about any focus group."

"It's standard procedure," Aaron replied, trying to keep his tone even. "Initial audience testing to gauge reactions before we lock picture. We have the MPAA screening next week."

"I should be there," Barry insisted. "Standing in for Kennedy."

"No actors or agents at focus groups," Cris stated flatly. "That's basic filmmaking. They'd either cry, try to defend their performances, or start editing on the spot."

"I should be there," Gabe declared, closing his iPad with a decisive snap. "To observe which musical cues resonate emotionally with the audience. Their unconscious physical responses will inform my final compositional approach."

Aaron checked his watch. Forty minutes until the screening, and he still needed to render the current cut and get it to the theater. "Here's what's happening," he announced, his tone leaving no room for negotiation. "We're keeping the orchestral score for now, Gabe. If the glass armonica is truly essential, we'll revisit after tonight's screening."

Gabe opened his mouth to protest, but Aaron raised a hand to silence him.

"Cris, include a shortened version of Kennedy's mirror scene; trim it to fifteen seconds, use the best emotional beat, and integrate it into the existing sequence where Eva learns about the assassination attempt."

"You're compromising the structural integrity," Cris began.

"And it undermines the emotional weight of," Barry jumped in simultaneously.

"This is my film!" Aaron's voice cut through their objections with unexpected force. Both men fell silent, startled by the outburst from the normally composed director. "I need this cut rendered and delivered to the screening room in thirty minutes, or Victoria Martinez will personally ensure none of us works in this town again. Now, can we please act like professionals for half an hour?"

A stunned silence fell over the editing bay. Even Gabe seemed momentarily subdued, blinking owlishly behind his designer frames.

"Ten seconds for the mirror scene," Cris finally muttered. "I'll integrate it, but under protest."

"Noted," Aaron replied, already turning to his phone to text Victoria: *Cut coming. Running late. Save me a seat behind the glass.*

Her response came instantly: *You'd better be bringing something extraordinary to justify this delay. Michelle is stress-eating the focus group's M&Ms.*

Aaron turned back to find the three men watching him expectantly. "Cris, render the cut with the mirror scene adjustment. Gabe, send me the specs and contact for the glass armonica rental; I'll review it tomorrow."

All three looked momentarily surprised by his authoritative tone before grudgingly nodding their assent. As they dispersed to their assigned tasks, Aaron sank into the nearest chair, suddenly aware of just how exhausted he was.

Three months of post-production battles had taken their toll. His hair was noticeably thinner; a fact Michelle had tactfully avoided mentioning during their last three meetings. He hadn't seen Emily awake in nearly two weeks, their communication reduced to apologetic text messages and notes left on the kitchen counter. The film had consumed him entirely, as unrelenting as the historical figure at its center.

But tonight would provide their first real audience feedback. Beyond the Twitter wars and TikTok conspiracies, beyond Kennedy's Instagram activism and journalists' think pieces: actual humans watching their film and responding to it as reality rather than as a concept or controversy.

Aaron's phone buzzed again. Victoria, with characteristic timing: *25 minutes and counting. Bring energy drinks. You look like hell in all your recent texts.*

"Hard at work on your producer documentation?" Cris asked, glancing over as he executed the edits with practiced efficiency.

Aaron nodded. "Every night after editing. Forms, budgets, schedules; documenting my producer contributions in triplicate. The PGA doesn't make it easy."

"Worth it though," Cris observed. "That mark changes everything in this business."

"Tell that to my receding hairline," Aaron replied, attempting humor despite his exhaustion.

Cris chuckled, his fingers flying over the keyboard as he worked. "Creative battles cause more hair loss than actual genetics in this town. I've seen fully-haired directors go completely bald during post-production."

"Comforting," Aaron muttered, checking his watch again. Twenty minutes until the screening. "How's the render coming?"

"Almost there," Cris replied. "And for what it's worth, you've handled these conflicting egos better than most. Barry's a shark in designer clothing, and Gabe lives in a parallel musical universe where budget constraints don't exist. Lesser directors would have cracked weeks ago."

The unexpected validation caught Aaron off guard. Coming from Cris St. Claire, the legendarily difficult "editor's editor" who'd once reportedly made Christopher Nolan cry, such praise was rarer than a studio executive admitting a mistake.

"Thanks," Aaron said simply. "That actually means a lot."

"Don't get sentimental," Cris warned, though a hint of a smile played at the corner of his mouth. "I still think your second act transition needs work, and the Berlin sequence runs two minutes too long."

"And we'll address all of that tomorrow," Aaron promised. "For now, let's just get this cut to the screening room before Victoria comes to extract us herself."

With a final keystroke, Cris initiated the export. "Rendering now. You'll have your cut in seven minutes."

Aaron grabbed his jacket, mentally preparing for the gauntlet ahead. Focus groups were notoriously unpredictable; those artificial collections of "representative viewers" whose offhand comments could reshape months of creative work in an instant. In Hollywood's strange ecosystem, their casual opinions carried the weight of scripture, capable of resurrecting or destroying projects with a single confused response.

"Ready?" Cris asked, USB drive in hand as the render completed.

Aaron took the drive, feeling its physical weight as disproportionately small compared to the creative burden it represented. "As ready as anyone can be to have their work dissected by strangers."

"That's the business we chose," Cris shrugged. "Better them than more executives with notes."

With that sobering thought, they headed for the door, USB clutched in Aaron's hand like the last lifeline on a sinking ship. Behind him, Barry was already on the phone with Kennedy's team, his voice shifting into the practiced smoothness he reserved for client management.

"Kennedy, darling! Yes, I was able to ensure your dressing table scene was included in the cut. That's what I am here for; after all, I am your representation and"

The elevator doors closed, mercifully cutting off the rest of Barry's elaborate deception. Aaron leaned against the wall, closing his eyes for a brief moment of silence before the storm ahead.

His phone buzzed one final time. Victoria again: *12 minutes. Running out of excuses for your absence. Nielsen guy getting annoyed.*

Aaron tucked the phone away and smiled exhaustedly at Cris as they watched the elevator numbers descend. The moment of truth approached: not just for *Gravity,* but for every career entangled in its controversial orbit. The next few hours would reveal whether they'd created genuine art from calculated provocation or simply an expensive exercise in algorithmic outrage.

Either way, he desperately needed a drink.

***

"He's still not here?" André looked up from his phone with an expression of disbelief. "The screening starts in twenty minutes and our director is MIA with the only copy of the cut? What happened to basic professional competence?"

Michelle dabbed perspiration from her forehead with a tissue, trying to maintain her composure despite the mounting tension as she worked through the already half-depleted bowl of M&Ms. The cramped monitoring room at Nielsen's Los Angeles facility had grown uncomfortably warm: partly from technical equipment running the live feed, partly from the collective anxiety of the marketing team awaiting their first audience feedback.

"Cris is apparently refusing to render the cut until he and Aaron reach an agreement on Kennedy's mirror scene," Michelle explained. "Barry's threatening to call Kennedy directly if they remove it entirely."

"Barry Hickson is the living embodiment of why agents shouldn't be allowed near the creative process," André muttered, checking his watch. "I've texted Aaron nine times in the last hour. If we delay this screening,

Nielsen charges us another twenty thousand dollars, which Victoria will personally deduct from my daughter's college fund."

Ravi looked up from his laptop. "Aaron just replied. Says he's 'handling final adjustments with Cris' and will be here in 'ten minutes max.'"

"He said that twenty minutes ago," André pointed out. "Are we sure he hasn't been taken hostage by Kennedy's team? Should we send a tactical extraction unit to the editing bay?"

"Aaron cares too much about this cut to let anyone rush it," Ravi said. "He's probably fighting for every frame."

"Caring is all well and good, but the Nielsen moderator is already prepping the audience," André replied, gesturing toward one of the monitors showing the screening room where participants were finding their seats. "We have one hundred and twenty-three real humans who've signed NDAs and agreed to fill out surveys, not to mention Dr. Price, whose last name is less a misnomer than a Yelp rating: four dollar signs."

The monitoring room, standard issue for professional testing facilities, was lined with screens showing multiple angles of the screening room and audience area. Unlike the traditional two-way mirror setup of smaller facilities, Nielsen's premium testing center offered comprehensive digital monitoring, allowing the team to observe audience reactions from multiple perspectives while listening to the pristine audio feed.

Through the main feed, they could see the participants settling into their comfortable theater-style seats, making awkward small talk while nibbling on provided snacks. They had been carefully selected by Nielsen's recruitment team to represent the film's potential audience demographics, balanced by age, gender, race, and viewing habits. All were pre-screened to ensure they weren't active in online film commentary spaces that might have exposed them to the "Black Hitler" controversy.

"Fresh eyes," as André had insisted during the selection process. "I want genuine reactions, not regurgitated Twitter discourse."

A tech appeared in the doorway, looking harried. "Just got a text from the security desk. Mr. Weisman in the building, moving swiftly."

"Thank god," Michelle breathed. "I was about to tell the Nielsen people we were experiencing 'technical difficulties,' which is apparently our code for 'our director is still arguing about Eva Braun's mirror scene.'"

"Is the cut actually ready?" André demanded. "Or is he bringing a hard drive and seventeen apologies?"

"USB drive with the final render, apparently completed eight minutes ago," Lucy confirmed.

André exhaled dramatically. "If Victoria were here, she'd have given him that look; you know the one, where you can physically feel your future job prospects withering."

"Probably why he's running late," Michelle muttered. "No Victoria means one less executive to disappoint."

Dr. Price, the Nielsen moderator, a polished woman in her forties with the blend of corporate efficiency and therapeutic warmth her profession required, appeared on one of the monitors, adjusting her microphone as she prepared to address the test audience.

"She's starting the introductions," André noted with rising alarm. "Where the hell is"

The door burst open as Aaron Weisman practically fell into the room, clutching a USB drive in one hand, his messenger bag dangling precariously from his shoulder. He looked like he'd aged a decade since morning: dark circles shadowed his eyes, his normally neat hair stood at odd angles, and his rumpled shirt suggested he'd been wearing it for longer than professional standards typically allowed.

"I'm here," he gasped, thrusting the USB drive toward the nearest technician. "Final cut. Five compromises, three threatened resignations, and one near-physical altercation over a glass instrument, but it's done."

"Jesus Christ, you look like you've been held hostage by editorial terror-ists," André observed as the Nielsen tech took the drive and rushed to load it. "What happened? Did they demand artistic ransom?"

"Barry wanted Kennedy's mirror scene expanded to establish her 'emo-tional imprisonment,'" Aaron explained, collapsing into the nearest chair. "Cris threatened to quit if it ran longer than ten seconds. And Gabe has spent the last two hours explaining why we need a historically authentic glass armonica for just fifteen thousand dollars a day."

"Wait, doesn't the Hitler hallucination sequence already have a glass armonica?" Michelle asked, confusion evident. "I remember seeing an ap-proval for that twenty-two-thousand-dollar expense months ago."

"That's a modern instrument," Aaron explained with the weary tone of someone who'd heard the argument too many times. "Apparently, Gabe has located an original built in 1782, and he's convinced it produces dis-tinctive overtones in a different kilohertz range that 'stimulate the limbic system.' I think it's magic."

"The Mesmer armonica," Ravi nodded. "He's not wrong about the overtones, actually."

Everyone turned to stare at him.

"What?" Ravi shrugged. "Juilliard. Two years, cello performance. It didn't work out."

"You might be the only person in Los Angeles who knows what Gabe is talking about without a Wikipedia search," Aaron said, looking genuinely impressed.

André handed Aaron a bottle of water and two aspirin. "Hydrate and medicate. You look like you've been through a war zone. Did you get any actual sleep last night?"

"Three hours," Aaron admitted, swallowing the pills gratefully. "I was up finalizing PGA documentation. The producers mark doesn't earn it-self. Actually, you're not allowed to earn it; the rules specifically prohibit treating the requirements as a checklist. You have to somehow show that you placed the production above all other considerations. It's not an application, it's a canonization inquiry."

"And what do you get at the end?" Michelle asked.

"Three lowercase letters and two periods after my name. It confers no compensation; the Guild is very clear on that." Aaron rubbed his eyes. "They also confidentially interview the crew to verify you actually produced anything. Department heads. The production designer." He paused. "The editor."

Cris burst through the door, silver ponytail swinging wildly, his expression suggesting he'd just narrowly escaped something apocalyptic. "Tell me they haven't started yet. I had to park two blocks away because some asshole in a Tesla took the last spot."

"Just loading the cut now," André confirmed. "What happened to 'editors stay in their caves and directors handle screenings'? I thought that was your mantra."

"Usually true," Cris agreed, dropping into a chair beside Aaron. "But I spent three months of my life on this absurdist masterpiece. I need to see these reactions firsthand, not filtered through Aaron's optimistic interpretation or marketing."

Dr. Price's voice came through the speakers as she addressed the test audience. "Good evening, everyone. Thank you for participating in today's screening. As I explained during your intake, we'll be showing you a new film and then discussing your reactions afterward. We ask that you not discuss your opinions during the screening itself; there will be plenty of time for conversation afterward."

The Nielsen technician gave a thumbs up. "Cut is loaded and ready to go."

"Here we go," Aaron murmured, suddenly looking nervous in a way he hadn't since film school screenings. "Moment of truth."

André settled in beside him, his expression uncharacteristically serious. "Whatever happens in there," he said quietly, "remember that focus groups told the studio to cut the 'Over the Rainbow' sequence from *The Wizard of Oz* and called *The Godfather* confusing and too long."

"Are you suggesting we ignore their feedback?" Aaron asked.

"I'm suggesting we interpret it through the lens of reality rather than panic," André replied. "These hundred and twenty-three random people aren't the final arbiters of artistic merit. They're just data points."

"Expensive data points," Aaron muttered, turning his attention to the screen as the lights dimmed in the test screening room.

Dr. Price's voice came through once more: "We're about to begin. Please give the film your full attention."

The screen shifted to show the opening scene: James Wright as Hitler, alone in his bunker, staring at a map of a Berlin now in ruins.

For the next two hours, the monitoring room fell into tense silence, all eyes focused on the audience's reactions through the multiple camera feeds. Aaron found himself watching the viewers more than his own work, searching their expressions for clues to their internal responses.

There was the expected moment of visible surprise when James first appeared clearly as Hitler: a ripple of shifting postures and widened eyes as viewers processed the visual. But remarkably, most seemed to adjust quickly, their attention focusing on the performance rather than the casting concept.

By the thirty-minute mark, they appeared genuinely engrossed. By the one-hour point, several were leaning forward in their seats. And during the mental breakdown scene, where James's Hitler showed the fracturing of his psyche, the focus group seemed as captivated as the extras playing his fictional followers.

When the film finally ended and the lights came up, Aaron realized he'd been holding his breath. The focus group sat in silence for a moment, many blinking as if awakening from a trance.

***

"Aaron, you should see this," Ravi called from his laptop. "The Nielsen real-time sentiment tracking during the screening is remarkable. Look at the engagement curve during James's first major speech scene."

Aaron moved to Ravi's side, studying the graph on screen. A jagged line tracked audience emotional engagement throughout the film, with notable spikes during key dramatic moments. The highest peak coincided with Hitler's beer hall speech: a scene James had quietly reshot eighteen times until he captured the precise balance of charisma and menace, a number that appeared in nobody's anecdotes.

"That's validation right there," Ravi said quietly. "They weren't just intellectually engaged; they were emotionally invested. That's what separates provocative stunts from actual cinema."

Aaron nodded, suddenly feeling the weight of the past year: from Victoria's whirlwind initial casting decision through production chaos to this moment of unexpected validation. What had begun as industry politics and algorithmic provocation had somehow, almost accidentally, become something authentic.

"So what's next?" Michelle asked, looking to Aaron expectantly.

"We finish the edit," he replied simply. "Address the pacing issues they identified. Fight more battles with Barry over Kennedy's screen time. Decide whether Gabe gets his precious Mesmer glass armonica."

"And then?" André prompted.

"And then," Aaron replied with the tone of a kid who realizes he's getting his birthday wish, "we see if our calculated risk can actually become what we've pretended it was all along: serious art worthy of serious awards consideration."

As they gathered their things to leave, Dr. Price approached with her tablet in hand. "The full recording and metrics report will be available tomorrow, but I wanted to share something interesting with you now."

She turned her tablet to show them a chart. "This tracks emotional engagement by demographic segments. Notice anything unusual?"

Aaron studied the data, quickly spotting the pattern. "The engagement levels are remarkably consistent across demographics. Age, race, gender; they're all following similar patterns."

"Exactly," Dr. Price nodded. "That's quite rare, especially for historically sensitive material. Typically we see significant variations based on demographic factors, but your film seems to be connecting with viewers regardless of their background."

"Universal appeal through specific execution," André murmured, his marketing brain already spinning the data into festival applications. "That's the holy grail."

"Victoria will want this data immediately," Michelle noted, already making notes on her tablet. "This is exactly the kind of metric that convinces executives to increase festival budgets."

"It's still early to draw definitive conclusions," Dr. Price cautioned, "but I've been running focus groups for fifteen years, and I would say this demographic consistency in response patterns is pretty good."

After Dr. Price departed, the team stood in momentary silence, absorbing the implications of the feedback.

"I need a drink," Aaron finally declared. "Possibly several."

"Seconded," Michelle agreed. "We've earned it."

"Earned it and then some," Cris added, running a hand through his silver ponytail.

"I know just the place," André said, guiding them toward the exit. "A new spot in Los Feliz where the bartenders don't know anything about the film industry, the music is too loud for serious conversation, and no one will ask us a single question about Hitler."

"Sounds perfect," Aaron replied, feeling the tension of the past months begin to ease slightly. "Just what the doctor ordered."

As they headed out into the Los Angeles evening, Aaron's phone buzzed. A text from Victoria: *Focus group metrics?*

Aaron quickly typed back: *Remarkably positive. Universal engagement across demographics. Strong emotional response during Hitler's speeches. Will send full report in morning.*

Victoria's response came instantly: *Sean's office. 9 AM tomorrow. Bring data AND requests. Festival budget window closing.*

As they walked toward their waiting cars, Aaron found himself experiencing an unfamiliar sensation: something close to optimism. After months of chaos, controversy, and compromise, they'd somehow navigated to this unexpected moment of validation.

***

CHAPTER 19

Victoria swept into her office with the triumphant stride of a general returning from a successful campaign. She'd spent the morning in Sean's office, armed with focus group data, demographic engagement metrics, and the blend of confidence and strategic flattery that had defined her rise through Pinnacle's executive ranks.

"The look on Sean's face," she announced to Lucy, who was already positioned at attention with a tablet in hand. "When I showed him the consistency in demographic engagement, he actually sat up straight. Do you know how rare it is to see Sean Lynch's perfect posture falter? It's like witnessing a solar eclipse."

Lucy smiled, clearly relieved. "So we secured the additional funding?"

"One million, exactly as requested." Victoria placed her portfolio on her desk with a decisive thud. "Of course, he acted like he was donating a kidney rather than allocating reasonable marketing funds, but that's just Sean performing fiscal responsibility for our corporate overlords."

"That's fantastic news," Lucy replied. "The full three million for festival positioning means we can implement the complete strategy."

"And the Oscar campaign after." Victoria's smile turned predatory. "One step at a time, of course, but Sean's already talking about being open to awards consideration. He actually used the phrase 'potential contender' without sounding like it was causing him physical pain."

Lucy hesitated, uncertainty flashing across her face before professional composure reasserted itself. "Speaking of, um, contenders."

"Later," Victoria waved her off, still riding her victory high. "First, show me that final TruthHunterRyan video you mentioned. Consider it our victory lap."

Lucy seemed relieved by the interruption, quickly pulling up the video on her tablet. "It's... something special. She's now filming from her car 'for safety reasons' while wearing sunglasses inside."

Victoria settled into her chair, accepting the tablet with anticipation. "Perfect. Nothing says 'credible source' like automotive paranoia."

The video began playing, showing Ryan glancing nervously around her car interior, sunglasses perched on her face despite the obvious lack of sunshine. Her performance had escalated from concerned citizen to full conspiracy theorist, complete with furtive glances and whispered revelations.

"The right says it's 'historically inaccurate.' The controlled left like Jade says it 'obscures White supremacy.' But BOTH arguments serve the same master: elites are terrified of people questioning the official WW2 narrative entirely!"

"She's cracked the code," Victoria deadpanned. "Our entire marketing strategy revealed by a woman filming in a Toyota Prius."

Ryan leaned closer to her camera, voice dropping to a conspiratorial whisper. "Ask yourself: Why can @LiftieInLipstick make four viral videos saying 'Hitler stays White' with no restrictions, but accounts questioning other historical events get instantly banned?"

"Because one is discussing a movie casting decision and the other is probably denying actual genocide?" Lucy offered.

"Details, details." Victoria waved dismissively, still watching with amused fascination.

"And the final proof?" Ryan declared, replacing her sunglasses. "Her last video got 8.4 million views in eighteen hours. Her follower count has increased by 800K since she started this 'series.' You tell me how that makes sense. She's PAID for and Big Tech is helping them stop our real questions about World War Two!"

Victoria burst out laughing. "That's incredible. Apparently we now communicate in secret with TikTok influencers. André will be thrilled to know we've achieved such precise algorithmic control."

"The comment section is even better," Lucy noted. "'This makes so much sense!' and 'Stay safe, brother! Truth will prevail!'"

"Brother?" Victoria raised an eyebrow. "Isn't Ryan a woman?"

"I think her followers are confused too," Lucy replied. "She's been referred to with every possible pronoun in the comments."

"Well, at least they're inclusive in their conspiracy theories," Victoria said, handing the tablet back to Lucy. "Send that to André. He'll appreciate the absurdity."

Her phone rang, interrupting the moment of levity. Victoria glanced at the screen, her expression brightening further. "It's Janice, my source at the MPAA. Perfect timing; we should have our official rating."

She answered with professional cheer. "Janice! Just the person I wanted to hear from. Tell me you have good news about our little Hitler movie."

Lucy watched as Victoria's triumphant expression faltered, then collapsed entirely. The transformation was so dramatic that Lucy found herself unconsciously taking a step backward, as if physical distance might protect her from whatever catastrophe had just been communicated.

"I see," Victoria said, her voice now glacial. "And what precisely was their rationale?"

A pause.

"Even without explicit content? That's highly unusual for this type of... I understand. Yes. We'll review the formal letter when it arrives."

Another, longer pause.

"No, I appreciate your call. Better to hear it directly. Yes, we'll be in touch about next steps."

Victoria ended the call and placed her phone on the desk with exaggerated care, as if handling an explosive device. When she looked up, her expression had transformed into something Lucy recognized from previous crises: focused, calculating, and absolutely determined.

"Get some proper coffees. Not the studio sludge; the good stuff from Alfred. Two shots. And tell Aaron and André to get down here ASAP. I need all hands on deck."

"What happened?" Lucy asked, already typing messages.

"We've been rated R," Victoria replied, her tone flat. "For, and I quote, 'disturbing thematic content throughout, including depictions of historical fascism and genocide ideology.'"

Lucy's fingers froze over her tablet. "R? But there's no explicit violence, no language issues, no sex."

"Apparently the 'psychological intensity' and 'realistic depiction' of Hitler is too much for tender teenage minds. Isn't half the internet telling us he's very *unrealistic*?" Victoria's voice dripped with sarcasm. "Meanwhile, *Jojo Rabbit* danced its way to a PG-13 with actual Nazi imagery and Hitler as an imaginary friend."

"What does this mean for release strategy?"

"It means," Victoria's expression hardened, "we need to strategize. R rating means we lose a significant portion of the younger demographic, which impacts our commercial potential."

Lucy was already sending SOS texts to Aaron and André. "They're both on the lot. Should be here within twenty minutes."

"Good. And Lucy?" Victoria's tone shifted slightly, revealing genuine concern beneath her executive armor. "That coffee? Make it three shots."

***

Eighteen minutes later, Lucy returned bearing premium caffeine, with Aaron and André arriving nearly simultaneously. The energy had shifted in the room from celebration to crisis management, with a hint of grim determination.

"R rating?" Aaron looked genuinely confused. "For what? We purposely avoided explicit content."

"For Hitler being Hitler, apparently," Victoria replied, sliding a printed copy of the MPAA letter across her desk. "They acknowledge we don't have the usual R-rating elements but claim our 'unflinching portrayal of fascist reasoning' and 'charismatic presentation of a genocidal figure' warrants the restriction."

André scanned the letter, his marketing brain already recalculating strategies. "This is... unexpected. But potentially workable."

"Workable?" Aaron echoed, sounding skeptical. "We just lost a significant portion of our potential audience."

"Actually," André countered, "this might offer certain advantages for our awards narrative. R-rated films often carry more prestige in voters' minds; they're perceived as more 'serious' artistic endeavors."

"So we're spinning this as 'too powerful for children'?" Aaron asked.

"Something like that," André nodded. "The suggested advisory about 'historical subject matter' practically writes itself as a marketing angle."

Victoria sipped her triple-shot coffee, her mind working through the implications. "We need to decide quickly whether to appeal. We have ten business days according to this letter."

"What's our historical precedent?" Aaron asked. "How are other Nazi-focused films typically rated?"

"Most genuine examinations of the Third Reich receive R ratings," André confirmed, consulting his tablet. "*Schindler's List, Downfall, The Pianist*: all Rs. Exceptions tend to be either lighter-toned or less direct in their portrayal."

"Like Jojo Fucking Rabbit," Victoria muttered. "A literal comedy with Hitler gets PG-13, but our serious historical drama is too intense? Who were they sleeping with to secure that rating?"

"Taika Waititi's Hitler was portrayed as an absurdist imaginary friend," André pointed out. "Ours is a psychologically accurate portrayal of how fascism takes root in human minds. The MPAA apparently finds reality more disturbing than satire."

"So we have options," Victoria summarized, standing to pace the office. "Appeal the decision, accept the R rating and adjust our strategy, or make cuts to secure a PG-13."

"Cuts to what, exactly?" Aaron asked, frustration evident. "The Nazi speeches? The parts where Hitler explains his twisted ideology? That's literally the point of the movie: to show how a monster rationalizes evil. If we remove that, what are we even making?"

"Not to mention," André added, "the cuts would likely undermine James's performance. The psychological elements are what make his Hitler transcend mere impersonation."

"That might work for the awards narrative," Victoria acknowledged, "but it still impacts our commercial potential. Teens are a significant market segment, especially for historically educational content."

"The important question," André said, "is whether we fight this on principle or pivot for awards. R-rated Nazi films have a stronger track record for nominations."

Victoria drummed her fingers on her desk, thinking. "Either way, we need to get ahead of any new controversy. The rating announcement will generate another round of debate."

"We could include a content advisory," André suggested. "Not just the standard rating disclaimer, but something that frames the historical context. It demonstrates our awareness and responsibility."

Aaron's expression shifted to amused disbelief. "So, we tell them this movie about Hitler will have Nazi symbols? Like people might accidentally buy tickets thinking it's a romance? 'Surprise! It's actually about fascism!'"

"You'd be surprised," André replied with the weariness of someone who'd witnessed genuine audience confusion about basic plot elements. "Remember when women went to see *It Ends With Us* thinking it was a standard rom-com?"

"Even so," Aaron persisted, "are people this obtuse? We're not making a movie about domestic violence and pretending it's a rom-com. All our posters have Hitler on them!"

"That's precisely why the disclaimer matters," André insisted. "It's not just about informing audiences; it's about showing the industry, critics, and awards voters that we're handling sensitive material responsibly. It's marketing and sensitivity theater, not just information."

Victoria considered this. "The disclaimer approach has merit. We could even lean into it; make it slightly meta, acknowledging the obvious while satisfying the industry's demand for performative sensitivity."

"You want us to create a tongue-in-cheek warning that our Hitler movie contains... Hitler?" Aaron asked incredulously.

"Not tongue-in-cheek," Victoria corrected. "Self-aware. There's a difference."

André was already typing notes. "I can draft language that walks that fine line. We've seen these advisories become increasingly specific over the years; probably to prevent lawsuits from people who somehow didn't realize what they were watching."

"Oh, absolutely," Aaron rolled his eyes. "Should we also include warnings about able-bodied actors throughout the production? Or that Kennedy's perfect Instagram face might make women feel bad about themselves?"

"I understand your frustration," Victoria said, her tone softening slightly. "But we're operating in an industry where optics matter as much as content. Often more."

Aaron sighed, the weight of compromise evident in his posture. "I just don't want to dilute the important moments; some of those speeches are crucial, and the flag scene was deliberate. The man is literally draped and doomed by his own ideology."

"Nobody's talking about cutting those elements," Victoria assured him. "Even with an R rating, they stay intact. But we need to think about framing."

"I'm just concerned people don't know the history," Aaron admitted. "Now they'll know even less if we restrict younger audiences."

"For what it's worth," André interjected, his tone lightening slightly, "when I was a teenager, an R rating just meant I found creative ways to sneak in. Forbidden content has its own appeal."

Victoria smiled despite herself. "True. Nothing enhances appeal quite like restriction."

"Speaking of appeal," André continued, pulling out his phone, "there's something you should see. A major YouTube film critic posted a surprisingly positive review of our teaser. The Drunk Critique, usually very skeptical about race-swapped historical figures, actually praised James's performance and the artistic concept."

He handed his phone to Victoria, who watched with growing interest.

"Y'know, when the first rumors about 'Black Hitler' started circulating, I was ready to drink myself into oblivion just to escape the inevitable garbage fire," the scruffy critic declared, glass of whiskey in hand. "But then the trailer dropped. And folks... I'm as surprised as you are... but it doesn't look completely terrible."

Victoria's eyebrows rose as the critic continued, praising James's transformation while humorously critiquing Kennedy's "Instagram Face" in 1940s Berlin.

"Here's the million-dollar question," the critic continued. "Is this a case of controversial casting for those dreaded 'Modern Audiences,' or is it actually... art? Because here's the thing: there's an actual artistic statement being made when you cast a Black man as Hitler. It creates an immediate visual contradiction between the actor and the character's ideology. It forces the audience to reconcile the historical reality with what they're seeing onscreen. It's uncomfortable, confrontational, and... well, isn't that what actual art is supposed to do sometimes?"

"He gets it," Aaron said quietly, genuine surprise in his voice. "He actually understands what we were trying to achieve."

"His channel has three million subscribers," André noted. "Primarily male, eighteen to forty-five, historically skeptical of 'woke casting'; exactly the demographic we might struggle with. If he's on board, that's a significant opinion leader in our corner."

"The focus group data supports this too," André reminded them. "Remember the uniform demographic engagement? This film is connecting across traditional audience divides. Even with an R rating, that's powerful."

Victoria nodded, decision crystallizing. "We accept the R rating. Frame it as artistic integrity: we refused to water down the psychological reality of fascism just to secure a more commercial rating. That narrative aligns with our awards strategy."

"I agree," Aaron said, surprising them all with his quick acceptance. "Better to embrace the restriction than compromise the content."

"So we're in agreement," Victoria confirmed. "We accept the rating, craft a thoughtful disclaimer that satisfies industry expectations without undermining our artistic vision, and position this as further validation of our film's power and authenticity."

As they discussed implementation details, Lucy's phone buzzed. She glanced at it, her expression shifting subtly as she read the message. Victoria, ever attentive to her assistant's micro-expressions, caught the change immediately.

"What is it?" she asked, cutting through André's explanation of content advisory language.

Lucy hesitated, clearly reluctant to puncture the room's renewed optimism. "It's... nothing urgent. Festival submission details."

Victoria's eyes narrowed. "Lucy. What did you just learn?"

Lucy sighed, recognizing defeat. "It's what I tried to mention earlier. Goldman's assistant texted me. They've secured an additional two million for *Journey's End* marketing and festival positioning. Their total budget now exceeds ours by nearly thirty percent."

The room went silent. Victoria's expression didn't change, but those who knew her well could detect the slight tightening around her eyes: the executive equivalent of a battle cry.

"So, Sean allocated an extra million to us and an extra two million to Marcus," she said, her voice dangerously calm. "After assuring me repeatedly that resources were 'extremely limited this quarter.'"

"Technically," Lucy replied cautiously, "the funds apparently came from a special allocation by the board, not Sean's discretionary budget."

Victoria stood perfectly still for a moment, processing this new information. When she finally spoke, her voice carried the determination and calculation that Hollywood's ruthless hierarchy had taught her.

"Well then," she said simply. "It seems our competition with Marcus has entered a new phase." She turned to André and Aaron. "Gentlemen, we now have an additional challenge. We need to outperform a refugee drama with a one-million-dollar disadvantage."

"Sounds like a challenge," André quipped, though his expression had turned serious. "What's our approach?"

"We do more with less," Victoria replied without hesitation. "Quality over quantity. Strategic rather than blanket coverage. The advantage of controversy is that it generates its own momentum. *Journey's End* may have more money, but *Gravity* has what no budget can buy: genuine cultural relevance."

Aaron stood, gathering his notes. "I should get back to the editing bay. If we're committed to the R rating, I want to ensure every frame justifies that restriction. No compromise on content, maximum impact."

"And I'll start drafting our messaging around the rating decision," André added. "Position it as artistic integrity rather than commercial limitation."

As they prepared to leave, Victoria's posture straightened imperceptibly, her expression shifting from reactive to proactive. "We'll use these constraints to sharpen our approach."

Lucy watched the transformation with quiet admiration. Victoria Martinez in battle mode was a force even Hollywood's most ruthless power players had learned to respect.

"Lucy," Victoria said once Aaron and André had departed, "see if you can get me Sean Lynch's complete calendar for the next two weeks. Board meetings, lunches, screenings; everything. And let's pull the latest data on similar films that secured nominations despite R ratings."

Lucy was already typing. "What are you planning?"

Victoria smiled; the smile that had preceded some of Pinnacle's most unexpected successes and several executives' career implosions.

"I'm planning," she replied calmly, "to remind our esteemed EVP that I don't require equal resources to outmaneuver the competition. Just equal opportunity. And if Sean thinks additional funding will secure Marcus the spotlight, he's gravely miscalculated the power of provocative art in a clickbait culture."

"After all," she added almost to herself, "history seldom remembers who spent the most. It remembers who made the greatest impact."

***

ReLease

Release began, as revisionist history often does in Hollywood, with everyone claiming credit for successes, disavowing failures, and desperately trying to salvage what they'd created before awards season.

CHAPTER 20

J ames Olayinka Wright sat in his childhood home in Hampstead, curled into the worn leather armchair that had witnessed his transformation from gangly teenager to acclaimed actor. Outside, London fog pressed against the windows, rendering the world beyond in soft focus: a welcome relief after months of California's relentless clarity.

"So she just...made you do the scene seventeen times?" his mother asked, refilling his teacup. Dr. Folake Wright had aged gracefully into her sixties, her academic intensity softened by the warmth she reserved exclusively for family. "That doesn't seem very... professional."

"Kennedy believes in what she calls 'emotional exploration,'" James explained, accepting the tea gratefully. "Seventeen takes to achieve one perfect tear that would convey Eva's 'internal imprisonment in the patriarchal constraints of the Third Reich.'"

His father, Professor Michael Wright, looked up from his dog-eared copy of the *Times Literary Supplement*. "That's a remarkably complex emotional journey for a woman who voluntarily attached herself to history's greatest monster."

"The very point I attempted to make," James replied with a wry smile. "Though I believe my exact words were 'Eva made choices, not just tears.'"

Thomas, his grandfather, chuckled from his favorite spot by the fireplace. At eighty-six, he remained remarkably spry, his weathered hands steady as he nursed his own tea. "And what did Miss Romantic Comedy have to say to that?"

"She thanked me for the 'brilliant character insight' and proceeded to cry exactly the same way for takes eight through seventeen."

His mother settled into the adjacent chair, her expression shifting to that blend of academic curiosity and maternal interest. "Is she as beautiful in person as she appears in films? The bone structure is quite remarkable for someone so young."

"More beautiful, actually," James admitted. "Though it's a highly engineered beauty: what André called 'algorithmic attractiveness.' Two hours of makeup each morning to achieve what her social media posts caption as 'just woke up like this.'"

"And Andrew Kline?" his father asked, eyes lighting up with genuine interest. "We were quite fans of his early work. That noir western: what was it called, Dad?"

"*Blood Meridian County*," Thomas supplied immediately. "Magnificent performance. Won him his first Oscar, didn't it?"

"Indeed it did," James nodded. "And he was... not at all what I expected. There's a dignity to him: a quiet professionalism I hadn't anticipated given his reputation. After all the stories about DUIs and drugs, I thought I'd be getting someone very... difficult."

"And instead?" his mother prompted.

"Instead I found a man carrying the weight of his mistakes with remarkable grace. In some ways, he reminded me of Grandad: that kind of quiet strength that doesn't need to announce itself."

Thomas looked genuinely touched by the comparison. "High praise coming from you, lad. Though I don't recall ever wearing a Confederate flag or marrying anyone on a plantation."

James laughed. "No, but you had that same quality: the ability to acknowledge past missteps without being defined by them." His expression grew more thoughtful. "Kline told me something interesting one night after filming. Said that growing up poor in Arkansas, places like plantations weren't symbols of oppression to him; they were where the rich people lived. Emblems of success he couldn't imagine achieving."

His father set down his magazine, intrigued. "That's a perspective you don't often hear in these public controversies. Context tends to be the first casualty of outrage."

"That's what made him interesting," James agreed. "His views were shaped by experiences I couldn't fully understand, just as mine were shaped by experiences he couldn't fully understand."

"Like when your dad brought me home?" his mother suggested with a mischievous smile. "Your grandfather wasn't exactly thrilled about having a Nigerian academic join the family."

Thomas had the good grace to look slightly embarrassed. "Different times. Never seen a Black person except on the telly. Didn't know what to make of it all."

James's mother reached over to pat Thomas's hand affectionately. "And yet here we are, thirty-five years later. All because I was stubborn enough to keep coming round, bringing Nigerian dishes and listening to your stories."

"You brought food and respect," Thomas corrected with a wink. "Two things no Englishman can resist for long."

"You insisted on waiting to marry until Grandad gave his blessing," James remembered, smiling at the family lore he'd heard dozens of times.

"The woman has always been impossible!" Thomas declared proudly. "She wears you down. Always gets her way."

James sank deeper into his chair, grateful for the grounding presence of these three people who had formed his worldview long before Hitler or Hollywood entered his life.

"So what's next for the famous James Olayinka Wright?" his father eventually asked. "I imagine offers are pouring in after all this publicity?"

James sighed, balancing his teacup on the chair's arm. "Three main possibilities at the moment. Another historical drama: playing Epictetus, the philosopher who influenced Marcus Aurelius and stoicism."

"Another White historical figure?" his mother asked, her academic eyebrow lifting slightly.

"Indeed. Apparently Hollywood may have discovered that race-swapping historical figures generates free publicity and potential virtue signaling."

"Or," his mother suggested thoughtfully, "perhaps they're acknowledging that Epictetus began as a slave, and they're falling into a different type of pigeonholing."

James nodded, conceding the point. "Fair observation. There's also a biopic of Carter G. Woodson, the founder of Black History Month in America. Fascinating figure, compelling script."

"But?" his father prompted, knowing his son well enough to hear the hesitation.

"But I'm British-Nigerian, not African American. There's a legitimate question about whether I'm the right person to portray such a significant figure in African American history. Cultural appropriation works in multiple directions."

Thomas snorted. "In my day, acting meant pretending to be someone you're not. Now it's all about being exactly who you are, just with different costumes."

"It's more complicated than that, Dad," James's father interjected gently.

"The third option is an action film: international spy thriller," James continued. "Blockbuster potential, substantially higher paycheck, considerably lower artistic merit."

"The Ferrari versus the bus pass dilemma," his father translated with a smile.

James laughed. "Something like that. Though Epictetus is probably the most intellectually interesting, I find myself wondering: am I destined to be the Black version of someone else's history? Is that progress or just a different kind of limitation?"

His mother studied him with the intensity she normally reserved for doctoral candidates. "What is it you actually want, James?"

The question hung in the air: simple yet profound. James considered it carefully before responding.

"I want roles that allow me to be seen as an actor first, not primarily as a representation of my race. Yet I'd like not to represent all black people either, it's a heavy burden. I want characters with complexity and depth, regardless of their historical accuracy or contemporary relevance. And I want to build a career that opens doors for others without being defined by that purpose."

He paused, sipping his tea. "The truth is, if *Gravity* succeeds, if it manages to transcend the controversy and be recognized for its artistic merit, it could create that opportunity. Not just for me, but for others."

"Well, I'd be thrilled to be your plus-one for this fancy premiere," Thomas interjected, bringing the conversation back to immediate practicalities.

James smiled, grateful for his grandfather's characteristic ability to cut through philosophical complexities. "I wish I could bring all of you. And you're all invited to be with me in Cannes, of course. But the official premiere only gives me one plus-one, and Grandad here is the reason I took this role."

"He's a perfect plus-one," his father agreed. "We used to watch so many movies in the theatre growing up."

"A fancy premiere at my age," Thomas marveled, genuine delight illuminating his weathered features. "That's one for the bucket list."

"Just don't tell them I play Hitler," James cautioned with mock seriousness. "Might cause some confusion given the family resemblance."

The room filled with laughter: the kind that exists only in spaces where people are loved for who they are rather than what they represent. In this modest Hampstead home, far from Hollywood's calculated machinery and social media's reactive discourse, James Olayinka Wright was simply James.

***

The Palais des Festivals et des Congrès in Cannes had seen eighty-six years of cinematic history: from artistic triumphs to commercial disasters, from Fellini to Tarantino, from *La Dolce Vita* to *Pulp Fiction*. Today, it would witness something entirely new: the world premiere of a film where a Black actor portrayed Adolf Hitler.

James emerged from the sleek black limousine, adjusting his impeccably tailored Dior tuxedo with the mix of confidence and anxiety unique to actors still adjusting to sudden spotlight. Behind him, Thomas Wright followed, eyes widening at the sea of photographers and reporters that stretched along the famous red carpet like a gauntlet of flashing lights and shouted questions.

"My word," Thomas murmured, adjusting his own rented tuxedo. "Quite the circus, isn't it?"

"Hollywood's most elaborate performance," James confirmed, guiding his grandfather forward as cameras clicked frantically. "The film before the film."

Their progress down the red carpet was immediately interrupted by reporters calling James's name with increasing urgency; each desperate to be the one whose question might generate a headline.

"James! How does it feel to make history with this controversial casting?"

"Do you consider your Hitler a political statement?"

"Why have you remained silent on social media during all the controversy?"

James navigated the questions with careful diplomacy, maintaining the measured poise that had become his public signature. When asked about his social media silence, he smiled politely. "I'm hoping the film will speak for itself tonight."

An especially persistent reporter from *Vanity Fair* pressed further. "But what do you feel about this historic casting?"

James's expression remained placid, though those who knew him well might have detected a flicker of weariness. "I'd love to hear how you feel about my acting after you get to see the movie!"

The delicate dance was mercifully interrupted by a commotion further down the carpet. Kennedy Oswald had arrived: a vision in custom Dior designed to evoke the "New Look" aesthetic of post-war Paris. Her entrance created the ripple that follows genuine star power, reporters and photographers immediately pivoting in her direction.

"Saved by the Romantic Comedy Queen," James murmured to his grandfather with a small smile.

André materialized beside them with the timing of a marketing executive who'd calculated exactly when to appear. Michelle and Lucy flanked him, all three dressed in the version of formal attire that signaled "important enough to be here but not important enough to be photographed."

"Want us to escort your grandfather inside while you face the remaining press gauntlet?" André offered with professional efficiency.

James looked to Thomas questioningly.

"Go on, lad," his grandfather encouraged. "Do your actor duties. I'm in good hands with these fine folks."

"Thank you," James said gratefully to André. "I owe you one."

"Not at all," André replied with a wink. "Though if you could mention our 'visionary marketing approach' in any interviews, I wouldn't object."

As André and the PR team gently guided Thomas toward the entrance, Michelle leaned in to whisper, "Good luck. Kennedy's coming."

Before James could ask for clarification, Kennedy herself approached, gliding across the red carpet with the grace of someone who could do this in her sleep. She embraced him with perfectly calibrated warmth, kissing his cheek at precisely the angle that photographers found most appealing. Intimate, but not salacious.

"James! You look absolutely magnificent," she declared, positioning herself so the cameras could capture them together. "Are you ready for our moment?"

"As ready as one can be," he replied politely, beneath the blinding camera flashes.

A reporter thrust a microphone toward them. "Kennedy! James! How does it feel to finally present this controversial film to the world?"

Kennedy stepped slightly forward, her posture shifting to what James recognized as her "serious artist mode."

"This project has been transformative on multiple levels," she began, her voice carrying the cadence she reserved for substantive statements. "Working on material this historically significant, with themes this profound, has made me recognize how crucial it is for us to find moments of centered awareness in these polarized times."

The press corps leaned in, sensing the practiced rhythm of a prepared announcement.

"That's why I'm so excited to share that I've created Franklly: a meditation app designed to help people reconnect with their authentic selves.

Named after Viktor Frankl, whose work became my spiritual guide during the intense filming process."

James fought to maintain his neutral expression, the only indication of his surprise being a slight tightening around his eyes. Kennedy continued, her delivery flawless.

"In our chaotic world, with its political divisions and constant outrage, Franklly offers a path to mindfulness and meaning. My voice will guide you on every breath. I'm so grateful that this film journey led me to this deeper purpose."

The photographers erupted in a new frenzy of flashes, capturing the perfect combination of Hollywood glamour and performed significance. As Kennedy continued to detail her app's features, James caught sight of Victoria Martinez arriving with Andrew Kline. Victoria's expression was a masterclass in executive composure; nothing in her perfectly arranged features betrayed her reaction to Kennedy's impromptu product launch except a nearly imperceptible tightening of her jaw.

***

Within moments of entering the lobby inside the Palais, Victoria had extracted André and Michelle from the crowd, pulling them into a quiet corner of the entrance area while James, Kennedy, and Andrew continued their press engagement.

"Please tell me Cynthia Teback is already here," Victoria hissed, her smile never faltering for the benefit of nearby onlookers. "Kennedy just hijacked our premiere to launch her fucking meditation app."

"What app?" André asked, genuinely confused.

"Franklly," Victoria spat, the word sounding like an especially offensive expletive in her mouth. "As in Viktor Frankl. The Holocaust survivor. She named her mindfulness app after a Holocaust survivor and announced it at our Hitler movie premiere."

Michelle's professional composure cracked momentarily. "She did what?"

"You heard me," Victoria replied, maintaining her public smile with remarkable discipline. "Our Eva Braun just leveraged our Holocaust film to launch her lifestyle brand with possibly the worst naming decision since Kendall Jenner's tequila."

"Damage control options?" André asked, already shifting to crisis management mode.

"Find Cynthia," Victoria ordered. "If anyone can spin this, it's her. We need to;"

She fell silent as Cynthia Teback herself approached: a commanding presence in Armani, her signature titanium glasses catching the light like weapons, framed by her sleek white bob. At fifty-eight, Hollywood's most legendary awards strategist moved through industry events with the confidence of someone who had engineered more Oscar campaigns than most executives had attended premieres.

"Was it your idea to have Kennedy launch an app today?" Cynthia asked without preamble, holding up her phone to display Kennedy's announcement already trending across multiple platforms.

Victoria looked momentarily flummoxed, her carefully prepared strategies collapsing in real time. "Cynthia, I can explain."

To everyone's surprise, Cynthia's expression shifted to something resembling approval. "It's brilliant."

"It's... what?" Victoria managed, genuinely shocked.

"Brilliant," Cynthia repeated, scrolling through her phone with practiced efficiency. "The media is buzzing. Usually, there's nothing to do from the Cannes media except take photos. Big announcements mean they have to get the ground team or colleagues to look up the information and share it in real time. Kennedy has the exact algorithmically appropriate audience for this content."

Her eyes remained on her screen as she continued her assessment. "Look: multiple Twitter threads expressing appreciation for her mental health advocacy. Her celebrity friends' accounts are already posting supportive messages. When celebrities unite to support something simultaneously cringe-worthy and well-intentioned, it creates the perfect engagement storm."

Victoria's expression remained carefully neutral, though those who knew her well could detect the calculation happening behind her eyes: the mental adjustment of someone recognizing an unexpected advantage.

"We did consider that the announcement might generate additional conversation beyond the film itself," she ventured cautiously.

Cynthia's look said quite clearly: *Please don't insult my intelligence by pretending this was planned.* But her words were measured: "It's certainly generating conversation. The app itself is being downloaded at remarkable rates. Timing is unusual, but in this attention economy, unusual often equates to successful."

André, ever adaptive, jumped in. "We're also seeing significant engagement growth due to the Rivera-Hughes interview."

Cynthia's expression shifted to something approaching genuine satisfaction. "Yes, remarkably fortunate timing that she was interviewed this morning. Almost as if someone arranged it."

"Interview?" James asked, finally joining the conversation after extricating himself from Kennedy's press orbit.

André quickly pulled up a video on his phone, showing the group a clip labeled "Conservative Senator DESTROYS Liberal Host on Black Hitler Controversy."

"Elena Rivera-Hughes," Michelle explained as they huddled around the small screen. "Conservative senator from Arizona. Very influential with moderate Republicans."

On screen, a polished Cuban American woman in her forties wearing a red suit was engaged in what appeared to be a confrontational interview about *Gravity*.

"Actually, Taylor, I think it's wonderful," Senator Rivera-Hughes was saying, her confident smile never wavering.

"I'm sorry; you support the casting?" the visibly surprised host asked.

"I do. This is what true diversity looks like. For too long, actors of color were relegated to side characters or stereotypes. Then we moved to this era where they could only be saints, victims, or 'inspiring' figures. How patronizing."

The segment continued, with the host visibly struggling to maintain control of the interview.

"But isn't there something troubling about casting a Black man as history's most notorious White supremacist?" the host pressed. "Some critics suggest this is attempting to shift the sins of White supremacy onto the Black community."

"Interesting," Rivera-Hughes replied, one perfectly shaped eyebrow rising. "So you only support race-blind casting when it's for easy, likable roles?"

"I didn't say."

"Are we BIPOC people not complex?" the senator continued smoothly, leaning forward. "Are we not a diverse group with the same range of human potential as anyone else? Do our actors not deserve to play the entire pantheon of characters?"

"Of course, but."

"When James Earl Jones voiced Darth Vader, was that 'shifting the sins' of the Empire onto Black people? Or was it recognizing a brilliant actor for his talent?"

"That's different."

"Is it? Or is this new form of diversity actually less patronizing than reducing Hispanic people to always playing maids or gangsters? Less patronizing than suggesting Black actors can only represent goodness?"

"Perfect triangulation," Cynthia murmured approvingly. "Conservative credentials intact while positioning traditional liberals as the actual patronizing force. She's giving permission to her base to view this casting as genuine equality rather than 'woke revisionism.' The clip is being shared across multiple platforms, generating precisely the kind of pre-screening discourse we want."

On screen, the interview continued its masterful demolition.

"But Hitler's entire ideology was based on White supremacy, so," the host attempted.

"Exactly," Rivera-Hughes smiled warmly. "Which makes this casting so powerful. What clearer statement that his ideology lost?"

"I think many would say."

"You know, my abuelita used to tell me, 'Elena, they'll only let you succeed if you play by their rules,'" the senator interjected, her tone softening with practiced nostalgia. "I see an industry finally allowing actors to succeed based on talent, not identity politics. Isn't that the goal? Or is the goal just to replace old stereotypes with new, more politically correct ones?"

"Let's talk about your position on," the host attempted to pivot.

"Actually, I'm curious, Taylor," Rivera-Hughes leaned forward with genuine-seeming interest. "Do you believe actors of color should only play heroes? Because that doesn't sound like equality to me. That sounds like a new form of typecasting."

James watched with quiet fascination, an actor recognizing another skilled performer at work. The senator's arguments were delivered with the warmth and authority that made even controversial positions seem reasonable: the political equivalent of Kennedy's practiced authenticity.

"We need to take a quick break," the host said, visibly relieved to escape. "When we return, we'll discuss the senator's new social media bill."

The clip ended with the senator maintaining her composed smile as the camera cut away.

"This is good?" James asked, genuinely unsure how to interpret this unexpected support.

"This is excellent," Cynthia confirmed, her gaze moving analytically between the remaining guests arriving on the red carpet. "Conservative validation creates permission for certain audience segments that might otherwise dismiss the film outright. Combined with liberal arts criticism praising the conceptual daring, we achieve the perfect cross-demographic intrigue."

She turned to Victoria, her assessment complete. "You're going to the dance, kid."

The phrase, Cynthia's shorthand for awards season, hung in the air like a promise. Victoria's expression shifted subtly, professional composure momentarily giving way to genuine ambition and hope.

James glanced around for his grandfather, spotting him engaged in animated conversation with Lucy near the entrance. Thomas had already acquired a flute of champagne and was gesturing enthusiastically, clearly deep into one of his stories. Lucy's expression suggested genuine interest rather than the polite tolerance usually offered to elderly relatives at industry events.

"I see your grandfather's settled in nicely," André remarked, following James's gaze. "He's already charmed half the PR team with stories about his favorite movies."

"He has that effect on people," James replied with affection. "Authenticity tends to stand out in rooms like this."

Thomas caught his eye across the crowded space and raised his champagne glass in a small toast, his face alight with the joy of someone enjoying a once-in-a-lifetime experience. James returned the gesture with a warm smile, grateful that at least one person in this calculated spectacle was simply enjoying the moment for what it was.

As they moved toward the theater entrance, James felt the weight of the moment settling around him. Here, in this temple to cinema, they would finally witness whether their controversial experiment had transcended its origins as provocative concept to become genuine art worthy of consideration.

The critics were seated. The jury was present. The world's press waited, pens poised.

It was time for *Gravity* to speak for itself.

***

CHAPTER 21

Whoever had invented the modern press junket, James decided, deserved to be studied as thoroughly as any historical monster he'd portrayed. The Presidential Suite at the Beverly Wilshire had been transformed into a precision-engineered machine designed for one purpose: to extract marketable soundbites from exhausted actors while maintaining the illusion of authentic conversation.

Two weeks after their unexpected triumph at Cannes, a Grand Prix and Best Actor award that had sent shockwaves through the industry, the *Gravity* team found themselves trapped in this elegant prison of their own success. Room after room of the palatial suite had been repurposed into interview stations, each with its own specific function in the publicity ecosystem.

The main living room had been reconfigured as the high-profile video interview space, complete with professional lighting, a tastefully branded backdrop, and the kind of furniture that photographed better than it felt. Here, top-tier outlets like *Variety*, *The Hollywood Reporter*, and *Deadline* would capture the carefully rehearsed insights that would define the film's narrative in the coming awards season.

The second living room handled print and magazine journalists. A more "intimate" setting designed to create the illusion of casual conversation while actual PR staff hovered just out of sight. The dining area had been repurposed as a holding pen for waiting journalists, stocked with the kind of premium snacks and beverages that made media types feel momentarily special before being ushered into their strictly-timed interview slots.

Even the outdoor terrace had been colonized, now serving as a photoshoot space where the gentle California light could be harnessed to make everyone look approximately twenty-seven percent more inspirational than they felt. Kennedy had already claimed this as her primary territory, citing "optimal lighting conditions" with the scientific authority of someone who'd spent more time being professionally photographed than most people spent sleeping.

James stood at the window of the makeshift greenroom, watching Los Angeles shimmer beneath him. The city seemed to ripple in the morning heat, as unreal as everything else about this carefully constructed day.

"Ten minutes until your first interview," Lucy announced, managing to sound both apologetic and firm. "You're paired with Kennedy for the first three: *Variety*, *Hollywood Reporter*, then *Deadline*."

"Thank you," James replied, adjusting his cuffs. The suit had been selected by André's team, approachable but dignified, not too formal but serious enough to suggest serious discussions. Every element of his appearance had been calculated for optimal impression management, down to the specific shade of his pocket square.

Cynthia Teback materialized beside him, moving with the stealth of someone who preferred to remain invisible. Her white bob looked even sleeker today. Her expression carried the intensity of someone who manufactured Oscar campaigns the way other people manufactured automobiles (with ruthless efficiency and uncompromising standards).

"James," she said, her voice carrying a blend of warmth and calculation that marked every interaction with potential nominees, "we need to discuss approach before your first interview."

"Good morning to you too, Cynthia," James replied with a polite smile.

"Morning. Talent, campaign, strategy; in that order of priority," she replied, not bothering with small talk. Her eyes scanned him with analytical precision, like someone appraising an investment property. "You're deliberately underplaying the representational angle."

It wasn't a question.

"I prefer to let the work speak for itself," James confirmed.

Cynthia's expression shifted to something rarely seen on her face: actual concern rather than strategic empathy. "That approach, while admirably dignified, is creating a vacuum. Nature abhors a vacuum. Twitter abhors it even more. Your silence is being interpreted as discomfort with your own identity."

"My identity isn't being Hitler," James pointed out mildly.

"Your identity as a Black actor in a groundbreaking role," Cynthia corrected, already scrolling through something on her phone. "Here: three major culture writers are questioning your 'reluctance to engage with the cultural significance' of your casting. The new *Vulture* piece suggests you've been 'media-trained into neutrality.' One suggested we've 'silenced' you."

James leaned against the windowsill, studying her with quiet interest. "And you think I should be more... what, exactly? Performatively grateful? Politically charged? Racially focused?"

"I think," Cynthia replied with precise emphasis, "you should acknowledge the reality that this casting is meaningful beyond artistic considerations. I think you should lean into your heritage, not as a stunt, but as context for why this particular actor playing this particular role carries unique resonance."

She glanced at her sleek rose gold Royal Oak, a gesture so fluid it seemed choreographed. "These journalists don't want to hear about your process or your craft, though those are excellent, obviously. They want to hear about representation. Give them enough to satisfy that hunger, or they'll create a narrative without your input."

Before James could respond, a new voice entered the conversation. "They're asking about your mother."

Both turned to see Lucy, looking slightly uncomfortable. "The *ET* correspondent just told the pre-interviewer they want to ask why your Nigerian mother wasn't at Cannes. Something about 'family division over the controversial role.'"

James's expression darkened slightly. "My mother is a full professor at UCL with teaching responsibilities that didn't allow international travel that week. I chose my grandfather for his specific connection to the material. There's no division; they're extraordinarily supportive."

"Facts are irrelevant," Cynthia stated flatly. "Narrative is everything. And right now, your narrative has a gap they're trying to fill with conflict."

She adjusted her glasses with the deliberate motion of someone shifting tactical approach. "Give them enough of your actual perspective that they don't manufacture one. Acknowledge your heritage, express pride in breaking barriers, then pivot to the universal themes of the film."

"That sounds suspiciously like a talking point," James observed.

"It is," Cynthia confirmed unapologetically. "One crafted to protect your authentic voice while giving the media enough to feel satisfied."

James considered this, then nodded once. "All right. I'll acknowledge the representational elements without letting them become the entire conversation."

"Excellent," Cynthia said, already turning to go. "Now I need to find Andrew before his first interview."

As she departed with the efficiency of someone with seven simultaneous crises to manage, Kennedy Oswald swept into the room with the practiced entrance of someone who knew exactly how many eyes would turn in her direction. She wore a cream-colored pantsuit that somehow managed to suggest both serious modern artist and photo-readiness, her blonde hair falling in those signature waves that had launched a thousand tutorial videos.

"James!" she exclaimed with rehearsed warmth, air-kissing somewhere in the vicinity of his cheek. "Isn't this exciting? The energy today is just electric."

"Indeed," James agreed politely, noting the subtle differences between Kennedy's public and private personas. The volume was higher, the gestures more expansive, the overall effect designed to read natural on camera while being anything but. "How are you holding up? These days can be rather exhausting."

"Oh, I thrive on this," Kennedy assured him, though the slight tightness around her eyes suggested otherwise. "It's all about energy management. I did forty minutes of kundalini breathing before my first coffee."

Behind her, Miguel, her eternally vigilant assistant, appeared with a monogrammed water bottle containing a precisely calibrated hydration solution to get her through her day.

"Your first interview starts in eight minutes," Miguel reminded her. "Dani is monitoring social responses to your meditation app announcement, and Barry is... discussing things with the *Vanity Fair* team."

"Discussing," in this context, clearly meant "terrorizing"; judging by Miguel's expression.

"Perfect," Kennedy beamed, accepting the water bottle and taking a precise sip. "James, we should coordinate on the Nazi questions. They always try to make us contradict each other about historical perspectives."

"Nazi questions?" James raised an eyebrow.

"You know, the ones like 'how does it feel playing such evil characters' and 'what responsibility do actors have when portraying fascists,'" Kennedy explained, making air quotes with perfect French-manicured nails. "I usually pivot to how Eva wasn't politically engaged but trapped in a patriarchal system that limited her choices."

"Interesting take," James replied diplomatically. "I tend to emphasize Hitler's belief in his own righteousness, how monsters rarely see themselves as monsters."

"That's good." Kennedy nodded, her expression suggesting she was mentally filing this away for potential appropriation.

As they moved toward the interview area, James caught sight of Andrew Kline entering from the terrace, looking remarkably at ease for a man whose career redemption hung on this very day. At sixty-one, the Oscar-winning actor carried himself with the dignity of someone who had survived his own worst instincts and emerged with hard-won wisdom.

"Morning." Kline nodded, his Arkansas drawl more pronounced than usual. "Ready for the firing squad?"

"Always," James replied with a genuine smile. He wondered if the industry could figure out what he had: that Kline was remarkably straightforward during production, none of the rumored difficult behavior or problematic remarks. Just a consummate professional with the wounded wariness of someone who knew exactly how much goodwill he'd squandered.

"They've got me paired with Aaron for the first round," Kline said. "Apparently, I'm not to be trusted alone with journalists yet."

"It'll be more dynamic this way," Cynthia confirmed without apology as she appeared beside them. "It's not personal; it's strategy. You are with Aaron, then with Kennedy, then with James. It'll protect you."

"Who's protecting who?" Kline asked with a sardonic half-smile. "Them from me or me from them?"

"Both," Cynthia replied frankly. "We control the narrative by controlling the combinations."

"Reassuring to know I'm being handled like nuclear material," Kline chuckled, though his eyes carried the resignation of a man who understood exactly how tenuous his position remained.

As they approached the interview space, James felt the familiar shift in atmosphere that accompanied these artificial encounters: the tension of rooms designed to extract performative authenticity from people who made their living pretending to be someone else.

Seated in the carefully arranged chairs were two journalists from Variety, their expressions carrying that blend of fatigued cynicism and professional enthusiasm unique to entertainment reporters. Their eyes lit up as Kennedy entered, then registered visible surprise at James's appearance, the practiced double-take of people who still couldn't quite reconcile the handsome British-Nigerian actor with the Hitler they'd witnessed on screen.

"Kennedy! James! Wonderful to meet you both," the lead journalist greeted them, rising to shake hands with the vigor of someone who wanted to establish immediate rapport before asking potentially offensive questions. "Congratulations on Cannes. Quite the achievement."

"Thank you," Kennedy beamed, settling into her chair with practiced ease. "It was a profound experience sharing this film with such a discerning audience."

As cameras began rolling and microphones were checked, James observed the subtle shift in Kennedy's posture: the almost imperceptible adjustment that optimized her appearance for the three-quarters angle that her team had likely determined received maximum engagement metrics.

"So, James," the journalist began, leaning forward with a deliberate show of interest, "you've made history with this role in multiple senses. What drew you to playing Hitler, and how did you approach such a controversial casting choice?"

And so it began: the delicately choreographed dance of questions and answers, of revelations that weren't really revelations, of insights manufactured to seem spontaneous. James settled in for what promised to be a very long day of explaining, yet again, why a Black actor playing Adolf Hitler might actually be art rather than simply algorithmic provocation.

***

In the additional suite they'd secured for PR operations, André and Michelle monitored the digital feeds with the wary attentiveness of bomb disposal experts. On multiple screens, interviews unfolded simultaneously. Kennedy and James with *Variety*, Aaron and Andrew with the *New York Times*, and B-roll footage being captured for the electronic press kit that would feed hungry content machines worldwide.

"Kennedy's leaning too heavily on her app promotion," Michelle observed, making notes on her tablet. "Third mention in twelve minutes."

"Let her," André replied, sipping his third espresso of the morning. "After that Cannes stunt, she's earned a few plugs. Besides, it keeps her from going off-script on the historical material."

The "Cannes stunt" had become their internal shorthand for Kennedy's impromptu meditation app launch at the premiere: a moment of such perfect brand synergy and tone-deaf historical insensitivity that even André had been momentarily speechless. Naming a mindfulness app after Viktor

Frankl, complete with Kennedy's dulcet tones guiding users through their spiritual journey, had generated precisely the kind of bewildered press coverage that somehow managed to benefit everyone involved.

"She just compared Hitler's charisma to 'toxic influencer culture,'" Michelle noted with a wince. "Dr. Friedman is going to have another aneurysm."

"Add it to the clarification list," André said, already scanning social media reactions. "The 'artistic interpretation' folder is getting thick enough to publish as its own historical text."

The door opened and Ravi entered from handing out schedules to the journalists in the dining area.

"Please tell me there's coffee in here," he said, making a beeline for the refreshment table. "I can't deal with journalists' egos jockeying for more time or schedule changes."

"Over by the monitors," André directed him. "Fresh from the place down the street."

"Thank god," Ravi declared, pouring himself a cup with the reverence usually reserved for religious rituals. "How are the interviews actually going?"

"About as expected," André replied. "Kennedy's promoting her app, James is being his usual thoughtful self, and journalists are trying desperately to generate click-worthy moments of conflict or controversy."

"The usual press junket kabuki theater," Michelle added. "Though we've had some close calls. *Entertainment Tonight* tried to create a narrative about James's mother being 'opposed' to the role because she wasn't at Cannes."

Ravi winced. "God, what is wrong with these people? Can't any of them just ask about the film?"

"Absolutely not," André replied with the cheerful cynicism of someone who had long since accepted the absurdity of his profession. "That would require actually watching it and forming genuine thoughts, which is far too much work when manufacturing outrage is so much more efficient."

Their attention was drawn to one of the monitors where Kennedy and James were finishing their third interview of the day with *Deadline*. As they stood to leave, Kennedy leaned in to whisper something that made James smile. A genuine expression rather than his media smile. The moment was brief but captured something unexpectedly authentic in the manufactured environment.

"That's good footage," Michelle noted. "Shows genuine rapport between our leads."

"Hmm." André nodded, studying the screen. "Make sure we get that clip for the EPK. 'Stars forming real connection despite controversial material' is exactly the kind of heartwarming narrative that plays well with Academy voters."

Ravi rolled his eyes. "Can't we just acknowledge they might actually respect each other as professionals?"

"Professionalism doesn't get retweets," André replied without irony.

The door opened again, and Cynthia Teback entered with the focused energy of someone perpetually operating at higher RPMs than everyone else in the room. Her titanium glasses gleamed perfectly in place despite the logistical chaos she'd been navigating since dawn.

"Crisis averted with Kline," she announced without preamble. "The *Access Hollywood* interviewer tried to ambush him with footage from the plantation wedding. Aaron intercepted and redirected to a softball about his 'creative process.' Puff piece secured."

André looked impressed. "That's some quick thinking by Aaron."

"That's why he gets paid the big bucks," Cynthia replied, scanning the monitors with analytical precision. "Where are we with the *Newsweek* situation?"

Michelle consulted her tablet. "Their request for a solo James interview is still pending. You wanted to pair him with Kennedy instead."

"Correct," Cynthia confirmed. "James alone gives them too much room to push the 'uncomfortable with his role' narrative. Kennedy adds strategic buffering and industry context."

Michelle watched Cynthia's strategic maneuvering with a mixture of fascination and mild horror. "You know, sometimes I remember that we're actually promoting a film about the human capacity for evil and self-deception, not launching a new flavor of breakfast cereal."

"In this industry, there's remarkably little difference," Cynthia observed dryly. "Both require manipulating perceptions to create artificial desire."

Their attention was suddenly drawn to a commotion on one of the monitors. In the print interview room, a female journalist was pressing Kennedy with unusual persistence.

"Turn up the volume on three," André instructed, reaching for the control panel.

The journalist's voice filled the room, carrying that blend of compliment and attack that characterized modern celebrity interviews.

"It must have been hard to watch your mother's public breakdown on Letterman all those years ago, now that you're close to her age. You've obviously had excellent work done, nothing like what was available in your mother's day," the journalist was saying. "But even with modern procedures, there's still a ticking clock, isn't there? Is that why this Hitler project felt so urgent? A last chance at legitimacy before you ran out of time?"

Kennedy's breathing had become shallow, visible despite her trained composure.

"I find that question fascinating," James interrupted, his British accent cutting through the tension like a scalpel. "Not for its content, which is deliberately cruel, but for what it reveals about our industry's imagination."

The journalist blinked, momentarily thrown.

"Ms. Oswald has spoken extensively about her artistic choices and the historical weight of this material," James continued with calm precision. "Yet you've reduced both her and her mother to commodities with expiration dates."

Kennedy's eyes, usually camera-perfect, had glazed slightly, seeing something beyond the room.

"I wasn't asking you," the journalist recovered, turning back to Kennedy. "I'm asking how it feels knowing you're facing the same thing she is."

"What exactly do you expect as a response to that question?" James persisted, his tone politely puzzled. "Should Ms. Oswald deny the obvious reality of industry sexism? That would seem disingenuous. Should she perform victimhood for your audience? That becomes clickbait. Or perhaps she should just accept the premise that her entire value is tied to her appearance rather than her considerable talents?"

Miguel had appeared at Kennedy's side, his professional smile not quite concealing his concern. "Ms. Oswald needs a moment. Blood sugar. She's been on press since five a.m.."

Kennedy's agent, Barry, burst into the frame, his silver hair perfectly coiffed despite his obvious fury. He was dressed in a Brioni suit, the expensive fabric stretching slightly as he physically inserted himself between Kennedy and the interviewer.

"This interview is concluded," he announced, his voice carrying the menace of someone who had ended careers with a single phone call. "What kind of journalistic hackery is this? You were briefed on the parameters. This isn't your little podcast basement where you fish for clickbait."

"It's a legitimate question about industry dynamics," the journalist protested, though she had already begun packing up her recorder.

"Is it?" Barry's smile had the warmth of a subpoena. "Because it sounded like deliberate provocation designed to generate a reaction you could monetize. Congratulations; you've just been blacklisted from every Pinnacle event for the foreseeable future. And when we pull your access credentials on the way out, I'll be personally calling your editor to discuss your novel approach to entertainment journalism."

As Kennedy's team executed their extraction maneuvers, she remained unnaturally still. The mask had slipped completely, revealing not just vulnerability but a flash of naked terror: the exact expression her mother had worn during the infamous Letterman meltdown that had ended her career.

"Kennedy," Miguel murmured, barely audible. "We need to move. Now."

She rose mechanically, posture perfect from decades of media training, but her eyes remained unfocused, not seeing the hotel room or anyone in it. Without a word, she allowed herself to be guided toward the exit.

James watched the procession with quiet interest before turning back to the journalist, who was still attempting to maintain professional composure.

"You know," he said conversationally, "I've been wondering why celebrities increasingly prefer podcasts to traditional media. I believe you've just provided an excellent case study."

In the command center, André, Michelle, Ravi, and Cynthia watched in silent assessment as the scene unfolded.

"That footage is toxic," Michelle said immediately. "We need to lock it down, Barry will be coming for it."

"Or," Cynthia countered, her expression calculating, "we could strategically leak it."

The three others turned to her in surprise.

"You can't be serious," Ravi said, genuinely shocked.

"Deadly serious," Cynthia replied, entirely unperturbed. "Look at what just happened. Kennedy had a vulnerable moment that humanizes her completely. James stepped in as her knight with eloquence and dignity. The journalist came across as a vulture. It's perfect material."

"It's exploitative," Michelle protested. "Using Kennedy's actual trauma as promotional content."

"It's authentic," Cynthia corrected. "Everything else today has been manufactured. This was real. That's what resonates with audiences, especially Academy voters."

"It would absolutely reframe the narrative," André said slowly, his marketing mind calculating the potential impact. "James transforms from 'uncomfortably silent Black Hitler' to 'dignified defender of women in Hollywood.' Kennedy shifts from 'privileged celebrity with meditation app' to 'vulnerable artist continuing her mother's legacy despite industry cruelty.'"

He turned to Michelle. "Strategically, it's brilliant."

"Morally, it's questionable," Michelle countered. "Even for us."

Victoria chose that moment to enter, looking like she'd just navigated a war zone rather than a press junket. Her tailored suit remained impeccable, but the slight tightness around her eyes revealed the strain of managing the day's controlled chaos.

"What did I miss?" she asked, taking in the intensity on their faces. "And why does it look like you're planning a coup in here?"

"Kennedy breakdown footage," André supplied, gesturing toward the monitor still displaying the aftermath of the incident. "Cynthia thinks we should leak it. Michelle thinks that's a step too far, even for Hollywood vultures like us."

Victoria glanced at the screen, then back at Cynthia. "The interview where the journalist attacked her about her mother and aging?"

"Yes," Cynthia confirmed. "James defended her beautifully, Barry went full shark, and Kennedy had a genuine moment of vulnerability. It's beautiful narrative material."

"It's also deeply personal," Victoria observed, her tone uncharacteristically gentle. "That wasn't acting; that was actual trauma response. Her mother's Letterman meltdown destroyed her career."

"Precisely why it would resonate so powerfully," Cynthia pressed. "This is the human story beneath the controversy, Victoria. This is what transforms a provocative film into an awards contender."

Victoria studied the screen for a long moment, clearly weighing the strategic benefits against other considerations. "Let me think about it," she said finally. "We don't need to decide immediately."

Cynthia looked like she wanted to press the issue but instead gave a curt nod. "Your call. But remember: in this business, authentic vulnerability is the rarest and most valuable currency."

"Speaking of currency," Ravi interjected, clearly eager to change the subject, "what's our plan for the *Entertainment Weekly* team? With Kennedy taking a break, they're waiting with no interview subject."

"We'll put James with Andrew," Cynthia decided immediately. "Tell them we're giving them an exclusive pairing that wasn't on the original schedule. I'll need to give Andrew some talking points."

Aaron Weisman chose that moment to enter the command center, his expression suggesting he'd come seeking refuge from his own interview gauntlet. "What happened? I just saw Kennedy being whisked into the service elevator looking like she'd seen a ghost."

"Inappropriate questioning about her mother's breakdown," Victoria supplied, keeping details minimal. "James shut it down before it got worse, but the damage was done."

"Christ," Aaron sighed, dropping into a chair. "As if this day wasn't complicated enough."

"How are things with Andrew?" Victoria asked, pivoting to the next potential crisis point.

"Surprisingly smooth," Aaron replied. "He's handling the redemption narrative questions with genuine humility. Almost makes me believe he's actually changed."

"Everyone changes when their career is on the line," André observed, not looking up from his phone. "The question is whether it sticks when the pressure's off."

Aaron rubbed his temples, the gesture of a man approaching his limit. "These journalists are relentless. Half the questions aren't even about the film; they're about controversy, representation politics, or trying to bait Andrew into saying something problematic."

"Welcome to modern press coverage," Victoria replied without sympathy. "Content farms need outrage to survive. Actually discussing the artistic merits doesn't generate sufficient engagement metrics."

Aaron's phone buzzed. His expression transformed as he read the message, a complex sequence of emotions flickering across his features: fear giving way to surprise, then excitement, and finally profound relief.

"The PGA mark," he said quietly, almost to himself. "It came through."

Victoria allowed herself a rare genuine smile. "Congratulations, Aaron. You're officially a proper producer now. Just in time to take full responsibility for this entire debacle."

"Thanks," Aaron laughed, the tension visibly draining from his shoulders. "After pursuing this for so long, I thought I'd feel different. But all I can think about is wanting this project to succeed."

"It is succeeding," André pointed out, gesturing toward the monitors where interviews continued unfolding. "Cannes triumph, critical acclaim, festival invitations rolling in; we've moved beyond merely controversial to legitimately prestigious."

"And Cynthia Teback is fully committed to the Oscar campaign," Victoria added. "Even though Marcus's refugee drama took the Palme d'Or, she says we're stronger contenders with the Academy."

"The Gold Derby experts agree," Michelle added. "Four out of seven have us in first position."

Aaron was only half listening. Beneath the Guild's notification sat a second email. Benjamin Friedman. Subject line: *Errata.*

Mr. Weisman. The studio's invitation list evidently predates my seventh and final departure, so I attended the premiere. Attached is a list of eleven historical errors in the finished film, ranging from incorrect collar insignia to a telephone that will not exist for another four years. None of them matter. The film understands what the period felt like, which is rarer than accuracy and considerably harder to fake. I stayed through the credits. It was good to see my name among them. B.F.

Aaron read it twice. Around him, the room went on trading prediction odds and cross-demographic appeal. He put the phone back in his pocket without mentioning it to anyone.

"Not bad for a movie we were going to walk away from," Aaron observed, standing to return to the interview gauntlet. "Back into the breach."

Michelle, who had been monitoring another screen, suddenly straightened with renewed interest. "You should see this."

She gestured to a monitor showing James and Andrew now seated together for their impromptu joint interview. The *Entertainment Weekly* journalist was already diving into the predictable territory.

"So, James," the interviewer was saying with practiced earnestness, "as an actor of color achieving mainstream success, what do you think should be done about systemic inequality and poverty? What is your unique perspective on it?"

The question hung in the air, wrapped in its familiar packaging of performative concern and thinly disguised tokenism. The unspoken expectation was clear: deliver an impassioned, quotable statement that would generate social shares without offending sponsors.

James, who'd been responding with thoughtful but calculated precision throughout the interview, suddenly did something unexpected. He smiled, a smile that reached his eyes, and glanced sideways at Andrew Kline.

"You know," James said, his voice carrying its distinctive British cadence, "I think I'm actually the wrong person to answer that question."

The interviewer blinked, momentarily thrown off script.

"I was raised by two university professors," James continued. "I attended private schools before RADA. My perspective on economic struggle is necessarily academic rather than lived." He gestured toward Kline. "Andrew would likely have far more insight on this issue."

A ripple of surprise moved through the press room. This wasn't how these interviews were supposed to work. The "social consciousness" question was meant for the Black actor, not the controversial white star attempting a comeback.

Kline looked startled, not just at being addressed, but at being acknowledged this way. For a moment, the practiced cynicism that normally armored his features fell away.

"I... uh..." Kline cleared his throat. "Yeah, I grew up in a trailer park outside Little Rock. Single mom working three jobs. Dad was more of a theoretical concept than a presence."

The interviewer, struggling to recalibrate, forced a smile. "That's... interesting background, but we were asking about solutions to..."

"Poverty isn't theoretical where I'm from," Kline continued, his Arkansas accent suddenly more pronounced. "When folks talk about 'food insecurity,' we just called it 'the last week of the month.' When politicians debate healthcare access, I remember my mom choosing between medicine and rent."

James watched quietly, his expression one of genuine interest rather than the performative allyship the cameras were hunting for.

"As for solutions?" Kline shrugged. "I'm just an actor. But I know that when you've got nothing, having one person, a teacher, a neighbor, a stranger, believe in you can make the difference." He glanced at James with a hint of grudging appreciation. "That's not policy, but it's what I know."

The interviewer, desperately trying to regain control of their narrative, pivoted. "James, is that why diversity in film is so important to you? Creating those opportunities for..."

"I think Andrew was making a rather more universal point," James interjected politely. "About human connection transcending policy. Though I appreciate your attempt to redirect the conversation back to my racial identity."

The slight emphasis on "attempt" hung in the air just long enough to register.

Kline snorted, a genuine laugh escaping before he could catch it. The publicist at the back of the room looked ready to swallow her tongue.

"Let's talk about the film," James suggested, extending a professional lifeline to the flustered interviewer. "After all, that's why we're here."

In the command center, André couldn't contain his delight. "This is gold. Absolute gold. James refuses to be tokenized, Kline comes across as authentically thoughtful rather than performatively rehabilitated, and they both gently expose the media's lazy framing."

"He's threading an impossible needle," Victoria observed, genuine admiration in her voice. "Acknowledging the representational significance without letting it become his entire identity. I didn't think it could be done."

"It's not calculation," Michelle noted quietly. "That's just James being genuine. That's why it works."

"Both liberal and conservative outlets are going to love this," André added. "Left Twitter will appreciate him refusing the burden of speaking for all Black people. Right Twitter will celebrate him not playing the victim card. It's the perfect cross-demographic appeal."

"Seven interviews down, twelve to go. Then it's onto the festivals, global release, and the awards gauntlet." Michelle calculated.

"One step at a time," Victoria cautioned, though her expression betrayed her confidence. "We still have to survive today without anyone saying something catastrophically unrecoverable. And off I go to help. I'll check in on the talent."

On the screen, James and Andrew continued their unexpected rapport, two men from entirely different worlds finding common ground in the artificial environment of a press junket.

"You know what I've been wondering?" Ravi asked suddenly when it was just the marketing team. He looked at Michelle. "You said you asked to be on this project, even before James was cast? Before it became the controversy machine?"

For a moment, Michelle's carefully maintained professional facade slipped, revealing something more contemplative.

"I've always loved movies," Michelle began, her tone unusually personal. "Growing up, they were my greatest source of escapism. Books let me create worlds in my imagination, but movies were something I could share with others. We'd all see the same thing, experience the same emotions together."

She paused, gathering her thoughts. "Films about World War II, especially: when we were still processing the complexity and atrocity of what had happened. There was something powerful about sitting in a darkened theater, feeling an entire audience collectively experiencing history's darkest moment and ultimately witnessing evil's defeat."

The room had grown quiet, everyone caught off guard by Michelle's unexpected sincerity.

"Watching *Life is Beautiful* or *The Boy in the Striped Pajamas* or even *Jojo Rabbit*, there was this sense, palpable and real, that we were all together. The Nazis lose every time we see their cruelty together, and all those who died somehow live again in our collective memory. It's our responsibility to let them haunt us occasionally, to remind us of human capacity for both cruelty and beauty."

She shrugged, suddenly self-conscious. "So when I heard about this project, about creating one of those experiences, I wanted to be part of it. Before the controversy, before the marketing angles; just to help create something that might make people feel together in the darkness."

The silence that followed felt reverent, unexpected in this cynical command center of calculated public relations.

"That's..." Ravi seemed genuinely at a loss for words. "That's not what I expected."

"You joined marketing to amplify togetherness?" André asked, his tone lacking its usual edge.

Michelle laughed, a touch embarrassed. "Maybe someone as cynical as you can't understand."

"No," André said quietly, his expression surprisingly genuine. "I think I do. It's refreshing to hear in this business."

The moment was interrupted by a production assistant bursting through the door. "Kennedy's ready to continue. Where do you want her?"

And then the machinery of publicity resumed. André issued rapid-fire instructions, Michelle returned to monitoring social media metrics, and Ravi coordinated the reshuffling of interview schedules. But something had shifted subtly in the room. A momentary glimpse beneath the carefully maintained professional facades to the human reasons they all found themselves in this strange business of manufacturing perception.

Outside, Los Angeles continued its relentless sunshine, oblivious to the careful dance of revelation and concealment unfolding in the Presidential Suite of the Beverly Wilshire.

And the machinery of modern entertainment continued its inexorable operation: transforming human experiences into content, content into conversation, and conversation into commerce.

***

CHAPTER 22

The Oscar campaign had entered its critical phase, and Victoria's office reflected the shift from creative ambition to tactical execution. Her awards shelf, frequently adjusted during moments of stress, had remained untouched for weeks. No point rearranging symbols of past glory when the ultimate prize loomed on the horizon.

Lucy entered without knocking, tablet in hand, expression caught between professional calm and genuine concern. "Have you seen the Fox News panel about *Gravity*? It's being clipped across social platforms, nearly fifteen million views since last night."

Victoria glanced up from budget spreadsheets, her coffee gone cold beside her. "Please tell me they're calling us 'Hollywood elites destroying history' again. That plays well with our festival positioning."

"Not exactly," Lucy grimaced. "They're calling the film a 'devastating takedown of progressive tactics' and comparing Hitler's propaganda methods to... transgender rights advocates and cancel culture."

Victoria's pen froze mid-calculation. "They're what?"

"It's trending under #HitlerWasWoke," Lucy continued, tapping her tablet. "Conservative commentators are praising the film for 'exposing how the radical left uses the same playbook as fascists.'"

"Jesus Christ." Victoria pushed aside her spreadsheets. "Show me."

Lucy passed her tablet across the desk, the video already queued up. Victoria watched with escalating horror as four panelists and a smirking host dissected *Gravity* through the peculiar prism of contemporary American culture wars.

"They're literally showing how language can be weaponized, how terms can be redefined, how dissenters can be silenced," a silver-haired commentator was saying, voice dripping with self-satisfaction. "Sound familiar? It's exactly what we're seeing from the radical left today."

Victoria's expression hardened as the panel continued, each conservative voice more gleeful than the last as they twisted her film into ammunition for their ideological battlefield.

"There's a scene where Hitler talks about how 'words must mean what we want them to mean' while discussing propaganda strategy," a blonde woman in a red blazer added. "If that's not a perfect description of what's happening with gender ideology right now, I don't know what is."

"This is a fucking nightmare," Victoria muttered, watching the lone progressive panelist struggle against the tide of false equivalencies. "They're co-opting our Holocaust film to attack transgender people. Sean will have an aneurysm."

She scrolled through the comments beneath the clip, each more alarming than the last:

"Finally someone said it! The REAL fascists are on the LEFT!"

"Mandatory viewing for every liberal. Show them what they've become."

"Best unintentional red-pilling in Hollywood history."

Victoria handed the tablet back to Lucy, her expression grim. "Get André on this immediately. We need to issue a statement clarifying the film's actual intentions before this narrative crystallizes. Draft something about honoring historical accuracy and the dangers of misappropriating Holocaust imagery for contemporary political battles."

"On it," Lucy confirmed. "Should I also tell..." she began.

The door swung open without a knock, cutting Lucy off mid-sentence. Cynthia Teback entered with the imperious confidence of someone who viewed closed doors as suggestions rather than barriers. Her white bob gleamed under the office lights, titanium glasses perched precisely on her nose.

"Lucy, be a dear and get me a piccolo," Cynthia said without bothering with greetings. "Extra shot, no sugar."

Lucy looked to Victoria, clearly surprised by the dismissal.

"It's fine," Victoria nodded. "But talk to André about shutting down this Fox segment before it metastasizes."

"Don't," Cynthia countermanded, not even turning to look at Lucy. "Leave it exactly as it is. And that piccolo, oat milk if they have it."

Lucy departed with a final questioning glance at Victoria, who gave an almost imperceptible nod. When the door closed, Cynthia settled into the visitor's chair, removing her glasses with deliberate precision.

"Are you serious about this Oscar?" she asked without waiting.

Victoria was momentarily thrown by the direct question. "Of course I'm serious. Why else would I be paying you more than my editing budget?"

"Because hiring me and not listening to me would be a tragic waste of resources," Cynthia replied, her voice carrying the blend of condescension and insight that had made her Hollywood's most feared awards strategist. "And after thirty years of engineering Academy campaigns, I've learned to recognize the difference between executives who want Oscars and those willing to do what it takes to win them."

"And which am I?" Victoria asked, her tone carefully neutral.

"That's what I'm here to determine." Cynthia folded her hands precisely in her lap. "Cannes worked because I know more than half the judges personally. Most owe me favors dating back to the nineties. The Academy is different, larger, more diffuse, subject to shifting alliances and competing interests."

Victoria leaned forward. "Marcus Goldman has his own awards specialist."

"Judith Myers." Cynthia nodded. "Competent but constrained by ethical boundaries I discarded during the Clinton administration."

Victoria studied the woman across from her, this legendary figure whose name was whispered in executive suites with equal parts fear and reverence. Cynthia Teback didn't just run campaigns; she engineered perceptions, manufacturing the precise emotional context that transformed good films into "important" ones worthy of golden statues.

"What exactly are you suggesting?" Victoria asked finally.

Cynthia gestured toward Victoria's award shelf. "How badly do you want that Best Picture to complete your collection?"

Victoria's gaze drifted to the carefully arranged trophies and plaques, tangible evidence of her career's ascent, each representing battles won and rivals vanquished. But the most coveted spot remained conspicuously empty, awaiting the ultimate validation.

"Whatever it takes," she said simply.

Something like approval flickered across Cynthia's face. "Then let's discuss what 'whatever' actually entails." She reached into her elegant Celine bag, extracting a slim folder. "First: that Fox News segment you're so eager to disavow? I arranged it."

"You *what*?" Victoria's composure slipped momentarily.

"I carefully selected the panelists, fed them specific talking points, and ensured the lone progressive was outmatched but articulate enough to maintain plausible legitimacy." Cynthia spoke as casually as if discussing lunch options. "The culture war exists whether we acknowledge it or not. Our job is to ensure *Gravity* appears to validate both sides' worldviews simultaneously."

"By letting conservatives claim our Holocaust film supports their persecution complex?"

"Precisely." Cynthia nodded. "The right believes your film exposes liberal fascism. The left believes your film warns against right-wing extremism. Both interpretations generate passionate advocacy. Both drive Academy voters to view the film as 'important' rather than merely 'well-crafted.'"

Victoria found herself caught between professional admiration and moral discomfort. "That's... diabolically clever."

"It's basic campaign strategy," Cynthia corrected. "You've already satisfied the progressive contingent by casting a Black actor in a traditionally White role. Now you need conservatives who think James Wright is 'one of the good ones' to neutralize potential backlash."

She tapped a manicured fingernail against the folder. "The second component is the Kennedy footage from the press junket."

"The mother meltdown incident?" Victoria asked. "André deemed it too personal for strategic use."

"André seems competent but sentimental," Cynthia replied dismissively. "That footage is your insurance policy. The other campaigns will eventually attempt a hit piece on Andrew Kline, your most vulnerable target. When they do, we'll release Kennedy's breakdown footage to redirect attention and generate sympathy."

Victoria contemplated this, turning the strategy over in her mind. "Her agent Barry Hickson will threaten legal action."

"Let him threaten." Cynthia waved away the thought dismissively. "Kennedy won't actually sue once she sees how the footage positions her as a sympathetic figure continuing her mother's legacy despite industry cruelty. It's the narrative she's been trying to manufacture for years."

"And the leak source?"

"Choose an expendable intern," Cynthia advised. "Preferably one of color, it complicates the optics of potential retaliation. Offer them a generous severance, a promising position elsewhere, and an ironclad NDA. Then have them issue a personal apology to Kennedy for their 'terrible mistake.'"

Victoria felt a familiar calculation happening in her mind, the cold assessment of human assets and liabilities that had defined her rise through Hollywood's ruthless ecosystem. "I know just the candidate."

"Perfect." Cynthia's smile contained zero warmth. "Now for the uncomfortable question: How much of your seven million Oscar budget remains?"

"Just under five million," Victoria replied. "Are you suggesting we need more?"

"I'm stating it categorically," Cynthia confirmed. "Academy voters enjoy feeling important almost as much as they enjoy free alcohol and celebrities pretending to care about their opinions."

She opened her folder to reveal a spreadsheet with meticulously categorized expenses:

"Organized Screenings: $1.8 million," she began. "That covers private viewings for all 9,500 Academy members. Each needs appropriate venue, premium catering, and talent appearances. You can't just rent an AMC and serve grocery store wine."

Victoria glanced at the figures with growing unease. "That's seven percent of our entire production budget just for screenings."

"You're not buying a screening; you're buying the illusion of exclusivity and importance," Cynthia corrected. "Then there's the 'For Your Consideration' campaign: $2.2 million minimum."

"*Two point two* million for advertisements?" Victoria balked.

"For ubiquity," Cynthia specified. "Full-page spreads in every trade publication. Digital takeovers of industry sites. Strategically placed billboards on routes Academy members travel daily. Your film must become inescapable without appearing desperate."

She continued down the list: "Events and parties: $1.4 million. Every 'intimate gathering' requires A-list venues, celebrity chef catering, and gift bags valuable enough to matter but not so valuable they violate Academy rules against explicit bribery."

Victoria did the quick mental math. "That's over five million dollars just for the visible aspects of campaigning. I have just under five."

"Hence 'categorically,'" Cynthia said. "And that's before we even address talent travel, accommodations, and appearance fees. James and Kennedy need to be everywhere, which means first-class flights, luxury hotels, and dedicated handlers to ensure they remain on message."

"All this to convince a few thousand people to check a box on a ballot?"

"No," Cynthia corrected, looking almost offended. "All this to create the perception that your film matters more than the others. That voting for it aligns voters with the right side of history, with good taste, with cultural relevance."

She closed the folder with a decisive snap. "This happens for three solid months of the year, every screening, every Q&A, every 'intimate gathering.' The Academy campaign isn't a sprint; it's a marathon of strategic spending."

Victoria leaned back, processing the incredible financial outlay. "So on a twenty-five million dollar production budget, we're spending almost half just to win recognition for it."

"Welcome to the industry's most open secret," Cynthia replied. "But money only buys access. Winning requires... additional measures."

Victoria's eyes narrowed slightly. "Such as?"

"Our research team discovered some questionable social media posts from Marcus's lead actor," Cynthia replied, her tone suggesting she was discussing weather forecasts rather than potential career assassination.

"Racially insensitive comments from five years ago. Nothing catastrophic, but sufficient to create doubt during a competitive Oscar season."

"And you want to leak them," Victoria stated rather than asked.

"I want to ensure they're discovered organically by the right entertainment journalist," Cynthia corrected. "Similar opportunities exist with our other competitors. The supporting actress from another contender has a previously undisclosed DUI. The cinematographer of another has sexual harassment allegations that were settled quietly two years ago."

Victoria was silent for a moment, processing the implications. "This sounds like mutually assured destruction. What happens when our competitors discover one of our own secrets, especially Andrew?"

"That's precisely why we have the Kennedy breakdown footage as counterprogramming," Cynthia explained. "I've had my team go through the socials and background information on every member of the cast and crew. It's mostly fine. As for Andrew, his redemption narrative is already established and immunized through strategic media placements. He has no media presence outside what we have organized for him. Any attack will look like cruel piling-on at this point. People don't like bullies."

Lucy returned with the coffee, setting it carefully before Cynthia before retreating without a word. The awards strategist took a measured sip, never taking her eyes off Victoria.

"I can handle everything with appropriate distance," Cynthia continued once they were alone again. "Plausible deniability for you and the studio. But this stays between us, no studio marketing or PR involvement. What we do for awards remains the unacknowledged secret of the industry. We only reveal what has been done. They compromised themselves."

Victoria studied the woman across from her, this elegant architect of perception whose methods existed in the shadowy territory between aggressive campaigning and outright sabotage.

"And if I decline these... additional measures?" Victoria asked carefully.

"Then you've spent 1.6 million dollars on my services only to ignore my most valuable advice," Cynthia replied with a thin smile. "And Marcus Goldman will finally have that Best Picture trophy he's been pursuing since you stole *Sarajevo* from him."

The mention of *Sarajevo*, Victoria's first major project and the source of her longest-running industry rivalry, hit its intended mark. Victoria's expression hardened with renewed determination.

"How much additional budget do you need?" she asked quietly.

"Two million minimum," Cynthia replied without hesitation. "And your explicit authorization to conduct opposition research at my discretion."

Victoria considered the prospect, the Oscar she'd coveted for years now within reach, requiring only the compromise of certain principles she'd already bent countless times throughout her career. Was this final ethical flexibility really any different from the calculated manipulations that had brought her this far? If there was nothing to find, they wouldn't find anything anyway.

"You'll have both by close of business tomorrow," Victoria decided, sealing whatever remained of her moral high ground in exchange for golden validation. "Just make sure we win."

Cynthia's smile widened fractionally as she slipped the folder back into her bag. "That's why they call me the Statue-Maker, darling. I don't enter races I can't engineer."

She rose with practiced elegance, straightening her immaculate suit. "Continue with the planned screenings and events. Focus on your specialty, making the creatives feel validated while I handle the unsavory aspects. Together, we'll deliver that Best Picture."

After the door closed behind her, Victoria remained motionless, contemplating what she'd just authorized. The quiet manipulation of public perception was standard industry practice, but this calculated character assassination of competitors crossed into territory even she had previously avoided.

She turned to gaze at her awards shelf, the carefully curated evidence of her professional journey. The empty space reserved for the Oscar seemed to mock her, as if questioning whether she was willing to pay the true price for completion.

Victoria Martinez, champion of diverse voices, strategic risk-taker, and calculating executive, had just authorized the darkest chapter of her career. And as she reached for her phone to arrange the additional funding, she found herself remarkably at peace with the decision.

In Hollywood's twisted moral economy, the ends had always justified the means. The only difference now was her willingness to acknowledge it.

A week later, the door to Victoria's office crashed open with such force that the framed *Gravity* teaser poster, tastefully minimalist, with James's silhouette cast in shadow, nearly toppled from its wall mount.

Barry Hickson stormed in like a silver-haired hurricane in a bespoke Savile Row suit, his sixty-year-old face flushed with a shade of rage that suggested his blood pressure had entered medically alarming territory.

"Which incompetent fucking intern leaked that footage?" he bellowed, skipping pleasantries entirely. "Because I want their head on a goddamn spike!"

Victoria, who had been reviewing Oscar campaign projections, maintained remarkable composure in the face of Barry's theatrical entrance. She slowly set down her pen with the deliberate calm of someone used to agents' emotional tempests.

"Good morning to you too, Barry," she said evenly. "I assume you're referring to the Kennedy interview footage."

"Don't play dumb with me, Victoria," Barry snapped, his silver mane seeming to bristle with indignation. "That footage was under strict embargo. FUCKING STRICT. My client is trending on every social platform because some bottom-feeding tabloid got hold of her most vulnerable moment in twenty years!"

Lucy, hovering uncertainly near the door, caught Victoria's subtle nod and quickly slipped out, presumably to summon reinforcements.

"I assure you," Victoria replied with practiced diplomacy, "we're conducting a thorough investigation to determine how this happened. The footage was supposed to be;"

"Supposed to be SECURE!" Barry interrupted, his John Lobbs wearing a path in Victoria's carpet. "Kennedy Oswald doesn't have vulnerable moments on camera. That's in her FUCKING CONTRACT."

He slammed both palms on Victoria's desk, leaning forward with the intensity of a courtroom attorney delivering a closing argument. "Do you have any idea what this does to her brand? Her carefully managed public persona? Her strategic positioning as an empowered female entrepreneur?"

"Actually," Victoria began, "the public response has been overwhelmingly sympathetic;"

"I don't give a flying fuck about 'public response'!" Barry's voice reached a volume that likely carried through several adjoining offices. "I care about my client, who called me at three in the fucking morning SOBBING because the most traumatic memory of her life, watching her mother's career die on national television, is now being replayed for public entertainment!"

The door opened again as André and Michelle entered with the synchronized timing of crisis management professionals. André carried his tablet like a shield, while Michelle's expression suggested she'd been mentally rehearsing de-escalation techniques during her sprint to Victoria's office.

"Barry," André began smoothly, "I understand your concern, but the footage has actually generated extraordinary goodwill for Kennedy. Look at these metrics;"

"METRICS?" Barry whirled on him, eyebrows nearly reaching his hairline. "Are you serious right now? My client is having a genuine emotional crisis, and you're talking about fucking ENGAGEMENT METRICS?"

Michelle stepped forward, her tone gentle but firm. "Mr. Hickson, we understand that this is deeply personal for Kennedy. We're taking this breach extremely seriously."

"Oh, I can see how seriously you're taking it," Barry replied, sarcasm dripping from every syllable. "No one even bothered to call her. Not one of you supposedly concerned executives picked up the phone to check if she was okay."

A momentary flash of something like guilt crossed Michelle's features, a fleeting expression so unexpected in the context of a publicity crisis that both Victoria and André glanced at her in surprise.

"I've been in contact with Dani for damage control," Michelle admitted quietly. "Kennedy has asked for a few days off. She's spending time with her mother."

This revelation, especially the detail about Kennedy seeking out her mother, sucked some of the righteous wind from Barry's sails. His shoulders dropped slightly, though his expression remained thunderous.

"Of course she can take whatever time she needs," Victoria said, seizing the opening. "The scheduled appearances can be rearranged."

Barry's eyes narrowed with renewed suspicion. "And the leak? The person responsible?"

"Will be identified and appropriately disciplined," Victoria assured him. "We're reviewing security protocols and interviewing everyone with access to the footage."

"I don't want 'appropriate discipline,'" Barry snarled, jabbing a manicured finger toward Victoria. "I want a fucking HEAD ON A STICK. And I'll be reviewing our contract for breach proceedings."

With that parting shot, he straightened his Italian silk tie and stalked toward the door, stopping only for a final glare. "Kennedy trusted you people. Remember that when you're calculating your precious metrics."

The door slammed behind him with enough force to rattle Victoria's awards shelf.

For a moment, the three executives stood in awkward silence, the echo of Barry's fury hanging in the air like an unpleasant aftershock.

"Well," André finally said, "that was invigorating. Nothing like starting the morning with a reminder of our moral bankruptcy."

Victoria sank back into her chair. "Is Kennedy really with her mother? I thought they barely spoke."

"According to Dani, yes," Michelle confirmed, settling into one of the visitor chairs. "Apparently the leaked footage created some kind of... reconciliation opportunity. Jennifer Oswald reached out to Kennedy after seeing it online."

"So in a twisted way, this leak might have actually helped her personally, if not professionally," André mused, taking the chair beside Michelle.

Victoria's expression remained carefully neutral. "How did this happen? We explicitly decided not to use that footage."

André studied her with sudden intensity. "That's what I was going to ask you. We all agreed it crossed a line. How exactly did it leak? Was it Cynthia?"

"We'll conduct a full investigation," Victoria said firmly, avoiding his direct question with skill. "This breach of protocol is unacceptable regardless of the outcome."

Michelle shifted in her seat, her posture suggesting professional discomfort. "I should start on some damage control. BuzzFeed is already running a listicle on 'Hollywood's Most Traumatic Press Junket Moments' with Kennedy at number one."

"Of course they are," André sighed. "Give me an hour to draft an official response addressing the leak. We'll position it as a security failure rather than strategic release."

André leaned forward, his expression shifting to one of genuine curiosity. "So, what else has been happening with our promotional circus? Any other fires I should know about?"

Victoria's relief at the topic change was nearly palpable. "Have you seen the *Entertainment Weekly* piece? Apparently James's mother is 'devastated' by his Hitler role."

"Complete fabrication," André waved dismissively. "I spoke with James this morning. His mother is doing fine. The reporter invented an anonymous 'university colleague' for dramatic effect."

Lucy returned, carrying fresh coffees and wearing the slightly shell-shocked expression of someone who had just witnessed Barry Hickson verbally eviscerate an intern who'd made the mistake of getting in his way.

"Ah, Lucy, you have such foresight." Victoria smiled as Lucy distributed the coffees to everyone.

Victoria took her coffee then turned to Michelle. "So, what's the latest from the press trenches?"

Michelle pulled up her tablet. "It's getting increasingly ridiculous out there. The Daily Beast is claiming James 'schooled' Kennedy on economic privilege, *Huffington Post* thinks his defense of Kennedy proves 'Hollywood's exhausting gender dynamics,' and *Page Six* claims he's having an affair with you."

"Me?" Victoria nearly choked on her coffee. "That's a new one."

"Apparently you're having a 'corrupting influence' on his career choices," Michelle continued, fighting a smile. "His mother is reportedly very concerned."

André snorted. "The telephone game of entertainment journalism at its finest. By next week, you'll have kidnapped him from Nigeria personally."

"BuzzFeed is running with '10 SHOCKING REVELATIONS From the *Gravity* Press Junket That Prove Hollywood Is Totally Broken,'" Michelle continued. "Number seven will apparently blow your mind."

"Let me guess," André deadpanned. "We're secretly funded by right-wing extremists?"

"Actually, it's 'Wright and Oswald HATE each other,'" Michelle read. "'Despite publicity photos showing them laughing together, multiple sources confirm the co-stars can barely stand being in the same room.'"

Victoria laughed despite herself. "They've literally had dinner together three times this month."

"My personal favorite," André chimed in, scrolling through his own phone, "is Fox News claiming James admitted he's 'too privileged to discuss real economic problems.' They've fully constructed a class warfare narrative where Andrew Kline is the working-class hero putting the elitist Black actor in his place."

"The Twitter cycle is even worse," Lucy added. "There's a viral thread claiming James's admission of privilege proves he's 'leveraging racial identity for career advancement while avoiding real conversations about class.'"

Michelle shook her head, absently tapping her own tablet. "Did anyone actually watch the interview? He was being thoughtful and self-aware about his background."

"Nuance doesn't generate engagement," André shrugged. "Outrage does."

"At least the actual reviews are positive," Michelle offered. "Have you seen The Drunk Critique's latest? Over two million views since yesterday."

André's eyes lit up. "Oh, you have to see this. He's the most profane, hard-to-impress reviewer on YouTube, and he actually loved the film. The subtitle is 'The Movie Hollywood Accidentally Got Right.'"

He pulled up the video on the conference screen, and they all turned to watch a disheveled man in his thirties, empty whiskey bottles visible in frame, gesturing animatedly about *Gravity*.

"Well, well, well. If it isn't the most surprising cinematic achievement since M. Night Shyamalan remembered how to make a decent film. Against all odds, logic, and the laws of the Hollywood universe, *Gravity* is... actually good."

Victoria leaned forward with genuine interest as the critic continued his profanity-laden but surprisingly insightful analysis.

"James Wright doesn't just act in this film, he delivers a performance of such nuanced monstrosity that you forget completely about the casting controversy within minutes. He's not playing 'Black Hitler.' He's playing Hitler, full stop."

The reviewer took another drink before continuing.

"And somehow. SOMEHOW, they got Kennedy Oswald to actually act. I know, I'm as shocked as you are. The woman who's been essentially playing herself in increasingly expensive wigs for the past decade actually disappears into a role."

Victoria couldn't suppress a smile at this unexpected validation.

"What makes this film work is that it never treats its premise as a gimmick," the critic concluded. "It doesn't wink at the camera or engage in meta-commentary about its casting. And it especially doesn't treat its audience as idiots who need a lecture. It simply commits fully to telling this story with these actors, trusting its audience to see past the surface and engage with the substance. And that's all we really want from Hollywood."

As the video ended, a moment of thoughtful silence fell over the room.

"The man has a point," André finally said. "We actually did make a good movie. Almost by accident."

"Not by accident," Victoria corrected. "Despite all the chaos and compromise and controversy, we did exactly what we set out to do, create something that mattered."

Michelle nodded in agreement, her expression softening.

André glanced at his phone as a notification appeared. "Speaking of matters, I've just received confirmation about the Oscar host."

"And?" Victoria prompted.

"It's Evan Hayes," André announced. "So we'll get to hear him make jokes about us for three excruciating hours."

"Could be worse," Michelle shrugged. "Remember last year when they let that TikTok influencer co-host? The Academy nearly dissolved in shame."

Victoria leaned back, contemplating the bizarre trajectory that had brought them to this moment, a genuinely acclaimed film encircled by manufactured controversy, calculated leaks, and multi-million-dollar campaigning. The Hollywood machine in all its absurd glory.

"Well," she said finally, raising her coffee cup in a mock toast, "here's to the enduring magic of cinema, where dreams come true through backstabbing, manipulation, and strategic character assassination."

"The dream factory," André agreed, returning the gesture while Michelle raised her cup with a slightly more conflicted expression. "Where nightmares are just part of the process."

They clinked cups, the sound punctuating their shared recognition of an industry that somehow produced art despite itself, or perhaps because of its very dysfunction. Oscar campaign battles, leaked footage, and Barry Hickson's threats aside, they had created something that genuinely resonated.

In Hollywood's strange moral economy, that counted as victory.

***

CHAPTER 23

The Dolby Theatre hummed with the energy that exists only when three thousand people in borrowed jewelry simultaneously pretend they aren't terrified. Red carpet arrivals had been unusually subdued: a calculated restraint that publicists had been drilling into their clients for weeks. "Dignified excitement" was the phrase repeated in green rooms and limousines throughout Los Angeles: an emotional state previously unknown to humanity that had been invented specifically for this occasion.

James emerged from his car with practiced poise. His mother, Dr. Folake Wright, stepped out behind him, radiant in a custom silk gown that incorporated traditional Nigerian patterns with modern silhouette. The photographers immediately erupted in a frenzy that seemed to physically manifest as visible light.

"James! Dr. Wright! Over here!"

"James! How does it feel to be making history tonight?"

"Dr. Wright! Are you proud of your son's controversial achievement?"

James guided his mother through the gauntlet with protective grace, stopping at strategic intervals for the photos that would define tomorrow's coverage. His expression maintained that precise balance between humility and confidence that came naturally.

"I wouldn't normally play into these rumors about family tensions," he whispered to his mother as they posed, "but my publicist and the studio insisted this was necessary."

"Darling, I've spent thirty years in academia," Dr. Folake replied with a serene smile that concealed her amusement. "I've faced tenure committees. This is nothing."

A few yards away, Kennedy Oswald was executing her own carefully choreographed entrance with her mother, Jennifer. The elder Oswald moved with the hesitant grace of someone who had been out of public scrutiny, her face bearing the kind of beauty that Hollywood had once celebrated before discarding her for the crime of aging naturally. Kennedy held her hand with protective affection that, for once, didn't appear calculated for cameras.

"Kennedy! Jennifer! This way!"

"Kennedy! Is this a mother-daughter reconciliation?"

"Jennifer! How does it feel to return to Hollywood after twenty years?"

"Just breathe," Kennedy murmured to her mother. "They're only people with cameras. They can't actually hurt you."

Jennifer's smile flickered with the memory of times when that hadn't felt true. "I'm here for you, sweetie. Tonight is your night."

"Our night," Kennedy corrected, squeezing her hand.

Near the theater entrance, Victoria Martinez observed the unfolding spectacle with the calculating gaze of a field general. Her Zuhair Murad gown, selected specifically to communicate both authority and artistic sensibility, drew appreciative glances from the crowd, but her attention remained fixed on the strategic positioning of her talent.

"James and his mother look so happy," Lucy noted, materializing beside her with the stealth of a personal assistant who had kept her job longer than any other by perfecting the art of appearing exactly when needed. "The visual of Dr. Wright supporting her son will finally end those 'family division' stories in one swoop. It was a great call to pick that gown for her, this way he leans into his heritage without having to say anything."

"And Kennedy bringing Jennifer is either genuine reconciliation or the most brilliant PR move of her career," Victoria replied. "Possibly both."

"Maybe it's both?" Lucy smiled. "The public loves them right now."

A few feet away, Marcus Goldman appeared with his wife, statuesque in an understated tuxedo. He caught Victoria's eye and approached with the smile of a worthy opponent.

"Victoria," he nodded. "You've had quite the year."

"Marcus," she replied, matching his tone precisely. "Enjoying the chaos?"

"I've always appreciated your ability to manufacture controversy," he said, his admiration seemingly genuine. "Though I admit, even I didn't think you'd actually pull it off."

"The nominations or the cultural meltdown?"

"Both," he chuckled. "But especially making James Wright the frontrunner despite everything. I'd wish you luck tonight, but with Cynthia Teback in your corner, you don't need it."

"But you have Judith Myers, quite a coup." Victoria finished for him, her smile sharp as a blade. "She is very... competent, I hear."

Their laugh, synchronized in its calculated warmth, drew attention from nearby photographers who immediately captured what would appear in trade papers as "rival producers share a moment of camaraderie."

Aaron approached with Emily on his arm, both glowing with the happiness of people whose professional achievements had temporarily silenced their personal insecurities.

"The PGA mark looks good on you, Aaron," Marcus said, extending his hand. "Hard-earned, I understand."

"Thank you, Marcus," Aaron replied, his handshake firm. "Emily, this is Marcus Goldman, who's also nominated tonight for *Journey's End*."

"The refugee drama." Emily nodded. "Beautifully shot. We were both moved."

"High praise from a literary agent," Marcus smiled. "I hear your client list is even more selective than Victoria's development slate."

"Only slightly more profitable," Emily replied without missing a beat, drawing genuine laughter from both executives.

As the industry's power players continued their elaborate social chess match, the crowds in the bleachers strained against barriers for glimpses of their favorite celebrities. Publicists whispered last-minute reminders about appropriate topics (industry solidarity, creative vision, gratitude) and forbidden landmines (politics, rival performances, that thing that happened at Sundance). Security personnel with earpieces maintained the invisible boundaries that separated Hollywood's royalty from its subjects.

James and Dr. Folake approached the group, his protective hand on her back suggesting authentic concern rather than performative chivalry.

"Dr. Wright," Victoria greeted her with genuine warmth. "Thank you for braving this circus tonight. Your presence means more than you know."

"The circus is familiar territory for academics," Dr. Folake replied with a smile. "Though our controversies typically involve footnote formats rather than identity politics."

"Mother specializes in understatement," James explained, his expression softening with affection. "She once described receiving death threats for her postcolonial analysis of Conrad as 'spirited academic disagreement.'"

Dr. Folake waved this away. "Compared to what you've endured these past months, my academic battles were merely papercuts."

"Speaking of battle scars," André interjected smoothly, "we should head inside. The ceremony starts in twenty minutes, and Cynthia's already texting me about seating arrangements."

Indeed, Cynthia Teback had been inside for an hour, her white hair visible as she directed the placement of key Academy voters with the tactical precision of a battlefield commander. Her Armani pantsuit, selected to communicate authority without unnecessary flourish, moved through the theater like a shark through shallow waters.

The group made their way inside, navigating the complex social protocols that determined who spoke to whom and for precisely how long. James found himself momentarily separated from his mother, caught in a brief exchange with a director who was "absolutely dying to work with him on something meaningful."

As the celebrities filed into the Dolby Theatre for their assigned seats, Kennedy spotted James near the fifth row center, the placement that signaled both honor and strategic camera positioning. Her own seat was just two rows behind, close enough to be captured in the same frame during reaction shots, a detail Cynthia Teback had negotiated with the precision of a nuclear arms treaty.

"James!" Kennedy called out, navigating the narrow aisle with the practiced grace of someone who'd spent years perfecting the art of moving in couture while appearing completely at ease. "Wait up!"

James turned, genuine warmth breaking through his composed expression. "Kennedy. You look stunning."

"Thank you. Though Mother is stealing the spotlight tonight," Kennedy replied, gesturing toward Jennifer who was engaged in animated conversation with a legendary director who'd once fired her for being "distractingly emotional" on set. "Three offers this week alone. Apparently, being unceremoniously dumped by the industry for aging while female is now marketable if you return with sufficient emotional baggage to exploit."

James laughed. A genuine sound that caught several nearby phones recording for social media. "Hollywood's capacity for commodifying trauma never ceases to amaze."

"Speaking of which," Kennedy leaned closer, lowering her voice to the theatrical whisper designed to seem intimate while remaining perfectly audible to anyone with recording capabilities nearby. "Franklly just hit six million downloads. The venture capital people are calling it 'mindfulness with authentic celebrity trauma' like I'm selling designer mental health."

"Congratulations?" James offered, his tone suggesting the appropriate response wasn't entirely clear.

"It's making more than my last two roles combined," Kennedy confirmed, her expression cycling through practiced humility to strategic pride in under a second. "Turns out having your deepest insecurities broadcast to the world creates what my new brand strategist calls 'unmanufactured authenticity,' apparently the holy grail of branding."

She glanced around the theater with newfound clarity. "The whole industry is suddenly treating me like I've discovered plutonium. Three pieces about my brave stand against Hollywood ageism!"

"And how does actual Kennedy feel about becoming the face of this movement?" James asked, his observant gaze catching what the cameras missed, the slight tension around her eyes that even perfect makeup couldn't conceal.

Kennedy's mask slipped momentarily, revealing something more genuine than she'd displayed in years of carefully curated Instagram stories. "Terrified? Exhilarated? Confused. When my mother called after seeing that footage, I thought she was going to freak, but it was... nice."

"That sounds..." James searched for the appropriate word.

"Thank you for what you did, for defending me." She adjusted her diamond bracelet, a nervous habit that her previous media coach had spent months trying to eliminate. "It's totally crazy, I spent my entire career trying to make them happy with my charity work, look relatable but the moment I accidentally show them something... real, it's like, they're interested in me again."

"Perhaps this is what people really want from you, something real." James suggested. "Behind all the filters and carefully worded captions."

"Maybe." Kennedy nodded, her expression shifting to something almost philosophical. "Or maybe this is just the next evolution of performance, monetizing genuine vulnerability. Either way, I'm leaning in."

James laughed again, drawing the attention of a nearby cinematographer who immediately angled for a candid shot of *Gravity's* leads sharing a moment of apparent camaraderie.

"What about you?" Kennedy asked. "Prepared for your speech when they call your name?"

"Let's not jinx it." James laughed. "Though I suspect whatever I actually say will bear little resemblance to my preparation."

Kennedy's expression softened with unexpected empathy. "That's the torture of this industry. We rehearse sincerity until the words lose all meaning, but panic when genuine emotion breaks through the performance."

"Kennedy Oswald, dispensing authentic wisdom. The world truly has shifted on its axis."

"Don't get used to it," she replied with a wink. "My new brand strategy includes 'occasional rawness amid calculated perfection' as my most engaging content pattern. This conversation has officially fulfilled my authenticity quota for the evening."

As the warning lights blinked, signaling everyone to take their seats, Kennedy touched James's arm with unexpected sincerity. "Whatever happens tonight, creating this absurd, controversial, accidentally meaningful film with you has been one of the top ten genuinely worthwhile experiences of my career."

"Even with seventeen takes for a single tear?" James asked.

"Especially then," Kennedy laughed. "That's just how long it takes to get perfect vulnerability, you'll learn. Good luck tonight!"

"You as well," he replied. "Though I suspect luck has very little to do with what happens in this room."

"There you are," Dr. Folake said, reappearing at James's side. "I was just cornered by someone who wanted to know my thoughts on 'decolonizing Hitler.' I told him I'd need at least a semester-long seminar to unpack that phrase."

As they separated toward their respective seats, Kennedy's mother caught her eye from across the theater. Kennedy gave her a small, genuine smile, not the camera-ready beam she'd perfected for red carpets, but something quieter and more real. The algorithm might not recognize the difference, but for once, Kennedy Oswald didn't much care.

Victoria and Aaron took their places on either side of him, with Dr. Folake beside her son. Behind them, Cynthia Teback materialized as if by teleportation, her expression suggesting she had successfully arranged several key voting blocs to maximum advantage.

"Remember," Victoria whispered to James as the house lights began to dim, "no matter what happens, we've already won."

"How exactly?" James asked quietly.

"People are watching the Oscars again," she replied with serene confidence. "Ratings are up sixty percent."

"Because they're hoping for a train wreck, with Evan Hayes hosting," Aaron added under his breath.

Victoria's smile didn't falter. "Attention is attention."

As the orchestra swelled with the bombastic arrangement that somehow suggested both artistic legitimacy and commercial appeal, the vast machine of Hollywood self-congratulation lurched into motion. Production assistants with headsets made frantic final adjustments. The ceremonial countdown began.

And onto the stage bounded Evan Hayes, the controversial comedian whose podcast reached twenty million listeners weekly, whose Netflix specials broke viewership records, and whose selection as host represented the Academy's desperate attempt to recapture cultural relevance.

"Good evening, Hollywood royalty, streaming content creators, and the seven people still watching network television!" Evan announced, his grin suggesting he might either deliver the performance of a lifetime or burn the entire institution to the ground. "Welcome to the ninety-eighth Academy Awards, the night when we celebrate the magic of movies while desperately hoping I don't say something that gets us all canceled."

Uncertain laughter rippled through the audience. In the control room, a technician hovered over the delay button with religious devotion.

"I want to address the elephant in the room right away: the Academy hiring me to host tonight shows just how desperate they've become for ratings. It's like hiring a food critic to run your restaurant, or asking a cardiologist to plan your bacon festival. I've spent my career pointing out everything wrong with this industry, and now you've handed me a live microphone and three hours of network television. Your optimism is adorable."

Genuine laughter now, tinged with the nervousness of people recognizing uncomfortable truths.

"For those who don't know me, I'm Evan Hayes. I'm what happens when a YouTube algorithm achieves sentience and decides to disappoint its parents. My rise to fame is actually a perfect metaphor for modern Hollywood. I started by saying what I actually thought, got fired for it, then got rich when people suddenly decided authenticity was marketable."

Dr. Folake leaned toward James with surprised delight. "He's quite good, isn't he? Rather like watching someone juggle chainsaws."

"I see the *Gravity* team is here tonight," Evan continued, his gaze finding their section. "Great performances. Truly. But I couldn't help thinking, this is what it took to get a Black actor an Oscar nomination? Playing Hitler? What's next year? Idris Elba in the remake of *Birth of a Nation*? Actually, that would really confuse the White supremacists. Half of them went to see *Gravity* and couldn't figure out if they were turned on by Hitler or by a Black man. Some of them had to give up their white robes from the sexual confusion."

The camera found James, who maintained perfect composure, his expression giving away nothing. Beside him, Dr. Folake radiated the pride of a mother who had raised a son capable of navigating absurdity with dignity.

"The studio says it was a bold artistic choice. Sure. Just like my alcoholism is a 'bold hydration choice.' We all know what happened. Some executive said, 'Quick, how can we get think pieces AND controversy AND pretend we're progressive while actually just being provocative for money?' The film generated so much online discourse that TikTok had to create a new server farm just to handle the hot takes."

The audience's laughter grew more genuine, the relief of people realizing they weren't the targets.

"But hey, it worked! People are watching again! Nothing brings America together like a good culture war. Left, right, Black, White, everyone got to be angry about this movie for completely different reasons. If that's not unity, what is?"

Victoria's smile grew fractionally wider. Aaron exhaled quietly. Behind them, Cynthia made a single, approving note on her phone.

"Of course, we also have *Journey's End* nominated tonight. Marcus Goldman's powerful refugee drama that checks every award-season box with such precision it's almost suspicious. Seriously, Marcus, did you run the script through an algorithm called 'OscarBait-4000'? Childhood trauma, historical injustice, inspirational teacher figure, and a tearful monologue in the rain? That's not a movie, that's a vision board for award strategists."

The camera found Marcus, who managed the smile of an executive recognizing a direct hit while refusing to acknowledge the wound.

"This industry collectively spent 3.6 billion dollars on movies this year for a 7 billion return, and that's not including all the awards campaigns taking a cut off the top to give you these little statuettes," Evan continued, holding up a mock Oscar. "Next year, I'd suggest just hiding your money offshore or doing cringy crypto ads!"

Victoria's expression remained perfectly composed, though those who knew her well might have detected the slight twitch at the corner of her mouth that indicated either amusement or murderous intent.

"But seriously, if you're willing to spend so much buying one of these, I have to tell you guys, the material and labor for this is only six hundred bucks. I'll sell it to you at cost! And for another one hundred, I'll let you pick the category!"

In the audience, several studio executives shifted uncomfortably in their seats while the audience's laughter grew more genuine.

Dr. Folake's laughter, genuine and unrestrained, cut through the carefully modulated responses around them. James glanced at his mother with affection, grateful for her authentic presence in this manufactured environment.

"Too real? My bad. Let's talk about the other elephant in the room, the fact that half of you are sitting there thinking, 'Please don't mention the thing everyone knows about me.' Don't worry! I signed an NDA. Just like all your assistants. And housekeepers. And drivers."

Kennedy almost reached for her phone until her mother put a gentle hand on her shoulder.

"You know what's fascinating," Evan continued, shifting to a more thoughtful tone. "Everyone's here pretending to be shocked by a Black Hitler, but we've been watching rich White guys greenlight atrocities for profit since Hollywood began. At least this time they were honest about it. 'Will this make money? Yes? Will people talk about it? Yes? Approved!'

The most authentic thing about this whole controversy is that absolutely no one involved asked if it was the right thing to do."

The laughter faltered. Evan had crossed into uncomfortable territory, the zone where comedy reveals truths that the audience preferred remained concealed.

Aaron leaned toward James. "I think this is actually good for us," he whispered.

"For whom exactly?" James replied without moving his lips.

"For the film. He's making everyone else look ridiculous, not us."

Victoria gripped both their arms. "Stop talking. Cameras."

The silence in the theater was absolute now. In the control room, executives debated whether to cut to commercial, though none dared press the button.

"So tonight, we celebrate the magic of movies, and by magic, I mean the incredible illusion that any of this matters beyond the money it generates. I'm Evan Hayes, and I will absolutely not be invited back next year!"

The orchestra hurriedly began playing as Evan grinned and walked off-stage, leaving three thousand of the most powerful people in entertainment sitting in stunned silence.

As the first presenter nervously approached the microphone, trying to rebuild the ceremony's dignity, James touched his mother's hand and thought about what his grandfather had told him months ago: "History isn't what you portray. It's who does the portraying, and why."

Tonight, at least, that felt truer than ever.

When the Best Supporting Actor category arrived, the tension in their row became palpable. Andrew Kline was nominated for his portrayal of Joseph Goebbels, a performance that critics had described as "disturbingly authentic" and "a master class in the banality of evil." As the montage played his most chilling scene, the camera found him in the audience, his expression carefully neutral.

"And the Oscar goes to..." The presenter paused dramatically. "Thomas Lachre for *The Last Bridge*."

A ripple of surprise moved through the theater, the unexpected pleasure of a genuinely unpredictable moment in an otherwise choreographed evening. As Lachre made his way to the stage, Aaron leaned toward Victoria.

"Too controversial," he murmured.

"The Academy will tolerate a Black Hitler but not a possible racist," Victoria replied with practiced cynicism.

When Best Supporting Actress was announced, Marcus Goldman's refugee drama claimed its first victory of the night. His supporting actress, a veteran character actor who had finally found a breakthrough role at sixty-two, delivered an acceptance speech of such genuine gratitude that even Victoria found herself momentarily moved.

"Nice win for Marcus," she whispered to Aaron. "Though Cynthia predicted this exact outcome two months ago."

"Is there anything she doesn't foresee?" Aaron asked.

"World peace," Victoria replied. "And reasonable catering budgets."

The night progressed with its familiar rhythm of expected victories and occasional surprises. When Best Original Score was announced, Gabriel Trent's name echoed through the Dolby Theatre for his work on *Gravity*. The composer bounded to the stage with the manic enthusiasm of someone who had been mainlining espresso since four a.m.

"This is extraordinary!" he declared, clutching his statue with the reverence usually reserved for religious artifacts. "I want to thank Victoria Martinez and Aaron Weisman for their visionary leadership, and especially for letting me use the historic Mesmer armonica despite the budgetary implications!"

Victoria and Aaron exchanged glances that could only be described as "weary vindication."

"The psycho-acoustic resonance of that 18th-century instrument created the precise emotional dissonance needed for Hitler's psychological deterioration," Gabe continued with increasing intensity. "This victory is for authentic instrumentation everywhere!"

"Worth every penny of the twelve thousand dollars per day," Aaron murmured.

As the ceremony progressed with its familiar rhythm of tributes, manufactured moments, and occasionally genuine emotion, James found himself experiencing an unusual sense of detachment. The machine of industry validation hummed around him, but his attention kept returning to his mother beside him, to the journey that had brought him from a London stage to this surreal pinnacle of Hollywood recognition.

In the backstage production room, technicians monitored the broadcast's global reach. One whispered to another: "Twitter's calling it the 'Evan Hayes massacre.' Trending in twenty-two countries."

Another responded: "The ratings are insane. Highest in fifteen years. The Academy is simultaneously furious and ecstatic."

When the presenter for Best Actor took the stage, a previous winner whose career had been built on the combination of classical training and commercial appeal that James himself embodied, the Dolby Theatre grew quiet with anticipation.

"The performances nominated this year represent the extraordinary range of what actors can achieve," the presenter began, his British accent lending gravitas to the proceedings. "From physical transformation to emotional vulnerability, these five artists have shown us the full spectrum of human experience."

The familiar montage played, five actors, five roles, five distinct approaches to the craft. When James appeared as Hitler, delivering the beer hall speech with the intensity that had first captivated Aaron in London, a palpable energy moved through the room.

"And the Oscar goes to..." The presenter opened the envelope with theatrical deliberation. His expression shifted to one of genuine pleasure. "James Olayinka Wright for *Gravity.*"

The applause erupted with the enthusiasm of an industry recognizing both artistic achievement and narrative satisfaction. James felt his mother's hand squeeze his own as he rose, accepting congratulations from Aaron and Victoria before making his way to the stage.

The statuette, heavier than he'd expected, gleamed under the lights as he accepted it from the presenter.

"Thank you," James said simply, his voice steady despite the enormity of the moment. "This recognition means more than I can express, especially given the extraordinary performances nominated alongside mine."

He paused, gathering his thoughts.

"When I first read this script, I was struck by its unflinching examination of how evil becomes normalized, how monstrous ideologies can be made to seem reasonable through charisma and calculated appeals to fear. The question that haunted me throughout filming was not 'How could this happen then?' but 'How might it happen again?'"

The audience grew still, sensing they were witnessing one of those rare Oscar moments when substance transcends spectacle.

"My grandfather's father fought against Hitler in World War II. He returned changed, carrying wounds both visible and invisible. My mother's research has explored how power shapes narrative, how history is written by those who control who gets to speak. These influences shaped my approach to this role more than any acting technique."

He glanced toward Dr. Folake, whose expression conveyed both pride and a mother's perpetual concern.

"I'd like to thank Aaron Weisman for his extraordinary direction, Victoria Martinez for her unwavering belief in this project despite its risks, and the entire cast and crew who brought such dedication to difficult material. To my mother, whose academic rigor and personal courage have always inspired me, and to my father and grandfather, whose perspectives on history helped shape my understanding of this character."

James took a breath, aware that his time was limited but determined to use this platform thoughtfully.

"Art at its best doesn't just entertain, it lays bare the mechanisms of the world and invites the audience to discover it through their lens. If my performance contributes even slightly to that understanding, then all the controversy surrounding this project will have been worthwhile."

He held up the Oscar with a mixture of gratitude and humility.

"Thank you for this honor. I promise to use whatever opportunities it brings to continue telling stories that matter."

As he exited the stage to renewed applause, James felt the weight of the moment, not just the golden statue in his hand, but the responsibility that came with recognition on this scale.

The ceremony continued its inexorable progression through categories and presentations, commercial breaks and musical performances. When the time came for Best Picture, the tension in the Dolby Theatre was palpable. Victoria sat with the stillness she reserved for moments of maximum pressure, her expression revealing nothing of her internal calculations.

The legendary director tasked with presenting the final award took the stage with the gravitas of someone who had witnessed Hollywood's cycles of excess and redemption for decades.

"The films nominated for Best Picture this year represent the extraordinary diversity of voices and visions that define contemporary cinema," he began, his voice carrying the weight of industry authority. "From intimate personal dramas to sweeping historical narratives, these ten films challenge, entertain, and illuminate the human experience."

The montage played, ten films, ten distinct approaches to storytelling.

"And the Oscar for Best Picture goes to..." The director opened the envelope, his expression shifting to something that might have been genuine surprise. "*Gravity*, produced by Victoria Martinez and Aaron Weisman."

The Dolby Theatre erupted in the kind of applause that suggested both genuine appreciation and strategic industry alignment. Victoria rose with the practiced grace of someone who had imagined this moment for decades, accepting Aaron's embrace before they made their way to the stage.

As they climbed the steps, Victoria caught sight of Marcus in the audience, his expression conveying that blend of professional disappointment and strategic recalculation. He nodded once, the executive's version of acknowledging a worthy opponent, and she returned the gesture with the slightest incline of her head.

Taking the microphone, Victoria delivered the acceptance speech she had been mentally refining for months.

"Thank you to the Academy for this extraordinary recognition," she began, her voice carrying the perfect blend of humility and authority. "And to everyone who believed in this project despite, or perhaps because of, its inherent challenges."

Aaron stood beside her, allowing Victoria her moment in the spotlight while scanning the audience for Emily, whose proud smile meant more to him than the golden statue in Victoria's hand.

"*Gravity* began as an artistic risk, an attempt to examine how the unthinkable becomes normalized through the alchemy of charisma, fear, and calculated manipulation. Our extraordinary cast, led by the incomparable James Wright, brought this vision to life with courage and nuance."

She continued with perfectly calibrated gratitude, acknowledging key contributors while maintaining the practiced rhythm of an executive who understood that even acceptance speeches were strategic opportunities.

As they exited the stage, Oscar in hand, Victoria found herself surrounded by the frenzy that accompanies industry validation, congratulatory embraces from people who had privately questioned her judgment, effusive praise from executives who had previously distanced themselves from the controversy, and the immediate shift in status that comes with holding the industry's most coveted trophy.

In the backstage press room, journalists jostled for position, cameras flashed, and the machinery of immediate commentary lurched into motion. Victoria found herself answering questions with the mix of candor and calculation that had defined her career.

"Was the controversial casting worth the backlash?" a journalist from *Variety* asked.

"Art that doesn't provoke conversation isn't doing its job," Victoria replied smoothly. "James Wright's extraordinary performance transcended the controversy and reminded us that great acting illuminates human truth, regardless of superficial considerations."

"Do you feel vindicated after the criticism you faced?"

Victoria's smile contained multitudes. "I feel grateful that the Academy recognized the artistic merit of our film. The criticism was always part of the conversation we hoped to inspire."

As the press conference continued, Aaron found his attention wandering to his phone, where Emily had sent him screenshots of social media reactions from everyday viewers, not the calculated hot takes of blue-checked influencers, but genuine responses from people who had been moved, disturbed, or challenged by their film.

"This," he whispered to himself, "is what matters. Not the statues. Just knowing someone actually got what we were trying to do."

Meanwhile, in the Sunset Tower Hotel's bar, Sean Lynch watched the ceremony on the discreetly positioned screens, nursing a Japanese whiskey. When Victoria and Aaron accepted their award, a complex expression crossed his features, pride mingled with the satisfaction of a gambit successfully executed.

He texted Victoria: *Breakfast tomorrow at the Polo Lounge?*

***

CHAPTER 24

Across town, in a spacious house in Los Feliz that managed to be both impressive and surprisingly homey, André sat on his comfortable sectional surrounded by family rather than industry calculations.

"Dad, you're trending!" Zoe announced, looking up from her phone. "Someone compiled all your tweets for *Gravity* with reaction shots from the ceremony broadcast. Half a million views and climbing."

"Perfect," André groaned, though his smile suggested he wasn't entirely displeased. "Soon I'll be the meme instead of the meme creator."

"The circle of life in digital marketing," Michelle quipped from the adjacent armchair, having accepted the invitation to join their small Oscar viewing party rather than attend the industry's more manufactured celebrations.

Nadia returned from the kitchen with a fresh bottle of champagne that André, out of industry-trained superstition, had refused to put on ice until the Best Picture envelope was opened. "I genuinely don't understand why you're not at some fancy after-party right now. You literally just won Best Picture."

"Because Victoria and Aaron are handling the industry theater," André replied, accepting a refilled glass. "My job was getting us to the ceremony. Their job is performing gratitude afterward."

"Also because you promised me we'd watch together this year," Zoe reminded him with a smile.

"That too," André acknowledged, glancing at his daughter with affection.

"So," Zoe began, attempting a question she knew the answer to but hoped might land while everyone was drunk on victory, "when can I start going to the actual ceremony with you? Jenna Schwartz's dad took her to the Globes last year and she's only three months older than me."

"We've talked about this," Nadia replied with the practiced patience of someone who'd had this exact conversation multiple times. "After you turn sixteen, we'll revisit."

"But that's two whole years!" Zoe protested with the specific teenage outrage that made two years sound like three decades.

"And by then," André added, "you'll be old enough to understand that those events are actually punishment disguised as privilege." He took a deliberate sip of champagne. "Trust me, you're getting the better experience right here."

Michelle's phone vibrated. "Real-time engagement is up 842% from projections. #BlackHitler and #GravityFilm are both trending globally. And The Drunk Critique posted his reaction video. He reviewed it sober."

"Sober," André repeated, with the respect the word deserved. "The only award tonight that wasn't campaigned for."

The word campaigned hung a moment longer than he'd intended. He turned his glass slowly by the stem.

"Whatever happened with Isa?" he asked. "One day she's running half the command center, the next her desk is cleared. Nobody ever said anything."

"She resigned," Michelle said. "The morning Barry came for his head on a spike. Coordinator position at another studio, very generous severance." She watched the bubbles rise in her glass. "And... a handwritten apology for Kennedy on her way out."

André stopped turning the glass. "She was with you the entire junket. She never even touched that footage."

"I know," Michelle said.

Nadia settled onto the couch beside him, tucking her feet beneath her. "So after all that, after all the controversy and think pieces and social media meltdowns... you guys actually won."

André took a moment before answering, weighing fifteen months of professional chaos against this moment of unexpected calm.

"We won," he confirmed, sounding almost surprised by his own words. "And more importantly, I'm home."

Meanwhile, at the *Vanity Fair* after-party, a carefully orchestrated convergence of power, talent, and strategic visibility, Aaron stood with Emily in a relatively quiet corner, scrolling through his phone with surprised delight.

"Look at this," he said, showing her a YouTube comment thread, his eyes alight in a way even his PGA mark couldn't ignite. "These are just regular people discussing the film's themes, debating character motivations, sharing personal responses. Not industry hot takes or controversy angles, they're just talking about the actual movie."

Emily smiled at her husband's enthusiasm. "Look at how happy you are, you're holding an Oscar but scrolling through audience reviews. For the audience rather than the industry?"

"I know, I thought this would bring me more joy," Aaron admitted. "The machinery of production makes it easy to forget that eventually, real humans will watch what we create and draw their own conclusions." He scrolled further, reading more comments with growing satisfaction. "This is really what I wanted."

James approached, having temporarily escaped the media frenzy of congratulations and photo opportunities that accompanied his new status as Oscar-winning actor. His mother had retired early, citing the exhaustion that comes from maintaining professional composure in surreal circumstances.

"Congratulations, Aaron," James said, genuine warmth in his voice. "Though I imagine the PGA mark means more to you than the Oscar."

"You've noticed my priorities," Aaron laughed, clapping him on the shoulder. "How does it feel to be in the rarefied stratosphere of the Best Actor winners?"

"Surprisingly normal," James replied thoughtfully. "Though I suspect that will change when I wake up tomorrow to discover what new meaning has been assigned to my victory by people who have seen my image but not the film."

Emily excused herself tactfully, leaving the two men to their moment of professional reflection.

"I've been meaning to ask," Aaron said, lowering his voice slightly. "With all the discourse and controversy, did you ever regret taking the role?"

James considered this with the thoughtfulness that had defined his approach throughout the entire strange journey. "No," he said finally. "Though I sometimes questioned the industry surrounding it. But the work itself, the actual process of laying bare a monster for the audience, seeing how he rationalized his actions, how evil becomes normalized through incremental steps, felt genuinely worthwhile."

He glanced around at the carefully choreographed spectacle of the after-party, where power dynamics and career calculations were performed with practiced precision beneath the veneer of celebration.

"What happens next for you?" Aaron asked. "I assume the offers have started."

"Seventeen since the nominations," James said. "Napoleon. Churchill. A Marvel villain called Mister Sinister. An Elvis biopic."

"Elvis."

"My agent assures me the script is 'a bold reclamation.'" James's delivery remained perfectly even. "I asked about Hamlet. They said it lacked an angle."

Before Aaron could decide whether laughing was appropriate, James's phone lit up. He read the alert, then turned the screen toward Aaron without comment. *DEADLINE: Netflix greenlights "The True Queen Charlotte"; TJ Jackson attached as executive producer and historical consultant.*

Neither of them said anything for a moment.

Aaron's phone buzzed with a text from Victoria: *Where are you? Variety wants photos of the whole team.*

"Duty calls," Aaron sighed. "The industry machine never stops, even on its most celebratory night." He hesitated, then added with sudden decisiveness: "When this publicity tour ends, I'm taking a long vacation. A very long vacation."

"Well deserved," James replied with a smile. "Though I doubt Victoria will approve."

"She already has," Aaron said with surprising confidence. "Her exact words were, 'I'll approve it personally.'"

***

Victoria arrived at her office the morning after the Oscars to find the statuette waiting on her desk, where Lucy had delivered it at some dawn hour with a note about engraving appointments. The space on her awards shelf, the vacancy she'd been maintaining for months, remained empty. There would be time for that.

Lucy entered with her usual efficiency, tablet in hand. "Congratulations again. The headlines are overwhelmingly positive, social mentions are up six thousand percent from yesterday, and *The Hollywood Reporter* is calling it 'a triumph of artistic vision over controversy.'"

"Perfect." Victoria nodded, studying the new arrangement of her collection. "And the other side of the conversation?"

"Fox News is calling it 'Hollywood elites rewarding each other for provocative casting,'" Lucy reported. "TruthHunterRyan claims the whole ceremony was rigged by 'deep state agents,' and LiftieInLipstick is filming a three-part series analyzing James's acceptance speech for 'hidden meanings.'"

"The ecosystem thrives," Victoria observed with clinical satisfaction. "Any word from Marcus?"

"A professionally gracious congratulatory email arrived at seven a.m.," Lucy confirmed. "Though his assistant told me he's taking a day off."

"Good," Victoria said, her smile containing the satisfaction of victory hard-won. "Let him channel that energy into his next project. Speaking of which, what's on our development slate for the coming year?"

Lucy consulted her tablet. "The board meeting to discuss greenlight priorities is scheduled for next week. Sean Lynch requested your presence specifically."

"I'm sure he did," Victoria murmured, her mind already calculating the next competition, the next controversy, the next opportunity to prove herself against artificial constraints.

***

The Polo Lounge at the Beverly Hills Hotel welcomed Victoria Martinez at lunch with the same pink-and-green tableau that had framed her other lunches with Sean months ago. This time, however, she arrived with the confidence of someone who had just secured Hollywood's ultimate validation.

Sean Lynch was already seated at a prime center table, another cup of coffee at his elbow, his expression suggesting he had been waiting the amount of time required to establish dominance without crossing into genuine inconvenience.

"Congratulations, Victoria," he said as she slid into her chair. "A historic achievement for 'Black Hitler.' Or should I say *Gravity*? I noticed the marketing department's frantic pivot to the more prestigious title, but internally never quite caught up, did it?"

"Thank you, Sean." Victoria signaled the waiter for her usual coffee. "I appreciate the support, especially given the... unconventional path this project took."

Sean's smile contained the knowledge of an executive who had seen the machinery of success from all angles. "Unconventional. That's one word for it. 'Calculated controversy leveraged into awards validation through strategic manipulation' might be another."

Victoria's expression remained carefully neutral. "I'm not sure what you're implying."

"I'm not implying anything," Sean replied, sipping his coffee. "I'm stating directly that you played the game exactly as designed, perhaps better than anyone expected."

The waiter delivered Victoria's coffee, and she took a precise sip before responding. "You make it sound like there was some grand design beyond making a film worthy of recognition."

Sean's laugh held genuine appreciation. "Victoria, please. You took a project you initially wanted to abandon, transformed it into a deliberate provocation that generated six months of free publicity, spent eleven million on awards campaigning, and weaponized controversy into prestige. It was a masterclass in industry manipulation."

Victoria studied him, reassessing the conversation. "You almost sound like you orchestrated this yourself."

"Let's just say I recognized the potential when Marcus tried to take the project from you," Sean replied with calculated casualness. "I've been in this business long enough to know that nothing motivates talented executives like competitive spite."

"So you deliberately set us against each other," Victoria said, the pieces falling into place. "You knew I'd fight to keep Hitler just to spite Marcus, and that the rivalry would push us both to create better films."

"Better? Questionable. More commercially viable and awards-worthy? Absolutely." Sean raised his glass in a mock toast. "Why settle for two mediocre movies when rivalry could give the studio two award contenders? Competition breeds excellence, or at least the industry's version of it."

Victoria absorbed this revelation with the stillness of someone recalculating every interaction of the past year. "I should be furious."

"But you're not," Sean observed. "Because you won. And because you know that without that manipulative push, *Gravity* might have remained an abandoned option rather than your crowning achievement."

"So this was all just a game to you?" Victoria asked, her tone revealing a rare glimpse of genuine emotion beneath her executive armor.

"Not a game," Sean corrected. "A strategic investment in human psychology. I know you, Victoria. I know what drives you. And I know that without Marcus as your white whale, you might never have pushed *Gravity* to its full potential."

Victoria took a measured sip of her coffee, processing this revelation with the blend of irritation and admiration that defined most industry relationships. "So the additional funding for Marcus, that was deliberate too?"

"Of course." Sean nodded. "Competition only works when both sides believe they can win. Marcus needed resources to make his refugee drama genuinely competitive, and you needed a worthy opponent to fuel your brand of vindictive excellence."

"Vindictive excellence," Victoria repeated, the phrase landing somewhere between insult and compliment. "That's how you see my process?"

"That's how I see your genius," Sean corrected. "Some executives are driven by artistic vision, others by commercial instinct. You're driven by the incessant need to prove everyone wrong, particularly those who've underestimated you."

He leaned forward, his expression shifting to something almost like genuine respect. "The studio won last night, regardless of which envelope they opened."

Victoria studied him, reassessing years of interactions through this new lens. "Did you do the same with the *Sarajevo* project?"

Sean's smile contained multitudes. "Let's just say Marcus still doesn't know how his initial interest in that script suddenly became a competitive bidding situation."

"You magnificent bastard," Victoria said softly, a reluctant smile playing at her lips.

"I prefer 'strategic executive,'" Sean replied, raising his coffee cup. "To Hollywood's most elegant machine, turning human insecurity into commercial art since 1927."

Victoria clinked her cup against his, the sound punctuating this strange moment of clarity. "Does it bother you?" she asked suddenly. "Manipulating people like this?"

"Does it bother you that eleven million in awards campaigning may have influenced last night's outcome more than the actual artistic merit of your film?" Sean countered.

They regarded each other with the recognition of industry veterans who had glimpsed behind the final curtain and chosen to remain in the theater anyway.

"My film deserved to win," Victoria said finally.

"Of course it did," Sean agreed. "Just as you deserved to make it. Just as Marcus deserved his nomination. Just as the audience deserves to believe that what they're watching matters."

He signaled for the check with the practiced efficiency of someone who had concluded countless such conversations. "Your next project starts pre-production in three months. Marcus begins his new film around the same time."

Victoria's eyebrow rose fractionally. "Another engineered rivalry?"

"Another opportunity for excellence," Sean corrected. "Unless, of course, you'd prefer to remove the competitive element that seems to fuel your best work?"

Victoria's smile contained a blend of irritation, amusement, and determination that had defined her entire career. "I'll see you at the greenlight meeting."

As she left the Polo Lounge, Victoria found herself experiencing an unfamiliar sensation: the clarity that comes with realizing you've been both manipulator and manipulated simultaneously. Her path to victory had been orchestrated in ways she hadn't fully perceived, yet her triumph remained indisputably her own.

The paradox felt oddly fitting for an industry built on manufacturing authentic emotion through calculated means.

***

Back at her office that evening, Victoria found the texts waiting. James: *Thank you for everything. This journey has been extraordinary, if occasionally absurd.* Aaron: *Emily says if we have a child, we should name her Victoria. I told her that's a terrible threat to make to an innocent baby.*

She placed the phone face-down on her desk and picked up the Oscar. Fingerprints clouded the gold: a night's worth of hands. Lucy's, the engraver's, half the Vanity Fair party's, her own.

She set him in the space she had kept empty for months and stepped back.

The golden knight of the Hollywood dream looked up at her, sword planted, his expression unreadable.

It was enough.

For now.

***

THE END